Middle School Literature for Christian Homeschoolers: 7th Grade

Volume 1:
Stories, Poems, and Essays

2nd Edition
(with Answer Key)

Scott Clifton

ISBN: 9798873877966

How to Use This Book to Make Homeschooling 7th Grade Literature Easy and Fun!

The three volumes of *Middle School Literature for Christian Homeschoolers: 7th Grade* are designed to make it easy for parents to help their homeschooled "seventh graders" enjoy reading great literature, presented from a Christian worldview. Here's all you need to do:

(1) **Purchase *Middle School Literature for Christian Homeschoolers: 7th Grade*.** The set contains these three volumes; all are available for purchase online at **www.homeschoolpartners.net/books**:

Volume 1:
Stories, Poems, and Essays

Volume 2:
North Woods Manhunt • Mary Louise • The Prisoner of Zenda

Volume 3:
The Time Machine • The Yellow Pearl • The Story of a Bad Boy

(2) **Use the 30-week, 4-days-per-week reading schedule to map out your student's reading for the year.** The reading plan is on the next page of this book.

    Suggestion: Start your Week 1 readings so that your student completes the Week 16 readings the week or two before Christmas (Week 16's readings are Christmas-themed!).

(3) **Use the answer key.** The answer key to the review questions is available at the back of this book.

(4) **Consider these other reading sets:**

- *Middle School Literature for Christian Homeschoolers: 8th Grade*
- *American Literature for Christian Homeschoolers (high school)*
- *Classic Literature for Christian Homeschoolers (high school)*
- *British Literature for Christian Homeschoolers (high school)*
- *World Literature for Christian Homeschoolers (high school)*

7th Grade Literature for Christian Homeschoolers
30-Week Reading Plan
(Gray boxes indicate material found in <u>this</u> volume.)

Week	Day 1	Day 2	Day 3	Day 4
1	John 1	The Highest Education	Casey at the Bat	Rikki-Tikki-Tavi
2	The First Telegraph Instrument	The Leak	The Boat	My Financial Career
3	*North Woods Manhunt*, Chapters 1-3	*North Woods Manhunt*, Chapters 4-5	*North Woods Manhunt*, Chapters 6-8	*North Woods Manhunt*, Chapters 9-10
4	An Address to Young Converts	John G.	He Leadeth Me • • • • • Temptation Resisted	In the Country of the Sioux
5	Psalm 1 • • • • • Psalm 97	The Largest Statues in the World • • • • • The Story of Alaska	A Poison Tree • • • • • A Ballad of Trees and the Master	Benjamin Franklin
6	*The Merry Adventures of Robin Hood*, Part 1	*The Merry Adventures of Robin Hood*, Part 2	My Kate	Cicely
7	*Mary Louise*, Chapters 1-4	*Mary Louise*, Chapters 5-8	*Mary Louise*, Chapters 9-11	*Mary Louise*, Chapters 12-13
8	*Mary Louise*, Chapters 14-16	*Mary Louise*, Chapters 17-19	*Mary Louise*, Chapters 20-22	*Mary Louise*, Chapters 23-26
9	Pug-Puggy and the Rattlesnake	From Morn Till Night on a Florida River	On the Grasshopper and the Cricket	The "'Gator"
10	Matthew 5	Uncle Remus: His Songs and His Sayings	What a Friend We Have in Jesus	The Lumber Room

Week	Day 1	Day 2	Day 3	Day 4
11	*The Prisoner of Zenda*, Chapters 1-2	*The Prisoner of Zenda*, Chapter 3	*The Prisoner of Zenda*, Chapters 4-5	*The Prisoner of Zenda*, Chapter 6
12	*The Prisoner of Zenda*, Chapters 7-8	*The Prisoner of Zenda*, Chapter 9	*The Prisoner of Zenda*, Chapter 10	*The Prisoner of Zenda*, Chapter 11
13	*The Prisoner of Zenda*, Chapter 12	*The Prisoner of Zenda*, Chapter 13	*The Prisoner of Zenda*, Chapter 14	*The Prisoner of Zenda*, Chapter 15
14	*The Prisoner of Zenda*, Chapters 16-17	*The Prisoner of Zenda*, Chapters 18-19	*The Prisoner of Zenda*, Chapters 20-21	*The Prisoner of Zenda*, Chapter 22
15	A Safety Match	On Raising Questions	Thankfulness	The Pimientia Pancakes
16	My First Christmas Tree	A Christmas Inspiration	Christmas Bells	Luke 2
17	*The Time Machine*, Intro.-Chapter II	*The Time Machine*, Chapters III-IV	*The Time Machine*, Chapters V-VI	*The Time Machine*, Chapters VII-VIII
18	*The Time Machine*, Chapters IX-X	*The Time Machine*, Chapter XI	*The Time Machine*, Chapters XII-XIII	*The Time Machine*, Chapter XIV-Epilogue
19	Have You Done Your Best?	*Billy Sunday: The Man and His Message*	Jim, Who Ran Away from His Nurse	The Adventure of the Norwood Builder
20	The Eagle · · · · · Ingratitude (Blow, Blow, Thou Winter Wind)	The Golden Windows · · · · · A Dilemma	Inscriptions on a Sun-Dial · · · · · Four Things	The Revolt of "Mother"
21	*The Yellow Pearl*, Part 1	*The Yellow Pearl*, Part 2	*The Yellow Pearl*, Part 3	*The Yellow Pearl*, Part 4
22	What Can I Do?	A Pioneer Mother	Up Hill	Quality

Week	Day 1	Day 2	Day 3	Day 4
23	Proverbs 13	Bears of High and Low Degree	The Children's Hour • • • • • I Like To See It Lap the Miles	The Doctor's Cow
24	The Right To What I Consider a Normal Standard of Living	Shandon Waters	Old Aunt Mary's	Do Insects Think?
25	*The Story of a Bad Boy*, Chapters 1-3	*The Story of a Bad Boy*, Chapter 4	*The Story of a Bad Boy*, Chapter 5	*The Story of a Bad Boy*, Chapter 6
26	*The Story of a Bad Boy*, Chapter 7	*The Story of a Bad Boy*, Chapters 8-9	*The Story of a Bad Boy*, Chapters 10-11	*The Story of a Bad Boy*, Chapters 12-13
27	*The Story of a Bad Boy*, Chapter 14	*The Story of a Bad Boy*, Chapter 15	*The Story of a Bad Boy*, Chapter 16	*The Story of a Bad Boy*, Chapter 17
28	*The Story of a Bad Boy*, Chapter 18	*The Story of a Bad Boy*, Chapter 19	*The Story of a Bad Boy*, Chapter 20	*The Story of a Bad Boy*, Chapters 21-22
29	*Missionary Travels and Researches*, Part 1	*Missionary Travels and Researches*, Part 2	Songs for My Mother • • • • • My Mother's Bible	Zero Hour
30	A Manual of Education	The Night Express	I Know Whom I Have Believed	Mabel Ashton's Dream
31	An Incredibly Important Question for Review			

Table of Contents

John 1:1-14

By the Apostle John

For our beginning selection, let's go to...the beginning! John 1 starts like Genesis 1, but focuses on Jesus, whom John calls "the beginning and the end" in Revelation, which he also wrote. In John 1, the disciple John—calls Jesus a Light, God, and the Word. The Greek word for "Word" is logos, *from which we get our English word* logic *and parts of other words like* biology *and* archaeology.

· · · · ·

1 – In the beginning was the Word, and the Word was with God, and the Word was God.

2 – The same was in the beginning with God.

3 – All things were made by him; and without him was not any thing made that was made.

4 – In him was life; and the life was the light of men.

5 – And the light shineth in darkness; and the darkness comprehended[1] it not.

6 – There was a man sent from God, whose name was John.

7 – The same came for a witness, to bear witness of the Light, that all men through him might believe.

8 – He was not that Light, but was sent to bear witness of that Light.

9 – That was the true Light, which lighteth every man that cometh into the world.

10 – He was in the world, and the world was made by him, and the world knew him not.

11 – He came unto his own, and his own received him not.

12 – But as many as received him, to them gave he power to become the sons of God, even to them that believe on his name:

---

[1] understood

13 – Which were born, not of blood, nor of the will of the flesh, nor of the will of man, but of God.

14 – And the Word was made flesh, and dwelt among us, (and we beheld his glory, the glory as of the only begotten of the Father,) full of grace and truth.

Questions for Review

1. What do you think verse five means?

2. Why was John the Baptist sent to the world, according to verse seven?

3. How is verse nine similar to verse seven?

4. How does someone become one of the "sons of God"? Who gets the credit for this, according to verse 14?

The Highest Education

By Booker T. Washington

"The Highest Education" is one of many talks that Booker T. Washington (1856-1915) gave on Sunday evenings to students at Tuskegee Institute, a teachers' college in Alabama. Washington was a former slave who worked extremely hard after he and his family were freed. He had to struggle to get an education, and partly because of his willingness to work and learn from many jobs, he eventually earned the position of principal at Tuskegee.

· · · · ·

It may seem to some of you that I am continually talking to you about education—the right kind of education, how to get an education, and such kindred[1] subjects—but surely no subject could be more pertinent,[2] since the object for which you all are here is to get an education; and if you are to do this, you wish to get the best kind possible.

You will understand, then, I am sure, if I speak often about this, or refer to the subject frequently, that it is because I am very anxious that all of you go out from here with a definite and correct idea of what is meant by education, of what an education is meant to accomplish, what it may be expected to do for one.

We are very apt to get the idea that education means the memorizing of a number of dates, of being able to state when a certain battle took place, of being able to recall with accuracy this event or that event. We are likely to get the impression that education consists in being able to commit to memory a certain number of rules in grammar, a certain number of rules in arithmetic, and in being able to locate correctly on the earth's surface this mountain or that river, and to name this lake and that gulf.

Now I do not mean to disparage[3] the value of this kind of training, because among the things that education should do for us is to give us strong, orderly, and well-developed minds. I do not wish to have you get the idea that I undervalue or overlook the strengthening of the mind. If there is one person more than another who is to be pitied, it is the individual who is all heart and no head. You will see numbers of persons going through the world

---

[1] related
[2] important, appropriate
[3] mock, criticize

whose hearts are full of good things—running over with the wish to do something to make somebody better, or the desire to make somebody happier—but they have made the sad mistake of being absolutely without development of mind to go with this willingness of heart. We want development of mind, and we want strengthening of the mind.

I have often said to you that one of the best things that education can do for an individual is to teach that individual to get hold of what he wants, rather than to teach him how to commit to memory a number of facts in history or a number of names in geography. I wish you to feel that we can give you here orderliness of mind—I mean a trained mind—that will enable you to find dates in history or to put your finger on names in geography when you want them. I wish to give you an education that will enable you to construct rules in grammar and arithmetic for yourselves. That is the highest kind of training.

But, after all, this kind of thing is not the end of education. What, then, do we mean by education? I would say that education is meant to give us an idea of truth. Whatever we get out of textbooks, whatever we get out of industry,[4] whatever we get here and there from any sources, if we do not get the idea of truth at the end, we do not get education. I do not care how much you get out of history, or geography, or algebra, or literature, I do not care how much you have got out of all your textbooks—unless you have got

---

[4] working

truth, you have failed in your purpose to be educated. Unless you get the idea of truth so pure that you cannot be false in anything, your education is a failure.

Then education is meant to make us just in our dealings with our fellow men. The man or woman who has learned to be absolutely just, so far as he can interpret, has, in that degree, an education, is to that degree an educated man or woman. Education is meant to make us change for the better, to make us more thoughtful, to make us so broad that we will not seek to help one man because he belongs to this race or that race of people, and seek to hinder another man because he does not belong to this race or that race of people.

Education in the broadest and truest sense will make an individual seek to help all people, regardless of race, regardless of color, regardless of condition. And you will find that the person who is most truly educated is the one who is going to be kindest, and is going to act in the gentlest manner toward persons who are unfortunate, toward the race or the individual that is most despised. The highly educated person is the one who is the most considerate of those individuals who are less fortunate. I hope that when you go out from here, and meet persons who are afflicted by poverty, whether of mind or body, or persons who are unfortunate in any way, that you will show your education by being just as kind and just as considerate toward those persons as it is possible for you to be. That is the way to test a person with education. You may see ignorant persons, who, perhaps, think themselves educated, going about the street, who, when they meet an individual who is unfortunate—lame, or with a defect of body, mind, or speech—are inclined to laugh at and make sport of that individual. But the highly educated person, the one who is really cultivated, is gentle and sympathetic to everyone.

Education is meant to make us absolutely honest in dealing with our fellows. I don't care how much arithmetic we have, or how many cities we can locate—it all is useless unless we have an education that makes us absolutely honest.

Education is meant to make us give satisfaction, and to get satisfaction out of giving it. It is meant to make us get happiness out of service for our fellows. And until we get to the point where we can get happiness and supreme satisfaction out of helping our fellows, we are not truly educated. Education is meant to make us generous. In this connection let me say that I very much hope that when you go out from here you will show that you have learned this lesson of being generous in all charitable objects, in the support of your churches, your Sunday schools, your hospitals, and in being generous in giving help to the poor.

I hope, for instance, that a large proportion of you—in fact all of you—will make it a practice to give something yearly to this institution. If you

cannot give but twenty-five cents, fifty cents, or a dollar a year, I hope you will put it down as a thing that you will not forget, to give something to this institution every year. We want to show to our friends who have done so much for us, who have supported this school so generously, how much interest we take in the institution that has given us so nearly all that we possess. I hope that every senior, in particular, will keep this in mind. I am glad to say that we have many graduates who send us such sums, even if small, and one graduate who for the last eight or ten years has sent us ten dollars annually. I hope a number of you in the senior class that I see before me will do the same thing.

Education is meant to make us appreciate the things that are beautiful in nature. A person is never educated until he is able to go into the swamps and woods and see something that is beautiful in the trees and shrubs there, is able to see something beautiful in the grass and flowers that surround him, is, in short, able to see something beautiful, elevating and inspiring in everything that God has created. Not only should education enable us to see the beauty in these objects which God has put about us, but it is meant to influence us to bring beautiful objects about us. I hope that each one of you, after you graduate, will surround himself at home with what is beautiful, inspiring, and elevating. I do not believe that any person is educated so long as he lives in a dirty, miserable shanty. I do not believe that any person is educated until he has learned to want to live in a clean room made attractive with pictures and books, and with such surroundings as are elevating.

In a word, I wish to say again, that education is meant to give us that culture, that refinement, that taste which will make us deal truthfully with our fellow men, and will make us see what is beautiful, elevating, and inspiring in what God has created. I want you to bear in mind that your textbooks, with all their contents, are not an end, but a means to an end, a means to help us get the highest, the best, the purest and the most beautiful things out of life.

Questions for Review

1. What does Washington say is the point of education? What does he say an education is *not*?

2. How can a young Christian compare Proverbs 23:23 and John 14:6 to the author's main point?

3. How does Washington say that a person can prove he has a *real* education?

4. Since you're a homeschooler, what's something *you* can do this year to "take charge" of your education, instead of waiting for Mom or Dad to *tell* you what to do all the time? (And be sure to give them a big hug and thank them for homeschooling you!)

Casey at the Bat

By Ernest Thayer

Ernest Thayer (1863-1940) wrote the funny "Casey at the Bat" in 1888, using a pen name.[1] The poem quickly became tremendously popular. (To understand the poem, it helps to know the game of baseball and its terms.) Pay attention to the poem's rhythmic use of the English language, which makes it smooth and even more enjoyable.

• • • • •

The outlook wasn't brilliant for the Mudville nine that day;
The score stood four to two, with but one inning more to play.
And then when Cooney died at first, and Barrows did the same,
A sickly silence fell upon the patrons[2] of the game.

A straggling few got up to go in deep despair. The rest
Clung to that hope which springs eternal in the human breast;
They thought, if only Casey could get but a whack at that—
They'd put up even money,[3] now, with Casey at the bat.

---

[1] A pen name is a false name writers use to hide their true identity—similar to why Clark Kent wears glasses (but it works a lot better).
[2] customers, fans
[3] gamble that Mudville would win

But Flynn preceded Casey, as did also Jimmy Blake,
And the former was a lulu, and the latter was a cake,
So upon that stricken multitude grim melancholy[4] sat,
For there seemed but little chance of Casey's getting to the bat.

But Flynn let drive a single, to the wonderment of all,
And Blake, the much despised, tore the cover off the ball;
And when the dust had lifted, and the men saw what had occurred,
There was Jimmy safe at second and Flynn a-hugging third.

Then from five thousand throats and more there rose a lusty yell;
It rumbled through the valley; it rattled in the dell;[5]
It knocked upon the mountain and recoiled upon the flat,
For Casey, mighty Casey, was advancing to the bat.

There was ease in Casey's manner as he stepped into his place;
There was pride in Casey's bearing[6] and a smile on Casey's face.
And when, responding to the cheers, he lightly doffed his hat,[7]
No stranger in the crowd could doubt 'twas Casey at the bat.

Ten thousand eyes were on him as he rubbed his hands with dirt;
Five thousand tongues applauded when he wiped them on his shirt.
Then while the writhing pitcher ground the ball into his hip,
Defiance gleamed in Casey's eye; a sneer curled Casey's lip.

And now the leather-covered sphere came hurtling through the air,
And Casey stood a-watching it in haughty grandeur[8] there.
Close by the sturdy batsman the ball unheeded sped—
"That ain't my style," said Casey. "Strike one," the umpire said.

From the benches, black with people, there went up a muffled roar,
Like the beating of the storm-waves on a stern and distant shore.
"Kill him! Kill the umpire!" shouted someone on the stand;
And it's likely they'd have killed him had not Casey raised his hand.

With a smile of Christian charity great Casey's visage[9] shone;
He stilled the rising tumult;[10] he bade the game go on;
He signaled to the pitcher, and once more the spheroid flew;
But Casey still ignored it, and the umpire said: "Strike two."

---

[4] sadness
[5] valley
[6] attitude
[7] tipped his hat to the crowd in thanks
[8] "haughty grandeur": arrogance
[9] face
[10] uproar

"Fraud!" cried the maddened thousands, and Echo answered fraud;
But one scornful look from Casey and the audience was awed.
They saw his face grow stern and cold, they saw his muscles strain,
And they knew that Casey wouldn't let that ball go by again.

The sneer is gone from Casey's lip; his teeth are clenched in hate;
He pounds with cruel violence his bat upon the plate.
And now the pitcher holds the ball, and now he lets it go,
And now the air is shattered by the force of Casey's blow.

Oh, somewhere in this favored land the sun is shining bright;
The band is playing somewhere, and somewhere hearts are light,
And somewhere men are laughing, and somewhere children shout;
But there is no joy in Mudville—mighty Casey has struck out.

Questions for Review

1. What are some things that happen in this poem that *you* might have seen
    while attending a baseball game, or another sporting event?

2. Since a batter only gets three strikes until he's out, why do you think
    Casey lets the first two strikes go by him without swinging?

3. Did the ending surprise you? Why or why not?

4. Find and watch the 1946 Walt Disney cartoon "Casey at the Bat," and
    compare it to the original poem.

Rikki-Tikki-Tavi

By Rudyard Kipling

Today British author Rudyard Kipling (1865-1936) is probably best known for his story about the boy Mowgli, taken from the 1894 collection The Jungle Book. *Also in that collection was the below "Rikki-Tikki-Tavi." Kipling set those two stories, as well as many others he wrote, in India. That nation had been a British colony for many years, and only won its independence in 1947. This story is about an English family in India—and their new little friend.*

• • • • •

At the hole where he went in
Red-Eye called to Wrinkle-Skin.
Hear what little Red-Eye saith:
"Nag, come up and dance with death!"
Eye to eye and head to head,
(Keep the measure, Nag.)
This shall end when one is dead;
(At thy pleasure, Nag.)
Turn for turn and twist for twist—
(Run and hide thee, Nag.)
Hah! The hooded Death has missed!
(Woe betide thee, Nag!)

This is the story of the great war that Rikki-tikki-tavi fought single-handed through the bathrooms of the big bungalow[1] in Segowlee cantonment. Darzee, the Tailorbird, helped him, and Chuchundra, the muskrat, who never comes out into the middle of the floor, but always creeps round by the wall, gave him advice, but Rikki-tikki did the real fighting.

He was a mongoose, rather like a little cat in his fur and his tail, but quite like a weasel in his head and his habits. His eyes and the end of his restless nose were pink. He could scratch himself anywhere he pleased with any leg, front or back, that he chose to use. He could fluff up his tail till it looked like a bottle brush, and his war cry as he scuttled through the long grass was: "Rikk-tikk-tikki-tikki-tchk!"

---

[1] cottage

One day, a high summer flood washed him out of the burrow where he lived with his father and mother, and carried him, kicking and clucking, down a roadside ditch. He found a little wisp of grass floating there, and clung to it till he lost his senses. When he revived, he was lying in the hot sun on the middle of a garden path, very draggled indeed, and a small boy was saying, "Here's a dead mongoose. Let's have a funeral."

"No," said his mother, "let's take him in and dry him. Perhaps he isn't really dead."

They took him into the house, and a big man picked him up between his finger and thumb and said he was not dead but half choked. So they wrapped him in cotton wool, and warmed him over a little fire, and he opened his eyes and sneezed.

"Now," said the big man (he was an Englishman who had just moved into the bungalow), "don't frighten him, and we'll see what he'll do."

It is the hardest thing in the world to frighten a mongoose, because he is eaten up from nose to tail with curiosity. The motto of all the mongoose family is "Run and find out," and Rikki-tikki was a true mongoose. He looked at the cotton wool, decided that it was not good to eat, ran all round the table, sat up and put his fur in order, scratched himself, and jumped on the small boy's shoulder.

"Don't be frightened, Teddy," said his father. "That's his way of making friends."

"Ouch! He's tickling under my chin," said Teddy.

Rikki-tikki looked down between the boy's collar and neck, snuffed at his ear, and climbed down to the floor, where he sat rubbing his nose.

"Good gracious," said Teddy's mother, "and that's a wild creature! I suppose he's so tame because we've been kind to him."

"All mongooses are like that," said her husband. "If Teddy doesn't pick him up by the tail, or try to put him in a cage, he'll run in and out of the house all day long. Let's give him something to eat."

They gave him a little piece of raw meat. Rikki-tikki liked it immensely, and when it was finished he went out into the veranda and sat in the sunshine and fluffed up his fur to make it dry to the roots. Then he felt better.

"There are more things to find out about in this house," he said to himself, "than all my family could find out in all their lives. I shall certainly stay and find out."

He spent all that day roaming over the house. He nearly drowned himself in the bathtubs, put his nose into the ink on a writing table, and burned it on the end of the big man's cigar, for he climbed up in the big man's lap to see how writing was done. At nightfall he ran into Teddy's nursery to watch how kerosene lamps were lighted, and when Teddy went to bed Rikki-tikki climbed up too. But he was a restless companion, because he had to get up and attend to every noise all through the night, and find out what made it. Teddy's mother and father came in, the last thing, to look at their boy, and Rikki-tikki was awake on the pillow.

"I don't like that," said Teddy's mother. "He may bite the child."

"He'll do no such thing," said the father. "Teddy's safer with that little beast than if he had a bloodhound to watch him. If a snake came into the nursery now—"

But Teddy's mother wouldn't think of anything so awful.

Early in the morning Rikki-tikki came to early breakfast in the veranda riding on Teddy's shoulder, and they gave him banana and some boiled egg. He sat on all their laps one after the other, because every well-brought-up mongoose always hopes to be a house mongoose some day and have rooms to run about in; and Rikki-tikki's mother (she used to live in the general's house at Segowlee) had carefully told Rikki what to do if ever he came across white men.

Then Rikki-tikki went out into the garden to see what was to be seen. It was a large garden, only half cultivated, with bushes, as big as summer houses, of Marshal Niel roses, lime and orange trees, clumps of bamboos, and thickets of high grass. Rikki-tikki licked his lips. "This is a splendid hunting ground," he said, and his tail grew bottle-brushy at the thought of it, and he scuttled up and down the garden, snuffing here and there till he heard very sorrowful voices in a thornbush.

It was Darzee, the Tailorbird, and his wife. They had made a beautiful nest by pulling two big leaves together and stitching them up the edges with fibers, and had filled the hollow with cotton and downy fluff. The nest swayed to and fro, as they sat on the rim and cried.

"What is the matter?" asked Rikki-tikki.

"We are very miserable," said Darzee. "One of our babies fell out of the nest yesterday and Nag ate him."

"H'm!" said Rikki-tikki, "that is very sad—but I am a stranger here. Who is Nag?"

Darzee and his wife only cowered down in the nest without answering, for from the thick grass at the foot of the bush there came a low hiss—a horrid cold sound that made Rikki-tikki jump back two clear feet. Then inch by inch out of the grass rose up the head and spread hood of Nag, the big black cobra, and he was five feet long from tongue to tail. When he had lifted one-third of himself clear of the ground, he stayed balancing to and fro exactly as a dandelion tuft balances in the wind, and he looked at Rikki-tikki with the wicked snake's eyes that never change their expression, whatever the snake may be thinking of.

"Who is Nag?" said he. "*I* am Nag. The great Brahm[2] put his mark upon all our people, when the first cobra spread his hood to keep the sun off Brahm as he slept. Look, and be afraid!"

---

[2] Brahma (Brahma) is a mythical "god" in the Indian religion of Buddhism.

He spread out his hood more than ever, and Rikki-tikki saw the spectacle-mark on the back of it that looks exactly like the eye part of a hook-and-eye fastening. He was afraid for the minute, but it is impossible for a mongoose to stay frightened for any length of time, and though Rikki-tikki had never met a live cobra before, his mother had fed him on dead ones, and he knew that all a grown mongoose's business in life was to fight and eat snakes. Nag knew that too and, at the bottom of his cold heart, he was afraid.

"Well," said Rikki-tikki, and his tail began to fluff up again, "marks or no marks, do you think it is right for you to eat fledglings out of a nest?"

Nag was thinking to himself, and watching the least little movement in the grass behind Rikki-tikki. He knew that mongooses in the garden meant death sooner or later for him and his family, but he wanted to get Rikki-tikki off his guard. So he dropped his head a little, and put it on one side.

"Let us talk," he said. "You eat eggs. Why should not I eat birds?" "Behind you! Look behind you!" sang Darzee.

Rikki-tikki knew better than to waste time in staring. He jumped up in the air as high as he could go, and just under him whizzed by the head of Nagaina, Nag's wicked wife. She had crept up behind him as he was talking, to make an end of him. He heard her savage hiss as the stroke missed. He came down almost across her back, and if he had been an old mongoose he would have known that then was the time to break her back with one bite; but he was afraid of the terrible lashing return stroke of the cobra. He bit, indeed, but did not bite long enough, and he jumped clear of the whisking tail, leaving Nagaina torn and angry.

"Wicked, wicked Darzee!" said Nag, lashing up as high as he could reach toward the nest in the thornbush. But Darzee had built it out of reach of snakes, and it only swayed to and fro.

Rikki-tikki felt his eyes growing red and hot (when a mongoose's eyes grow red, he is angry), and he sat back on his tail and hind legs like a little kangaroo, and looked all round him, and chattered with rage. But Nag and Nagaina had disappeared into the grass. When a snake misses its stroke, it never says anything or gives any sign of what it means to do next. Rikki-tikki did not care to follow them, for he did not feel sure that he could manage two snakes at once. So he trotted off to the gravel path near the house, and sat down to think. It was a serious matter for him.

If you read the old books of natural history, you will find they say that when the mongoose fights the snake and happens to get bitten, he runs off and eats some herb that cures him. That is not true. The victory is only a matter of quickness of eye and quickness of foot—snake's blow against mongoose's jump—and as no eye can follow the motion of a snake's head when it strikes, this makes things much more wonderful than any magic herb. Rikki-tikki knew he was a young mongoose, and it made him all the more pleased to think that he had managed to escape a blow from behind. It gave him confidence in himself, and when Teddy came running down the path, Rikki-tikki was ready to be petted.

But just as Teddy was stooping, something wriggled a little in the dust, and a tiny voice said: "Be careful. I am Death!" It was Karait, the dusty brown snakeling that lies for choice on the dusty earth; and his bite is as dangerous as the cobra's. But he is so small that nobody thinks of him, and so he does the more harm to people.

Rikki-tikki's eyes grew red again, and he danced up to Karait with the peculiar rocking, swaying motion that he had inherited from his family. It looks very funny, but it is so perfectly balanced a gait that you can fly off from it at any angle you please, and in dealing with snakes this is an advantage.

If Rikki-tikki had only known, he was doing a much more dangerous thing than fighting Nag, for Karait is so small, and can turn so quickly, that unless Rikki bit him close to the back of the head, he would get the return stroke in his eye or his lip. But Rikki did not know. His eyes were all red, and he rocked back and forth, looking for a good place to hold. Karait struck out. Rikki jumped sideways and tried to run in, but the wicked little dusty gray head lashed within a fraction of his shoulder, and he had to jump over the body, and the head followed his heels close.

Teddy shouted to the house: "Oh, look here! Our mongoose is killing a snake." And Rikki-tikki heard a scream from Teddy's mother. His father ran out with a stick, but by the time he came up, Karait had lunged out once too far, and Rikki-tikki had sprung, jumped on the snake's back, dropped his head far between his forelegs, bitten as high up the back as he could get hold, and rolled away. That bite paralyzed Karait, and Rikki-tikki was just going to eat him up from the tail, after the custom of his family at dinner, when he remembered that a full meal makes a slow mongoose, and if he wanted all his strength and quickness ready, he must keep himself thin.

He went away for a dust bath under the castor-oil bushes, while Teddy's father beat the dead Karait. "What is the use of that?" thought Rikki-tikki. "I have settled it all;" and then Teddy's mother picked him up from the dust and hugged him, crying that he had saved Teddy from death, and Teddy's father said that he was a providence, and Teddy looked on with big scared eyes. Rikki-tikki was rather amused at all the fuss, which, of course, he did not understand. Teddy's mother might just as well have petted Teddy for playing in the dust. Rikki was thoroughly enjoying himself.

That night at dinner, walking to and fro among the wine-glasses on the table, he might have stuffed himself three times over with nice things. But he remembered Nag and Nagaina, and though it was very pleasant to be patted and petted by Teddy's mother, and to sit on Teddy's shoulder, his eyes would get red from time to time, and he would go off into his long war cry of "Rikk-tikk-tikki-tikki-tchk!"

Teddy carried him off to bed, and insisted on Rikki-tikki sleeping under his chin. Rikki-tikki was too well bred to bite or scratch, but as soon as Teddy was asleep he went off for his nightly walk round the house, and in the dark he ran up against Chuchundra, the muskrat, creeping around by the wall. Chuchundra is a broken-hearted little beast. He whimpers and cheeps all the night, trying to make up his mind to run into the middle of the room. But he never gets there.

"Don't kill me," said Chuchundra, almost weeping. "Rikki-tikki, don't kill me!"

"Do you think a snake-killer kills muskrats?" said Rikki-tikki scornfully.

"Those who kill snakes get killed by snakes," said Chuchundra, more sorrowfully than ever. "And how am I to be sure that Nag won't mistake me for you some dark night?"

"There's not the least danger," said Rikki-tikki. "But Nag is in the garden, and I know you don't go there."

"My cousin Chua, the rat, told me—" said Chuchundra, and then he stopped.

"Told you what?"

"H'sh! Nag is everywhere, Rikki-tikki. You should have talked to Chua in the garden."

"I didn't—so you must tell me. Quick, Chuchundra, or I'll bite you!"

Chuchundra sat down and cried till the tears rolled off his whiskers. "I am a very poor man," he sobbed. "I never had spirit enough to run out into the middle of the room. H'sh! I mustn't tell you anything. Can't you *hear*, Rikki-tikki?"

Rikki-tikki listened. The house was as still as still, but he thought he could just catch the faintest scratch-scratch in the world—a noise as faint as that of a wasp walking on a window-pane—the dry scratch of a snake's scales on brickwork.

"That's Nag or Nagaina," he said to himself, "and he is crawling into the bathroom sluice.[3] You're right, Chuchundra; I should have talked to Chua."

He stole off to Teddy's bathroom, but there was nothing there, and then to Teddy's mother's bathroom. At the bottom of the smooth plaster wall there was a brick pulled out to make a sluice for the bath water, and as Rikki-tikki stole in by the masonry curb where the bath is put, he heard Nag and Nagaina whispering together outside in the moonlight.

"When the house is emptied of people," said Nagaina to her husband, "he will have to go away, and then the garden will be our own again. Go in quietly, and remember that the big man who killed Karait is the first one to bite. Then come out and tell me, and we will hunt for Rikki-tikki together."

"But are you sure that there is anything to be gained by killing the people?" said Nag.

"Everything. When there were no people in the bungalow, did we have any mongoose in the garden? So long as the bungalow is empty, we are king and queen of the garden; and remember that as soon as our eggs in the melon bed hatch (as they may tomorrow), our children will need room and quiet."

"I had not thought of that," said Nag. "I will go, but there is no need that we should hunt for Rikki-tikki afterward. I will kill the big man and his wife, and the child if I can, and come away quietly. Then the bungalow will be empty, and Rikki-tikki will go."

Rikki-tikki tingled all over with rage and hatred at this, and then Nag's head came through the sluice, and his five feet of cold body followed it. Angry as he was, Rikki-tikki was very frightened as he saw the size of the big cobra. Nag coiled himself up, raised his head, and looked into the bathroom in the dark, and Rikki could see his eyes glitter.

"Now, if I kill him here, Nagaina will know; and if I fight him on the open floor, the odds are in his favor. What am I to do?" said Rikki-tikki-tavi.

Nag waved to and fro, and then Rikki-tikki heard him drinking from the biggest water-jar that was used to fill the bath. "That is good," said the snake. "Now, when Karait was killed, the big man had a stick. He may have that stick still, but when he comes in to bathe in the morning he will not have a stick. I shall wait here till he comes. Nagaina—do you hear me?—I shall wait here in the cool till daytime."

There was no answer from outside, so Rikki-tikki knew Nagaina had gone away. Nag coiled himself down, coil by coil, round the bulge at the bottom of the water jar, and Rikki-tikki stayed still as death. After an hour he began to move, muscle by muscle, toward the jar. Nag was asleep, and Rikki-tikki looked at his big back, wondering which would be the best place for a good hold. "If I don't break his back at the first jump," said Rikki, "he

---

[3] drain

can still fight. And if he fights—O Rikki!" He looked at the thickness of the neck below the hood, but that was too much for him; and a bite near the tail would only make Nag savage.

"It must be the head"' he said at last; "the head above the hood. And, when I am once there, I must not let go."

Then he jumped. The head was lying a little clear of the water jar, under the curve of it; and, as his teeth met, Rikki braced his back against the bulge of the red earthenware to hold down the head. This gave him just one second's purchase, and he made the most of it. Then he was battered to and fro as a rat is shaken by a dog—to and fro on the floor, up and down, and around in great circles, but his eyes were red, and he held on as the body cart-whipped over the floor, upsetting the tin dipper and the soap dish and the flesh brush, and banged against the tin side of the bath. As he held he closed his jaws tighter and tighter, for he made sure he would be banged to death, and, for the honor of his family, he preferred to be found with his teeth locked. He was dizzy, aching, and felt shaken to pieces when something went off like a thunderclap just behind him. A hot wind knocked him senseless, and red fire singed his fur. The big man had been wakened by the noise, and had fired both barrels of a shotgun into Nag just behind the hood.

Rikki-tikki held on with his eyes shut, for now he was quite sure he was dead. But the head did not move, and the big man picked him up and said, "It's the mongoose again, Alice. The little chap has saved *our* lives now." Then Teddy's mother came in with a very white face, and saw what was left of Nag, and Rikki-tikki dragged himself to Teddy's bedroom and spent half the rest of the night shaking himself tenderly to find out whether he really was broken into forty pieces, as he fancied.

When morning came he was very stiff, but well pleased with his doings. "Now I have Nagaina to settle with, and she will be worse than five Nags, and there's no knowing when the eggs she spoke of will hatch. Goodness! I must go and see Darzee," he said.

Without waiting for breakfast, Rikki-tikki ran to the thornbush where Darzee was singing a song of triumph at the top of his voice. The news of Nag's death was all over the garden, for the sweeper had thrown the body on the rubbish-heap.

"Oh, you stupid tuft of feathers!" said Rikki-tikki angrily. "Is this the time to sing?"

"Nag is dead—is dead—is dead!" sang Darzee.

"The valiant Rikki-tikki caught him by the head and held fast. The big man brought the bang-stick, and Nag fell in two pieces! He will never eat my babies again."

"All that's true enough. But where's Nagaina?" said Rikki-tikki, looking carefully round him.

"Nagaina came to the bathroom sluice and called for Nag," Darzee went on, "and Nag came out on the end of a stick—the sweeper picked him up on the end of a stick and threw him upon the rubbish heap. Let us sing about the great, the red-eyed Rikki-tikki!" And Darzee filled his throat and sang.

"If I could get up to your nest, I'd roll your babies out!" said Rikki-tikki. "You don't know when to do the right thing at the right time. You're safe enough in your nest there, but it's war for me down here. Stop singing a minute, Darzee."

"For the great, the beautiful Rikki-tikki's sake I will stop," said Darzee. "What is it, O Killer of the terrible Nag?"

"Where is Nagaina, for the third time?"

"On the rubbish heap by the stables, mourning for Nag. Great is Rikki-tikki with the white teeth."

"Bother my white teeth! Have you ever heard where she keeps her eggs?"

"In the melon bed, on the end nearest the wall, where the sun strikes nearly all day. She hid them there weeks ago."

"And you never thought it worthwhile to tell me? The end nearest the wall, you said?"

"Rikki-tikki, you are not going to eat her eggs?"

"Not eat, exactly; no. Darzee, if you have a grain of sense you will fly off to the stables and pretend that your wing is broken, and let Nagaina chase you away to this bush. I must get to the melon-bed, and if I went there now she'd see me."

Darzee was a feather-brained little fellow who could never hold more than one idea at a time in his head. And just because he knew that Nagaina's children were born in eggs like his own, he didn't think at first that it was fair to kill them. But his wife was a sensible bird, and she knew that cobra's eggs meant young cobras later on. So she flew off from the nest, and left Darzee to keep the babies warm, and continue his song about the death of Nag. Darzee was very like a man in some ways.

She fluttered in front of Nagaina by the rubbish heap and cried out, "Oh, my wing is broken! The boy in the house threw a stone at me and broke it." Then she fluttered more desperately than ever.

Nagaina lifted up her head and hissed, "You warned Rikki-tikki when I would have killed him. Indeed and truly, you've chosen a bad place to be lame in." And she moved toward Darzee's wife, slipping along over the dust.

"The boy broke it with a stone!" shrieked Darzee's wife.

"Well! It may be some consolation to you when you're dead to know that I shall settle accounts with the boy. My husband lies on the rubbish heap this morning, but before night the boy in the house will lie very still. What is the use of running away? I am sure to catch you. Little fool, look at me!"

Darzee's wife knew better than to do that, for a bird who looks at a snake's eyes gets so frightened that she cannot move. Darzee's wife fluttered on, piping sorrowfully, and never leaving the ground, and Nagaina quickened her pace.

Rikki-tikki heard them going up the path from the stables, and he raced for the end of the melon patch near the wall.

There, in the warm litter above the melons, very cunningly hidden, he found twenty-five eggs, about the size of a bantam's eggs,[4] but with whitish skin instead of shell.

"I was not a day too soon," he said, for he could see the baby cobras curled up inside the skin, and he knew that the minute they were hatched they could each kill a man or a mongoose. He bit off the tops of the eggs as fast as he could, taking care to crush the young cobras, and turned over the litter from time to time to see whether he had missed any. At last there were only three eggs left, and Rikki-tikki began to chuckle to himself, when he heard Darzee's wife screaming:

"Rikki-tikki, I led Nagaina toward the house, and she has gone into the veranda, and—oh, come quickly—she means killing!" Rikki-tikki smashed two eggs, and tumbled backward down the melon-bed with the third egg in his mouth, and scuttled to the veranda as hard as he could put foot to the

---

[4] A bantam is a small chicken.

ground. Teddy and his mother and father were there at early breakfast, but Rikki-tikki saw that they were not eating anything. They sat stone-still, and their faces were white. Nagaina was coiled up on the matting by Teddy's chair, within easy striking distance of Teddy's bare leg, and she was swaying to and fro, singing a song of triumph.

"Son of the big man that killed Nag," she hissed, "stay still. I am not ready yet. Wait a little. Keep very still, all you three! If you move I strike, and if you do not move I strike. Oh, foolish people, who killed my Nag!"

Teddy's eyes were fixed on his father, and all his father could do was to whisper, "Sit still, Teddy. You mustn't move. Teddy, keep still."

Then Rikki-tikki came up and cried, "Turn round, Nagaina. Turn and fight!"

"All in good time," said she, without moving her eyes. "I will settle my account with you presently. Look at your friends, Rikki-tikki. They are still and white. They are afraid. They dare not move, and if you come a step nearer I strike."

"Look at your eggs," said Rikki-tikki, "in the melon bed near the wall. Go and look, Nagaina!"

The big snake turned half around, and saw the egg on the veranda.

"Ah-h! Give it to me," she said. Rikki-tikki put his paws one on each side of the egg, and his eyes were blood-red.

"What price for a snake's egg? For a young cobra? For a young king cobra? For the last—the very last of the brood? The ants are eating all the others down by the melon bed."

Nagaina spun clear round, forgetting everything for the sake of the one egg.

Rikki-tikki saw Teddy's father shoot out a big hand, catch Teddy by the shoulder, and drag him across the little table with the teacups, safe and out of reach of Nagaina.

"Tricked! Tricked! Tricked! Rikk-tck-tck!" chuckled Rikki-tikki. "The boy is safe, and it was I—I—I that caught Nag by the hood last night in the bathroom." Then he began to jump up and down, all four feet together, his head close to the floor. "He threw me to and fro, but he could not shake me off. He was dead before the big man blew him in two. I did it! Rikki-tikki-tck-tck! Come then, Nagaina. Come and fight with me. You shall not be a widow long."

Nagaina saw that she had lost her chance of killing Teddy, and the egg lay between Rikki-tikki's paws.

"Give me the egg, Rikki-tikki. Give me the last of my eggs, and I will go away and never come back," she said, lowering her hood.

"Yes, you will go away, and you will never come back. For you will go to the rubbish heap with Nag. Fight, widow! The big man has gone for his gun! Fight!"

Rikki-tikki was bounding all round Nagaina, keeping just out of reach of her stroke, his little eyes like hot coals.

Nagaina gathered herself together and flung out at him. Rikki-tikki jumped up and backward. Again and again and again she struck, and each time her head came with a whack on the matting of the veranda, and she gathered herself together like a watch spring.

Then Rikki-tikki danced in a circle to get behind her, and Nagaina spun round to keep her head to his head, so that the rustle of her tail on the matting sounded like dry leaves blown along by the wind.

He had forgotten the egg. It still lay on the veranda, and Nagaina came nearer and nearer to it, till at last, while Rikki-tikki was drawing breath, she caught it in her mouth, turned to the veranda steps, and flew like an arrow down the path, with Rikki-tikki behind her. When the cobra runs for her life, she goes like a whiplash flicked across a horse's neck.

Rikki-tikki knew that he must catch her, or all the trouble would begin again. She headed straight for the long grass by the thornbush, and as he was running Rikki-tikki heard Darzee still singing his foolish little song of triumph. But Darzee's wife was wiser. She flew off her nest as Nagaina came along, and flapped her wings about Nagaina's head. If Darzee had helped they might have turned her, but Nagaina only lowered her hood and went on. Still, the instant's delay brought Rikki-tikki up to her, and as she plunged into the rat-hole where she and Nag used to live, his little white teeth were clenched on her tail, and he went down with her—and very few mongooses, however wise and old they may be, care to follow a cobra into its hole. It was dark in the hole; and Rikki-tikki never knew when it might open out and give Nagaina room to turn and strike at him. He held on savagely, and stuck out his feet to act as brakes on the dark slope of the hot, moist earth.

Then the grass by the mouth of the hole stopped waving, and Darzee said, "It is all over with Rikki-tikki! We must sing his death song. Valiant Rikki-tikki is dead! For Nagaina will surely kill him underground."

So he sang a very mournful song that he made up on the spur of the minute, and just as he got to the most touching part, the grass quivered again, and Rikki-tikki, covered with dirt, dragged

himself out of the hole leg by leg, licking his whiskers. Darzee stopped with a little shout. Rikki-tikki shook some of the dust out of his fur and sneezed. "It is all over," he said. "The widow will never come out again." And the red ants that live between the grass stems heard him, and began to troop down one after another to see if he had spoken the truth.

Rikki-tikki curled himself up in the grass and slept where he was—slept and slept till it was late in the afternoon, for he had done a hard day's work.

"Now," he said, when he awoke, "I will go back to the house. Tell the Coppersmith, Darzee, and he will tell the garden that Nagaina is dead."

The Coppersmith is a bird who makes a noise exactly like the beating of a little hammer on a copper pot; and the reason he is always making it is because he is the town crier to every Indian garden, and tells all the news to everybody who cares to listen. As Rikki-tikki went up the path, he heard his "attention" notes like a tiny dinner gong, and then the steady "Ding-dong-tock! Nag is dead—dong! Nagaina is dead! Ding-dong-tock!" That set all the birds in the garden singing, and the frogs croaking, for Nag and Nagaina used to eat frogs as well as little birds.

When Rikki got to the house, Teddy and Teddy's mother (she looked very white still, for she had been fainting) and Teddy's father came out and almost cried over him; and that night he ate all that was given him till he could eat no more, and went to bed on Teddy's shoulder, where Teddy's mother saw him when she came to look late at night.

"He saved our lives and Teddy's life," she said to her husband. "Just think, he saved all our lives."

Rikki-tikki woke up with a jump, for the mongooses are light sleepers.

"Oh, it's you," said he. "What are you bothering for? All the cobras are dead. And if they weren't, I'm here."

Rikki-tikki had a right to be proud of himself. But he did not grow too proud, and he kept that garden as a mongoose should keep it, with tooth and jump and spring and bite, till never a cobra dared show its head inside the walls.

Questions for Review

1. What makes Rikki-tikki-tavi a likable character, almost like a person? What other characters did you think acted like humans?

2. Describe Nag and Nagaina's plans to get rid of Rikki-tikki-tavi. What plans does he make after he kills Nag?

3. Why do you think Kipling chose snakes as the enemies in the story? What Bible account is this similar to?

4. Look up two things and watch them: first, a real mongoose-cobra fight (watch the mongoose's strategy!), and second, the 1975 animated version of "Rikki-Tikki-Tavi," directed by Chuck Jones. How do these compare to the original story?

The First Telegraph Instrument

By Samuel Morse

Samuel Morse (1797-1872) was a Christian artist who was also interested in electricity. He labored for years on his telegraph invention, which sent instant messages via a series of clicks (representing letters of the alphabet) through wires. Today, the telegraph seems old-fashioned, but it was a giant step in history when Morse sent the first telegraph message in 1844 ("What hath God wrought?"[1]) from Washington, D.C. to Baltimore—38 miles away.

• • • • •

I immediately commenced,[2] with very limited means, to experiment upon my invention. My first instrument was made up of an old picture or canvas frame fastened to a table; the wheels of an old wooden clock, moved by a weight to carry the paper forward; three wooden drums, upon one of which the paper was wound and passed over the other two; a wooden pendulum[3] suspended to the top piece of the picture or stretching frame, and vibrating across the paper as it passes over the center wooden drum; a pencil at the lower end of the pendulum, in contact with the paper; an electromagnet fastened to a shelf across the picture or stretching frame, opposite to an armature[4] made fast to the pendulum; a type rule and type for breaking the circuit, resting on an endless band, composed of carpet-binding, which passed over two wooden rollers, moved by a wooden crank, and carried forward by points projecting from the bottom of the rule downward into the carpet-binding; a lever, with

Morse's Telegraph Instrument

a small weight on the upper side, and a tooth projecting downward at one end, operated on by the type, and a metallic fork also projecting downward over two mercury-cups, and a short circuit of wire, embracing the helices[5] of the electromagnet connected with the positive and negative poles of the battery and terminating in the mercury-cups.

---

[1] See Numbers 23:23.
[2] began
[3] a weight that swings back and forth
[4] frame
[5] spirals, springs

When the instrument was at rest the circuit was broken at the mercury-cups; as soon as the first type in the type-rule (put in motion by turning the wooden crank) came in contact with the tooth on the lever, it raised that end of the lever and depressed the other, bringing the prongs of the fork down into the mercury, thus closing the circuit; the current passing through the helices of the electro-magnet caused the pendulum to move and the pencil to make an oblique[6] mark upon the paper, which, in the mean-time, had been put in motion over the wooden drum. The tooth in the lever falling into the first two cogs of the types, the circuit was broken when the pendulum returned to its former position, the pencil making another mark as it returned across the paper. Thus, as the lever was alternately raised and depressed by the points of the type, the pencil passed to and fro across the slip of paper passing under it, making a mark resem-bling a succession of V's. The spaces between the types caused the pencil to mark horizontal lines, long or short, in propor-tion to the length of the spaces.

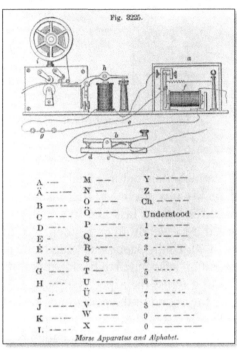

A Morse Code Chart

With this apparatus, rude[7] as it was, and completed before the first of the year 1836, I was enabled to and did mark down telegraphic intelligible signs, and to make and did make distinguishable sounds for telegraphing; and, having arrived at that point, I exhibited it to some of my friends early in that year, and among others to Professor Leonard D. Gale, who was a college professor in the university. I also experimented with the chemical power of the electric current in 1836, and succeeded in marking my telegraphic signs upon paper dipped in tur-meric and a solution of the sulphate of soda (as well as other salts), by pass-ing the current through it. I was soon satisfied, however, that the electro-magnetic power was more available for telegraphic purposes and possessed many advantages over any other, and I turned my thoughts in that direction.

---

[6] slanted
[7] simple, basic

Early in 1836 I procured[8] forty feet of wire, and putting it in the circuit I found that my battery of one cup was not sufficient to work my instrument. This result suggested to me the probability that the magnetism to be obtained from the electric current would diminish in proportion as the circuit was lengthened, so as to be insufficient for any practical purposes at great distances; and to remove that probable obstacle to my success I conceived the idea of combining two or more circuits together in the manner described in my first patent, each with an independent battery, making use of the magnetism of the current on the first to close and break the second; the second, the third, and so on. This contrivance[9] was fully set forth in my patents.[10] My chief concern, therefore, on my subsequent

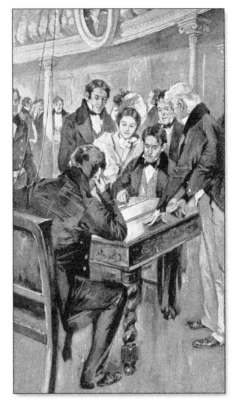

patents was to ascertain[11] to what distance from the battery sufficient magnetism could be obtained to vibrate a piece of metal, knowing that, if I could obtain the least motion at the distance of eight or ten miles, the ultimate object was within my grasp. A practical mode of communicating the impulse of one circuit to another, such as that described in my patent of 1840, was matured as early as the spring of 1837, and exhibited then to Professor Gale, my confidential friend.

Up to the autumn of 1837 my telegraphic apparatus existed in so rude a form that I felt a reluctance to have it seen. My means were very limited— so limited as to preclude[12] the possibility of constructing an apparatus of such mechanical finish as to warrant my success in venturing upon its public exhibition. I had no wish to expose to ridicule the representative of so many hours of laborious thought. Prior to the summer of 1837, at which time Mr. Alfred Vail's attention became attracted to my Telegraph, I depended upon

---

[8] obtained
[9] setup, plan
[10] A patent is a legal document giving an inventor credit for an invention.
[11] find out
[12] prevent

my pencil for subsistence.[13] Indeed, so straitened[14] were my circumstances that, in order to save time to carry out my invention and to economize my scanty means, I had for many months lodged and eaten in my studio, procuring my food in small quantities from some grocery, and preparing it myself. To conceal from my friends the stinted manner in which I lived, I was in the habit of bringing my food to my room in the evenings, and this was my mode of life for many years.

Morse's First-Ever Telegraph Message: "What Hath God Wrought"

Questions for Review

1. Even without knowing much about the machinery Morse talks about in this selection, how do you know his work is impressive?

2. What difficult situation did Morse endure to be able to work on his telegraph invention?

3. In 1825, Samuel Morse's wife, Lucretia, died after giving birth to their child. She was then in Connecticut, and he was in New York. News traveled so slowly that Samuel didn't know for a week that she had died, and he was too late to even attend her funeral. How do you think this incident might have his motivated him to invent the telegraph?

4. Watch a video of a person sending and receiving a telegraph. How hard do you think it would be to learn this skill?

---

[13] survival
[14] severe, difficult

The Leak

By Jacques Futrelle

Former news writer Jacques Futrelle (1875-1912), like the best news writers, learned to write in a way that quickly and efficiently got the facts out, often in the very first paragraph. When Futrelle, who was a Sherlock Holmes fan, created the Thinking Machine stories, he employed the same snappy writing style. (Check out the first paragraph!) Try to use the same logic that The Thinking Machine uses to figure out how the story's crimes are being committed.

• • • • •

"Really great criminals are never found out, for the simple reason that the greatest crimes—their crimes—are never discovered," remarked Professor Augustus S. F. X. Van Dusen positively. "There is genius in the perpetration of crime, Mr. Grayson, just as there must be in its detection, unless it is the shallow work of a bungler. In this latter case there have been instances where even the police have uncovered the truth. But the expert criminal, the man of genius—the professional, I may say—regards as perfect only that crime which does not and cannot be made to appear a crime at all; therefore one that can never under any circumstances involve him, or anyone else."

The financier, J. Morgan Grayson, regarded this wizened[1] little man of science—The Thinking Machine—thoughtfully, through the smoke of his cigar.

"It is a strange psychological fact that the casual criminal glories in his crime beforehand, and from one to ten minutes afterward," The Thinking Machine continued. "For instance, the man who kills for revenge wants the world to know it is his work; but at the end of ten minutes comes fear, and then paradoxically[2] enough, he will seek to hide his crime and protect himself. With fear comes panic, with panic irresponsibility, and then he makes

---

[1] wrinkly, withered
[2] illogically, in contradiction

the mistake—hews a pathway which the trained mind follows from motive to a prison cell."

"These are the men who are found out. But there are men of genius, Mr. Grayson, professionally engaged in crime. We never hear of them because they are never caught, and we never even suspect them because they make no mistake. Imagine the great brains of history turned to crime. Well, there are today brains as great as any of those of history; there is murder and theft and robbery under our noses that we never dream of. If I, for instance, should become an active criminal—" He paused.

Grayson, with a queer expression on his face, puffed steadily at his cigar.

"I could kill you now, here in this room," The Thinking Machine went on calmly, "and no one would ever know, never even suspect. Why? Because I would make no mistake."

It was not a boast as he said it; it was merely a statement of fact. Grayson appeared to be a little startled. Where there had been only impatient interest in his manner, there was now fascination.

"How would you kill me, for instance?" he inquired curiously.

"With any one of a dozen poisons, with virulent[3] germs, or even with a knife or revolver," replied the scientist placidly. "You see, I know how to use poisons; I know how to inoculate[4] with germs; I know how to produce a suicidal appearance perfectly with either a revolver or knife. And I never make mistakes, Mr. Grayson. In the sciences we must be exact—not approximately so, but absolutely so. We must know. It isn't like carpentry. A carpenter may make a trivial mistake in a joint, and it will not weaken his house; but if the scientist makes one mistake, the whole structure tumbles down. We must know. Knowledge is progress. We gain knowledge through observation and logic—inevitable logic. And logic tells us that two and two make four—not sometimes, but all the time."

Grayson flicked the ashes off his cigar thoughtfully, and little wrinkles appeared about his eyes as he stared into the drawn, inscrutable[5] face of the scientist. The enormous, straw-yellow head was cushioned against the chair, the squinting, watery blue eyes turned upward, and the slender white fingers at rest, tip to tip. The financier drew a long breath. "I have been informed that you were a remarkable man," he said at last slowly. "I believe it. Quinton Frazer, the banker who gave me the letter of introduction to you, told me how you once solved a remarkable mystery in which—"

"Yes, yes," interrupted the scientist shortly, "the Ralston Bank burglary—I remember."

---

[3] dangerous, contagious
[4] inject someone with a needle
[5] mysterious, unreadable

"So I came to you to enlist your aid in something which is more inexplicable than that," Grayson went on hesitatingly. "I know that no fee I might offer would influence you; yet it is a case which—"

"State it," interrupted The Thinking Machine again.

"It isn't a crime—that is, a crime that can be reached by law," Grayson hurried on, "but it has cost me millions, and—"

For one instant The Thinking Machine lowered his squint eyes to those of his visitor, then raised them again. "Millions!" he repeated. "How many?"

"Six, eight, perhaps ten," was the reply. "Briefly, there is a leak in my office. My plans become known to others almost by the time I have perfected them. My plans are large; I have millions at stake; and the greatest secrecy is absolutely essential. For years I have been able to preserve this secrecy; but half a dozen times in the last eight weeks my plans have become known, and I have been caught. Unless you know the Street, you can't imagine what a tremendous disadvantage it is to have someone know your next move to the minutest detail and, knowing it, defeat you at every turn."

"No, I don't know your world of finance, Mr. Grayson," remarked The Thinking Machine. "Give me an instance."

"Well, take this last case," said the financier earnestly. "Briefly, without technicalities,[6] I had planned to unload the securities of the P., Q. & X. Railway, protecting myself through brokers, and force the outstanding stock down to a price where other brokers, acting for me, could buy far below the actual value. In this way I intended to get complete control of the stock. But my plans became known, and when I began to unload everything was snapped up by the opposition, with the result that instead of gaining control of the road I lost heavily. This same thing has happened, with variations, half a dozen times."

"I presume that is strictly honest?" inquired the scientist mildly.

"Honest?" repeated Grayson. "Certainly—of course."

"I shall not pretend to understand all that," said The Thinking Machine curtly. "It doesn't seem to matter, anyway. You want to know where the leak is. Is that right?"

"Precisely."

"Well, who is in your confidence?"

"No one, except my stenographer."[7]

"Who is he, please?"

"It's a woman—Miss Evelyn Winthrop. She has been in my employ for six years in the same capacity—more than five years before this leak appeared. I trust her absolutely."

---

[6] complicated details

[7] A stenographer is a secretary who takes notes by hand, types them up, or both.

"No man knows your business?"

"No," replied the financier grimly. "I learned years ago that no one could keep my secrets as well as I do—there are too many temptations. Therefore, I never mention my plans to anyone—never—to anyone!"

"Except your stenographer," corrected the scientist.

"I work for days, weeks, sometimes months, perfecting plans, and it's all in my head, not on paper—not a scratch of it," explained Grayson. "When I say that she is in my confidence, I mean that she knows my plans only half an hour or less before the machinery is put into motion. For instance, I planned this P., Q. & X. deal. My brokers didn't know of it; Miss Winthrop never heard of it until twenty minutes before the Stock Exchange opened for business. Then I dictated to her, as I always do, some short letters of instructions to my agents. That is all she knew of it."

"You outlined the plan in those letters?"

"No; they merely told my brokers what to do."

"But a shrewd person, knowing the contents of all those letters, could have learned what you intended to do?"

"Yes; but no one person knew the contents of all the letters. No one broker knew what was in the other letters. Miss Winthrop and I were the only two human beings who knew all that was in them."

The Thinking Machine sat silent for so long that Grayson began to fidget in his chair. "Who was in the room besides you and Miss Winthrop before the letters were sent?" he asked at last.

"No one," responded Grayson emphatically. "For an hour before I dictated those letters, until at least an hour afterward, after my plans had gone to smash, no one entered that room. Only she and I work there."

"But when she finished the letters, she went out?" insisted The Thinking Machine.

"No," declared the financier, "she didn't even leave her desk."

"Or perhaps sent something out—carbon copies of the letters?"

"No."

"Or called up a friend on the telephone?" continued The Thinking Machine quietly.

"Nor that," retorted Grayson.

"Or signaled to someone through the window?"

"No," said the financier again. "She finished the letters, then remained quietly at her desk, reading a book. She hardly moved for two hours."

The Thinking Machine lowered his eyes and glared straight into those of the financier. "Someone listened at the window?" he went on after a moment.

"No. It is sixteen stories up, fronting the street, and there is no fire escape."

"Or the door?"

"If you knew the arrangement of my offices, you would see how utterly impossible that would be, because—"

"Nothing is impossible, Mr. Grayson," snapped the scientist abruptly. "It might be improbable, but not impossible. Don't say that—it annoys me exceedingly." He was silent for a moment. Grayson stared at him blankly. "Did either you or she answer a call on the phone?"

"No one called; we called no one."

"Any holes or cracks—in your flooring or walls or ceilings?" demanded the scientist.

"Private detectives whom I had employed looked for such an opening, and there was none," replied Grayson.

Again The Thinking Machine was silent for a long time. Grayson lighted a fresh cigar and settled back in his chair patiently. Faint cobweb-by lines began to appear on the dome-like brow of the scientist, and slowly the squint eyes were narrowing.

"The letters you wrote were intercepted?" he suggested at last.

"No," exclaimed Grayson flatly. "Those letters were sent direct to the brokers by a dozen different methods, and every one of them had been delivered by five minutes of ten o'clock, when business begins. The last one left me at ten minutes of ten."

"Dear me! Dear me!" The Thinking Machine rose and paced the length of the room.

"You don't give me credit for the extraordinary precautions I have taken, particularly in this last P., Q. & X. deal," Grayson continued. "I left positively nothing undone to insure absolute secrecy. And Miss Winthrop, I know, is innocent of any connection with the affair. The private detectives suspected her at first, as you do, and she was watched in and out of my office for weeks. When she was not under my eyes, she was under the eyes of men to whom I had promised an extravagant sum of money if they found the leak. She didn't know it then, and doesn't know it now. I am heartily ashamed of it all, because the investigation proved her absolute loyalty to me. On this last day she was directly under my eyes for two hours; and she didn't make one movement that I didn't note, because the thing meant millions to me. That proved beyond all question that it was no fault of hers. What could I do?"

The Thinking Machine didn't say. He paused at a window, and for minute after minute stood motionless there, with eyes narrowed to mere slits.

"I was on the point of discharging[8] Miss Winthrop," the financier went on, "but her innocence was so thoroughly proved to me by this last affair that it would have been unjust, and so—"

---

[8] firing

Suddenly the scientist turned upon his visitor. "Do you talk in your sleep?" he demanded.

"No," was the prompt reply. "I had thought of that too. It is beyond all ordinary things, Professor. Yet there is a leak that is costing me millions."

"It comes down to this, Mr. Grayson," The Thinking Machine informed him crabbedly. "If only you and Miss Winthrop knew those plans, and no one else, and they did leak, and were not deduced from other things, then either you or she permitted them to leak, intentionally or unintentionally. That is as pure logic as two and two make four; there is no need to argue it."

"Well, of course, I didn't," said Grayson.

"Then Miss Winthrop did," declared The Thinking Machine finally, positively; "unless we credit the opposition, as you call it, with telepathic[9] gifts hitherto[10] unheard of. By the way, you have referred to the other side only as the opposition. Do the same men, the same clique,[11] appear against you all the time, or is it only one man?"

"It's a clique," explained the financier, "with millions back of it, headed by Ralph Matthews, a young man to whom I give credit for being the prime factor against me." His lips were set sternly.

"Why?" demanded the scientist.

"Because every time he sees me he grins," was the reply. Grayson seemed suddenly discomfited.

The Thinking Machine went to a desk, addressed an envelope, folded a sheet of paper, placed it inside, then sealed it. At length he turned back to his visitor. "Is Miss Winthrop at your office now?"

"Yes."

"Let us go there, then."

A few minutes later the eminent[12] financier ushered the eminent scientist into his private office on the Street. The only person there was a young woman—a woman of twenty-six or-seven, perhaps—who turned, saw Grayson, and resumed reading. The financier motioned to a seat. Instead of sitting, however, The Thinking Machine went straight to Miss Winthrop and extended a sealed envelope to her.

"Mr. Ralph Matthews asked me to hand you this," he said.

The young woman glanced up into his face frankly, yet with a certain timidity, took the envelope, and turned it curiously in her hand.

"Mr. Ralph Matthews," she repeated, as if the name was a strange one. "I don't think I know him."

---

[9] signaling and/or reading others' minds
[10] up until now
[11] group
[12] well-known, respected

The Thinking Machine stood staring at her aggressively, as she opened the envelope and drew out the sheet of paper. There was no expression save surprise—bewilderment, rather—to be read on her face.

"Why, it's a blank sheet!" she remarked, puzzled.

The scientist turned suddenly toward Grayson, who had witnessed the incident with frank astonishment in his eyes. "Your telephone a moment, please," he requested.

"Certainly; here," replied Grayson.

"This will do," remarked the scientist.

He leaned forward over the desk where Miss Winthrop sat, still gazing at him in a sort of bewilderment, picked up the receiver, and held it to his ear. A few moments later he was talking to Hutchinson Hatch, reporter.

"I merely wanted to ask you to meet me at my apartment in an hour," said the scientist. "It is very important."

That was all. He hung up the receiver, paused for a moment to admire an exquisitely wrought silver box—a "vanity" box[13]—on Miss Winthrop's desk, beside the telephone, then took a seat beside Grayson and began to discourse[14] almost pleasantly upon the prevailing meteorological conditions. Grayson merely stared; Miss Winthrop continued her reading.

• • • • •

Professor Augustus S. F. X. Van Dusen, distinguished scientist, and Hutchinson Hatch, newspaper reporter, were poking round among the chimney pots and other obstructions on the roof of a skyscraper. Far below them the slumber-enshrouded city was spread out like a panorama, streets dotted brilliantly with lights, and roofs hazily visible through mists of night. Above, the infinite blackness hung like a veil, with starpoints breaking through here and there.

"Here are the wires," Hatch said at last, and he stooped.

The Thinking Machine knelt on the roof beside him, and for several minutes they remained thus in the darkness, with only the glow of a flash-light to indicate their presence. Finally, The Thinking Machine rose.

"That's the wire you want, Mr. Hatch," he said. "I'll leave the rest of it to you."

"Are you sure?" asked the reporter.

"I am always sure," was the tart response.

Hatch opened a small hand satchel and removed several queerly wrought[15] tools. These he spread on the roof beside him; then, kneeling

---

[13] used to hold makeup, hairbrushes, and so on
[14] chat
[15] shaped

again, began his work. For half an hour he labored in the gloom, with only the flashlight to aid him, and then he rose.

"It's all right," he said.

The Thinking Machine examined the work that had been done, grunted his satisfaction, and together they went to the skylight, leaving a thin, insulated wire behind them, stringing along to mark their path. They passed down through the roof and into the darkness of the hall of the upper story. Here the light was extinguished. From far below came the faint echo of a man's footsteps as the watchman passed through the silent, deserted building.

"Be careful!" warned The Thinking Machine.

They went along the hall to a room in the rear, and still the wire trailed behind. At the last door they stopped. The Thinking Machine fumbled with some keys, then opened the way. Here an electric light was on. The room was bare of furniture, the only sign of recent occupancy being a telephone instrument on the wall.

Here The Thinking Machine stopped and stared at the spool of wire which he had permitted to wind off as he walked, and his thin face expressed doubt.

"It wouldn't be safe," he said at last, "to leave the wire exposed as we have left it. True, this floor is not occupied; but someone might pass this way and disturb it. You take the spool, go back to the roof, winding the wire as you go, then swing the spool down to me over the side of the building, so that I can bring it in through the window. That will be best. I will catch it here, and thus there will be nothing to indicate any connection." Hatch ent out quietly and closed the door.

• • • • •

Twice the following day The Thinking Machine spoke to the financier over the telephone. Grayson was in his private office, Miss Winthrop at her desk, when the first call came.

"Be careful in answering my questions," warned The Thinking Machine when Grayson answered. "Do you know how long Miss Winthrop has owned the little silver box which is now on her desk, near the telephone?"

Grayson glanced round involuntarily to where the girl sat idly turning over the leaves of her book. "Yes," he answered, "for seven months. I gave it to her last Christmas."

"Ah!" exclaimed the scientist. "That simplifies matters. Where did you buy it?"

Grayson mentioned the name of a well-known jeweler.

Considerably later in the day The Thinking Machine called Grayson to the telephone again.

"What make of typewriter does she use?" came the querulous[16] voice over the wire.

Grayson named it.

While Grayson sat with deeply perplexed lines in his face, the diminutive[17] scientist called upon Hutchinson Hatch at his office.

"Do you use a typewriter?" demanded The Thinking Machine.

"Yes."

"What kind?"

"Oh, four or five kinds—we have half a dozen different makes in the office."

They passed along through the city room, at that moment practically deserted, until finally the watery blue eyes settled upon a typewriter with the name emblazoned on the front.

"That's it!" exclaimed The Thinking Machine. "Write something on it," he directed Hatch.

Hatch drew up a chair and rolled off several lines of the immortal practice sentence, beginning, "Now is the time for all good men—"

The Thinking Machine sat beside him, squinting across the room in deep abstraction, and listening intently. His head was turned away from the reporter, but his ear was within a few inches of the machine. For half a minute he sat there listening, then shook his head.

"Strike your vowels," he commanded; "first slowly, then rapidly."

Again Hatch obeyed, while the scientist listened. And again he shook his head. Then in turn every make of machine in the office was tested the same way. At the end The Thinking Machine rose and went his way. There was an expression nearly approaching complete bewilderment on his face.

• • • • •

For hour after hour that night The Thinking Machine half lay in a huge chair in his laboratory, with eyes turned uncompromisingly upward, and an expression of complete concentration on his face. There was no change either in his position or his gaze as minute succeeded minute; the brow was deeply wrinkled now, and the thin line of the lips was drawn taut. The tiny clock in the reception room struck ten, eleven, twelve, and finally one. At just half-past one The Thinking Machine rose suddenly.

"Positively I am getting stupid!" he grumbled half aloud. "Of course! Of course! Why couldn't I have thought of that in the first place?"

So it came about that Grayson did not go to his office on the following morning at the usual time. Instead, he called again upon The Thinking

---

[16] grouchy
[17] tiny

Machine in eager, expectant response to a note which had reached him at his home just before he started to his office.

"Nothing yet," said The Thinking Machine as the financier entered. "But here is something you must do today. At one o'clock," the scientist went on, "you must issue orders for a gigantic deal of some sort; and you must issue them precisely as you have issued them in the past; there must be no variation. Dictate the letters as you have always done to Miss Winthrop—*but don't send them!* When they come to you, keep them until you see me."

"You mean that the deal must be purely imaginative?" inquired the financier.

"Precisely," was the reply. "But make your instructions circumstantial; give them enough detail to make them absolutely logical and convincing."

Grayson asked a dozen questions, answers to which were curtly denied, then went to his office. The Thinking Machine again called Hatch on the telephone.

"I've got it," he announced briefly. "I want the best telegraph operator you know. Bring him along and meet me in the room on the top floor where the telephone is at precisely fifteen minutes before one o'clock today."

"Telegraph operator?" Hatch repeated.

"That's what I said—telegraph operator!" replied the scientist irritably. "Goodbye."

Hatch smiled whimsically[18] at the other end as he heard the receiver banged on the hook—smiled because he knew the eccentric ways of this singular man, whose mind so accurately illuminated every problem to which it was directed. Then he went out to the telegraph room and borrowed the principal operator. They were in the little room on the top floor at precisely fifteen minutes of one.

The operator glanced about in astonishment. The room was still unfurnished, save for the telephone box on the wall.

"What do I do?" he asked The Thinking Machine.

"I'll tell you when the time comes," responded the scientist, as he glanced at his watch.

At three minutes of one o'clock he handed a sheet of blank paper to the operator, and gave him final instructions.

There was ludicrous mystification[19] on the operator's face; but he obeyed orders, grinning cheerfully at Hatch as he tilted his cigar up to keep the smoke out of his eyes. The Thinking Machine stood impatiently looking on, watch in hand. Hatch didn't know what was happening, but he was interested.

---

[18] amusingly
[19] "ludicrous mystification": ridiculous, funny confusion

At last the operator heard something. His face became suddenly alert. He continued to listen for a moment, and then came a smile of recognition.

• • • • •

Less than ten minutes after Miss Winthrop had handed over the type-written letters of instruction to Grayson for signature, and while he still sat turning them over in his hands, the door opened, and The Thinking Machine entered. He tossed a folded sheet of paper on the desk before Grayson, and went straight to Miss Winthrop.

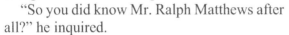

"So you did know Mr. Ralph Matthews after all?" he inquired.

The girl rose from her desk, and a flash of some subtle emotion passed over her face. "What do you mean, sir?" she demanded.

"You might as well remove the silver box," The Thinking Machine went on mercilessly. "There is no further need of the connection."

Miss Winthrop glanced down at the telephone extension on her desk, and her hand darted toward it. The silver "vanity" box was directly under the receiver,[20] supporting it, so that all weight was removed from the hook, and the line was open. She snatched the box and the receiver dropped back on the hook. The Thinking Machine turned to Grayson.

"It was Miss Winthrop," he said.

"Miss Winthrop!" exclaimed Grayson, "I can't believe it!"

"Read the paper I gave you, Mr. Grayson," directed The Thinking Machine coldly. "Perhaps that will enlighten her."

The financier opened the sheet, which had remained folded in his hand, and glanced at what was written there. Slowly he read it aloud: "PEABODY— Sell ten thousand shares L. & W. at 97. MCCRACKEN Co.—Sell ten thousand shares L. & W. at 97." He read on down the list, bewildered. Then gradually, as he realized the import[21] of what he read, there came a hardening of the lines about his mouth.

"I understand, Miss Winthrop," he said at last. "This is the substance of the orders I dictated, and in some way you made them known to persons for whom they were not intended. I don't know how you did it, of course; but I understand that you did do it, so—" He stepped to the door and opened it with grave courtesy. "You may go now."

---

[20] the telephone receiver
[21] seriousness

Miss Winthrop made no plea—merely bowed and went out. Grayson stood staring after her for a moment, then turned to The Thinking Machine and motioned him to a chair. "What happened?" he asked briskly.

"Miss Winthrop is a tremendously clever woman," replied The Thinking Machine. "She neglected to tell you, however, that besides being a stenographer and typist she is also a telegraph operator. She is so expert in each of her lines that she combined the two, if I may say it that way. In other words, in writing on the typewriter, she was clever enough to be able to *give the click of the machine the patterns in the Morse telegraphic code*—so that another telegraph operator at the other end of the phone could hear her machine and translate the clicks into words."

Grayson sat staring at him incredulously. "I still don't understand," he said finally.

The Thinking Machine rose and went to Miss Winthrop's desk. "Here is an extension telephone with the receiver on the hook. It happens that the little silver box which you gave Miss Winthrop is just tall enough to lift this receiver clear of the hook, and the minute the receiver is off the hook the line is open. When you were at your desk and she was here, you couldn't see this telephone; therefore it was a simple matter for her to lift the receiver, and place the silver box underneath, thus holding the line open permanently. That being true, the sound of the typewriter—*the striking of the keys*—would go over the open wire to whoever was listening at the other end. Then, if the striking of the keys typed out your letters and, by their frequency and pauses, simultaneously tapped out telegraphic code, an outside operator could read your letters at the same moment they were being written. That is all. It required extreme concentration on Miss Winthrop's part to type accurately in Morse rhythms."

"Oh, I see!" exclaimed Grayson.

"When I knew that the leak in your office was not in the usual way," continued The Thinking Machine, "I looked for the unusual. There is nothing very mysterious about it now—it was merely clever."

"Clever!" repeated Grayson, and his jaws snapped. "It is more than that. Why, it's criminal! She should be prosecuted."

"I shouldn't advise that, Mr. Grayson," returned the scientist coldly. "If it is honest—merely business—to juggle stocks as you told me you did, this is no more dishonest. And besides, remember that Miss Winthrop is backed by the people who have made millions out of you, and—well, I wouldn't prosecute. It is betrayal of trust, certainly; but—" He rose as if that were all, and started toward the door. "I would advise you, however, to discharge the person who operates your switchboard."

"Was she in the scheme, too?" demanded Grayson. He rushed out of the private office into the main office. At the door he met a clerk coming in.

"Where is Miss Mitchell?" demanded the financier hotly.

"I was just coming to tell you that she went out with Miss Winthrop just now without giving any explanation," replied the clerk.

"Good day, Mr. Grayson," said The Thinking Machine.

The financier nodded his thanks, then stalked back into his room.

• • • • •

In the course of time The Thinking Machine received a check for ten thousand dollars, signed, "J. Morgan Grayson."[22] He glared at it for a little while, then endorsed it in a crabbed hand, *Pay to the Trustees' Home for Crippled Children*, and sent Martha, his housekeeper, out to mail it.

Questions for Review

1. Why does The Thinking Machine say that the best criminals aren't even known as criminals at all?

2. What is Grayson's basic problem? What does The Thinking Machine say *must* be the source of the leak?

3. How is the crime committed? Were you able to guess, based on yesterday's reading?

---

[22] Ten thousand dollars at the time of this story's writing is equivalent to nearly half a million dollars today.

The Boat

By George MacDonald

 *Scottish minister and poet George MacDonald (1824-1905) also wrote many works of Christian fantasy. He was a key influence on later author C. S. Lewis, who wrote* The Chronicles of Narnia *and other Christian-themed fantasy novels. "The Boat" is a fictionalized take on several inter-actions between Jesus and Peter.*

· · · · ·

I owned a little boat a while ago,
And sailed the morning sea without a fear.
And whither[1] any breeze might fairly blow,
I steered my little craft afar and near.

Mine was the boat,
And mine the air.
And mine the sea.
Nor mine a care.

My boat became my place of mighty toil.[2]
I sailed at evening to the fishing ground.
At morn my boat was freighted with the spoil[3]
Which my all-conquering work had found.

Mine was the boat,
And mine the net,
And mine the skill
And power to get.

One day there came along that silent shore,
While I my net was casting in the sea,
A man who spoke as never man before.
I followed Him; new life began in me.[4]

Mine was the boat,
But His the voice,

---

[1] to whatever place
[2] labor
[3] "freighted with the spoil": filled with the goods
[4] See John 7:46.

And His the call.
Yet mine the choice.

Ah! 'twas a fearful night out on the lake.
And all my skill availed not, at the helm.
Till Him asleep I waked, crying, "Take
Thou the helm—lest water overwhelm!"

And His the boat,
And His the sea,
And His the peace
O'er all and me.

Once from the boat He taught the curious throng.[5]
Then bade[6] me cast my net into the sea;
I murmured, but obeyed, nor was it long
Before the catch amazed and humbled me.

His was the boat,
And His the skill,
And His the catch,
And His my will.

Questions for Review

1. Study the poem to figure out its rhyme scheme. How would you describe it?

2. How does Peter's attitude toward his life and change slowly over the course of the poem, as shown by the second, fourth, sixth, eight, and tenth stanzas?

---

[5] crowd
[6] told, invited

My Financial Career

By Stephen Leacock

The Canadian writer and humorist Stephen Leacock (1869-1944) was one of the funniest and most popular writers in the early 1900s. (Canadian writers still compete for the "Stephen Leacock Award," which is awarded yearly to the best humorous writing.) Leacock poked fun at many different subjects, and he wasn't afraid to take aim at himself now and then, either. Have you ever been in a situation like the one the young man finds himself in this story?

• • • • •

When I go into a bank I get rattled. The clerks rattle me; the wickets[1] rattle me; the sight of the money rattles me; everything rattles me.

The moment I cross the threshold of a bank and attempt to transact business there, I become an irresponsible idiot.

I knew this beforehand, but my salary had been raised to fifty dollars a month, and I felt that the bank was the only place for it.

So I shambled in and looked timidly round at the clerks. I had an idea that a person about to open an account must needs consult the manager.

I went up to a wicket marked "Accountant." The accountant was a tall, cool devil. The very sight of him rattled me. My voice was sepulchral.[2]

"Can I see the manager?" I said, and added solemnly, "alone." I don't know why I said "alone."

"Certainly," said the accountant, and fetched him.

The manager was a grave, calm man. I held my fifty-six dollars clutched in a crumpled ball in my pocket.

"Are you the manager?" I said. Heaven knows I didn't doubt it.

---

[1] service windows where customers talk to bank tellers
[2] gloomy, like someone speaking at a funeral

"Yes," he said.

"Can I see you," I asked, "alone?" I didn't want to say "alone" again, but without it the thing seemed self-evident.

The manager looked at me in some alarm. He felt that I had an awful secret to reveal.

"Come in here," he said, and led the way to a private room. He turned the key in the lock.

"We are safe from interruption here," he said; "sit down."

We both sat down and looked at each other. I found no voice to speak.

"You are one of Pinkerton's men, I presume," he said.[3]

He had gathered from my mysterious manner that I was a detective. I knew what he was thinking, and it made me worse.

"No, not from Pinkerton's," I said, seeming to imply that I came from a rival[4] agency.

"To tell the truth," I went on, as if I had been prompted to lie about it, "I am not a detective at all. I have come to open an account. I intend to keep all my money in this bank."

The manager looked relieved, but still serious; he concluded now that I was a son of Baron Rothschild or a young Gould.[5]

"A large account, I suppose," he said.

"Fairly large," I whispered. "I propose to deposit fifty-six dollars now and fifty dollars a month regularly."

The manager got up and opened the door. He called to the accountant.

"Mr. Montgomery," he said unkindly loud, "this gentleman is opening an account; he will deposit fifty-six dollars. Good morning."

I rose.

A big iron door stood open at the side of the room.

"Good morning," I said, and stepped into the safe.

"Come out," said the manager coldly, and showed me the other way.

I went up to the accountant's wicket and poked the ball of money at him with a quick convulsive[6] movement as if I were doing a conjuring[7] trick.

My face was ghastly pale.

"Here," I said, "deposit it." The tone of the words seemed to mean, "Let us do this painful thing while the fit is on us."

He took the money and gave it to another clerk.

He made me write the sum on a slip and sign my name in a book. I no longer knew what I was doing. The bank swam before my eyes.

---

[3] Allan Pinkerton (1819-1894) ran a famous detective agency.

[4] competing

[5] The Rothschild and Gould families are bankers and investors. Rich ones.

[6] jerky

[7] magic

"Is it deposited?" I asked in a hollow, vibrating voice.

"It is," said the accountant.

"Then I want to draw a check."

My idea was to draw out six dollars of it for present use. Someone gave me a checkbook through a wicket, and someone else began telling me how to write it out. The people in the bank had the impression that I was an invalid millionaire. I wrote something on the check and thrust it in at the clerk. He looked at it.

"What! are you drawing it all out again?" he asked in surprise. Then I realized that I had written fifty-six instead of six. I was too far gone to reason now. I had a feeling that it was impossible to explain the thing. All the clerks had stopped writing to look at me.

Reckless with misery, I made a plunge.

"Yes, the whole thing."

"You withdraw your money from the bank?"

"Every cent of it."

"Are you not going to deposit any more?" said the clerk, astonished.

"Never."

An idiot hope struck me that they might think something had insulted me while I was writing the check and that I had changed my mind. I made a wretched attempt to look like a man with a fearfully quick temper.

The clerk prepared to pay the money.

"How will you have it?" he said.

"What?"

"How will you have it?"

"Oh"—I caught his meaning and answered without even trying to think—"in fifties."

He gave me a fifty-dollar bill.

"And the six?" he asked dryly.

"In sixes," I said.

He gave it me and I rushed out.

As the big door swung behind me I caught the echo of a roar of laughter that went up to the ceiling of the bank. Since then I bank no more. I keep my money in cash in my trousers pocket and my savings in silver dollars in a sock.

Question for Review

Have you ever been in a situation where you got rattled and didn't know what to say? If so, what could you have done better, now that you look back on it? What could the bank customer in this story have done?

An Address to Young Converts

By George Müller

George Müller (1805-1898) led a sinful life in his youth, and at age 14 he was half-drunk and gambling at the same time his mother was dying. He became a Christian and ran orphanages in England, caring for more than 10,000 children in his lifetime. Müller never once asked for money, relying on God to answer his prayers for funds; many millions of dollars were sent to him to use. The following excerpts are from a sermon he preached in England.

• • • • •

As one who for fifty years has known the Lord, and has labored in word and doctrine,[1] I ought to be able, in some little measure, to lend a helping hand to these younger believers. And if God will only condescend[2] to use the acknowledgment of my own failures to which I refer, and of my experience, as a help to others in walking on the road to heaven, I trust that your coming here will not be in vain. This was the very purpose of my leaving home—that I might help these dear young brethren.

The Manner of Reading the Word

One of the most deeply important points is that of attending to the careful, prayerful reading of the Word of God, and meditation thereon. I would therefore ask your particular attention to one verse in the Epistle of Peter, where we are especially exhorted by the Holy Ghost through the apostle, regarding this subject. For the sake of the connection, let us read the first verse: "Wherefore laying aside all malice, and all guile and hypocrisies, and envies, and all evil-speakings, as newborn babes, desire the sincere milk of the Word, that ye may grow thereby; if so be ye have tasted that the Lord is gracious" (1 Peter 2:2).

The particular point to which I refer is contained in the second verse, "as newborn babes, desire the sincere milk of the Word." As growth in the natural life is attained by proper food, so in the spiritual life, if we desire to grow, this growth is only to be attained through the instrumentality of the Word of God. It is not stated here, as some might be very willing to say,

---

[1] "Let the elders that rule well be counted worthy of double honour, especially they who labour in the word and doctrine" (1 Timothy 5:17).
[2] come down (to Müller's level)

that "the reading of the Word may be of importance under some circumstances." Nor is it stated that you may gain profit by reading the statement which is made here; it is of the "Word," and of the Word alone, that the apostle speaks, and nothing else.

Cleave to the Word

You say that the reading of this tract or of that book often does you good. I do not question it. Nevertheless, the instrumentality which God has been specially pleased to appoint and to use is that of the Word itself; and just in the measure in which the disciples of the Lord Jesus Christ attend[3] to this, they will become strong in the Lord; and in so far as it is neglected, so far will they be weak. There is such a thing as babes being neglected, and what is the consequence? They never become healthy men or women, because of that early neglect.

Perhaps—and it is one of the most hurtful forms of this neglect—they obtain improper food, and therefore do not attain the full vigor of maturity. So with regard to the divine life. It is a most deeply important point, that we obtain right spiritual food at the very beginning of that life. What is that food? It is "the sincere milk of the Word"; that is the proper nourishment for the strengthening of the new life. Listen, then, my dear brethren and sisters, to some advice with regard to the Word...

[F]or the first four years of my Christian life I did not carefully read the Word of God. I used to read a tract, or an interesting book; but I knew nothing of the power of the Word. I read very little of it, and the result was, that, although a preacher then, yet I made no progress in the divine life. And why? Just for this reason—I neglected the Word of God. But it pleased God, through the instrumentality of a beloved Christian brother, to rouse in me an earnestness about the Word, and ever since then I have been a lover of it....

And though I have read the Word nearly a hundred times right through, I have never got tired of reading it, and this is more especially through reading it regularly, consecutively, day by day, and not merely reading a chapter here and there, as my own thoughts might have led me to do.

[W]e should read the Scripture prayerfully, never supposing that we are clever enough or wise enough to understand God's Word by our own wisdom. In all our reading of the Scriptures let us seek carefully to have the help of the Holy Spirit; let us ask, for Jesus' sake, that He will enlighten us. He is willing to do it.

I will tell you how it fared with me at the very first; it may be for your encouragement. It was in the year 1829, when I was living in Hack-

---

[3] pay attention

ney.[4] My attention had been called to the teaching of the Spirit by a dear brother of experience. "Well," I said, "I will try this plan; and will give myself, after prayer, to the careful reading of the Word of God, and to meditation, and I will see how much the Spirit is willing to teach me in this way."

An Illustration of This

I went accordingly to my room, and locked my door, and putting the Bible on a chair, I went down on my knees at the chair. There I remained for several hours in prayer and meditation over the Word of God; and I can tell you that I learned more in those three hours which I spent in this way, than I had learned for many months previously. I thus obtained the teaching of the Divine Spirit, and I cannot tell you the blessedness which it was to my own soul. I was praying in the Spirit, and putting my trust in the power of the Spirit, as I had never done before.

You cannot, therefore, be surprised at my earnestness in pressing this upon you, when you have heard how precious to my heart it was, and how much it helped me.

Read in Faith

Another point. It is of the utmost moment in reading the Word of God, that the reading should be accompanied with faith. "The word preached did not profit them, not being mixed with faith in them that heard it" (Hebrews 4:2). As with the preaching, so with the reading it must be mixed with faith. Not simply reading it as you would read a story, which you may receive or not; not simply as a statement, which you may credit or not; or as an exhortation,[5] to which you may listen or not; but as the revealed will of the Lord: that is, receiving it with faith. Received thus, it will nourish us, and we shall reap benefit. Only in this way will it benefit us; and we shall gain from it health and strength in proportion as we receive it with real faith.

Be Doers of the Word

Lastly, if God does bless us in reading His Word, He expects that we should be obedient children, and that we should accept the Word as His will, and carry it into practice. If this be neglected, you will find that the reading of the Word, even if accompanied by prayer, meditation, and faith, will do you little good. God does expect us to be obedient children, and will have us practice what He has taught us. The Lord Jesus Christ says: "If ye know these things, happy are ye if ye do them" (John 13:17). And in the measure

---

[4] an area in London
[5] encouragement, piece of advice

in which we carry out what our Lord Jesus taught, so much in measure are we happy children. And in such measure only can we honestly look for help from our Father, even as we seek to carry out His will.

If there is one single point I would wish to have spread all over this country, and over the whole world, it is just this, that we should seek, beloved Christian friends, not to be hearers of the Word only, but "doers of the Word" (James 1:22). I doubt not that many of you have sought to do this already, but I speak particularly to those younger brethren and sisters who have not yet learned the full force of this. Oh! seek to attend earnestly to this, it is of vast importance. Satan will seek with much earnestness to put aside the Word of God; but let us seek to carry it out and to act upon it. The Word must be received as a legacy from God, which has been communicated to us by the Holy Ghost. Therefore, it is the will of the Lord that we should always own our dependence upon Him in prayer.

The Fullness of the Revelation Given in His Word

To the faithful reader of this blessed Word, it reveals all that we need to know about the Father, all that we need to know about the Lord Jesus Christ, all about the power of the Spirit, all about the world that lieth in the wicked one, all about the road to heaven, and the blessedness of the world to come. In this blessed book we have the whole Gospel, and all rules necessary for our Christian life and warfare. Let us see than that we study it with our whole heart and with prayer, meditation, faith, and obedience.

Prayer

The next point on which I will speak for a few moments has been more or less referred to already, it is that of prayer. You might read the Word and seem to understand it very fully, yet if you are not in the habit of waiting continually upon God, you will make little progress in the divine life. We have not naturally in us any good thing; and cannot expect, save by the help of God, to please Him.

The blessed Lord Jesus Christ gave us an example in this particular. He gave whole nights to prayer. We find Him on the lonely mountain engaged by night in prayer. And as in every way He is to be an example to us, so, in particular, on this point. He is an example to us. The old evil corrupt nature is still in us, though we are born again; therefore, we have to come in prayer to God for help. We have to cling to the power of the Mighty One. Concerning everything, we have to pray. Not simply when great troubles come, when the house is on fire, or a beloved wife is on the point of death, or dear children are laid down in sickness—not simply at such times, but also in little things. From the very early morning, let us make everything a matter of prayer, and let it be so throughout the day, and throughout our whole life.

A Christian lady said lately, that thirty-five years ago she heard me speak on this subject in Devonshire; and that then I referred to praying about little things. I had said, that suppose a parcel[6] came to us, and it should prove difficult to untie the knot, and you cannot cut it; then you should ask God to help you, even to untie the knot. I myself had forgotten the words, but she has remembered them, and the remembrance of them, she said, had been a great help to her again and again. So I would say to you, my beloved friends, there is nothing too little to pray about. In the simplest things connected with our daily life and walk, we should give ourselves to prayer; and we shall have the living, loving Lord Jesus to help us. Even in the most trifling[7] matters I give myself to prayer and often in the morning, even ere[8] I leave my room I have two or three answers to prayer in this way.

Young believers, in the very outset of the divine life in your souls, learn, in childlike simplicity, to wait upon God for everything! Treat the Lord Jesus Christ as your personal Friend, able and willing to help you in everything. How blessed it is to be carried in His loving arms all the day long! I would say, that the divine life of the believer is made up of a vast number of little circumstances and little things. Every day there comes before us a variety of little trials, and if we seek to put them aside in our own strength and wisdom, we shall quickly find that we are confounded. But if, on the contrary, we take everything to God, we shall be helped, and our way shall be made plain. Thus our life will be a happy life!

A Word to the Unconverted

I am here tonight addressing believers, those who have felt the burden of their sins, and have accepted Christ as their Savior, and who now through Him have peace with God and seek to glorify Him. But if there be any here who are still in their sins, in a state of alienation from God, let me say, if they die in this state, the terrible punishment of sin must fall upon them. Unless their sins are pardoned, and they are made fit for the Divine presence, they can never enter heaven. But, dear friends, Christ came to save the lost, and as sinners, you are lost, and you have no power of your own to save yourselves. The world talks of turning over a new leaf, but that will not satisfy Divine justice. Sin must be punished, or God's righteousness would be set aside. Jesus came into the world to bear that punishment. He has borne it in our room and stead. He has suffered for us. Now what God

---

[6] a package in the mail
[7] unimportant
[8] before

looks for from us is, that we accept Jesus as our Savior, and put our trust in Him for the salvation of our souls. Whosoever looks really and entirely to Him shall assuredly be saved. Let his sins be ever so many, he shall have the forgiveness of them all. Nay, more, he will be accepted by God as His child. He will become an heir of God and a joint-heir with Christ. Oh, what great and glorious salvation, so freely given! May it be as thankfully accepted!

And may we who rejoice in Him stand boldly out and confess Christ, and work for Him. May we not be half-hearted, but be valiant soldiers of Christ. Let us be decided for Christ. Let us walk as in God's sight, in holy, peaceful, happy fellowship with Him, in the enjoyment of that nearness into which we are brought in Christ. Oh, the blessedness of this privilege of living near to God in this life! May we, then, seek His guidance in everything, so that we may be a blessing to others, and thus we shall be greatly blessed in our own souls.

Orphanage Buildings Run by George Muller in Bristol, England

Questions for Review

1. Describe the author's encouragements about reading God's Word.

2. What does Müller mean by "reading in faith"? Other than just reading the Word, what does he encourage Christians to do?

3. What does Müller say about prayer? Explain the "parcel" example.

4. Have *you* accepted Jesus Christ and asked Him to pay for your sins, like Müller encourages unbelievers at the end of this selection?

John G.

By Katherine Mayo

Pennsylvania native Katherine Mayo (1867-1940) became well-known from her articles and short stories in popular magazines. "John G." comes from her 1918 work titled The Standard Bearers, *a collection of short stories, based on fact, about the Pennsylvania State Police. (She spent much time with the police, interviewing and researching.) The year before, she wrote a work titled* Justice for All: A History of the Pennsylvania State Police.

• • • • •

It was nine o'clock of a wild night in December. For forty-eight hours it had been raining, raining, raining, after a heavy fall of snow. Still the torrents descended, lashed by a screaming wind, and the song of rushing water mingled with the cry of the gale.[1] Each steep street of the hill-town of Greensburg lay inches deep under a tearing flood. The cold was as great as cold may be while rain is falling. A night to give thanks for shelter overhead, and to hug the hearth with gratitude.

First Sergeant Price, at his desk in the Barracks office, was honorably grinding law.[2] Most honorably, because, when he had gone to take the book from its shelf in the day-room, "Barrack-Room Ballads"[3] had smiled down upon him with a heart-aching echo of the soft, familiar East; so that of a sudden he had fairly smelt the sweet, strange, heathen smell of the temples in Tien Tsin[4]—had seen the flash of a parrot's wing in the bolo-toothed Philippine jungle. And the sight and the smell, on a night like this, were enough to make any man lonely.

Therefore it was with honor indeed that, instead of dreaming off into the radiant past through the well-thumbed book of magic, he was digging between dull sheepskin covers after the key to the bar of the State, on which his will was fixed.

Now, a man who, being a member of the Pennsylvania State Police, aspires to qualify for admission to the bar, has his work cut out for him. The calls of his regular duty, endless in number and kind, leave him no certain leisure, and few and broken are the hours that he gets for books.

---

[1] strong wind
[2] "grinding law": studying to pass an exam ("the bar") to become a lawyer
[3] a book of poems by British author Rudyard Kipling
[4] area in northern China

"Confound the Latin!" grumbled the Sergeant, grabbing his head in his two hands. "Well—anyway, here's my night for it. Even the crooks will lie snug in weather like this." And he took a fresh hold on the poser.[5]

Suddenly "buzz" went the bell beside him. Before its voice ceased, he stood at salute in the door of the Captain's office.

"Sergeant," said Captain Adams, with a half-turn of his desk-chair, "how soon can you take the field?"

"Five minutes, sir."

"There's trouble over in the foundry[6] town. The local authorities have jailed some I. W. W. plotters.[7] They state that a jail delivery is threatened, that the Sheriff can't control it, and that they believe the mob will run amuck generally and shoot up the town. Take a few men; go over and attend to it."

"Very well, sir."

In the time that goes to saddling a horse, the detail rode into the storm, First Sergeant Price on John G., leading.

John G. had belonged to the Force exactly as long as had the First Sergeant himself, which was from the dawn of the Force's existence. And John G. is a gentleman and a soldier, every inch of him. Horse-show judges have affixed their seal to the self-evident fact by the sign of the blue ribbon, but the best proof lies in the personal knowledge of "A" Troop, soundly built on twelve years' brotherhood. John G., on that diluvian[8] night, was twenty-two years old, and still every whit as clean-limbed, alert, and plucky as his salad days[9] had seen him.

Men and horses dived into the gale[10] as swimmers dive into a breaker. It beat their eyes shut with wind and driven water, and, as they slid down the harp-pitched city streets, the flood banked up against each planted hoof till it split in folds above the fetlock.[11]

Down in the country beyond, mud, slush, and water clogged with chunks of frost-stricken clay made worse and still worse going. And so they pushed on through blackest turmoil toward the river road that should be their highway to Logan's Ferry.

They reached that road at last, only to find it as lost as Atlantis,[12] under twenty feet of water! The Allegheny had overflowed her banks, and now

---

[5] problem

[6] A foundry is a factory where metal is produced (Pennsylvania, specifically, Pittsburgh, is known for its steel production).

[7] The I. W. W. ("Industrial Workers of the World") was a radical, violent group that aimed to get rid of free trade and replace it government-run trade (socialism or communism).

[8] extremely rainy (the author compares it to Noah's flood)

[9] days of youth and energy

[10] storm

[11] horse's leg joint below the knee

[12] mythical island

there remained no way across, short of following the stream up to Pittsburgh and so around, a detour of many miles, long and evil.

"And that," said First Sergeant Price, "means getting to the party about
four hours late. Baby-talk and nonsense! By that time they might have
burned the place and killed all the people in it. Let's see, now: there's a
railroad bridge close along here, somewhere."

They scouted till they found the bridge. But behold, its floor was of cross-
ties only—of sleepers to carry the rails, laid with wide breaks between,
gaping down into deep, dark space whose bed was the roaring river.

"Nevertheless," said First Sergeant Price, whose spirits ever soar at the
foolish onslaughts of trouble—"nevertheless, we're *not* going to ride
twenty miles farther for nothing. There's a railroad yard on the other side.
This bridge, here, runs straight into it. You two men go over, get a couple
of good planks, and find out when the next train is due."

The two Troopers whom the Sergeant indicated gave their horses to a
comrade and started away across the trestle.

For a moment those who stayed behind could distinguish the rays of their
pocket flashlights as they picked out their slimy foothold. Then the whirling
night engulfed them, lights and all.

The Sergeant led the remainder of the detail down into the lee of an
abutment,[13] to avoid the full drive of the storm. Awhile they stood waiting,
huddled together. But the wait was not for long. Presently, like a code signal
spelled out on the black overhead, came a series of steadily lengthening
flashes—the pocket-light glancing between the sleepers, as the returning
messengers drew near.

---

[13] shelter

Scrambling up to rail level, the Sergeant saw with content that his emissaries bore on their shoulders between them two new pine "two-by-twelves."

"No train's due till five o'clock in the morning," reported the first across.

"Good! Now lay the planks. In the middle of the track. End to end. So."

The Sergeant, dismounting, stood at John G.'s wise old head, stroking his muzzle, whispering into his ear.

"Come along, John; it's all right, old man!" he finished with a final caress.

Then he led John G. to the first plank.

"One of you men walk on each side of him. Now, John!"

Delicately, nervously, John G. set his feet, step by step, till he had reached the center of the second plank.

Then the Sergeant talked to him quietly again, while two Troopers picked up the board just quitted to lay it in advance.

And so, length by length, they made the passage, the horse moving with extremest caution, shivering with full appreciation of the unaccustomed danger, yet steadied by his master's presence and by the friend on either hand. As they moved, the gale wreaked all its fury on them. It was growing colder now, and the rain, changed to sleet, stung their skins with its tiny, sharp-driven blades. The skeleton bridge held them high suspended in the very heart of the storm. Once and again a sudden more violent gust bid fair to sweep them off their feet. Yet, slowly progressing, they made their port unharmed.

Then came the next horse's turn. More than a single mount they dared not lead over at once, lest the contagious fears of one, reacting on another, produce panic. The horse that should rear or shy, on that wide-meshed footing, would be fairly sure to break a leg, at best. So, one by one, they followed over, each reaching the farther side before his successor began the transit.

And so, at last, all stood on the opposite bank, ready to follow John G. once more, as he led the way to duty.

"Come along, John, old man. You know how you'd hate to find a lot of dead women and babies because we got there too late to save them! Make a pace, Johnny boy!"

The First Sergeant was talking gently, leaning over his pommel.[14] But John G. was listening more from politeness than because he needed a lift. His stride was as steady as a clock.

It was three hours after midnight on that bitter black morning as they entered the streets of the town. And the streets were as quiet, as peaceful, as empty of men, as the heart of the high woods.

---

[14] upper front part of a saddle

"Where's their mob?" growled the Sergeant.

"Guess its mother's put it to sleep," a cold, wet Trooper growled back.

"Well, we *thought* there was going to be trouble," protested the local power, roused from his feather bed. "It really did look like serious trouble, I assure you. And we could not have handled serious trouble with the means at our command. Moreover, there may easily be something yet. So, gentlemen, I am greatly relieved you have come. I can sleep in peace now that you are here. Good-night! *Good*-night!"

All through the remaining hours of darkness the detail patrolled the town. All through the lean, pale hours of dawn it carefully watched its wakening, guarded each danger-point. But never a sign of disturbance did the passing time bring forth.

At last, with the coming of the business day, the Sergeant sought out the principal men of the place, and from them ascertained[15] the truth.

Threats of a jail delivery there had been, and a noisy parade as well, but nothing had occurred or promised beyond the power of an active local officer to handle. Such was the statement of one and all.

"I'll just make sure," said the Sergeant to himself.

Till two o'clock in the afternoon the detail continued its patrols. The town and its outskirts remained of an exemplary[16] peace. At two o'clock the Sergeant reported by telephone to his Captain:

"Place perfectly quiet, sir. Nothing seems to have happened beyond the usual demonstration of a sympathizing crowd over an arrest. Unless something more breaks, the Sheriff should be entirely capable of handling the situation."

"Then report back to Barracks at once," said the voice of the Captain of "A" Troop. "There's *real* work waiting here."

The First Sergeant, hanging up the receiver, went out and gathered his men.

Still the storm was raging. Icy snow, blinding sheets of sharp-fanged smother, rode on the racing wind. Worse overhead, worse underfoot, would be hard to meet in years of winters.

But once again men and horses, without an interval of rest, struck into the open country. Once again on the skeleton bridge they made the precarious[17] crossing. And so, at a quarter to nine o'clock at night, the detail topped Greensburg's last ice-coated hill and entered the yard of its high-perched Barracks.

---

[15] learned
[16] perfect
[17] risky, unsure

As the First Sergeant slung the saddle off John G.'s smoking back, Corporal Richardson, farrier[18] of the Troop, appeared before him wearing a mien[19] of solemn and grieved displeasure.

"It's all very well," said he— "all very well, no doubt. But eighty-six miles in twenty-four hours, in weather like this, is a good deal for any horse. And John G. is twenty-two years old, as perhaps you may remember. *I've brought the medicine.*"

Three solid hours from that very moment the two men worked over John G., and when, at twelve o'clock, they put him up for the night, not a wet hair was left on him. As they washed and rubbed and bandaged, they talked together, mingling the Sergeant's trenchantly[20] humorous common sense with the Corporal's mellow philosophy. But mostly it was the Corporal that spoke, for twenty-four hours is a fair working day for a Sergeant as well as a Troop horse.

"I believe in my soul," said the Sergeant, "that if a man rode into this stable with his two arms shot off at the shoulder, you'd make him groom his horse with his teeth and his toes for a couple of hours before you'd let him hunt a doctor."

"Well," rejoined Corporal Richardson, in his soft Southern tongue, "and what if I did? Even if that man died of it, he'd thank me heartily afterward. You know, when you and I and the rest of the world, each in our turn, come to Heaven's gate, there'll be St. Peter before it, with the keys safe in his pocket. And over the shining wall behind—*from the inside*, mind you—will be poking a great lot of heads—innocent heads with innocent eyes—heads of horses and of all the other animals that on this earth are the friends of man, put at his mercy and helpless.

"And it's clear to me—over, John! So, boy!—that before St. Peter unlocks the gate for a single one of us, he'll turn around to that long row of heads, and he'll say:

"'Blessed animals in the fields of Paradise, is this a man that should enter in?'

"And if the animals—they that were placed in his hands on earth to prove the heart that was in him—if the immortal animals have aught[21] to say against that man—never will the good Saint let him in, with his dirty, mean stain upon him. Never. *You'll see, Sergeant, when your time comes. Will you give those tendons another ten minutes?*"

---

[18] horseshoer
[19] expression
[20] sharply
[21] anything

Next morning John G. walked out of his stall as fresh and as fit as if he had come from pasture. And to this very day, in the stable of "A" Troop, John G., handsome, happy, and able, does his friends honor.

Questions for Review

1. What is John G. like?

2. What situation do the police face? How does John G. handle it?

3. What do the men feel about John G.? How can you tell?

4. Compare Proverbs 12:10 to the main idea of this story.

He Leadeth Me

By Joseph H. Gilmore

Joseph Gilmore (1834-1918) wrote this hymn in 1862, during the North/South War. He got the idea from Psalm 23:2: "...he leadeth me beside the still waters." Gilmore's wife secretly sent his words to Christian publications, and three years after writing "He Leadeth Me," he found his hymn in a hymnbook in a church where he was preaching!

• • • • •

He leadeth me! O blessed thought!
O words with heavenly comfort fraught![1]
Whate'er I do, where'er I be,
Still 'tis God's hand that leadeth me.

He leadeth me, He leadeth me,
By His own hand He leadeth me:
His faithful follower I would be,
For by His hand He leadeth me.

Sometimes 'mid scenes of deepest gloom,
Sometimes where Eden's bowers[2] bloom,
By waters still, o'er troubled sea,
Still 'tis His hand that leadeth me!

He leadeth me, He leadeth me,
By His own hand He leadeth me:
His faithful follower I would be,
For by His hand He leadeth me.

Lord, I would clasp thy hand in mine,
Nor ever murmur nor repine,[3]
Content, whatever lot I see,
Since 'tis my God that leadeth me!

He leadeth me, He leadeth me,
By His own hand He leadeth me:
His faithful follower I would be,
For by His hand He leadeth me.

---

[1] filled
[2] gardens, trees
[3] complain, have regrets

Questions for Review

1. This selection lists three of the hymn's "stanzas" (verses) and "refrains" (sections sung after every stanza). Compare the third stanza's words to Philippians 2:14-16.

2. Listen to a choir sing "He Leadeth Me." Do you think the music fits the words?

Temptation Resisted

By T. S. Arthur

New York-born Timothy Shay Arthur (1809-1885) was a popular author who is almost forgotten today. He was homeschooled, and much of his lessons involved Bible study, reading and writing, and teaching himself various subjects. He began to write and publish a weekly magazine, then started writing novels and short stories with strong morals. "Temptation Resisted" is exactly the story you think it'll be, based on the title. But it is still enriching to read it!

• • • • •

Charles Murray left home, with his books in his satchel, for school. Before starting, he kissed his little sister, and patted Juno on the head, and as he went singing away, he felt as happy as any little boy could wish to feel. Charles was a good-tempered lad, but he had the fault common to a great many boys, that of being tempted and enticed by others to do things which he knew to be contrary to the wishes of his parents. Such acts never made him feel any happier; for the fear that his disobedience would be found out, and the consciousness of having done wrong, were far from being pleasant companions.

On the present occasion, as he walked briskly in the direction of the school, he repeated over his lessons in his mind, and was intent upon having them so perfect as to be able to repeat every word. He had gone nearly half the distance, and was still thinking over his lessons, when he stopped suddenly, as a voice called out,

"Halloo, Charley!"

Turning in the direction from which the voice came, he saw Archy Benton, with his school basket in his hand; but he was going from, instead of in the direction of the school.

"Where are you going, Archy?" asked Charles, calling out to him.

"Into the woods, for chestnuts."

"Ain't you going to school, today?"

"No, indeed. There was a sharp frost last night, and Uncle John says the wind will rattle down the chestnuts like hail."

"Did your father say you might go?"

"No, indeed. I asked him, but he said I couldn't go until Saturday. But the hogs are in the woods, and will eat the chestnuts all up, before Saturday. So I am going today. Come, go along, won't you? It is such a fine day, and the ground will be covered with chestnuts. We can get home at the usual time, and no one will suspect that we were not at school."

"I should like to go, very well," said Charley; "but I know father will be greatly displeased, if he finds it out, and I am afraid he will get to know it, in some way."

"How could he get to know it? Isn't he at his store all the time?"

"But he might think to ask me if I was at school. And I never will tell a lie."

"You could say yes, and not tell a lie, either," returned Archy. "You were at school yesterday."

"No, I couldn't. A lie, father says, is in the intent to deceive. He would, of course, mean to ask whether I was at school today, and if I said yes, I would tell a lie."

"It isn't so clear to me that you would. At any rate, I don't see such great harm in a little fib. It doesn't hurt anybody."

"Father says a falsehood hurts a boy a great deal more than he thinks for. And one day he showed me in the Bible where liars were classed with murderers, and other wicked spirits, in hell.[1] I can't tell a lie, Archy."

"There won't be any need of your doing so," urged Archy; "for I am sure he will never think to ask you about it. Why should he?"

"I don't know. But whenever I have been doing anything wrong, he is sure to begin to question me, and lead me on until I betray the secret of my fault."

"Never mind. Come and go with me. It is such a fine day. We shan't have another like it. It will rain on Saturday, I'll bet anything. So come along, now, and let us have a day in the woods, while we can."

Charles was very strongly tempted. When he thought of the confinement of school, and then of the freedom of a day in the woods, he felt much inclined to go with Archy.

"Come along," said Archy, as Charles stood balancing the matter in his mind. And he took hold of his arm, and drew him in a direction opposite from the school. "Come! you are just the boy I want. I was thinking about you the moment before I saw you."

---

[1] "But the fearful, and unbelieving, and the abominable, and murderers, and whoremongers, and sorcerers, and idolaters, and all liars, shall have their part in the lake which burneth with fire and brimstone: which is the second death" (Revelation 21:8).

The temptation to Charles was very strong. "I don't believe I will be found out," he said to himself; "and it is such a pleasant day to go into the woods!"

Still he held back, and thought of his father's displeasure if he should discover that he had played the truant.[2] The word "truant," that he repeated mentally, decided the matter in his mind, and he exclaimed, in a loud and decided voice, as he dragged away from the hand of Archy, that had still retained its hold on his arm, "I've never played truant yet, and I don't think I ever will. Father says he never played truant when he was a boy; and I'd like to say the same thing when I get to be a man."

"Nonsense, Charley! come, go with me," urged Archy.

But Charles Murray's mind was made up not to play the truant. So he started off for school, saying, as he did so—

"No, I can't go, Archy; and if I were you, I would wait until Saturday. You will enjoy it so much better when you have your father's consent. It always takes away more than half the pleasure of any enjoyment to think that it is obtained at the cost of disobedience. Come! go to school with me now, and I will go into the woods with you on Saturday."

"No, I can't wait until Saturday. I'm sure it will rain by that time; and if it don't, the hogs will eat up every nut that has fallen before that time."

"There'll be plenty left on the trees, if they do. It's as fine sport to knock them down as to pick them up."

But Archy's purpose was settled, and nothing that Charles Murray could say had any influence with him. So the boys parted, the one for his school, and the other for a stolen holiday in the woods.

The moment Charles was alone again, he felt no longer any desire to go with Archy. He had successfully resisted the temptation, and the allurement was gone. But even for listening to temptation he had some small punishment, for he was late to school by nearly ten minutes, and had not his lessons as perfect as usual, for which the teacher felt called upon to reprimand[3] him. But this was soon forgotten; and he was so good a boy through the whole day, and studied all his lessons so diligently, that when evening came, the teacher, who had not forgotten the reprimand, said to him:

"You have been the best boy in the school today, Charles. Tomorrow morning try and come in time, and be sure that your lessons are all well committed to memory."

Charles felt very light and cheerful as he went running, skipping, and singing homeward. His day had been well spent, and happiness was his reward. When he came in sight of home, there was no dread of meeting his father and mother, such as he would have felt if he had played the truant.

---

[2] school-skipper
[3] scold

Everything looked bright and pleasant, and when Juno came bounding out to meet him, he couldn't help hugging the favorite dog in the joy he felt at seeing her.

When Charles met his mother, she looked at him with a more earnest and affectionate gaze than usual. And then the boy noticed that her countenance[4] became serious.

"Ain't you well, mother?" asked Charles.

"Yes, my dear, I am very well," she replied; "but I saw something an hour ago which has made me feel sad. Archy Benton was brought home from the woods this afternoon, where he had gone for chestnuts, instead of going to school, as he should have done, dreadfully hurt. He had fallen from a tree. Both his arms are broken, and the doctor fears that he has received some inward injury that may cause his death."

Charles turned pale when his mother said this.

"Boys rarely get hurt, except when they are acting disobediently, or doing some harm to others," remarked Mrs. Murray. "If Archy had gone to school, this dreadful accident would not have happened. His father told him that he might go for chestnuts on Saturday, and if he had waited until then, I am sure he might have gone into the woods and received no harm, for all who do right are protected from evil."

"He tried to persuade me to go with him," said Charles, "and I was strongly tempted to do so. But I resisted the temptation, and have felt glad about it ever since."

Mrs. Murray took her son's hand, and pressing it hard, said, with much feeling,

"How rejoiced I am that you were able to resist his persuasions to do wrong. Even if you had not been hurt yourself, the injury received by Archy would have discovered to us that you were with him, and then how unhappy your father and I would have been I cannot tell. And you would have been unhappy, too. Ah! my son, there is only one true course for all of us, and that is, to do right. Every deviation[5] from this path brings trouble. An act of a moment may make us wretched for days, weeks, months, or perhaps years. It will be a long, long time before Archy is free from pain of body or mind—it may be that he will never recover. Think how miserable his parents must feel; and all because of this single act of disobedience."

We cannot say how often Charles said to himself, that evening and the next day, when he thought of Archy, "Oh, how glad I am that I did not go with him!"

When Saturday came, the father and mother of Charles Murray gave him permission to go into the woods for chestnuts. Two or three other boys, who

---

[4] expression, face
[5] turning away

were his school companions, likewise received liberty to go; and they joined Charles, and altogether made a pleasant party. It did not rain, nor had the hogs eaten up all the nuts, for the lads found plenty under the tall old trees, and in a few hours filled their bags and baskets. Charles said, when he came home, that he had never enjoyed himself better, and was so glad that he had not been tempted to go with Archy Benton.

It was a lesson he never afterward forgot. If he was tempted to do what he knew was wrong, he thought of Archy's day in the woods, and the tempter instantly left him. The boy who had been so badly hurt did not die, as the doctor feared; but he suffered great pain, and was ill for a long time.

Questions for Review

1. How does Charley say his father defines a lie?

2. What does Charley feel, and also tell Archy, that lying does to his enjoyment of whatever he gets to do because of a lie?

3. Has someone tried to tempt you to do something wrong, like Archy tempting Charley? Write out a two- or three-sentence response you could give to someone who tries to tempt you in this way.

In the Country of the Sioux

By Meriwether Lewis

The following selection...attributed to Captain Lewis, is taken from...the journals of Lewis and Clark, the leaders of the celebrated expedition of 1804-1806, sent out by President Jefferson to explore the country which he had obtained by treaty from France as part of the Louisiana Purchase. The explorers passed across the plains and the Rocky Mountains....We take up their story in their journey through the Sioux country, on the Missouri.[1]

· · · · ·

Twenty miles farther on [continues the narrative] we reached and encamped at the foot of a round mountain on the south, having passed two small islands. This mountain, which is about three hundred feet at the base, forms a cone at the top, resembling a dome at a distance, and seventy feet or more above the surrounding highlands. As we descended from this dome, we arrived at a spot on the gradual descent of the hill, nearly four acres in extent, and covered with small holes; these are the residence of a little animal, called by the French *petit chien* (little dog), which sit erect near the mouth, and make a whistling noise, but, when alarmed, take refuge in their holes. In order to bring them out, we poured into one of the holes five barrels of water, without filling it, but we dislodged and caught the owner. After digging down another of the holes for six feet, we found, on running a pole into it, that we had not yet dug halfway to the bottom; we discovered, however, two frogs in the hole, and near it we killed a dark rattlesnake, which had swallowed a small prairie dog. We were also informed, though we never witnessed the fact, that a sort of lizard and a snake live habitually with these animals. The *petit chien* are justly named, as they resemble a small dog in some particulars, although they have also some points of similarity to the squirrel. The head resembles the squirrel in every respect, except that the ear is shorter; the tail like that of the ground squirrel; the toenails are long, the fur is fine, and the long hair is gray.

The following days they saw large herds of buffalo, and the copses[2] of timber appeared to contain elk and deer. Just below Cedar Island [adds the journal], on a hill to the south, is the backbone of a fish, forty-five feet long,

---

[1] From the original publication.
[2] group of small trees

tapering towards the tail, and in a perfect state of petrifaction, fragments of which were collected and sent to Washington....

September 17. While some of the party were engaged in the same way as yesterday, others were employed in examining the surrounding country. About a quarter of a mile beyond our camp, and at an elevation of twenty feet above it, a plain extends nearly three miles parallel to the river, and about a mile back to the hills, towards which it gradually ascends. Here we saw a grove of plum trees, loaded with fruit, now ripe, and differing in nothing from those of the Atlantic States, except that the tree is smaller and more thickly set. The ground of the plain is occupied by the burrows of multitudes of barking squirrels, who entice hither the wolves of a small kind, hawks, and polecats,[3] all of which animals we saw, and presumed that they fed on the squirrel. This plain is intersected, nearly in its whole extent, by deep ravines, and steep, irregular rising grounds, from one to two hundred feet. On ascending the range of hills which border the plain, we saw a second high level plain, stretching to the south as far as the eye could reach. To the westward a high range of hills, about twenty miles distant, runs nearly north and south, but not to any great extent, as their rise and termination is embraced by one view, and they seemed covered with a verdure[4] similar to that of the plains. The same view extended over the irregular hills which border the northern side of the Missouri.

All around, the country had been recently burned, and a young green grass about four inches high covered the ground, which was enlivened by herds of antelopes and buffalo, the last of which were in such multitudes that we cannot exaggerate in saying that at a single glance we saw three thousand of them before us. Of all the animals we had seen, the antelope seems to possess the most wonderful fleetness.[5] Shy and timorous, they generally repose[6] only on the ridges, which command a view of all the approaches of an enemy; the acuteness of their sight distinguishes the most distant danger; the delicate sensibility of their smell defeats the precautions of concealment; and, when alarmed, their rapid career seems more like the flight of birds than the movements of a quadruped.[7] After many unsuccessful attempts, Captain Lewis at last, by winding around the ridges, approached a party of seven, which were on an eminence[8] towards which the wind was unfortunately blowing. The only male of the party frequently encircled the summit of the hill, as if to announce any danger to the females, which formed a group at the top. Although they did not see Captain Lewis,

---

[3] skunks
[4] greenery (of plants, trees, and bushes)
[5] speed
[6] rest
[7] four-legged animal
[8] hill

the smell alarmed them, and they fled when he was at the distance of two hundred yards; he immediately ran to the spot where they had been; a ravine concealed them from him; but the next moment they appeared on a second ridge, at a distance of three miles. He doubted whether they could be the same; but their number, and the extreme rapidity with which they continued their course, convinced him that they must have gone with a speed equal to that of the most distinguished race-horse. Among our acquisitions today were a mule deer, a magpie,[9] a common deer, and a buffalo. Captain Lewis also saw a hare, and killed a rattlesnake near the burrows of the barking squirrels.

September 18. Having everything in readiness, we proceeded, with the boat much lightened, but the wind being from the northwest, we made but little way. At one mile we reached an island in the middle of the river, nearly a mile in length, and covered with red cedar; at its extremity a small creek comes in from the north. We then met some sandbars, and the wind being very high and ahead, we encamped on the south, having made only seven miles. In addition to the common deer, which were in great abundance, we saw goats, elk, buffalo, and the black-tailed deer; the large wolves, too, are very numerous, and have long hair with coarse fur, and are of a light color. A small species of wolf, about the size of a gray fox, was also killed, and proved to be the animal which we had hitherto[10] mistaken for a fox. There are also many porcupines, rabbits, and barking squirrels in the neighborhood....

On the 20th they arrived at the Grand Detour, or Great Bend, and two men were despatched with the only horse, to hunt, and wait the arrival of the boats beyond it. After proceeding twenty-seven and a half miles farther, they encamped on a sandbar in the river. Captain Clarke [continues the narrative], who early this morning had crossed the neck of the bend, joined us in the evening. At the narrowest part the gorge is composed of high and irregular hills of about one hundred and eighty or one hundred and ninety feet in elevation; from this descends an unbroken plain over the whole of the bend, and the country is separated from it by this ridge. Great numbers of buffalo, elk, and goats are wandering over these plains, accompanied by grouse and larks. Captain Clarke saw a hare, also, on the Great Bend.

Of the goats killed today, one is a female, differing from the male in being smaller in size; its horns, too, are smaller and straighter, having one short prong, and no black about the neck. None of these goats have any beard, but are delicately formed and very beautiful.

Shortly after midnight the sleepers were startled by the sergeant on guard crying out that the sandbar was sinking, and the alarm was given; for scarce-

---

[9] bird
[10] up until then

ly had they got off with the boats before the bank under which they had been lying fell in; and by the time the opposite shore was reached the ground on which they had been encamped sunk also. A man who was sent to step off the distance across the head of the bend made it but two thousand yards, while its circuit is thirty miles. On the 22d they passed a creek and two islands, known by the name of the Three Sisters, where a beautiful plain extended on both sides of the river. This is followed by an island on the north, called Cedar Island, about one mile and a half in length, and the same distance in breadth, and deriving its name from the quality of its timber. On the south side of this island is a fort and a large trading-house, built by a Mr. Loisel in order to trade with the Sioux,[11] the remains of whose camps are in great numbers about this place. The establishment is sixty or seventy feet square, built with red cedar, and picketed in with the same materials.

The next day, in the evening, three boys of the Sioux nation swam across the river, and informed them that two parties of Sioux were encamped on the next river, one consisting of eighty and the second of sixty lodges, at some distance above. After treating them kindly, they sent them back with a present of two carrots of tobacco to their chiefs, whom they invited to a conference in the morning.

September 24. At an island a few miles above Highwater Creek they were joined by one of their hunters, who [proceeds the narrative] procured four elk; but while he was in pursuit of the game the Indians had stolen his horse. We left the island, and soon overtook five Indians on the shore; we anchored, and told them from the boat we were friends, and wished to continue so, but were not afraid of any Indians; that some of their young men had stolen the horse which their great father had sent for their great chief, and that we could not treat with them until he was restored. They said they knew nothing of the horse, but if he had been taken he should be given up. We went on, and at thirteen and a half miles we anchored one hundred yards off the mouth of a river on the south side, where we were joined by both the pirogues,[12] and encamped; two-thirds of the party remained on board, and the rest went as a guard on shore, with the cooks and one pirogue; we have seen along the sides of the hills on the north a great deal of stone; besides the elk, we also observed a hare; the five Indians whom we had seen followed us, and slept with the guard on shore. Finding one of them was a chief, we smoked with him, and made him a present of tobacco. This river is about seventy yards wide, and has a considerable current...

[On the 25th they met a party of Indians who threatened violence, and attempted to detain them by force, but were induced to desist by a threatening attitude on the part of the whites.]

---

[11] a Native American Indian tribe
[12] canoes

September 26. Our conduct yesterday seemed to have inspired the Indians with fear of us; and as we were desirous of cultivating their acquaintance,[13] we complied with their wish that we should give them an opportunity of treating us well, and also suffer their squaws and children to see us and our boat, which would be perfectly new to them. Accordingly, after passing, at one and a half miles, a small willow island and several sandbars, we came to on the south side, where a crowd of men, women, and children were waiting to receive us. Captain Lewis went on shore, and remained several hours; and observing that their disposition was friendly, we resolved to remain during the night to a dance, which they were preparing for us. Captains Lewis and Clarke, who went on shore one after the other, were met on landing by ten well-dressed young men, who took them up in a robe, highly decorated, and carried them to a large council-house, where they were placed on a dressed buffalo-skin by the side of the grand chief. The hall, or council-room, was in the shape of three-quarters of a circle, covered at the top and sides with skins well dressed and sewed together. Under this shelter sat about seventy men, forming a circle round the chief, before whom were placed a Spanish flag and the one we had given them yesterday.

This left a vacant circle of about six feet in diameter, in which the pipe of peace was raised on two forked sticks, about six or eight inches from the ground, and under it the down of the swan was scattered; a large fire, in

---

[13] "cultivating their acquaintance": getting to know them

which they were cooking provisions, stood near, and in the center about four hundred pounds of excellent buffalo-meat, as a present for us.

As soon as we were seated an old man got up, and after approving what we had done, begged us to take pity on their unfortunate situation. To this we replied with assurances of protection. After he had ceased, the great chief rose and delivered an harangue[14] to the same effect; then, with great solemnity, took some of the most delicate parts of the dog which was cooked for the festival, and held it to the flag by way of sacrifice; this done, he held up the pipe of peace, and first pointed it towards the heavens, then to the four quarters of the globe, and then to the earth, made a short speech, lighted the pipe, and presented it to us. We smoked, and he again harangued his people, after which the repast[15] was served up to us. It consisted of the dog which they had just been cooking, this being a great dish among the Sioux, and used on all festivals; to this were added pemitigon, a dish made of buffalo-meat, dried or jerked, and then pounded and mixed raw with grease and a kind of ground potato, dressed like the preparation of Indian corn called hommony, to which it is little inferior. Of all these luxuries, which were placed before us in platters with horn spoons, we took the pemitigon and the potato, which we found good, but we could as yet partake but sparingly of the dog.

We ate and smoked for an hour, when it became dark; everything was then cleared away for the dance, a large fire being made in the center of the house, giving at once light and warmth to the ballroom. The orchestra was composed of about ten men, who played on a sort of tambourine, formed of skin stretched across a hoop, and made a jingling noise with a long stick to which the hoofs of deer and goats were hung; the third instrument was a small skin bag with pebbles in it; these, with five or six young men for the vocal part, made up the band. The women then came forward, highly décor-ated; some with poles in their hands, on which were hung the scalps of their enemies; others with guns, spears, or different trophies taken in war by their husbands, brothers, or connections.

Having arranged themselves in two columns, one on each side of the fire, as soon as the music began they danced towards each other till they met in the centre, when the rattles were shaken, and they all shouted and returned back to their places. They have no step, but shuffle along the ground; nor does the music appear to be anything more than a confusion of noises, distinguished only by hard or gentle blows upon the buffalo-skin; the song is perfectly extemporaneous.[16] In the pauses of the dance some man of the

---

[14] address, speech
[15] meal
[16] made up on the spot

company comes forward and recites, in a sort of low guttural[17] tone, some little story or incident, which is either martial[18] or ludicrous...; this is taken up by the orchestra and the dancers, who repeat it in a higher strain and dance to it. Sometimes they alternate, the orchestra first performing, and when it ceases the women raise their voices, and make a music more agreeable, that is, less intolerable, than that of the musicians.

The dances of the men, which are always separate from those of the women, are conducted very nearly in the same way, except that the men jump up and down instead of shuffling; and in the war-dances the recitations are all of a military cast. The harmony of the entertainment had nearly been disturbed by one of the musicians, who, thinking he had not received a due share of the tobacco we had distributed during the evening, put himself into a passion, broke one of the drums, threw two of them into the fire, and left the band. They were taken out of the fire; a buffalo robe, held in one hand, and beaten with the other by several of the company, supplied the place of the lost drum or tambourine, and no notice was taken of the offensive conduct of the man. We stayed till twelve o'clock at night, when we informed the chiefs that they must be fatigued with all these attempts to amuse us, and retired, accompanied by four chiefs, two of whom spent the night with us on board....

The tribe which we this day saw are a part of the great Sioux nation, and are known by the name of the Teton Okandandas: they are about two hundred men in number, and their chief residence is on both sides of the Missouri, between the Chayenne and Teton Rivers....

Their lodges are very neatly constructed, in the same form as those of the Yanktons: they consist of about one hundred cabins (made of white buffalo dressed hide), with a larger one in the center for holding councils and dances. They are built round with poles, about fifteen or twenty feet high, covered with white skins. These lodges may be taken to pieces, packed up, and carried with the nation wherever they go, by dogs which bear great burdens. The women are chiefly employed in dressing buffalo-skins; they seem perfectly well disposed, but are addicted to stealing anything which they can take without being observed. This nation, although it makes so many ravages among its neighbors, is badly supplied with guns. The water which they carry with them is contained chiefly in the paunches of deer and other animals, and they make use of wooden bowls. Some had their heads shaved, which we found was a species of mourning for their relations. Another usage on these occasions is to run arrows through the flesh, both above and below the elbow.

---

[17] harsh, grunting
[18] warlike

While on shore today we witnessed a quarrel between two squaws, which appeared to be growing every moment more boisterous,[19] when a man came forward, at whose approach everyone seemed terrified and ran. He took the squaws, and without any ceremony whipped them severely. On inquiring into the nature of such summary justice, we learned that this man was an officer well known to this and many other tribes. His duty is to keep the peace; and the whole interior police of the village is confided to two or three of these officers, who are named by the chief, and remain in power some days, at least till the chief appoints a successor: they seem to be a sort of constable or sentinel,[20] since they are always on the watch to keep tranquility during the day, and guarding the camp in the night. The short duration of their office is compensated by its authority. Their power is supreme, and in the suppression of any riot or disturbance no resistance to them is suffered....

Questions for Review

1. Which discoveries do you think readers would be most interested in from these selections?

2. What details did you remember about Lewis's notes after you finished reading this selection?

3. What is your take on the visit with the Sioux?

4. If you were an American at the time of Lewis and Clark's expedition and you read about these and other adventures of theirs, would it encourage you or discourage you from moving west? Why?

---

[19] rowdy

[20] A constable is like a police officer, a sentinel a guard.

Psalm 1, Psalm 97

By King David

· · · · ·

Psalm 1

1 – Blessed is the man that walketh not in the counsel of the ungodly, nor standeth in the way of sinners, nor sitteth in the seat of the scornful.

2 – But his delight is in the law of the LORD; and in his law doth he meditate[1] day and night.

3 – And he shall be like a tree planted by the rivers of water, that bringeth forth his fruit in his season; his leaf also shall not wither; and whatsoever he doeth shall prosper.

4 – The ungodly are not so: but are like the chaff[2] which the wind driveth away.

5 – Therefore the ungodly shall not stand in the judgment, nor sinners in the congregation of the righteous.

6 – For the LORD knoweth the way of the righteous: but the way of the ungodly shall perish.

Psalm 97

1 – The LORD reigneth; let the earth rejoice; let the multitude of isles be glad thereof.

2 – Clouds and darkness are round about him: righteousness and judgment are the habitation of his throne.

3 – A fire goeth before him, and burneth up his enemies round about.

4 – His lightnings enlightened the world: the earth saw, and trembled.

5 – The hills melted like wax at the presence of the LORD, at the presence of the Lord of the whole earth.

6 – The heavens declare his righteousness, and all the people see his glory.

---

[1] study, think carefully about
[2] Chaff is the part of grain that is thrown away after it's harvested, leaving just the grain (like wheat).

7 – Confounded[3] be all they that serve graven images, that boast themselves of idols: worship him, all ye gods.

8 – Zion heard, and was glad; and the daughters of Judah rejoiced because of thy judgments, O LORD.

9 – For thou, LORD, art high above all the earth: thou art exalted far above all gods.

10 – Ye that love the LORD, hate evil: he preserveth the souls of his saints; he delivereth them out of the hand of the wicked.

11 – Light is sown for the righteous, and gladness for the upright in heart.

12 – Rejoice in the LORD, ye righteous; and give thanks at the remembrance of his holiness.

Questions for Review

1. What do you think it means (1:1) to walk "in the counsel of the ungodly," to stand "in the way of sinners," and to sit "in the seat of the scornful"?

2. When the Bible says a person who delights in the "law of the LORD" will prosper in whatever he does (1:3), do you think that means he will become rich?

3. What do you think it means that "The heavens declare his righteousness" (97:6)?

4. What does God command those who love the Lord to do (97:10, 12)?

---

[3] ashamed, disappointed, confused

The Largest Statues in the World, Ancient and Modern

This selection comes from the July 26, 1884 issue of Chambers's Journal of Popular Literature, Science, and Art, *a weekly magazine that began in 1832 and ran until 1956. Publication of* Chambers's Journal *began in Edinburgh, Scotland, but moved to London around 20 years later.*

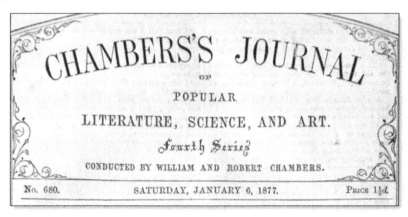

• • • • •

A piece of interesting news comes to us from Egypt regarding a discovery recently made in Lower Egypt, by Mr. Flinders Petrie, of the fragments of a colossal statue of King Rameses II, which, calculating the height from the fragments which remain, must have stood considerably over one hundred feet in height! The material employed is granite; and the executing of such a work in such a material, and when completed, rearing it into position, must have involved a profound[1] knowledge not only of high art, but of engineering skill. Is it possible that the statue could have been cut out whole in one piece? If so, what lever-power did the Egyptians possess to raise such an enormous weight into a perpendicular position?

Certain it is that these ancient builders knew well how to get over, and did get over, prodigious[2] difficulties, as witness their obelisks,[3] and the enormous stones which compose the platform of the magnificent Temple of the Sun at Baalbec.[4] As there is no stone quarry[5] near, how these vast

---

[1] deep
[2] enormous
[3] tall monuments pointed at the end (like the Washington Monument)
[4] This is now known as the Temple of Bacchus.
[5] A quarry is a pit or site for mining stone.

stones could possibly have been conveyed thither[6] in the first place, and then raised to their position, has been an enigma[7] to all modern architects and engineers by whom the temple has been critically examined, and who have freely confessed that, even with all our modern science of steam-cranes, hydraulic jacks, and railways, the transport and raising of such immense cyclopean[8] masses would have undoubtedly presented many serious difficulties, if indeed it could be accomplished at all.

Temple of the Sun (Temple of Bacchus)

Many of our readers will doubtless remember Mr. [Edward] Poynter's grand picture [painted in 1867] in the Royal Academy of London, a few years ago, entitled *Israel in Egypt*. It represented an enormous mass of sculpture mounted on a wheeled truck, dragged along by hundreds of the unfortunate captive Israelites, who are smarting under the whips of their cruel drivers. Mr. Poynter had good authority for his "motive-power" as shown in his picture. So far as we can discover from ancient works or ancient sculptures, the hugest stone masses were transported mainly by force of human muscles, with few mechanical expedients. Levers and rollers seem to have been almost, if not altogether, unknown. The mass was gener-

---

[6] there
[7] puzzle, mystery
[8] fitted together with huge, various-sized stones

ally placed on a kind of sledge, the ground over which it was to pass lubricated with some oily substance, and the sheer strength of human shoulders was then applied.

The most colossal and by far the most remarkable statue of modern days is that most elaborate and rather eccentric gift of the French nation to the people of America. Not only is it remarkable for its enormous height and gigantic proportions, but for the very singular and ingenious[9] manner in which it has been constructed, so singular, indeed, that at first sight it is somewhat difficult to comprehend the manner in which it has been built up piece by piece, especially when we mention that the several pieces of copper composing the figure have *not* been cast. How, then, have they been made? This we will try to explain.

The statue is a female figure of Liberty, having on her head a crown, and holding aloft in her hand a torch.[10] The figure is one hundred and five feet high; but, reckoning the extreme height to the top of the torch, the marvelous altitude of one hundred and thirty-seven feet nine inches is reached. The statue is to be reared on a pedestal of solid granite eighty-three feet high, so that the entire work will rise to the immense height of two hundred and twenty feet nine inches! The artist is M. Bartholdi (the family name, by-the-bye,[11] of the great composer best known as "Mendelssohn").

Having first carefully constructed a model in clay about life-size, this was repeatedly enlarged until the necessary form and size were obtained. The next step was to obtain plaster casts from the clay, and these casts were then reproduced by clever artists in hard wood. The wooden blocks were then in their turn placed in the hands of copper-smiths, who by the hammer alone, it is stated, gave the copper sheets the exact form of the wooden

---

[9] creative, inventive

[10] This essay was written in 1884. The Statue of Liberty was brought to the U. S. (in pieces on ships) in 1885, and construction was finished in 1886.

[11] by the way

molds or models; and thus, in this peculiar and laborious manner, the outside copper "skin" of the statue was formed and, to all outward appearance, completed. But as the copper is only one-eighth of an inch thick, an inner skin is also provided, placed about a foot behind the first, whilst the intermediate space will be filled in with sand, especially at the lower extremities, to give the whole a steadfast foundation.

The stability of the figure will not, however, be left to depend solely on these sheets of thin copper and loose sand; and therefore the interior, from top to bottom, will be strengthened by a framework of girders and supports, by which the whole will be knit together in one firm, compact, unyielding mass. As the sheets of copper and the interior framework are simply secured in the ordinary manner by rivets, when it is desired to remove this metallic mountain, all that has to be done is to unrivet the several plates, take down, and pack on board ship for New York.

It is proposed to place this gigantic "Liberty" on Bedloe's Island, a very small islet lying about two miles south of the Battery and Castle Garden, the lowest point of the island of Manhattan on which the city of New York is built, so that travelers approaching the city by water on that side will get a fine view of the statue of "Liberty enlightening the World."

This mighty work of art, after many years of close and anxious labor, has recently been formally handed over by M. Jules Ferry to the minister of the United States, as a free gift from the people of France to the people of America—a token of love and admiration from the one republic to the other—and measures are being adopted to take the statue to pieces, with a view to its immediate transmission to New York, in which go-ahead city we shall doubtless soon hear of its final erection.

If Mr. Flinders Petrie's discovery of the remains of the gigantic statue of Rameses II in Lower Egypt, one hundred feet high of solid granite, is the largest statue of antiquity, the "Liberty" of M. Bartholdi may certainly take rank as the most colossal production of modern days.

Questions for Review

1. What do the two statues in this selection have in common? How are they different in both their structure and what they represent?

2. Research Sir Flinders Petrie's discovery of the statue of Rameses II, and the building and transporting of the Statue of Liberty. What interesting discoveries did you make?

The Story of Alaska

By Rupert Sargent Holland

Author Rupert Sargent Holland (1878-1952) spe-cialized in writing interesting historical stories. The colorful "Story of Alaska" below comes from Hol-land's 1913 collection of non-fiction stories Historic Adventures: Tales from American History. *This nar-rative describes some of the fascinating details of how the United States obtained Alaska, and how it was settled. The special discovery in 1897 and the wild rush that followed add even more fun!*

• • • • •

In the far northwestern corner of North America is a land that has had few stirring scenes in its history. It is an enormous tract,[1] close to the Arctic Sea, and far from the busy cities of the United States. Not until long after the English, French, and Spanish discoverers had explored the country in the Temperate Zone did any European find Alaska. Even when it was found it seemed to offer little but ice fields and desolate[2] prairies, leading to wild mountain ranges that did not tempt men to settle. Seal hun-ters came and went, but generally left the native Indians in peace. Most of these hunters came from Siberia, for the Russians were the first owners of this land.

An officer in the Russian Navy named Vitus Bering found the strait[3] that is called by his name in 1728. Some years later he was sent into the Arctic Sea again by the Empress Anne of Russia to try to find the wonderful country that Vasco de Gama had sought. He sailed in summer, and after weathering heavy storms finally reached Kayak Island on St. Elias Day, July 17, 1741, and named the great mountain peak in honor of that saint. More storms followed, and soon afterward the brave sailor was ship-wrecked and drowned off the Comandorski Islands. His crew managed to get back to Siberia, having lived on the meat of the seals they were able to shoot. Russian traders saw the sealskins they brought home, and sent out expeditions to obtain more furs. Some returned richly laden,[4] but others were lost in storms and never heard from. There was so much danger in the hunting that it was not until 1783 that Russian merchants actually estab-

---

[1] area, territory
[2] wild, isolated
[3] passage, channel
[4] loaded

Kayak Island

lished trading posts in Alaska. Then a rich merchant of Siberia named Gregory Shelikoff built a post on Kadiak Island, and took into partnership with him a Russian named Alexander Baranof. Baranof built a fort on an island named for him, some three miles north of the present city of Sitka. The two men formed the Russian American Fur Company, and Baranof became its manager in America.

One day a seal hunter came to Baranof at his fortress, and took from his pocket a handful of nuggets of gold. He held them out to the Russian, and said that he knew where many more like them were to be found. "Ivan," said Baranof, "I forbid you to seek for any more. You must not say a word about this, or there will be trouble. If the Americans or the English know that there is gold in these mountains, we will be ruined. They will rush in here by the thousands, and crowd us to the wall." Baranof was a fur merchant, and did not want to see miners flocking to his land, as his company was growing rich from the seals and fur trading with the natives.

Little by little, however, the news leaked out that the northwestern country had rich minerals, and soon the King of Spain began to covet some of that wealth for himself. The Spaniards claimed that they owned all of the country that had not yet been mapped out, and they sent an exploring party, under Perez, to make charts of the northwest. Perez sailed along the coast, and finding two capes,[5] named them Santa Margarita and Santa Magdalena, but beyond that he did little to help the cause of Spain. Some years later, exploring parties were sent out from Mexico, but they found that the wild ice-covered country was already claimed by the Russians, and that the Czar[6] had no intention of giving it up. Other nations, therefore, soon ceased to claim it, and the Russian hunters and traders were allowed to enjoy the country in peace.

Alexander Baranof made a great success of the trade in skins, but the men who took his place were not equal to him. The company began to lose

---

[5] pieces of land that extend beyond the regular coast
[6] ruler of Russia (in this case, Alexander II)

money, and the Czar of Russia decided that the country was too far away from his capital to be properly looked after. The United States finally made an offer to buy the great territory from the Czar, although the government at Washington was not very anxious to make the purchase. The tract, large as it was, did not seem to promise much, and it was almost as far from Washington as it was from St. Petersburg.[7] The Czar was quite willing to sell, however, and so the United States bought the country from him in 1867, paying him $7,200,000 for it.[8]

On a fine October afternoon in 1867 Sitka Bay saw the Stars and Stripes flying from three United States warships, while the Russian Eagle waved from the flagstaffs and houses in the small town. On the shore soldiers of the two nations were drawn up in front of the old castle, and officers stood waiting at the foot of the flagpole on the parade ground. Then a gun was fired from one of the United States warships, and instantly the Russian batteries[9] returned the salute. A Russian officer lowered his country's flag from the parade ground pole, and an American pulled the Stars and Stripes to the peak. Guns boomed and regimental bands played, and then the Russian troops saluted and left the fortress, and the territory became part of the United States.

Up to that time the country had been known as Russian America, but now a new name had to be found. Some suggested American Siberia, and others the Zero Islands; but an American statesman, Charles Sumner, urged the name of Alaska, a native word meaning "the Great Land," and this was the name that was finally adopted.

It took many years to explore the western part of the United States, and men who were in search of wealth in mines and forests did not have to go as far as Alaska to find it. That bleak country was separated from the United States by a long, stormy sea voyage on the Pacific, or a tedious[10] and difficult overland journey through Canada. Alaska might have remained for years as little known as while Russia owned it had it not been for a small party of men who set out to explore the Yukon and the Klondike Rivers.

On June 16, 1897, a small ship called the *Excelsior* sailed into San Francisco Harbor, and half an hour after she had landed at her wharf the news was spreading far and wide that gold had been discovered in large quantities on the Klondike. Some of the men had gone out years before; some only a few months earlier, but they all brought back fortunes. Not one had left with less than $5,000[11] in gold, gathered in nuggets or flakes, in tin cans, canvas

---

[7] a city in Russia
[8] This is hundreds of millions of dollars today.
[9] military weapons
[10] dull, wearying
[11] hundreds of thousands of dollars today

bags, wooden boxes, or wrapped up in paper. The cry of such sudden wealth was heard by many adventurers, and the old days of 'Forty-Nine in California began over again when the wild rush started north to the Klondike.

On June 17th another ship, the *Portland*, arrived at Seattle, with sixty more miners and $800,000 in gold. This was the largest find of the precious mineral that had been made anywhere in the world, and Seattle followed the example of San Francisco in going gold-crazy. Immediately hundreds of people took passage on the outward-bound steamers, and hundreds more were turned away because of lack of room. Ships set out from all the seaports along the Pacific coast of the United States, and from the Canadian ports of Victoria and Vancouver. As in the old days of 1849 men gave up their business to seek the gold fields, but now they had to travel to a wilder and more desolate country than California had been.

There were many ways of getting to the Klondike country. Those who went by ocean steamer had to transfer to flat-bottomed boats to go up the Yukon River. This was the easiest route, but the boats could only be used on the Yukon from June until September, and the great rush of gold-seekers came later that autumn. A second route was by the Chilkoot trail, which had been used for many years by miners going into the country of the Yukon. Over this trail horses could be used as far as the foot of the great Chilkoot Pass, but from there luggage had to be carried by hand. Another trail, much like this one, was the White Pass trail, but it led through a less-known country than the Chilkoot, and was not so popular. The Canadian government laid out a trail of its own, which was called "the Stikeen route," and which ran altogether through Canadian territory. Besides these there were innumerable other roads through the mountains, and along the rivers; but the farther men got from the better known trails the more danger they were in of losing their way, or suffering from hunger and hardships.

Towns blossomed along the coast of Alaska almost overnight, but they were strange looking villages. The ships that landed at Skagway in the summer of 1897 found a number of rough frame houses, with three or four larger than the rest, which hung out hotel signs. The only government officer lived in a tent over which flew the flag of the United States. The passengers landed their outfits themselves, for labor was scarce, and found shelter wherever they could until they might start on the trail.

No one seemed to know much about the country they were going through, but fortunately most of the men were experienced woodsmen. They loaded their baggage on their packhorses, and started out, ready for any sort of country they might have to cross. Sometimes the trail lay over miry[12] ground, where a false step to the right or left would send the horses or men deep into the bog; sometimes it led up steep and rocky mountain-sides, where a man had to guard his horse's footing as carefully as his own; and much of the way was in the bed of an old river, where each step brought a splash of mud, and left the travelers at the end of the day spattered from head to foot. The journey was harder on the horses than on the men. The heavy packs they carried, and the wretched footing, caused them to drop along the road from time to time, and then the travelers had to make the best shift they could with their luggage. Had the men journeyed alone, or in small companies, they would have suffered greatly, but the Chilkoot trail was filled with miners who were ready to help each other, and to give en-couragement to any who lagged behind. At Dyea they came to an old Alaskan settlement, an Indian trading post, where a number of native tribes lived in their little wooden cabins. These men were the Chilkats, the Stikeen Indians, and the Chilkoots, short, heavy men....Both men and women were accustomed to painting their faces jet black or chocolate brown, in order to protect their eyes and skin from the glare of the sunlight on the snow. The traveler could here get Indians to act as guides, or if he had lost his horses might obtain dogs and sleds to carry some of his packs.

Each of the little settlements through which the travelers went boasted of a hotel, usually a frame building with two or three large rooms. Each day

---

[12] swampy

meals were served to three or four hundred hungry travelers at rude[13] board tables, and at night the men would spread their blankets on the floor and lie down to sleep. But as the trail went farther inland these little settlements grew fewer, and the men had to find whatever shelter they could. From Dyea they pushed on through the Chilkoot Pass, where the cliffs rose high above them. The winds blew cold from the north, and the mists kept every-thing wet. In the Pass some men turned back, finding the trip too difficult. Those who went on met with increasing hardships. They came to a place called Sheep Camp, where a stream of water and rocks from the mountain top had swept down upon a town of tents and carried them all away. Stories of similar happenings at other places were passed from mouth to mouth along the trail. More men turned back, finding such accidents a good excuse, and only the most determined stuck to the road.

In time they came to a chain of lakes and rivers. The travelers stopped to build rude boats and paddles, and navigated them as best they could. The rivers were full of rapids, and it was only by a miracle that the little clum-sily-built skiffs went dancing over the waters safely, and escaped the jutting rocks on either bank. In the rivers there was good trout fishing, and in the wild country good hunting, and Indian boys brought game to the tents at night. To the trees at each stopping-place papers were fastened, telling of the marvelous adventures of the miners who had just gone over the trail. As they neared Dawson City, they found the Yukon River more and more covered with floating ice, and travel by boat became harder. After a time, the oars, paddles, and all the baggage in the boats was encrusted with ice, and the boatmen had to make their way slowly among the floes. Then they came to a turn in the river, and on the bank saw a great number of tents and people. "How far is it to Dawson?" the boatman would call. "This is Daw-son. If you don't look out you'll be carried past," the men on shore an-swered. Paddles were thrust into the ice, and the boat brought to shore. The trip from Seattle had so far taken ninety-two days.

Food was scarce in Dawson, and men were urged to leave as soon as they could. Winter was now setting in, and the miners traveled with dog teams and sleds to the place where they meant to camp. Little work could be done in the winter, and the time was spent in preparing to work the gold fields in the early spring. All through the cold weather the men talked of the fortunes waiting for them, and when the warm weather came they staked out their claims and set to work. Stories of fabulous finds spread like wildfire, and those who were not finding gold rushed to the places that were proving rich. That summer many new towns sprang up, and in a few weeks the Bonanza and Eldorado mines made their owners rich, and all the tributaries of the Klondike River were yielding a golden harvest.

---

[13] simple, basic

When men found land that they thought would prove rich they made haste to claim it. Sometimes wild races followed, rivals trying to beat each other to the government offices at Dawson in order to claim the land. Frequently after such a wild race the claim would amount to nothing, while another man, who had picked out some place that no one wanted, would find a rich lode and make a fortune from it. Then there would be great excitement, for sudden wealth usually went to the miner's head. He would go down to Dawson, and spend his money freely, while everyone in the town would crowd around him to share in his good luck. One of the most successful was a Scotchman, Alexander McDonald. At the time of the Klondike strike he was employed by a company at the town of Forty-Mile. He had a little money and began to buy separate pieces of land. He could not afford the rich ground, but managed to purchase more than forty claims through the Klondike. At the end of that first season his fortune was said to be $5,000,000,[14] and might well have been more, as all his claims had not been fully worked. He was called "the King of the Klondike," and pointed out to newcomers as an example of what men might do in the gold fields.

That was only the beginning of the story of the Alaskan gold fields, and each year brought news of other discoveries. But the one season of 1897 was enough to prove the great value of Alaska, and to show that the United States had done well to buy that great territory from the Czar of Russia. Yet gold is only a small part of its riches, and even should the fields of the Klondike yield no more of the precious mineral, the seals, the fur trade, and the cities springing up along its coast are worth much more than the $7,000,000 paid for it. It is still a land of adventure, one of the few waste places that beckon men to come and find what wealth lies hidden within its borders.

Questions for Review

1. Tell a few facts about Alaska that you remember from the story.

2. What did the discovery of gold do for Alaska?

3. Find out a few more facts about Alaska. (Suggestions: when it became a state, other gold discoveries since 1897, how many hours of sunlight it receives, what the lowest recorded temperature was, and so on.)

---

[14] Easily $100 million, or maybe $200 million, today!

A Poison Tree

By William Blake

In 1794, British poet and artist William Blake (1757-1827) published "A Poison Tree" in a collection of poems called Songs of Experience. *Before reading "A Poison Tree," it would be helpful to read Matthew 5, verses 22 and 43-48; and Ephesians 4:26. What do these passages tell us to do about anger and dealing with our enemies?*

· · · · ·

I was angry with my friend:
I told my wrath, my wrath did end.
I was angry with my foe:
I told it not, my wrath did grow.

And I watered it in fears,
Night and morning with my tears:
And I sunned it with smiles,
And with soft deceitful wiles.[1]

And it grew both day and night,
Till it bore an apple bright,
And my foe beheld[2] it shine,
And he knew that it was mine—

And into my garden stole[3]
When the night had veiled the pole;[4]
In the morning, glad, I see
My foe outstretched beneath the tree.

Questions for Review

1. How does the poet handle his "two angers" differently in the first stanza? What happens to those angers?

2. What happens to the poet's anger toward his foe?

→

---

[1] tricks, deceits

[2] saw

[3] entered secretly

[4] that is, the trunk of the tree

3. What do you think the apple represents? How does this relate to Genesis, chapter 3?

4. Explain what happens to the author's foe in the last stanza, and compare this to the Bible passages referenced in the introduction.

A Ballad of Trees and the Master

By Sidney Lanier

*Georgia-born poet and musician Sidney Lanier (1842-1881) wrote "A Ballad of Trees and the Master" in 1880, the year before he died. A **ballad** is a poem that tells a story, and it is often set to music and sung. Before you read the following poem, it will help to first read Deuteronomy 21:23, Galatians 3:13, and Philippians 2:5-8.*

• • • • •

Into the woods my Master went,
    Clean forspent,[1] forspent.
Into the woods my Master came,
    Forspent with love and shame.
But the olives they were not blind to Him,
The little gray leaves were kind to Him:
The thorn-tree had a mind to Him
    When into the woods He came.

Out of the woods my Master went,
    And He was well content.
Out of the woods my Master came,
    Content with death and shame.
When Death and Shame would woo[2] Him last,
From under the trees they drew Him last:
'Twas on a tree they slew Him—last
    When out of the woods He came.

Questions for Review

1. How are the two stanzas of this poem alike? (What repetition or rhymes connect?)

2. How does "A Ballad of Trees and the Master" compare to the passages referenced in the introduction?

---

[1] exhausted
[2] persuade

Benjamin Franklin

By Nathaniel Hawthorne

One of America's finest writers, Nathaniel Hawthorne's (1804-1864) novels and short stories helped to make American literature respected throughout the world. The below "Benjamin Franklin" comes from Hawthorne's 1851 collection True Stories from History and Biography. *The attitude that young Benjamin Franklin displays in this little tale—without his meaning any real harm—is shown to be very destructive indeed.*

· · · · ·

In the year 1716, or about that period, a boy used to be seen in the streets of Boston, who was known among his schoolfellows and playmates by the name of Ben Franklin. Ben was born in 1706; so that he was now about ten years old. His father, who had come over from England, was a soap-boiler and tallow-chandler,[1] and resided in Milk Street, not far from the old South Church.

Ben was a bright boy at his book, and even a brighter one when at play with his comrades. He had some remarkable qualities which always seemed to give him the lead, whether at sport or in more serious matters. I might tell you a number of amusing anecdotes[2] about him. You are acquainted, I suppose, with his famous story of the WHISTLE, and how he bought it with a whole pocketful of coppers, and afterwards repented of his bargain. But Ben had grown a great boy since those days, and had gained wisdom by experience; for it was one of his peculiarities, that no incident ever happened to him without teaching him some valuable lesson. Thus he generally profited more by his misfortunes, than many people do by the most favorable events that could befall them.

Ben's face was already pretty well known to the inhabitants of Boston. The selectmen, and other people of note, often used to visit his father, for the sake of talking about the affairs of the town or province. Mr. Franklin was considered a person of great wisdom and integrity, and was respected by all who knew him, although he supported his family by the humble trade of boiling soap and making tallow-candles.

---

[1] someone who sells candles made from animal fat
[2] stories

While his father and the visitors were holding deep consultations about public affairs, little Ben would sit on his stool in a corner, listening with the greatest interest, as if he understood every word. Indeed, his features were so full of intelligence, that there could be but little doubt, not only that he understood what was said, but that he could have expressed some very sagacious[3] opinions out of his own mind. But, in those days, boys were expected to be silent in the presence of their elders. However, Ben Franklin was looked upon as a very promising lad, who would talk and act wisely by and by.

"Neighbor Franklin," his father's friends would sometimes say, "you ought to send this boy to college and make a minister of him."

"I have often thought of it," his father would reply; "and my brother Benjamin promises to give him a great many volumes of manuscript sermons in case he should be educated for the church. But I have a large family to support, and cannot afford the expense."

In fact, Mr. Franklin found it so difficult to provide bread for his family, that, when the boy was ten years old, it became necessary to take him from school. Ben was then employed in cutting candlewicks into equal lengths, and filling the molds with tallow;[4] and many families in Boston spent their evenings by the light of the candles which he had helped to make. Thus, you see, in his early days, as well as in his manhood his labors contributed to throw light upon dark matters.

Busy as his life now was, Ben still found time to keep company with his former schoolfellows. He and the other boys were very fond of fishing, and spent any of their leisure hours on the margin of the mill-pond, catching flounders, perch, eels, and tom-cod, which came up thither[5] with the tide. The place where they fished is now, probably, covered with stone-pavements and brick buildings, and thronged[6] with people, and with vehicles of all kinds. But, at that period, it was a marshy spot on the outskirts of the town, where gulls flitted and screamed overhead, and salt meadow-grass grew under foot. On the edge of the water there was a deep bed of clay, in which the boys were forced to stand, while they caught their fish. Here they dabbled in mud and mire like a flock of ducks.

"This is very uncomfortable," said Ben Franklin one day to his comrades, while they were standing mid-leg deep in the quagmire.[7]

"So it is," said the other boys. "What a pity we have no better place to stand!"

---

[3] wise
[4] animal fat
[5] there
[6] crowded
[7] swamp

If it had not been for Ben, nothing more would have been done or said about the matter. But it was not in his nature to be sensible of an inconvenience, without using his best efforts to find a remedy. So, as he and his comrades were returning from the water-side, Ben suddenly threw down his string of fish with a very determined air:

"Boys," cried he, "I have thought of a scheme, which will be greatly for our benefit, and for the public benefit!"

It was queer enough, to be sure, to hear this little chap—this rosy-cheeked, ten-year-old boy—talking about schemes for the public benefit! Nevertheless, his companions were ready to listen, being assured that Ben's scheme, whatever it was, would be well worth their attention. They remembered how sagaciously he had conducted all their enterprises, ever since he had been old enough to wear small-clothes.[8]

They remembered, too, his wonderful contrivance[9] of sailing across the mill-pond by lying flat on his back, in the water, and allowing himself to be drawn along by a paper-kite. If Ben could do that, he might certainly do anything.

"What is your scheme, Ben?—what is it?" cried they all.

It so happened that they had now come to a spot of ground where a new house was to be built. Scattered round about lay a great many large stones, which were to be used for the cellar and foundation. Ben mounted upon the highest of these stones, so that he might speak with the more authority.

"You know, lads," said he, "what a plague it is, to be forced to stand in the quagmire yonder—over shoes and stockings (if we wear any) in mud and water. See! I am bedaubed[10] to the knees of my small-clothes, and you are all in the same pickle. Unless we can find some remedy for this evil, our fishing-business must be entirely given up. And, surely, this would be a terrible misfortune!"

"That it would!—that it would!" said his comrades, sorrowfully.

"Now I propose," continued Master Benjamin, "that we build a wharf, for the purpose of carrying on our fisheries. You see these stones. The workmen mean to use them for the underpinning of a house; but that would be for only one man's advantage. My plan is to take these same stones, and carry them to the edge of the water and build a wharf with them. This will not only enable us to carry on the fishing business with comfort, and to better advantage, but it will likewise be a great convenience to boats passing up and down the stream. Thus, instead of one man, fifty, or a hundred, or a thousand, besides ourselves, may be benefited by these stones. What say you, lads?—shall we build the wharf?"

---

[8] knee-length pants
[9] setup, device
[10] smeared

Ben's proposal was received with one of those uproarious shouts, wherewith boys usually express their delight at whatever completely suits their views. Nobody thought of questioning the right and justice of building a wharf, with stones that belonged to another person.

"Hurrah, hurrah!" shouted they. "Let's set about it!"

It was agreed that they should all be on the spot, that evening, and commence[11] their grand public enterprise by moonlight. Accordingly, at the appointed time, the whole gang of youthful laborers assembled, and eagerly began to remove the stones. They had not calculated how much toil would be requisite,[12] in this important part of their undertaking. The very first stone which they laid hold of, proved so heavy, that it almost seemed to be fastened to the ground. Nothing but Ben Franklin's cheerful and resolute[13] spirit could have induced them to persevere.

Ben, as might be expected, was the soul of the enterprise. By his mechanical genius, he contrived methods to lighten the labor of transporting the stones; so that one boy, under his directions, would perform as much as half a dozen, if left to themselves. Whenever their spirits flagged, he had some joke ready, which seemed to renew their strength by setting them all into a roar of laughter. And when, after an hour or two of hard work, the stones were transported to the water-side, Ben Franklin was the engineer, to superintend[14] the construction of the wharf.

The boys, like a colony of ants, performed a great deal of labor by their multitude, though the individual strength of each could have accomplished but little. Finally, just as the moon sank below the horizon, the great work was finished.

---

[11] begin
[12] needed
[13] determined
[14] supervise

"Now, boys," cried Ben, "let's give three cheers, and go home to bed. Tomorrow, we may catch fish at our ease!" "Hurrah! hurrah! hurrah!" shouted his comrades.

Then they all went home, in such an ecstasy of delight that they could hardly get a wink of sleep.

In the morning, when the early sunbeams were gleaming on the steeples and roofs of the town, and gilding the water that surrounded it, the masons came, rubbing their eyes, to begin their work at the foundation of the new house. But, on reaching the spot, they rubbed their eyes so much the harder. What had become of their heap of stones?

"Why, Sam," said one to another, in great perplexity,[15] "here's been some witchcraft at work, while we were asleep. The stones must have flown away through the air!"

"More likely they have been stolen!" answered Sam.

"But who on earth would think of stealing a heap of stones?" cried a third. "Could a man carry them away in his pocket?"

The master-mason, who was a gruff kind of man, stood scratching his head, and said nothing, at first. But, looking carefully on the ground, he discerned innumerable tracks of little feet, some with shoes, and some barefoot. Following these tracks with his eye, he saw that they formed a beaten path towards the water-side.

"Ah, I see what the mischief is," said he, nodding his head. "Those little rascals, the boys! they have stolen our stones to build a wharf with!"

The masons immediately went to examine the new structure. And to say the truth, it was well worth looking at, so neatly, and with such admirable skill, had it been planned and finished. The stones were put together so securely, that there was no danger of their being loosened by the tide, however swiftly it might sweep along. There was a broad and safe platform to stand upon, whence the little fishermen might cast their lines into deep water, and draw up fish in abundance. Indeed, it almost seemed as if Ben and his comrades might be forgiven for taking the stones, because they had done their job in such a workmanlike manner.

"The chaps, that built this wharf, understood their business pretty well," said one of the masons. "I should not be ashamed of such a piece of work myself."

But the master-mason did not seem to enjoy the joke. He was one of those unreasonable people, who care a great deal more for their own rights and privileges, than for the convenience of all the rest of the world.

"Sam," said he, more gruffly than usual, "go call a constable."

So Sam called a constable, and inquiries were set on foot to discover the perpetrators of the theft. In the course of the day, warrants were issued, with

---

[15] puzzlement

the signature of a Justice of the Peace, to take the bodies of Benjamin Franklin and other evil-disposed persons, who had stolen a heap of stones. If the owner of the stolen property had not been more merciful than the master-mason, it might have gone hard with our friend Benjamin and his fellow-laborers. But, luckily for them, the gentleman had a respect for Ben's father, and moreover, was amused with the spirit of the whole affair. He therefore let the culprits[16] off pretty easily.

But, when the constables were dismissed, the poor boys had to go through another trial, and receive sentence, and suffer execution too, from their own fathers. Many a rod I grieve to say, was worn to the stump, on that unlucky night.

As for Ben, he was less afraid of a whipping than of his father's disapprobation.[17] Mr. Franklin, as I have mentioned before, was a sagacious man, and also an inflexibly upright one. He had read much, for a person in his rank of life, and had pondered upon the ways of the world, until he had gained more wisdom than a whole library of books could have taught him. Ben had a greater reverence for his father, than for any other person in the world, as well on account of his spotless integrity, as of his practical sense and deep views of things.

Consequently, after being released from the clutches of the law, Ben came into his father's presence, with no small perturbation[18] of mind.

"Benjamin, come hither," began Mr. Franklin, in his customary solemn and weighty tone.

The boy approached, and stood before his father's chair, waiting reverently to hear what judgment this good man would pass upon his late offense. He felt that now the right and wrong of the whole matter would be made to appear.

"Benjamin," said his father, "what could induce you to take property which did not belong to you?"

"Why, father," replied Ben, hanging his head, at first, but then lifting his eyes to Mr. Franklin's face, "if it had been merely for my own benefit, I never should have dreamed of it. But I knew that the wharf would be a public convenience. If the owner of the stones should build a house with them, nobody will enjoy any advantage except himself. Now, I made use of them in a way that was for the advantage of many persons. I thought it right to aim at doing good to the greatest number."

"My son," said Mr. Franklin, solemnly, "so far as it was in your power, you have done a greater harm to the public, than to the owner of the stones."

"How can that be, father?" asked Ben.

---

[16] guilty persons
[17] disapproval
[18] unrest

"Because," answered his father, "in building your wharf with stolen materials, you have committed a moral wrong. There is no more terrible mistake, than to violate what is eternally right, for the sake of a seeming expediency. Those who act upon such a principle, do the utmost in their power to destroy all that is good in the world."

"Heaven forbid!" said Benjamin.

"No act," continued Mr. Franklin, "can possibly be for the benefit of the public generally, which involves injustice to any individual. It would be easy to prove this by examples. But, indeed, can we suppose that our all-wise and just Creator would have so ordered the affairs of the world, that a wrong act should be the true method of attaining a right end? It is impious[19] to think so! And I do verily[20] believe, Benjamin, that almost all the public and private misery of mankind arises from a neglect of this great truth—that evil can produce only evil—that good ends must be wrought out by good means."

"I will never forget it again," said Benjamin, bowing his head.

"Remember," concluded his father, "that, whenever we vary from the highest rule of right, just so far we do an injury to the world. It may seem otherwise for the moment; but, both in Time and in Eternity, it will be found so."

To the close of his life, Ben Franklin never forgot this conversation with his father; and we have reason to suppose, that in most of his public and private career, he endeavored to act upon the principles which that good and wise man had then taught him.

After the great event of building the wharf, Ben continued to cut wick-yarn and fill candle-molds for about two years. But, as he had no love for that occupation, his father often took him to see various artisans at their work, in order to discover what trade he would prefer. Thus Ben learned the use of a great many tools, the knowledge of which afterwards proved very useful to him. But he seemed much inclined to go to sea. In order to keep him at home, and likewise to gratify his taste for letters, the lad was bound apprentice to his elder brother, who had lately set up a printing-office in Boston.

Here he had many opportunities of reading new books, and of hearing instructive conversation. He exercised himself so successfully in writing composition, that, when no more than thirteen or fourteen years old, he became a contributor to his brother's newspaper. Ben was also a versifier,[21] if not a poet. He made two doleful[22] ballads; one about the ship-wreck of

---

[19] wicked

[20] truly

[21] a writer of poor poetry

[22] sad

Captain Worthilake,[23] and the other about the pirate Black Beard, who not long before, infested the American seas.

When Ben's verses were printed, his brother sent him to sell them to the townspeople, wet from the press. "Buy my ballads!" shouted Benjamin, as he trudged through the streets, with a basketful on his arm. "Who'll buy a ballad about Black Beard? A penny a piece! a penny a piece! who'll buy my ballads?"

If one of those roughly composed and rudely printed ballads could be discovered now, it would be worth more than its weight in gold.

In this way our friend Benjamin spent his boyhood and youth, until, on account of some disagreement with his brother, he left his native town and went to Philadelphia. He landed in the latter city, a homeless and hungry young man, and bought three-pence worth of bread to satisfy his appetite. Not knowing where else to go, he entered a Quaker meeting-house, sat down, and fell fast asleep. He has not told us whether his slumbers were visited by any dreams. But it would have been a strange dream, indeed, and an incredible one, that should have foretold how great a man he was destined to become, and how much he would be honored in that very city, where he was now friendless, and unknown.

So here we finish our story of the childhood of Benjamin Franklin. One of these days, if you would know what he was in his manhood, you must read his own works, and the history of American Independence.

Questions for Review

1. Why was Benjamin Franklin's taking of the stones wrong? How does what the Bible says about one of government's proper duties in Jeremiah 22:3 related to Ben's action?

2. Ben's father says, "No act can possibly be for the benefit of the public generally, which involves injustice to any individual." Explain what this statement means.

3. Ask your Mom or Dad to tell you one thing that our government does, while *claiming* it's for the benefit of the public, and at the same time violating the rights of an individual or many individuals.

---

[23] George Worthilake (1673-1718) was a lighthouse keeper who drowned near Boston Harbor. Franklin's poem in honor of Worthilake is called "The Lighthouse Tragedy."

The Merry Adventures of Robin Hood

By Howard Pyle

American artist and author Howard Pyle (1853-1911) not only wrote these excerpts from his 1883 updating of the Robin Hood tales, but illustrated them too! Pyle's Robin Hood stories sparked a new popularity with the character, partly because Pyle's version made him more of a hero than an outlaw. The book and its illustrations influenced other Robin Hood works, including the great 1938 color film The Adventures of Robin Hood.

• • • • •

Preface: From the Author to the Reader

You who so plod amid serious things that you feel it shame to give yourself up even for a few short moments to mirth[1] and joyousness in the land of Fancy; you who think that life hath nought to do with innocent laughter that can harm no one; these pages are not for you. Clap to the leaves and go no farther than this, for I tell you plainly that if you go farther, you will be scandalized by seeing good, sober folks of real history so frisk and caper in gay colors and motley[2] that you would not know them but for the names tagged to them. Here is a stout, lusty fellow with a quick temper, yet none so ill for all that, who goes by the name of Henry II. Here is a fair, gentle lady before whom all the others bow and call her Queen Eleanor. Here is a fat rogue of a fellow, dressed up in rich robes of a clerical kind, that all the good folk call my Lord Bishop of Hereford. Here is a certain fellow with a sour temper and a grim look—the worshipful, the Sheriff of Nottingham. And here, above all, is a great, tall, merry fellow that roams the greenwood and joins in homely sports, and sits beside the Sheriff at merry feast, which same beareth the name of the proudest of the Plantagenets[3]—Richard of the Lion's Heart. Beside these are a whole host of knights, priests, nobles, burghers,[4] yeomen,[5] pages, ladies, lasses, landlords, beggars, peddlers, and whatnot, all living the merriest of merry lives, and all bound by nothing but a few odd strands of certain old ballads (snipped and clipped and tied together again in a score of knots) which draw these jocund[6] fellows here and there, singing as they go.

---

[1] laughter, humor
[2] assorted, varied
[3] line of British kings
[4] citizens
[5] officials who serve noble households or in government positions
[6] jolly, merry

Here you will find a hundred dull, sober, jogging places, all tricked out with flowers and what not, till no one would know them in their fanciful dress. And here is a country bearing a well-known name, wherein no chill mists press upon our spirits, and no rain falls but what rolls off our backs like April showers off the backs of sleek drakes;[7] where flowers bloom forever and birds are always singing; where every fellow hath a merry catch as he travels the roads....

This country is not Fairyland. What is it? 'Tis the land of Fancy, and is of that pleasant kind that, when you tire of it—whisk!—you clap the leaves of this book together and 'tis gone, and you are ready for everyday life, with no harm done.

And now I lift the curtain that hangs between here and No-man's-land. Will you come with me, sweet Reader? I thank you. Give me your hand.

How Robin Hood Came to Be an Outlaw

In merry England in the time of old, when good King Henry the Second ruled the land, there lived within the green glades of Sherwood Forest, near Nottingham Town, a famous outlaw whose name was Robin Hood. No archer ever lived that could speed a gray goose shaft with such skill and cunning as his, nor were there ever such yeomen as the sevenscore[8] merry men that roamed with him through the green-wood shades. Right merrily they dwelled within the depths of Sherwood Forest, suffering neither care nor want, but passing the time in merry games of archery or bouts of cudgel[9] play, living upon the King's venison, washed down with draughts of ale of October brewing.

Not only Robin himself but all the band were outlaws and dwelled apart from other men, yet they were beloved by the country people round about, for no one ever came to jolly Robin for help in time of need and went away again with an empty fist.

And now I will tell how it came about that Robin Hood fell afoul of the law.

When Robin was a youth of eighteen, stout of sinew and bold of heart, the Sheriff of Nottingham proclaimed a shooting match and offered a prize of a butt of ale to whosoever should shoot the best shaft in Nottinghamshire. "Now," quoth Robin, "will I go too, for fain[10] would I draw a string for the bright eyes of my lass and a butt of good October brewing." So up he got and took his good stout yew bow and a score or more of broad clothyard arrows, and started off from Locksley Town through Sherwood Forest to Nottingham.

---

[7] ducks
[8] A score is 20, so sevenscore is 140.
[9] A cudgel is a club or stick.
[10] gladly

It was at the dawn of day in the merry Maytime, when hedgerows are green and flowers bedeck the meadows; daisies pied[11] and yellow cuckoo buds and fair primroses all along the briery hedges; when apple buds blossom and sweet birds sing, the lark at dawn of day, the throstle cock and cuckoo; when lads and lasses look upon each other with sweet thoughts; when busy housewives spread their linen to bleach upon the bright green grass. Sweet was the greenwood as he walked along its paths, and bright the green and rustling leaves, amid which the little birds sang with might and main: and blithely[12] Robin whistled as he trudged along, thinking of Maid Marian and her bright eyes, for at such times a youth's thoughts are wont[13] to turn pleasantly upon the lass that he loves the best.

As thus he walked along with a brisk step and a merry whistle, he came suddenly upon some foresters seated beneath a great oak tree. Fifteen there were in all, making themselves merry with feasting and drinking as they sat around a huge pasty,[14] to which each man helped himself, thrusting his hands into the pie, and washing down that which they ate with great horns of ale which they drew all foaming from a barrel that stood nigh. Each man was clad in Lincoln green, and a fine show they made, seated upon the sward[15] beneath that fair, spreading tree. Then one of them, with his mouth full, called out to Robin, "Hulloa, where goest thou, little lad, with thy one-penny bow and thy farthing shafts?"

Then Robin grew angry, for no stripling[16] likes to be taunted with his green years.

"Now," quoth he, "my bow and eke[17] mine arrows are as good as shine; and moreover, I go to the shooting match at Nottingham Town, which same has been proclaimed by our good Sheriff of Nottinghamshire; there I will shoot with other stout yeomen, for a prize has been offered of a fine butt of ale."

Then one who held a horn of ale in his hand said, "Ho! listen to the lad! Why, boy, thy mother's milk is yet scarce dry upon thy lips, and yet thou pratest[18] of standing up with good stout men at Nottingham butts,[19] thou who art scarce able to draw one string of a two-stone bow."

---

[11] multicolored
[12] happily
[13] inclined
[14] pie
[15] grass
[16] young man, teenager
[17] also
[18] chatter, babble on
[19] targets

"I'll hold the best of you twenty marks," quoth bold Robin, "that I hit the clout at threescore rods,[20] by the good help of Our Lady fair."

At this all laughed aloud, and one said, "Well boasted, thou fair infant, well boasted! And well thou knowest that no target is nigh[21] to make good thy wager."

And another cried, "He will be taking ale with his milk next."

At this Robin grew right mad. "Hark ye," said he, "yonder, at the glade's end, I see a herd of deer, even more than threescore rods distant. I'll hold you twenty marks that, by leave of Our Lady, I cause the best hart among them to die."

"Now done!" cried he who had spoken first. "And here are twenty marks. I wager that thou causest no beast to die, with or without the aid of Our Lady."

Then Robin took his good yew bow in his hand, and placing the tip at his instep, he strung it right deftly; then he nocked a broad clothyard arrow and, raising the bow, drew the gray goose feather to his ear; the next moment the bowstring rang, and the arrow sped down the glade as a sparrowhawk skims in a northern wind. High leaped the noblest hart of all the herd, only to fall dead, reddening the green path with his heart's blood.

---

[20] A rod is 16½ feet, so threescore rods is $60 \times 16.5 = 900$ feet!

[21] near

"Ha!" cried Robin, "how likest thou that shot, good fellow? I wot the wager were mine, an it were three hundred pounds."

Then all the foresters were filled with rage, and he who had spoken the first and had lost the wager was more angry than all.

"Nay," cried he, "the wager is none of thine, and get thee gone, straight-way, or, by all the saints of heaven, I'll baste thy sides until thou wilt ne'er be able to walk again." "Knowest thou not," said another, "that thou hast killed the King's deer, and, by the laws of our gracious lord and sovereign King Harry, thine ears should be shaven close to thy head?"

"Catch him!" cried a third.

"Nay," said a fourth, "let him e'en go because of his tender years."

Never a word said Robin Hood, but he looked at the foresters with a grim face; then, turning on his heel, strode away from them down the forest glade. But his heart was bitterly angry, for his blood was hot and youthful and prone to boil.

Now, well would it have been for him who had first spoken had he left Robin Hood alone; but his anger was hot, both because the youth had gotten the better of him and because of the deep draughts of ale that he had been quaffing. So, of a sudden, without any warning, he sprang to his feet, and seized upon his bow and fitted it to a shaft. "Ay," cried he, "and I'll hurry thee anon."[22] And he sent the arrow whistling after Robin.

It was well for Robin Hood that that same forester's head was spinning with ale, or else he would never have taken another step. As it was, the arrow whistled within three inches of his head. Then he turned around and quickly drew his own bow, and sent an arrow back in return.

"Ye said I was no archer," cried he aloud, "but say so now again!"

The shaft flew straight; the archer fell forward with a cry, and lay on his face upon the ground, his arrows rattling about him from out of his quiver, the gray goose shaft wet with his; heart's blood. Then, before the others could gather their wits about them, Robin Hood was gone into the depths of the greenwood. Some started after him, but not with much heart, for each feared to suffer the death of his fellow; so presently they all came and lifted the dead man up and bore him away to Nottingham Town.

Meanwhile Robin Hood ran through the greenwood. Gone was all the joy and brightness from everything, for his heart was sick within him, and it was borne in upon his soul that he had slain a man.

"Alas!" cried he, "thou hast found me an archer that will make thy wife to wring! I would that thou hadst ne'er said one word to me, or that I had never passed thy way, or e'en that my right forefinger had been stricken off ere that this had happened! In haste I smote, but grieve I sore at leisure!"

---

[22] now, immediately

And then, even in his trouble, he remembered the old saw[23] that "What is done is done; and the egg cracked cannot be cured."

And so he came to dwell in the greenwood that was to be his home for many a year to come, never again to see the happy days with the lads and lasses of sweet Locksley Town; for he was outlawed, not only because he had killed a man, but also because he had poached upon the King's deer, and two hundred pounds were set upon his head, as a reward for whoever would bring him to the court of the King.

Now the Sheriff of Nottingham swore that he himself would bring this knave Robin Hood to justice, and for two reasons: first, because he wanted the two hundred pounds, and next, because the forester that Robin Hood had killed was of kin to him.

But Robin Hood lay hidden in Sherwood Forest for one year, and in that time there gathered around him many others like himself, cast out from other folk for this cause and for that. Some had shot deer in hungry winter-time, when they could get no other food, and had been seen in the act by the foresters, but had escaped, thus saving their ears; some had been turned out of their inheritance, that their farms might be added to the King's lands in Sherwood Forest; some had been despoiled[24] by a great baron or a rich abbot or a powerful esquire—all, for one cause or another, had come to Sherwood to escape wrong and oppression.

So, in all that year, fivescore or more good stout yeomen gathered about Robin Hood, and chose him to be their leader and chief. Then they vowed that even as they themselves had been despoiled they would despoil their oppressors, whether baron, abbot, knight, or squire, and that from each they would take that which had been wrung from the poor by unjust taxes, or land rents, or in wrongful fines. But to the poor folk they would give a helping hand in need and trouble, and would return to them that which had been unjustly taken from them. Besides this, they swore never to harm a child nor to wrong a woman, be she maid, wife, or widow; so that, after a while, when the people began to find that no harm was meant to them, but that money or food came in time of want to many a poor family, they came to praise Robin and his merry men, and to tell many tales of him and of his doings in Sherwood Forest, for they felt him to be one of themselves.

Up rose Robin Hood one merry morn when all the birds were singing blithely among the leaves, and up rose all his merry men, each fellow washing his head and hands in the cold brown brook that leaped laughing from stone to stone. Then said Robin, "For fourteen days have we seen no sport, so now I will go abroad to seek adventures forthwith.[25] But tarry ye,

---

[23] saying

[24] robbed

[25] without delay

my merry men all, here in the greenwood; only see that ye mind well my call. Three blasts upon the bugle horn I will blow in my hour of need; then come quickly, for I shall want your aid."

So saying, he strode away through the leafy forest glades until he had come to the verge of Sherwood. There he wandered for a long time, through highway and byway, through dell and forest skirts. Now he met a fair lass in a shady lane, and each gave the other a merry word and passed their way; now he saw a fair lady upon an ambling pad, to whom he doffed[26] his cap, and who bowed sedately in return to the fair youth; now he saw a fat monk on a pannier[27]-laden ass; now a gallant knight, with spear and shield and armor that flashed brightly in the sunlight; now a page clad in crimson; and now a stout burgher from good Nottingham Town, pacing along with serious footsteps; all these sights he saw, but adventure found he none. At last he took a road by the forest skirts, a by-path that dipped toward a broad, pebbly stream spanned by a narrow bridge made of a log of wood. As he drew nigh this bridge, he saw a tall stranger coming from the other side. Thereupon Robin quickened his pace, as did the stranger likewise, each thinking to cross first.

"Now stand thou back," quoth Robin, "and let the better man cross first."

"Nay," answered the stranger, "then stand back shine own self, for the better man, I wet, am I."

"That will we presently see," quoth Robin, "and meanwhile stand thou where thou art, or else, by the bright brow of Saint Alfrida, I will show thee right good Nottingham play with a clothyard shaft betwixt thy ribs."

"Now," quoth the stranger, "I will tan thy hide till it be as many colors as a beggar's cloak, if thou darest so much as touch a string of that same bow that thou holdest in thy hands."

"Thou pratest like an ass," said Robin, "for I could send this shaft clean through thy proud heart before a curtal friar[28] could say grace over a roast goose at Michaelmastide."[29]

"And thou pratest like a coward," answered the stranger, "for thou standest there with a good yew bow to shoot at my heart, while I have nought in my hand but a plain blackthorn staff wherewith to meet thee."

"Now," quoth Robin, "by the faith of my heart, never have I had a coward's name in all my life before. I will lay by my trusty bow and eke my arrows, and if thou darest abide my coming, I will go and cut a cudgel to test thy manhood withal."[30]

---

[26] took off or tipped in respect

[27] a large basket

[28] a friar with a short gown

[29] a Christian feast celebrated on September 29 to honor the angel Michael

[30] still

"Ay, marry,[31] that will I abide thy coming, and joyously, too," quoth the stranger; whereupon he leaned sturdily upon his staff to await Robin.

Then Robin Hood stepped quickly to the coverside and cut a good staff of ground oak, straight, without new, and six feet in length, and came back trimming away the tender stems from it, while the stranger waited for him, leaning upon his staff, and whistling as he gazed round about. Robin observed him furtively[32] as he trimmed his staff, measuring him from top to toe from out the corner of his eye, and thought that he had never seen a lustier or a stouter man. Tall was Robin, but taller was the stranger by a head and a neck, for he was seven feet in height. Broad was Robin across the shoulders, but broader was the stranger by twice the breadth of a palm, while he measured at least an ell around the waist.

"Nevertheless," said Robin to himself, "I will baste thy hide right merrily, my good fellow;" then, aloud, "Lo, here is my good staff, lusty and tough. Now wait my coming, an thou darest, and meet me an thou fearest not. Then we will fight until one or the other of us tumble into the stream by dint of blows."

"Marry, that meeteth my whole heart!" cried the stranger, twirling his staff above his head, betwixt his fingers and thumb, until it whistled again.

Never did the Knights of Arthur's Round Table meet in a stouter fight than did these two. In a moment Robin stepped quickly upon the bridge where the stranger stood; first he made a feint,[33] and then delivered a blow at the stranger's head that, had it met its mark, would have tumbled him speedily into the water. But the stranger turned the blow right deftly and in return gave one as stout, which Robin also turned as the stranger had done.

---

[31] indeed
[32] secretly
[33] a movement to trick his opponent

So they stood, each in his place, neither moving a finger's-breadth back, for one good hour, and many blows were given and received by each in that time, till here and there were sore bones and bumps, yet neither thought of crying "Enough," nor seemed likely to fall from off the bridge. Now and then they stopped to rest, and each thought that he never had seen in all his life before such a hand at quarterstaff. At last Robin gave the stranger a blow upon the ribs that made his jacket smoke like a damp straw thatch in the sun. So shrewd was the stroke that the stranger came within a hair's-breadth of falling off the bridge, but he regained himself right quickly and, by a dexterous[34] blow, gave Robin a crack on the crown that caused the blood to flow. Then Robin grew mad with anger and smote with all his might at the other. But the stranger warded the blow and once again thwacked Robin, and this time so fairly that he fell heels over head into the water, as the queen pin falls in a game of bowls.

"And where art thou now, my good lad?" shouted the stranger, roaring with laughter.

"Oh, in the flood and floating adown with the tide," cried Robin, nor could he forbear[35] laughing himself at his sorry plight. Then, gaining his feet, he waded to the bank, the little fish speeding hither and thither, all frightened at his splashing.

"Give me thy hand," cried he, when he had reached the bank. "I must needs own thou art a brave and a sturdy soul and, withal, a good stout stroke with the cudgels. By this and by that, my head hummeth like to a hive of bees on a hot June day."

Then he clapped his horn to his lips and winded a blast that went echoing sweetly down the forest paths. "Ay, marry," quoth he again, "thou art a tall lad, and eke a brave one, for ne'er, I bow, is there a man betwixt here and Canterbury Town could do the like to me that thou hast done."

"And thou," quoth the stranger, laughing, "takest thy cudgeling like a brave heart and a stout yeoman."

But now the distant twigs and branches rustled with the coming of men, and suddenly a score or two of good stout yeomen, all clad in Lincoln green, burst from out the covert, with merry Will Stutely at their head.

"Good master," cried Will, "how is this? Truly thou art all wet from head to foot, and that to the very skin."

"Why, marry," answered jolly Robin, "yon stout fellow hath tumbled me neck and crop into the water and hath given me a drubbing[36] beside."

"Then shall he not go without a ducking and eke a drubbing himself!" cried Will Stutely. "Have at him, lads!"

---

[34] skillful
[35] hold back from
[36] beating

Then Will and a score of yeomen leaped upon the stranger, but though they sprang quickly they found him ready and felt him strike right and left with his stout staff, so that, though he went down with press of numbers, some of them rubbed cracked crowns[37] before he was overcome.

"Nay, forbear!" cried Robin, laughing until his sore sides ached again. "He is a right good man and true, and no harm shall befall him. Now hark ye, good youth, wilt thou stay with me and be one of my band? Three suits of Lincoln green shalt thou have each year, beside forty marks in fee, and share with us whatsoever good shall befall us. Thou shalt eat sweet venison and quaff the stoutest ale, and mine own good right-hand man shalt thou be, for never did I see such a cudgel player in all my life before. Speak! Wilt thou be one of my good merry men?"

"That know I not," quoth the stranger surlily, for he was angry at being so tumbled about. "If ye handle yew bow and apple shaft no better than ye do oaken cudgel, I wot ye are not fit to be called yeomen in my country; but if there be any man here that can shoot a better shaft than I, then will I bethink me of joining with you."

"Now by my faith," said Robin, "thou art a right saucy varlet,[38] sirrah; yet I will stoop to thee as I never stooped to man before. Good Stutely, cut thou a fair white piece of bark four fingers in breadth, and set it fourscore yards distant on yonder oak. Now, stranger, hit that fairly with a gray goose shaft and call thyself an archer."

"Ay, marry, that will I," answered he. "Give me a good stout bow and a fair broad arrow, and if I hit it not, strip me and beat me blue with bowstrings."

---

[37] heads
[38] rascal

Then he chose the stoutest bow among them all, next to Robin's own, and a straight gray goose shaft, well-feathered and smooth, and stepping to the mark—while all the band, sitting or lying upon the greensward, watched to see him shoot—he drew the arrow to his cheek and loosed the shaft right deftly, sending it so straight down the path that it clove the mark in the very center. "Aha!" cried he, "mend thou that if thou canst;" while even the yeomen clapped their hands at so fair a shot.

"That is a keen shot indeed," quoth Robin. "Mend it I cannot, but mar it I may, perhaps."

Then taking up his own good stout bow and nocking an arrow with care, he shot with his very greatest skill. Straight flew the arrow, and so true that it lit fairly upon the stranger's shaft and split it into splinters. Then all the yeomen leaped to their feet and shouted for joy that their master had shot so well.

"Now by the lusty yew bow of good Saint Withold," cried the stranger, "that is a shot indeed, and never saw I the like in all my life before! Now truly will I be thy man henceforth and for aye. Good Adam Bell[39] was a fair shot, but never shot he so!"

"Then have I gained a right good man this day," quoth jolly Robin. "What name goest thou by, good fellow?"

"Men call me John Little whence I came," answered the stranger.

Then Will Stutely, who loved a good jest, spoke up. "Nay, fair little stranger," said he, "I like not thy name and fain would I have it otherwise. Little art thou indeed, and small of bone and sinew, therefore shalt thou be christened Little John, and I will be thy godfather."

Then Robin Hood and all his band laughed aloud until the stranger began to grow angry.

"An thou make a jest of me," quoth he to Will Stutely, "thou wilt have sore bones and little pay, and that in short season."

"Nay, good friend," said Robin Hood, "bottle thine anger, for the name fitteth thee well. Little John shall thou be called henceforth, and Little John shall it be. So come, my merry men, we will prepare a christening feast for this fair infant."

So turning their backs upon the stream, they plunged into the forest once more, through which they traced their steps till they reached the spot where they dwelled in the depths of the woodland. There had they built huts of bark and branches of trees, and made couches of sweet rushes spread over with skins of fallow[40] deer. Here stood a great oak tree with branches spreading broadly around, beneath which was a seat of green moss where Robin Hood was wont to sit at feast and at merrymaking with his stout men

---

[39] an English outlaw and archer
[40] light brown

about him. Here they found the rest of the band, some of whom had come in with a brace of fat does. Then they all built great fires and after a time roasted the does and broached a barrel of humming ale. Then when the feast was ready they all sat down, but Robin placed Little John at his right hand, for he was henceforth to be the second in the band.

Then when the feast was done Will Stutely spoke up. "It is now time, I ween,[41] to christen our bonny babe, is it not so, merry boys?" And "Aye! Aye!" cried all, laughing till the woods echoed with their mirth.

"Then seven sponsors shall we have," quoth Will Stutely, and hunting among all the band, he chose the seven stoutest men of them all.

"Now by Saint Dunstan," cried Little John, springing to his feet, "more than one of you shall rue[42] it an you lay finger upon me."

But without a word they all ran upon him at once, seizing him by his legs and arms and holding him tightly in spite of his struggles, and they bore him forth while all stood around to see the sport. Then one came forward who had been chosen to play the priest because he had a bald crown, and in his hand he carried a brimming pot of ale. "Now, who bringeth this babe?" asked he right soberly.

"That do I," answered Will Stutely.

"And what name callest thou him?"

"Little John call I him."

"Now Little John," quoth the mock priest, "thou hast not lived heretofore, but only got thee along through the world, but henceforth thou wilt live indeed. When thou livedst not thou wast called John Little, but now that thou dost live indeed, Little John shalt thou be called, so christen I thee." And at these last words he emptied the pot of ale upon Little John's head.

Then all shouted with laughter as they saw the good brown ale stream over Little John's beard and trickle from his nose and chin, while his eyes blinked with the smart of it. At first he was of a mind to be angry but found he could not, because the others were so merry; so he, too, laughed with the

---

[41] suppose
[42] regret

rest. Then Robin took this sweet, pretty babe, clothed him all anew from top to toe in Lincoln green, and gave him a good stout bow, and so made him a member of the merry band.

And thus it was that Robin Hood became outlawed; thus a band of merry companions gathered about him, and thus he gained his right-hand man, Little John; and so the prologue[43] ends. And now I will tell how the Sheriff of Nottingham three times sought to take Robin Hood, and how he failed each time.

Questions for Review

1. Even though you've probably heard this tale from the Robin Hood legend before, what details in Howard Pyle's telling of it were new to you, or made the story more enjoyable?

2. In our day Robin Hood is commonly referred to as someone who "robs from the rich and gives to the poor." How is this picture of him incorrect, based on Pyle's version?

---

[43] introduction

The Merry Adventures of Robin Hood

By Howard Pyle

• • • • •

The Shooting Match at Nottingham Town

Then the sheriff was very wroth[1] because of this failure to take jolly Robin, for it came to his ears, as ill news always does, that the people laughed at him and made a jest of his thinking to serve a warrant upon such a one as the bold outlaw. And a man hates nothing so much as being made a jest of; so he said: "Our gracious lord and sovereign King himself shall know of this, and how his laws are perverted and despised by this band of rebel outlaws. As for yon traitor Tinker, him will I hang, if I catch him, upon the very highest gallows tree in all Nottinghamshire."

Then he bade all his servants and retainers to make ready to go to London Town, to see and speak with the King.

At this there was bustling at the Sheriff's castle, and men ran hither and thither upon this business and upon that, while the forge fires of Nottingham glowed red far into the night like twinkling stars, for all the smiths of the town were busy making or mending armor for the Sheriff's troop of escort. For two days this labor lasted, then, on the third, all was ready for the journey. So forth they started in the bright sunlight, from Nottingham Town to Fosse Way and thence to Watling Street; and so they journeyed for two days, until they saw at last the spires and towers of great London Town; and many folks stopped, as they journeyed along, and gazed at the show they made riding along the highways with their flashing armor and gay plumes and trappings.

In London King Henry and his fair Queen Eleanor held their court, gay with ladies in silks and satins and velvets and cloth of gold, and also brave knights and gallant courtiers.

Thither came the Sheriff and was shown into the King's presence.

"A boon,[2] a boon," quoth he, as he knelt upon the ground.

"Now what wouldst thou have?" said the King. "Let us hear what may be thy desires."

"O good my Lord and Sovereign," spake the Sheriff, "in Sherwood Forest in our own good shire of Nottingham, liveth a bold outlaw whose name is Robin Hood."

---

[1] angry
[2] blessing

"In good sooth,"[3] said the King, "his doings have reached even our own royal ears. He is a saucy, rebellious varlet, yet, I am fain to own, a right merry soul withal."

"But hearken, O my most gracious Sovereign," said the Sheriff. "I sent a warrant to him with thine own royal seal attached, by a right lusty knave, but he beat the messenger and stole the warrant. And he killeth thy deer and robbeth thine own liege[4] subjects even upon the great highways."

"Why, how now," quoth the King wrathfully. "What wouldst thou have me do? Comest thou not to me with a great array of men-at-arms and retainers, and yet art not able to take a single band of lusty knaves without armor on breast, in thine own county! What wouldst thou have me do? Art thou not my Sheriff? Are not my laws in force in Nottinghamshire? Canst thou not take thine own course against those that break the laws or do any injury to thee or thine? Go, get thee gone, and think well; devise some plan of thine own, but trouble me no further. But look well to it, Master Sheriff, for I will have my laws obeyed by all men within my kingdom, and if thou art not able to enforce them thou art no sheriff for me. So look well to thyself, I say, or ill may befall thee as well as all the thieving knaves in Nottinghamshire. When the flood cometh it sweepeth away grain as well as chaff."

Then the Sheriff turned away with a sore and troubled heart, and sadly he rued his fine show of retainers, for he saw that the King was angry because he had so many men about him and yet could not enforce the laws. So, as they all rode slowly back to Nottingham, the Sheriff was thoughtful and full of care. Not a word did he speak to anyone, and no one of his men spoke to him, but all the time he was busy devising some plan to take Robin Hood.

"Aha!" cried he suddenly, smiting his hand upon his thigh "I have it now! Ride on, my merry men all, and let us get back to Nottingham Town as speedily as we may. And mark well my words: before a fortnight[5] is passed, that evil knave Robin Hood will be safely clapped into Nottingham gaol."

But what was the Sheriff's plan?

As a usurer[6] takes each one of a bag of silver angels,[7] feeling each coin to find whether it be clipped[8] or not, so the Sheriff, as all rode slowly and sadly back toward Nottingham, took up thought after thought in turn, feeling around the edges of each but finding in every one some flaw. At last he

---

[3] "In good sooth": "Yes, that's true."
[4] faithful
[5] two weeks ("fourteen nights")
[6] money lender
[7] English coins stamped with the image of the angel Michael
[8] A coin with some of the gold or silver scraped off the edges is "clipped."

thought of the daring soul of jolly Robin and how, as he the Sheriff knew, he often came even within the walls of Nottingham.

"Now," thought the Sheriff, "could I but persuade Robin nigh to Nottingham Town so that I could find him, I warrant I would lay hands upon him so stoutly that he would never get away again." Then of a sudden it came to him like a flash that were he to proclaim a great shooting match and offer some grand prize, Robin Hood might be overpersuaded by his spirit to come to the butts; and it was this thought which caused him to cry "Aha!" and smite his palm upon his thigh.

So, as soon as he had returned safely to Nottingham, he sent messengers north and south, and east and west, to proclaim through town, hamlet, and countryside, this grand shooting match, and everyone was bidden that could draw a longbow, and the prize was to be an arrow of pure beaten gold.

When Robin Hood first heard the news of this he was in Lincoln Town, and hastening back to Sherwood Forest he soon called all his merry men about him and spoke to them thus:

"Now hearken, my merry men all, to the news that I have brought from Lincoln Town today. Our friend the Sheriff of Nottingham hath proclaimed a shooting match, and hath sent messengers to tell of it through all the countryside, and the prize is to be a bright golden arrow. Now I fain would have one of us win it, both because of the fairness of the prize and because our sweet friend the Sheriff hath offered it. So we will take our bows and shafts and go there to shoot, for I know right well that merriment will be a-going. What say ye, lads?"

Then young David of Doncaster spoke up and said, "Now listen, I pray thee, good master, unto what I say. I have come straight from our friend Eadom o' the Blue Boar, and there I heard the full news of this same match. But, master, I know from him, and he got it from the Sheriff's man Ralph o' the Scar, that this same knavish Sheriff hath but laid a trap for thee in this shooting match and wishes nothing so much as to see thee there. So go not, good master, for I know right well he doth seek to beguile[9] thee, but stay within the greenwood lest we all meet dole and woe."

"Now," quoth Robin, "thou art a wise lad and keepest thine ears open and thy mouth shut, as becometh a wise and crafty woodsman. But shall we let it be said that the Sheriff of Nottingham did cow bold Robin Hood and sevenscore as fair archers as are in all merry England? Nay, good David, what thou tellest me maketh me to desire the prize even more than I else should do. But what sayeth our good gossip Swanthold? Is it not 'A hasty man burneth his mouth, and the fool that keepeth his eyes shut falleth into the pit'? Thus he says, truly, therefore we must meet guile with guile. Now some of you clothe yourselves as curtal friars, and some as rustic peasants,

---

[9] lure

and some as tinkers,[10] or as beggars, but see that each man taketh a good bow or broadsword, in case need should arise. As for myself, I will shoot for this same golden arrow, and should I win it, we will hang it to the branches of our good greenwood tree for the joy of all the band. How like you the plan, my merry men all?"

Then "Good, good!" cried all the band right heartily.

A fair sight was Nottingham Town on the day of the shooting match. All along upon the green meadow beneath the town wall stretched a row of benches, one above the other, which were for knight and lady, squire and dame, and rich burghers and their wives; for none but those of rank and quality were to sit there. At the end of the range, near the target, was a raised seat bedecked with ribbons and scarfs and garlands of flowers, for the Sheriff of Nottingham and his dame. The range was twoscore paces broad. At one end stood the target, at the other a tent of striped canvas, from the pole of which fluttered many-colored flags and streamers. In this booth were casks of ale, free to be broached by any of the archers who might wish to quench their thirst.

Across the range from where the seats for the better folk were raised was a railing to keep the poorer people from crowding in front of the target. Already, while it was early, the benches were beginning to fill with people of quality, who kept constantly arriving in little carts or upon palfreys that

---

[10] metalsmiths

curveted gaily to the merry tinkle of silver bells at bridle reins. With these came also the poorer folk, who sat or lay upon the green grass near the railing that kept them from off the range. In the great tent the archers were gathering by twos and threes; some talking loudly of the fair shots each man had made in his day; some looking well to their bows, drawing a string betwixt the fingers to see that there was no fray upon it, or inspecting arrows, shutting one eye and peering down a shaft to see that it was not warped, but straight and true, for neither bow nor shaft should fail at such a time and for such a prize. And never was such a company of yeomen as were gathered at Nottingham Town that day, for the very best archers of merry England had come to this shooting match. There was Gill o' the Red Cap, the Sheriff's own head archer, and Diccon Cruikshank of Lincoln Town, and Adam o' the Dell, a man of Tamworth, of threescore years and more, yet hale[11] and lusty still, who in his time had shot in the famous match at Woodstock, and had there beaten that renowned archer, Clym o' the Clough. And many more famous men of the longbow were there, whose names have been handed down to us in goodly ballads of the olden time.

But now all the benches were filled with guests, lord and lady, burgher and dame, when at last the Sheriff himself came with his lady, he riding with stately mien[12] upon his milk-white horse and she upon her brown filly. Upon his head he wore a purple velvet cap, and purple velvet was his robe, all trimmed about with rich ermine; his jerkin[13] and hose were of sea-green silk, and his shoes of black velvet, the pointed toes fastened to his garters with golden chains. A golden chain hung about his neck, and at his collar was a great carbuncle[14] set in red gold. His lady was dressed in blue velvet, all trimmed with swan's down. So they made a gallant sight as they rode along side by side, and all the people shouted from where they crowded across the space from the gentlefolk; so the Sheriff and his lady came to their place, where men-at-arms, with hauberk and spear, stood about, waiting for them.

Then when the Sheriff and his dame had sat down, he bade his herald wind upon his silver horn; who thereupon sounded three blasts that came echoing cheerily back from the gray walls of Nottingham. Then the archers stepped forth to their places, while all the folks shouted with a mighty voice, each man calling upon his favorite yeoman. "Red Cap!" cried some; "Cruikshank!" cried others; "Hey for William o' Leslie!" shouted others yet again; while ladies waved silken scarfs to urge each yeoman to do his best.

---

[11] healthy, fit

[12] appearance

[13] vest

[14] precious stone

Then the herald stood forth and loudly proclaimed the rules of the game as follows:

"Shoot each man from yon mark, which is sevenscore yards and ten from the target. One arrow shooteth each man first, and from all the archers shall the ten that shooteth the fairest shafts be chosen for to shoot again. Two arrows shooteth each man of these ten, then shall the three that shoot the fairest shafts be chosen for to shoot again. Three arrows shooteth each man of those three, and to him that shooteth the fairest shafts shall the prize be given."

Then the Sheriff leaned forward, looking keenly among the press of archers to find whether Robin Hood was among them; but no one was there clad in Lincoln green, such as was worn by Robin and his band. "Nevertheless," said the Sheriff to himself, "he may still be there, and I miss him among the crowd of other men. But let me see when but ten men shoot, for I wot[15] he will be among the ten, or I know him not."

And now the archers shot, each man in turn, and the good folk never saw such archery as was done that day. Six arrows were within the clout, four within the black, and only two smote the outer ring; so that when the last arrow sped and struck the target, all the people shouted aloud, for it was noble shooting.

And now but ten men were left of all those that had shot before, and of these ten, six were famous throughout the land, and most of the folk gathered there knew them. These six men were Gilbert o' the Red Cap, Adam o' the Dell, Diccon Cruikshank, William o' Leslie, Hubert o' Cloud, and Swithin o' Hertford. Two others were yeomen of merry Yorkshire, another was a tall stranger in blue, who said he came from London Town, and the last was a tattered stranger in scarlet, who wore a patch over one eye.

"Now," quoth the Sheriff to a man-at-arms who stood near him, "seest thou Robin Hood among those ten?"

"Nay, that do I not, Your Worship," answered the man. "Six of them I know right well. Of those Yorkshire yeomen, one is too tall and the other too short for that bold knave. Robin's beard is as yellow as gold, while yon tattered beggar in scarlet hath a beard of brown, besides being blind of one eye. As for the stranger in blue, Robin's shoulders, I ween, are three inches broader than his."

"Then," quoth the Sheriff, smiting his thigh angrily, "yon knave is a coward as well as a rogue, and dares not show his face among good men and true."

Then, after they had rested a short time, those ten stout men stepped forth to shoot again. Each man shot two arrows, and as they shot, not a word was spoken, but all the crowd watched with scarce a breath of sound; but when

---

[15] know

the last had shot his arrow another great shout arose, while many cast their caps aloft for joy of such marvelous shooting.

"Now by our gracious Lady fair," quoth old Sir Amyas o' the Dell, who, bowed with fourscore years and more, sat near the Sheriff, "ne'er saw I such archery in all my life before, yet have I seen the best hands at the longbow for threescore years and more."

And now but three men were left of all those that had shot before. One was Gill o' the Red Cap, one the tattered stranger in scarlet, and one Adam o' the Dell of Tamworth Town. Then all the people called aloud, some crying, "Ho for Gilbert o' the Red Cap!" and some, "Hey for stout Adam o' Tamworth!" But not a single man in the crowd called upon the stranger in scarlet.

"Now, shoot thou well, Gilbert," cried the Sheriff, "and if thine be the best shaft, fivescore broad silver pennies will I give to thee beside the prize."

"Truly I will do my best," quoth Gilbert right sturdily. "A man cannot do aught but his best, but that will I strive to do this day." So saying, he drew forth a fair smooth arrow with a broad feather and fitted it deftly to the string, then drawing his bow with care he sped the shaft. Straight flew the arrow and lit fairly in the clout, a finger's-breadth from the center. "A Gilbert, a Gilbert!" shouted all the crowd; and, "Now, by my faith," cried the Sheriff, smiting his hands together, "that is a shrewd shot."

Then the tattered stranger stepped forth, and all the people laughed as they saw a yellow patch that showed beneath his arm when he raised his elbow to shoot, and also to see him aim with but one eye. He drew the good yew bow quickly, and quickly loosed a shaft; so short was the time that no man could draw a breath betwixt the drawing and the shooting; yet his arrow lodged nearer the center than the other by twice the length of a barley-corn.

"Now by all the saints in Paradise!" cried the Sheriff, "that is a lovely shaft in very truth!"

Then Adam o' the Dell shot, carefully and cautiously, and his arrow lodged close beside the stranger's. Then after a short space they all three shot again, and once more each arrow lodged within the clout, but this time Adam o' the Dell's was farthest from the center, and again the tattered stranger's shot was the best. Then, after another time of rest, they all shot for the third time. This time Gilbert took great heed to his aim, keenly measuring the distance and shooting with shrewdest care. Straight flew the arrow, and all shouted till the very flags that waved in the breeze shook with the sound, and the rooks and daws[16] flew clamoring about the roofs of the

---

[16] "rooks and daws": crow-like birds

old gray tower, for the shaft had lodged close beside the spot that marked the very center.

"Well done, Gilbert!" cried the Sheriff right joyously. "Fain am I to believe the prize is thine, and right fairly won. Now, thou ragged knave, let me see thee shoot a better shaft than that."

Nought spake the stranger but took his place, while all was hushed, and no one spoke or even seemed to breathe, so great was the silence for wonder what he would do. Meanwhile, also, quite still stood the stranger, holding his bow in his hand, while one could count five; then he drew his trusty yew, holding it drawn but a moment, then loosed the string. Straight flew the arrow, and so true that it smote a gray goose feather from off Gilbert's shaft, which fell fluttering through the sunlit air as the stranger's arrow lodged close beside his of the Red Cap, and in the very center. No one spoke a word for a while, and no one shouted, but each man looked into his neighbor's face amazedly.

"Nay," quoth old Adam o' the Dell presently, drawing a long breath and shaking his head as he spoke, "twoscore years and more have I shot shaft, and maybe not all times bad, but I shoot no more this day, for no man can match with yon stranger, whosoe'er he may be." Then he thrust his shaft into his quiver, rattling, and unstrung his bow without another word.

Then the Sheriff came down from his dais and drew near, in all his silks and velvets, to where the tattered stranger stood leaning upon his stout bow, while the good folk crowded around to see the man who shot so wondrously well. "Here, good fellow," quoth the Sheriff, "take thou the prize, and well and fairly hast thou won it, I bow. What may be thy name, and whence[17] comest thou?"

"Men do call me Jock o' Teviotdale, and thence am I come," said the stranger.

---

[17] from where

"Then, by Our Lady, Jock, thou art the fairest archer that e'er mine eyes beheld, and if thou wilt join my service I will clothe thee with a better coat than that thou hast upon thy back; thou shalt eat and drink of the best, and at every Christmastide fourscore marks shall be thy wage. I trow thou drawest better bow than that same coward knave Robin Hood, that dared not show his face here this day. Say, good fellow, wilt thou join my service?"

"Nay, that will I not," quoth the stranger roughly. "I will be mine own, and no man in all merry England shall be my master."

"Then get thee gone, and a murrain[18] seize thee!" cried the Sheriff, and his voice trembled with anger. "And by my faith and troth, I have a good part of a mind to have thee beaten for thine insolence!"[19] Then he turned upon his heel and strode away.

It was a right motley company that gathered about the noble greenwood tree in Sherwood's depths that same day. A score and more of barefoot friars were there, and some that looked like tinkers, and some that seemed to be sturdy beggars and rustic hinds; and seated upon a mossy couch was one all clad in tattered scarlet, with a patch over one eye; and in his hand he held the golden arrow that was the prize of the great shooting match. Then, amidst a noise of talking and laughter, he took the patch from off his eye and stripped away the scarlet rags from off his body and showed himself all clothed in fair Lincoln green; and quoth he, "Easy come these things away, but walnut stain cometh not so speedily from yellow hair." Then all laughed louder than before, for it was Robin Hood himself that had won the prize from the Sheriff's very hands.

Then all sat down to the woodland feast and talked among themselves of the merry jest that had been played upon the Sheriff, and of the adventures that had befallen each member of the band in his disguise. But when the feast was done, Robin Hood took Little John apart and said, "Truly am I vexed in my blood, for I heard the Sheriff say today, 'Thou shootest better than that coward knave Robin Hood, that dared not show his face here this day.' I would fain let him know who it was who won the golden arrow from out his hand, and also that I am no coward such as he takes me to be."

Then Little John said, "Good master, take thou me and Will Stutely, and we will send yon fat Sheriff news of all this by a messenger such as he doth not expect."

That day the Sheriff sat at meat in the great hall of his house at Nottingham Town. Long tables stood down the hall, at which sat men-at-arms and household servants and good stout villains,[20] in all fourscore and more. There they talked of the day's shooting as they ate their meat and quaffed

---

[18] plague, disease

[19] disrespect

[20] bond servants

their ale. The Sheriff sat at the head of the table upon a raised seat under a canopy, and beside him sat his dame.

"By my troth,"[21] said he, "I did reckon full roundly that that knave Robin Hood would be at the game today. I did not think that he was such a coward. But who could that saucy knave be who answered me to my beard so bravely? I wonder that I did not have him beaten; but there was something about him that spoke of other things than rags and tatters."

Then, even as he finished speaking, something fell rattling among the dishes on the table, while those that sat near started up wondering what it might be. After a while one of the men-at-arms gathered courage enough to pick it up and bring it to the Sheriff. Then everyone saw that it was a blunted gray goose shaft, with a fine scroll, about the thickness of a goose quill, tied near to its head. The Sheriff opened the scroll and glanced at it, while the veins upon his forehead swelled and his cheeks grew ruddy with rage as he read, for this was what he saw:

"Now Heaven bless Thy Grace this day,"
Say all in sweet Sherwood,
For thou didst give the prize away
To merry Robin Hood.

"Whence came this?" cried the Sheriff in a mighty voice.

"Even through the window, Your Worship," quoth the man who had handed the shaft to him.

Questions for Review

1. The Sheriff of Nottingham says he is angry because Robin Hood breaks the laws of England, but what is he *really* angry about?

2. If you've never read or seen this particular Robin Hood story, did you guess the identity of Jock o' Teviotdale before the reveal at the end?

3. What is especially satisfying about the very last few paragraphs?

---

[21] promise

My Kate

By Elizabeth Barrett Browning

Elizabeth Moulton-Barrett (1806-1861) wrote poetry ad-mired by poet Robert Browning, who later married her. She wrote for him her most famous poems, Sonnets from the Portuguese*; one of these poems contains the famous line "How do I love thee? Let me count the ways." The be-low "My Kate" is a fine poem about a fine woman.*

• • • • •

She was not as pretty as women I know,
And yet all your best made of sunshine and snow
Drop to shade, melt to nought[1] in the long-trodden ways,
While she's still remember'd on warm and cold days—
   My Kate.

Her air had a meaning, her movements a grace;
You turn'd from the fairest to gaze on her face:
And when you had once seen her forehead and mouth,
You saw as distinctly her soul and her truth—
   My Kate.

Such a blue inner light from her eyelids outbroke,
You look'd at her silence and fancied she spoke:
When she did, so peculiar yet soft was the tone,
Though the loudest spoke also, you heard her alone—
   My Kate.

I doubt if she said to you much that could act
As a thought or suggestion: she did not attract
In the sense of the brilliant or wise: I infer[2]
'Twas her thinking of others, made you think of her—
   My Kate.

She never found fault with you, never implied
Your wrong by her right; and yet men at her side
Grew nobler, girls purer, as through the whole town
The children were gladder that pull'd at her gown—
   My Kate.

---

[1] nothing
[2] conclude, deduce

None knelt at her feet confess'd lovers in thrall;[3]
They knelt more to God than they used—that was all;
If you praised her as charming, some ask'd what you meant,
But the charm of her presence was felt when she went—
        My Kate.

The weak and the gentle, the ribald[4] and rude,
She took as she found them, and did them all good:
It always was so with her: see what you have!
She has made the grass greener even here...with her grave—
        My Kate.

My dear one!—when thou wast alive with the rest,
I held thee the sweetest and lov'd thee the best:
And now thou art dead, shall I not take thy part
As thy smiles used to do for thyself, my sweet Heart—
        My Kate?

Questions for Review

1. Describe the poem's rhythm—that is, how many syllables does nearly every line have? Which syllables are stressed more than the others?

2. Even though Kate isn't particularly pretty or brilliant or wise, what is it about her that impresses the author?

3. What effect does Kate have on those she is around? What does the author vow to do in the last stanza?

4. Compare Kate's qualities with Proverbs 31:30 and 1 Peter 3:1-5.

---

[3] "in thrall": enchanted, fascinated
[4] bad mannered, crude

Cicely

By Annie F. Johnston

When her husband died after she had been married only three years, Annie F. Johnston (1863-1931) began writing, becoming a million-selling author. The character Cicely in the below story is a poor orphan. On that subject the Bible says, "Blessed is he that considereth the poor" (Psalm 41:1) and "Defend the poor and fatherless: do justice to the afflicted and needy" (Psalm 82:3). "Cicely" beautifully expresses how this can be done.

• • • • •

There was a noisy whir of sewing machines in Madame Levaney's large dressmaking establishment. Cicely Leeds's head ached as she bent over the ruffles she was hemming. She was the youngest seamstress in the room, and wore her hair hanging in two long braids.

It seemed a pity that such girlish shoulders should be learning to stoop, and that her eyes had to bear such a constant strain. The light was particularly bad this afternoon. Every curtain was rolled to the top of its big window, but the dull December sky was as gray as a fog. Even the snow on the surrounding housetops looked gray and dirty in the smoky haze.

Now and then Cicely looked up from her work and glanced out of the window. The cold grayness of the outdoor world made her shiver. It was a world of sooty chimney-tops as she saw it, with a few chilly sparrows huddled in a disconsolate[1] row along the eaves. It would soon be time to be going home, and the only home Cicely had now was a cheerless little back bedroom in a cheap boarding house. She dreaded going back to it. It was at least warm in Madame Levaney's steam-heated workrooms, and it was better to have the noise and confusion than the cold solitude.

Cicely's chair was the one nearest the entrance to the parlor where madame received her customers, and presently someone passing through the door left it ajar. Above the hum of the machines Cicely could hear a voice that she recognized. It was that of Miss Shelby, a young society girl, who was one of madame's wealthiest customers.

"I've brought my cousin, Miss Balfour," Cicely heard her say, "and we want to ask *such* a favor of you, madame. You see my cousin stopped here yesterday on her way East, intending to remain only one night with us, but

---

[1] unhappy

we've persuaded her to stay over to our party on New Year's eve. Her trunks have gone on, and of course she hasn't a thing with her in the way of an evening dress. But I told her you would come to the rescue. You are always so clever—you could get her up a simple little party gown in no time. So, on the way down, we stopped at Bailey's, and she bought the material for it. Show it to madame, Rhoda. It's a perfect dream!"

Cicely heard the snapping of a string, the rustling of paper, and then madame's affected[2] little cry of admiration. But at the next word she knew just how the little Frenchwoman was shrugging her shoulders, with clasped hands and raised eyebrows.

"But, mademoiselle," Cicely heard her protesting, "it is *impossible*! If you will but step to ze door one instant and obsairve! Evair' one is beesy. Evair' one work, work, work to ze fullest capacitee. Look! All ze gowns zat mus' be complete before ze New Year dawn, and only two more day!"

She stepped to the door, and with a dramatic gesture pointed to the busy sewing women and the chairs and tables covered with dresses in all stages of construction.

"Only two day, and all zese yet to be feenish for zat same ball! Much as I desire, it is not *possible*!"

Everyone looked up as the two girls stood for a moment in the doorway. Miss Shelby glanced around in a coldly indifferent way, holding up her broadcloth skirt that it might escape the ravelings and scraps scattered over the floor. She was a tall brunette as elegantly dressed as any figure in madame's latest Parisian fashion plate.[3]

"Why can't you put somebody else off to accommodate me just this once?" she said. "It is a matter of great importance. My cousin has already bought the material on my promise that you would make it up for her. I think you might make a little extra effort in this case, madame, when you remember that I was one of your first customers, and that I really brought you half your trade."

The little Frenchwoman wrung her hands. "I *do* remember, mademoiselle! Indeed! Indeed! But you see for yourself ze situation. What can I do?"

"Make some of the women come back at night," answered Miss Shelby, turning back into the parlor, "and have them take some of the work home to finish. I'm sure you might be obliging enough to favour me."

Miss Balfour had taken no part in the conversation. She stood beside her cousin, fully as tall and handsome as she, and resembling her in both face and figure, but there was something in her expression that attracted Cicely as much as the other girl had repelled her.

---

[2] exaggerated

[3] A fashion plate is a picture and/or an advertisement showing the latest fashions.

Miss Shelby had not seemed to distinguish the sewing women from their machines, but Rhoda Balfour noticed how pallid[4] were some of the faces, and how gray was the hair on the temples of the old woman in the corner bending over her buttonholes. When her glance reached Cicely, the appealing little figure in the black gown, she could not help but notice the admiration that showed so plainly in the girl's face, and involuntarily she smiled in response, a bright, friendly smile.

As she turned away she did not see the sudden flush that rose to Cicely's cheeks, and did not know that her recognition had sent the blood surging warmly through the sad and discouraged heart. It had been two months since Cicely Leeds had been left alone in the strange city, and this was the first time in all those weeks that anyone had smiled at her.

Sometimes it seemed to her that the loneliness would kill her if she knew it must go on indefinitely. But Marcelle's promise helped her to bear it. Marcelle was her older sister, the only person in the world left to her, and Marcelle was teaching the village school at home. In another year the last penny of the debts their father had left when he died would be paid, and Marcelle would be free to send for Cicely then, and life would not be so hard. Just now there was no other way for Cicely to live but to take the small wages madame offered, and be thankful that she was having such an opportunity to learn the dressmaker's trade. She could set up a little establishment of her own someday, when she went back to Marcelle.

Cicely did not hear the final words of Miss Shelby's argument, but a few minutes later madame came back to the workroom with a bundle in her arms. There was a worried frown on her face as she unrolled it and called sharply to her forewoman.

Every seamstress in the room bent forward with an exclamation of pleasure as the piece of dress-goods was unrolled. It was a soft, shimmering silk, whose creamy surface was covered with rosebuds, as dainty and pink as if they had been blown across it from some June garden. Cicely caught her breath with a little gasp of delight, and thought again of the sweet face that had smiled on her. Miss Balfour would look like a rose herself in such a dress.

The next day Cicely saw the cutter at work on it, and then the forewoman distributed the various parts into different hands. Cicely wished that she could have a part in making it. She would have enjoyed putting her finest stitches into something to be worn by the beautiful girl who had smiled on her. It would be almost like doing it for a friend. But she was kept busy stitching monotonous[5] bias folds.

---

[4] pale, sickly
[5] dull, repetitive

Just as she was slipping on her jacket to go home that evening, the forewoman came up to her with a bundle. "I am sorry, Cicely," she said, "but I shall have to ask you to take some work home with you tonight. We are so rushed with all these orders we never can get through unless every one of you works over-hours. Miss Shelby's extra order is just the last straw that'll break the camel's back, I'm afraid. Try to get every bit of this hand work done some way or other before morning."

It was no part of the rose-pink party dress that Cicely had to work on; only more monotonous bias folds. But as she turned up the lamp in her chilly little room and began the weary stitching again, she felt that in a way it was for Miss Balfour, and she sewed on uncomplainingly.

She had intended to write to Marcelle that evening in order that her sister might have a letter on New Year's day, but there would be no time now. She wrapped a shawl around her and spread a blanket over her feet, but more than once she had to stop and warm her stiff fingers over the lamp. It was long after midnight when she finished, and she crept into bed, her head still throbbing with a dull ache.

"The last day of the old year!" she said to herself, as she waded through a newly fallen snow to her work the next morning. "Oh, Marcelle, how can I ever hold out ten months longer? Nobody in this whole city cares that I caught cold sitting up in a room without a fire, or that I feel so lonely and bad this minute that I can't keep back the tears."

It seemed to Cicely that she had never had such a wretched morning. The loss of sleep the night before left her languid[6] and nervous. Her cold seemed to grow worse every moment, and madame and the forewoman were both unusually cross. She felt ill and feverish when she took her seat again after the lunch hour.

Presently madame came in, looking sharply about her, and walked up to Cicely with the rosebud silk skirt in her hands. "Here!" she said, hurriedly. "Put ze band on zis. Ze ozair woman who do zis alway have gone home ill. An' be in one beeg haste, also, for ze time have arrive for ze las' fitting. You hear?"

Cicely took it up, pleased and smiling. After all, she was to have a part in making the beautiful rose gown that would surely give Miss Balfour such pleasure. Her quick needle flew in and out, but her thoughts flew still faster.

She had had a gown like that herself once; at least it was something like that pattern, although the material was nothing but lawn. She had worn it first on the day when she was fifteen years old, and her mother had surprised her by a birthday party. And they had had tea out in the old rose garden, and had pelted one another with the great velvety king roses, and she had torn

---

[6] sleepy

her hand on a thorn. Ah, how cruelly it hurt! It was a very present pain that made her cry out now, not the memory of that old one.

Someone had overturned a chair just behind her, and Cicely's nervousness made her jump forward with a violent start. With that sudden movement the sharp needle she held was thrust deep into her hand and two great drops of blood spurted out. With that sudden movement, also, the silk skirt slipped from her lap, and she clutched it to save it from touching the floor. Before she was aware of anything but the sharp pain, before she saw the blood that the needle had brought to the surface, two great stains blotted the front breadth of the dainty skirt.

She gave a stifled scream, and grew white and numb. Almost instantly madame saw and heard, and pounced down upon her. "I am ruin'!" she shrieked, pointing to the stains. "Nozzing will take zem out! Mademoiselle will be so angry I will lose ze trade of her!"

The irate woman took Cicely by the shoulders and shook her violently, just as Miss Shelby and Miss Balfour were announced. They had come for the final fitting, expecting to take the dress home with them.

Madame, still wildly indignant,[7] went storming in to meet them, and poor Cicely shrank back into the corner, with her face hidden against the wall. Never in her life had she been so utterly friendless and alone.

Miss Balfour's disappointed exclamation over the stained dress reached the girl's ears. She heard madame's eager suggestions of possible remedies, and then Miss Shelby's cold tones:

"Now if it had been the bodice, it would not have been so bad. It could have been hidden by some of the ribbons or lace or flowers; but to have it right down the middle of the front breadth—that's *too* hopeless! There's nothing for it but to make over the skirt and put in a whole new breadth. There isn't time for that, I suppose, before this evening."

Madame looked at the clock and shook her head. "Ze women air rush to ze grave now," she said. "Zay work half ze night las' night. Zat is why zis girl say she air so nairvous zat she could not help ze needle stab herself."

"I could just sit down and cry, I am so disappointed!" exclaimed Miss Balfour. "I had set my heart on going to the party, and in that dress."

Cicely's sobs shook her harder than ever as the words reached her, and her tears started afresh. Miss Shelby's voice broke in:

"I am surprised that you would keep such a careless assistant, madame. Of course, you will expect to make the loss good to my cousin. It will ruin your trade to keep incompetent employees. It would be better to let the woman go."

"It is a young girl which I have jus' take," said madame, with another shrug. "I have feel for her because she was an orphan, and I take her in ze

---

[7] angry

goodness of my heart. Behold how she repay me! Disappoint my customers, ruin my beesness!"

She was pointing to the stains and working herself up into a passion again, when Miss Balfour interrupted her.

"I should like to see the girl, madame. Will you please call her?"

"*Certainement!* Willingly, mademoiselle! Ze pleasure shall be yours for to scold ze careless creature."

Cicely heard and shivered. It had been hard enough to bear madame's angry reproaches, but to have the added burden of Miss Balfour's displeasure was more than she could endure—the displeasure of the only one who had smiled on her since she left Marcelle! A moment later madame confronted her, and Rhoda could hear the girl's sobs.

"Oh, I can't go in! Indeed I can't, madame! It nearly kills me to think I have spoiled that lovely dress, and that she cannot go tonight after all. I wouldn't have done it for the world, for it was almost like having her for my friend. She—she smiled at me—the other day."

Rhoda looked at her cousin wonderingly. Could it be someone that she knew, who seemed to care so much about her pleasure?

Then her eyes fell on the shrinking Cicely, whom madame was pushing somewhat unceremoniously into the room. Rhoda saw the little black-gowned figure with the tear-swollen face, and suddenly the crimson spots on her evening gown held a new significance.

It flashed through her mind that the very life-blood of such girls was being sacrificed for her own selfish pleasure. If she had not hurried madame so, there would have been no night-work for this poor child, no fagged-out[8] nerves for her the next day.

Suddenly Miss Balfour crossed the room and, to her cousin's astonishment, caught Cicely's cold hands in hers.

"Look up here, you poor little thing," she said, kindly. "Now don't cry another tear, or grieve another bit about this. It's no matter at all. I'll just get some new stuff to replace the front of the skirt, and madame can make it over next week for me and send it on East after me. I'll pay for it myself, of course, for I'll be very glad to have the silk that must be ripped out. Mamma is making me a silk quilt, and the rosebuds will work in beautifully. I shall have it put in, blood-spots and all, to remind me that my selfish pleasure may often prove a cruel thorn to somebody else. I don't want to go through the world leaving scratches behind me."

"Why, Rhoda!" gasped Miss Shelby; but with a proud lifting of her head, Miss Balfour went on:

"I realize it is my own fault in rushing you with the work, madame, and the consequences of my own unreasonableness are not to be laid at this

---

[8] exhausted

girl's door. Do you understand, madame? Not a cent is to come out of her wages, and you are to keep her and be good to her, if you want my good-will. I am coming back this way in the spring, and this gown is so beautifully made that I shall be glad to order my entire summer wardrobe from you."

"Why, Rhoda Balfour!" exclaimed her cousin again, while madame bowed and smiled and bowed again.

As for Cicely, she went back to the workroom almost dazed, and tingling with the remembrance of Miss Balfour's friendly tones. It was several hours later when she climbed the stairs to her little back bedroom to light her coal-oil stove, and make her toast and tea. Her eyes were still swollen from crying, but she had not felt so light-hearted for weeks.

Just inside her door she stumbled over a big pasteboard box. There was a note on top, and she hurried to light her lamp. "I know that you will be glad to hear I am going to the party, after all," she read. "I have found a very pretty white dress in my cousin's wardrobe that fits me well enough. As long as you have had such a thorny time on my account, it is only fair that you should share my roses; so I send them with the earnest wish that the coming year may bring you no thorn without some rose to cover it, and that it may be a very, very happy New Year indeed to you. Sincerely your friend, Rhoda Balfour."

Cicely tore aside the paraffine paper, and found six great roses, each with a leafy stem half as long as Cicely herself. She caught them up in her arms and laid her face against their velvety petals. For a moment, as she stood with closed eyes, drinking in their summer fragrance, she could have almost believed she was back in the old garden.

"Marcelle, dear," she murmured, "I can be brave now! I can hold out a little longer, for she wrote, 'Sincerely your friend.'"

The little room was glorified in Cicely's eyes that night by the flowers she loved best. She ate her scant supper as if she were at a festival, sent a little letter of thanks that made the tears come to Miss Balfour's handsome eyes, and afterward wrote a bright, hopeful letter to Marcelle that lifted a burden from the elder sister's heart. Marcelle had been half afraid that Cicely would be growing bitter against all the world.

"Think of it, sister!" Cicely wrote. "American Beauties[9] are a dollar apiece, and I have *six*![10] There is a music teacher who has the room across the hall from mine. She is at home this week with a cold on her lungs, and tomorrow, when I go to work, I am going to loan her all my beautiful roses.

---

[9] a type of rose
[10] This would have cost Rhoda a few hundred dollars today.

It's too bad to have them 'wasting their sweetness on the desert air' all day while I am gone. So she shall have them until I come home at night."[11]

Madame Levaney gave no holiday to her employees on New Year's day, but Cicely did not care. She left her roses at Miss Waite's door with the announcement that they were hers for the day, but that she would have to call for them and claim them at night. The oddness of the arrangement, and the quaint way in which Cicely made it, won Miss Waite's heart, and when she heard the girl's step in the hall that evening, she opened the door.

"Come right in," she called, cordially. "I can't spare the roses until after supper, so you will have to come in and eat with me. You've no idea how much I have enjoyed them!"

Cicely paused timidly on the threshold. There were the gorgeous American Beauties in a tall vase in the middle of the table, between some softly shaded candles. And there was a bright lamp on the open piano, and a glowing coal fire in the grate. The little table was spread for two, and a savory smell of oysters stole out from the chafing-dish Miss Wade had just uncovered.

"We'll celebrate the New Year together, and drink to our friendship in good strong coffee," said Miss Waite, lifting the steaming pot from the hearth. "Draw your chair right up to the table, please, while everything is hot."

Only one who has been as cold and hungry and homesick as Cicely was, can know how much that evening meant to her, or how the cheer and the warmth of it all comforted her lonely little heart. The best of it was that it was only a beginning, and there were few nights afterward, during that long winter, when the warmth and light of Miss Waite's room was not shared for awhile, at least, with the little seamstress.

The roses lasted more than a week; then Miss Waite helped Cicely to gather up the petals as they fell, and together they packed them away in a little rose-jar, according to an old recipe that Miss Waite read out of her grandmother's time-yellowed notebook.

Then Cicely brought Miss Balfour's note.

"I want to preserve this, too," she said, dropping it in among the dried rose leaves. "You told me that Rhoda means 'little rose,' and that line, 'Sincerely your friend,' was as sweet to me that day as the flowers themselves. As long as I live I shall think of her as an 'American Beauty.'"

She lifted the little rose-jar for one more whiff of its faint, sweet fragrance, and said, slowly, as she closed it again, "And as long as I live the thought of her will help to take the sting out of all my thorns."

---

[11] The line "wasting their sweetness on the desert air" comes from the 1750 poem "Elegy Written in a Country Churchyard," by English poet Thomas Gray.

Questions for Review

1. What about Miss Shelby makes her so unattractive, compared to her cousin? What does Rhoda give Cicely for the first time in two months?

2. Why is Cicely in the miserable situation she's in? What is she hanging on for?

3. When Rhoda sees Cicely so upset from spoiling the dress, she realizes that "the crimson spots on her evening gown held a new significance." What do you think this means?

4. How does Cicely's generosity with her roses do her even more good? What does she appreciate just as much as the roses themselves? Why?

Puc-Puggy and His Notes on the Rattlesnake

By William Bartram

It's one thing to be a brilliant botanist and ornithologist.[1] It's another thing to be a great artist. And it's something else to be a skilled writer. But William Bartram (1739-1823) was all these! He traveled through the southern U. S., observing unexplored areas and writing about—and drawing—its new and fascinating natural world. This selection comes from his 1791 book Travels through North and South Carolina, Georgia, East and West Florida.

• • • • •

I was in the forenoon busy in my apartment in the council-house, drawing some curious flowers; when, on a sudden, my attention was taken off by a tumult without,[2] at the Indian camp. I stepped to the door opening to the piazza, where I met my friend the old interpreter, who informed me that there was a very large rattlesnake in the Indian camp, which had taken possession of it, having driven the men, women and children out, and he heard them saying that they would send for Puc-Puggy (for that was the name which they had given me, signifying "the Flower Hunter") to kill him or take him out of their camp. I answered that I desired to have nothing to do with him, apprehending some disagreeable consequences; and desired that the Indians might be acquainted that I was engaged in business that required application and quiet, and was deter-mined to avoid it if possible.

My old friend turned about to carry my answer to the Indians. I presently heard them approaching and calling for Puc-Puggy. Starting up to escape from their sight by a back door, a party consisting of three young fellows, richly dressed and ornamented, stepped in, and with a countenance[3] and action of noble simplicity, amity,[4] and complaisance,[5] requested me to accompany them to their encampment. I desired them to excuse me at this time; they pleaded and entreated me to go with them, in order to free them from a great rattlesnake which had entered their camp; that none of them had freedom or courage to expel him; and understanding that it was my pleasure to collect all their animals and other natural productions of their

---

[1] bird scientist and plant scientist

[2] "tumult without": uproar outside

[3] expression

[4] friendship, goodwill

[5] agreeability

land, desired that I would come with them and take him away, that I was welcome to him. I at length consented and attended on them to their encampment, where I beheld[6] the Indians greatly disturbed indeed.

The men with sticks and tomahawks, and the women and children collected together at a distance in affright and trepidation,[7] whilst the dreaded and revered serpent leisurely traversed their camp, visiting the fireplaces from one to another, picking up fragments of their provisions and licking their platters. The men gathered around me, exciting me to remove him; being armed with a lightwood knot, I approached the reptile, who instantly collected himself in a vast coil (their attitude of defense); I cast my missile weapon at him, which, luckily taking his head, despatched him instantly, and laid him trembling at my feet. I took out my knife, severed his head from his body, then turning about, the Indians complimented me with every demonstration of satisfaction and approbation[8] for my heroism, and friendship for them. I carried off the head of the serpent bleeding in my hand as a trophy of victory; and taking out the mortal fangs, deposited them carefully amongst my collections.

I had not been long retired to my apartment, before I was again roused from it by a tumult in the yard; and hearing Puc-Puggy called on, I started up, when instantly the old interpreter met me again, and told me the Indians were approaching in order to scratch me. I asked him for what? He answered, for killing the rattlesnake within their camp. Before I could make any reply or effect my escape, three young fellows singing, arm in arm, came up to me. I observed one of the three was a young prince who had, on my first interview with him, declared himself my friend and protector, when he told me

Seminole Chief Drawn By William Bartram

that if ever occasion should offer in his presence, he would risk his life to defend mine or my property. This young champion stood by his two associates, one on each side of him; the two affecting a countenance and air of

---

[6] saw, watched
[7] anxiety
[8] admiration

displeasure and importance, instantly presenting their scratching instruments, and flourishing them, spoke boldly, and said that I was too heroic and violent, that it would be good for me to lose some of my blood to make me more mild and tame, and for that purpose they were come to scratch me. They gave me no time to expostulate[9] or reply, but attempted to lay hold on me, which I resisted; and my friend, the young prince, interposed and pushed them off, saying that I was a brave warrior and his friend; that they should not insult me; when instantly they altered their countenance and behavior: they all whooped in chorus, took me friendly by the hand, clapped me on the shoulder, and laid their hands on their breasts in token of sincere friendship, and laughing aloud, said I was a sincere friend to the Seminoles, a worthy and brave warrior, and that no one should hereafter attempt to injure me. They then all three joined arm in arm again and went off, shouting and proclaiming Puc-Puggy was their friend, etc. Thus it seemed that the whole was a ludicrous farce to satisfy their people and appease the manes of the dead rattlesnake. These people never kill the rattlesnake or any other serpent, saying if they do so, the spirit of the killed snake will excite or influence his living kindred or relatives to revenge the injury or violence done to him when alive....

But let us again resume the subject of the rattlesnake: a wonderful creature, when we consider his form, nature, and disposition. It is certain that he is capable by a puncture or scratch of one of his fangs, not only to kill the largest animal in America, and that in a few minutes' time, but to turn the whole body into corruption;[10] but such is the nature of this dreadful reptile, that he cannot run or creep faster than a man or child can walk, and he is never known to strike until he is first assaulted or fears himself in danger, and even then always gives the earliest warning by the rattles at the extremity of the tail. I have in the course of my travels in the Southern States (where they are the largest, most numerous, and supposed to be the most venomous and vindictive[11]) stepped unknowingly so close as almost to touch one of them with my feet, and when I perceived him he was already drawn up in circular coils ready for a blow. But however incredible it may appear, the generous, I may say magnanimous[12] creature lay as still and motionless as if inanimate, his head crouched in, his eyes almost shut. I precipitately[13] withdrew, unless when I have been so shocked with surprise and horror as to be in a manner riveted to the spot, for a short time not having strength to go away: when he often slowly extends himself and quietly

---

[9] protest
[10] sickness, injury
[11] nasty, mean
[12] kindly, generous
[13] quickly

moves off in a direct line, unless pursued, when he erects his tail as far as the rattles extend, and gives the warning alarm by intervals. But if you pursue and overtake him with a show of enmity,[14] he instantly throws himself into the spiral coil; his tail by the rapidity of its motion appears like a vapor, making a quick tremulous[15] sound; his whole body swells through rage, continually rising and falling as a bellows; his beautiful parti-colored skin becomes speckled and rough...; his head and neck are flattened, his cheeks swollen and his lips constricted, discovering his mortal fangs; his eyes red as burning coals, and his brandishing forked tongue, of the color of the hottest flame, continually menaces death and destruction, yet never strikes unless sure of his mark....

When on the sea coast of Georgia, I consented, with a few friends, to make a party of amusement at fishing and fowling on Sapello, one of the sea coast islands. We accordingly descended the Altamaha,[16] crossed the sound, and landed on the north end of the island, near the inlet, fixing our encampment at a pleasant situation, under the shade of a grove of live-oaks and laurels, on the high banks of a creek, which we ascended, winding through a salt marsh, which had its source from a swamp and savanna in the island: our situation, elevated and open, commanded a comprehensive landscape; the great ocean, the foaming surf breaking on the sandy beach, the snowy breakers on the bar, the endless chain of islands, checkered sound, and high continent all appearing before us. The diverting toils of the day were not fruitless, affording us opportunities of furnishing ourselves plentifully with a variety of game, fish, and oysters for our supper.

About two hundred yards from our camp was a cool spring, amidst a grove of the odoriferous[17] myrica: the winding path to this salubrious[18] fountain led through a grassy savanna. I visited the spring several times in the night, but little did I know, or any of my careless drowsy companions, that every time we visited the fountain we were in imminent danger, as I am going to relate. Early in the morning, excited by unconquerable thirst, I arose and went to the spring; and having, thoughtless of harm or danger, nearly half passed the dewy vale, along the serpentine footpath, my hasty steps were suddenly stopped by the sight of a hideous serpent, the formidable rattlesnake, in a high spiral coil, forming a circular mound half the height of my knees, within six inches of the narrow path. As soon as I recovered my senses and strength from so sudden a surprise, I started back out of his reach, where I stood to view him: he lay quiet whilst I surveyed

---

[14] hostility

[15] shaking

[16] the Altamaha River

[17] sweet-smelling

[18] clean, wholesome

him, appearing no way surprised or disturbed, but kept his half-shut eyes fixed on me. My imagination and spirits were in a tumult, almost equally divided betwixt thanksgiving to the supreme Creator and preserver, and the dignified nature of the generous though terrible creature, who had suffered us all to pass many times by him during the night, without injuring us in the least, although we must have touched him, or our steps guided therefrom by a supreme guardian spirit. I hastened back to acquaint my associates, but with a determination to protect the life of the generous serpent. I presently brought my companions to the place, who were, beyond expression, surprised and terrified at the sight of the animal, and in a moment acknowledged their escape from destruction to be miraculous; and I am proud to assert, that all of us, except one person, agreed to let him lie undisturbed, and that person at length was prevailed upon to suffer him to escape.

Again, when, in my youth, attending my father on a journey to the Catskill Mountains, in the government of New York, having nearly ascended the peak of Giliad, being youthful and vigorous in the pursuit of botanical[19] and novel[20] objects, I had gained the summit of a steep rocky

Nature Illustration by William Bartram

---

[19] having to do with plants
[20] new, undiscovered

precipice, ahead of our guide; when just entering a shady vale, I saw, at the root of a small shrub, a singular and beautiful appearance, which I remember to have instantly apprehended to be a large kind of fungus which we called Jews' ears, and was just drawing back my foot to kick it over; when at the instant, my father being near, cried out, "A rattlesnake, my son!" and jerked me back, which probably saved my life. I had never before seen one. This was of the kind which our guide called a yellow one; it was very beautiful, speckled and clouded. My father pleaded for his life, but our guide was inexorable,[21] saying he never spared the life of a rattlesnake, and killed him; my father took his skin and fangs.

Some years after this, when again in company with my father on a journey into East Florida, on the banks of St. Juan, at Port Picolata, attending the congress at a treaty between that government and the Creek Nation, for obtaining a territory from that people to annex to the new government; after the Indians and a detachment from the garrison of St. Augustine had arrived and encamped separately, near the fort, some days elapsed before the business of the treaty came on, waiting the arrival of a vessel from St. Augustine, on board of which were the presents for the Indians. My father employed this time of leisure in little excursions round about the fort; and one morning, being the day the treaty commenced, I attended him on a botanical excursion. Some time after we had been rambling in a swamp about a quarter of a mile from the camp, I being ahead a few paces, my father bid me observe the rattlesnake before and just at my feet. I stopped and saw the monster formed in a high spiral coil, not half his length from my feet: another step forward would have put my life in his power, as I must have touched if not stumbled over him. The fright and perturbation[22] of my spirits at once excited resentment; at that time I was entirely insensible to gratitude or mercy. I instantly cut off a little sapling and soon despatched him: this serpent was about six feet in length, and as thick as an ordinary man's leg.

The encounter deterred us from proceeding on our researches for that day. So I cut off a long tough withe or vine, which, fastening round the neck of the slain serpent, I dragged him after me, his scaly body sounding over the ground, and entering the camp with him in triumph, was soon surrounded by the amazed multitude, both Indians and my countrymen. The adventure soon reached the ears of the commander, who sent an officer to request that, if the snake had not bit himself, he might have him served up for his dinner. I readily delivered up the body of the snake to the cooks, and being that day invited to dine at the governor's table, saw the snake served up in several dishes; Governor Grant being fond of the flesh of the rattlesnake. I tasted of it but could not swallow it. I, however, was sorry after killing the

---

[21] stubborn
[22] distress

serpent, when coolly recollecting every circumstance. He certainly had it in his power to kill me almost instantly, and I make no doubt but that he was conscious of it. I promised myself that I would never again be accessory to the death of a rattlesnake, which promise I have invariably kept to. This dreaded animal is easily killed; a stick no thicker than a man's thumb is sufficient to kill the largest at one stroke, if well directed, either on the head or across the back; nor can they make their escape by running off, nor indeed do they attempt it when attacked.

Questions for Review

1. Why do the Indians call Bartram "Puc-Puggy"? How would you describe their relationship?

2. Why do the Indians try to hold Bartram down and "scratch" him? Does he seem too "heroic and violent," as they say?

3. What is it about snakes that makes them so frightening to many? Have *you* ever encountered a venomous snake? If so, what kind?

4. How does Bartram make rattlesnakes into sympathetic, almost likable creatures?

From Morn Till Night on a Florida River

By Sidney Lanier

In 1876 poet Sidney Lanier[1] published Florida: Its Scenery, Climate, and History. *The following selection is an excerpt from that book, in which Lanier describes a trip he took down the 74-mile-long Ocklawaha River.*

• • • • •

F or a perfect journey God gave us a perfect day. The little Ocklawaha steamboat *Marion* had started on her voyage some hours before daylight. She had taken on her passengers the night previous. By seven o'clock on such a May morning as no words could describe we had made twenty-five miles up the St. Johns. At this point the Ocklawaha flows into the St. Johns, one hundred miles above Jacksonville.

Presently we abandoned the broad highway of the St. Johns, and turned off to the right into the narrow lane of the Ocklawaha. This is the sweetest water lane in the world, a lane which runs for more than one hundred and fifty miles of pure delight betwixt hedge rows of oaks and cypresses and palms and magnolias and mosses and vines; a lane clean to travel, for there is

---

[1] Remember "A Ballad of Trees and the Master"?

never a speck of dust in it save the blue dust and gold dust which the wind blows out of the flags[2] and lilies.

As we advanced up the stream our wee craft seemed to emit her steam in leisurely whiffs, as one puffs one's cigar in a contemplative[3] walk through the forest. Dick, the pole-man,[4] lay asleep on the guards, in great peril of rolling into the river over the three inches between his length and the edge; the people of the boat moved not, and spoke not; the white crane, the curlew, the heron, the water-turkey, were scarcely disturbed in their quiet avoca-

tions[5] as we passed, and quickly succeeded in persuading themselves after each momentary excitement of our gliding by, that we were really no monster, but only some daydream of a monster.

"Look at that snake in the water!" said a gentleman, as we sat on deck with the engineer, just come up from his watch.

The engineer smiled. "Sir, it is a water-turkey," he said, gently.

The water-turkey is the most preposterous bird within the range of ornithology.[6] He is not a bird; he is a neck with such subordinate[7] rights, members, belongings, and heirlooms as seem necessary to that end. He has just enough stomach to arrange nourishment for his neck, just enough wings to fly painfully along with his neck, and just big enough legs to keep his neck from dragging on the ground; and his neck is light-colored, while the rest of him is black. When he saw us he jumped up on a limb and stared. Then suddenly he dropped into the water, sank like a leaden ball out of sight, and made us think he was drowned. Presently the tip of his beak appeared, then the length of his neck lay along the surface of the water. In this position, with his body submerged, he shot out his neck, drew it back, wriggled it, twisted it, twiddled it, and poked it spirally into the east, the west, the north, and the south, round and round with a violence and energy that made one

---

[2] plants with long leaves
[3] thoughtful
[4] someone who tests how deep water is by using a pole
[5] tasks
[6] the study of birds
[7] lesser, inferior

think in the same breath of corkscrews and of lightnings. But what nonsense! All that labor and perilous contortion[8] for a beggarly sprat[9] or a couple of inches of water snake.

Some twenty miles from the mouth of the Ocklawaha, at the right-hand edge of the stream, is the handsomest residence in America. It belongs to a certain alligator of my acquaintance, a very honest and worthy reptile of good repute. A little cove of water, dark-green under the overhanging leaves, placid[10] and clear, curves round at the river edge into the flags and lilies, with a curve just heartbreaking for its pure beauty. This house of the alligator is divided into apartments, little bays which are scalloped out by the lily pads, according to the winding fancies of their growth. My reptile, when he desires to sleep, has but to lie down anywhere; he will find marvelous mosses for his mattress beneath him; his sheets will be white lily petals; and the green disks of the lily pads will straightway embroider themselves together above him for his coverlet. He never quarrels with his cook, he is not the slave of a kitchen, and his one housemaid—the stream—forever sweeps his chambers clean. His conservatories[11] there under the glass of that water are ever, without labor, filled with the enchantments of underwater growths.

His parks and his pleasure grounds are larger than any king's. Upon my saurian's[12] house the winds have no power, the rains are only a new delight to him, and the snows he will never see. Regarding fire, as he does not use it as a slave, so he does not fear it as a tyrant.

Thus all the elements are the friends of my alligator's house. While he sleeps he is being bathed. What glory to awake sweetened and freshened by the sole, careless act of sleep!

Lastly, my saurian has unnumbered mansions, and can change his dwelling as no human householder may; it is but a flip of his tail, and lo! he is established in another place as good as the last, ready furnished to his liking.

On and on up the river! We find it a river without banks. The swift, deep current meanders[13] between tall lines of trees; beyond these, on either side, there is water also—a thousand shallow rivulets[14] lapsing past the bases of a multitude of trees.

Along the edges of the stream every tree trunk, sapling, and stump is wrapped about with a close-growing vine. The edges of the stream are also

---

[8] "perilous contortion": dangerous moving around
[9] "beggarly sprat": pathetically small fish
[10] calm
[11] rooms, houses
[12] reptile's
[13] weaves
[14] streams

defined by flowers and water-leaves. The tall blue flags, the lilies sitting on their round lily pads like white queens on green thrones, the tiny stars and long ribbons of the water grasses—all these border the river in an infinite variety of adornment.

And now, after this day of glory, came a night of glory. Deep down in these shaded lanes it was dark indeed as the night drew on. The stream which had been all day a girdle of beauty, blue or green, now became a black band of mystery.

But presently a brilliant flame flares out overhead: They have lighted the pine-knots on top of the pilot-house. The fire advances up these dark windings.

The startled birds suddenly flutter into the light and after an instant of illuminated flight melt into the darkness. From the perfect silence of these short flights one derives a certain sense of awe.

Now there is a mighty crack and crash: limbs and leaves scrape and scrub along the deck; a little bell tinkles; we stop. In turning a short curve, the boat has run her nose smack into the right bank, and a projecting stump has thrust itself sheer through the starboard side. Out, Dick! Out, Henry! Dick and Henry shuffle forward to the bow, thrust forth their long white pole against a tree trunk, strain and push and bend to the deck as if they were salaaming[15] the god of night and adversity. Our bow slowly rounds into the stream, the wheel turns, and we puff quietly along.

And now it is bedtime. Let me tell you how to sleep on an Ocklawaha steamer in May. With a small bribe persuade Jim, the steward, to take the mattress out of your berth and lay it slanting just along the railing that en-

---

[15] bowing to

closes the lower part of the deck in front and to the left of the pilot-house. Lie flat on your back down on the mattress, draw your blanket over you, put your cap on your head, on account of the night air, fold your arms, say some little prayer or other, and fall asleep with a star looking right down on your eye. When you wake in the morning you will feel as new as Adam.

Questions for Review

1. How does Lanier keep the reader interested in his little tale of a trip down the Ocklawaha? (What does he do instead of just listing off one thing after another that he did on that day?)

2. Think of a trip you've taken or an interesting place you've visited. Now, focus on one thing you did that day (or one part of the place you visited), and write an interesting description of what happened. Think of an effective opening sentence (like Lanier's opening sentence in this selection!), write colorfully about events that you experienced, and give your essay a nice closing that wraps up *your* little tale.

On the Grasshopper and the Cricket

By John Keats

*This poem by English poet John Keats (1795-1821) is a **sonnet**. A sonnet has 14 lines and is written in **iambic pentameter**, which means that each line has five "beats" ("pentameter"), and the second, fourth, sixth, eighth, and tenth "beats," or syllables, are stressed. Read the following poem twice before you look at the review questions!*

• • • • •

The poetry of earth is never dead:
When all the birds are faint with the hot sun,
And hide in cooling trees, a voice will run
From hedge to hedge about the new-mown mead:[1]
That is the grasshopper's—he takes the lead
In summer luxury—he has never done
With his delights, for, when tired out with fun,
He rests at ease beneath some pleasant weed.
The poetry of earth is ceasing never:
On a lone winter evening, when the frost
Has wrought[2] a silence, from the stove[3] there shrills
The cricket's song, in warmth increasing ever,
And seems to one in drowsiness half lost,
The grasshopper's among some grassy hills.

Questions for Review

1. Describe how the poem fits the pattern of "iambic pentameter." What is the poem's rhyme scheme?

2. What similar lines break the poem up into two parts? How are the two parts similar—and different?

3. What main message do you think the poet is trying to express?

4. Think of a nature topic that interests you, and write a two-line or four-line poem about that topic in rhyming iambic pentameter.

---

[1] meadow
[2] created
[3] a small house or cottage

The "'Gator"

By Clarence B. Moore

A traveling archaeologist, Clarence B. Moore (1852-1936) went around the world in search of artifacts and knowledge. In his steam-powered paddle-boat named Gopher, *Moore spent years exploring the southern United States and its unique plant and animal life. In the below essay, he relates some fascinating stories and facts about that potentially monstrous creature, the alligator—an animal American southerners know well, and often fear.*

• • • • •

The alligator, or "'gator," as it is usually called throughout its home, the Southern States, is an object of great curiosity at the North. Every winter many tourists visit Florida and carry back baby alligators, together with more or less magnified accounts of the creature's doings and habits, and their stories are probably the cause of this very widespread interest.

Though the alligator is rapidly disappearing from the banks of the lower St. John's River, in Lake Washington and in the Saw Grass Lake (where that river has its source), and in waters still farther south, they are still to be found in almost undiminished numbers, and are hunted for a living by native hunters. They are commonly sought at night, by torchlight, for in this way they can be approached with the utmost ease.

A rifle-ball will readily penetrate an alligator's hide, although there exists an unfounded belief to the contrary. The creatures will "stand a deal of killing," however, and frequently roll off a bank and are lost even after being shot through and through.

The alligator builds a nest of mud and grass, and lays a large number of oblong[1] white eggs, but the little ones when hatched often serve as lunch for their unnatural papa, and this cannibalism, more than the rifle, prevents their numbers from increasing. The alligator is not particular as to diet. I once found the stomach of a ten-footer to be literally filled with pine chips from some tree which had been felled[2] near the river's bank! They are fond of wallowing in marshes, and many a man out snipe shooting has taken an involuntary bath by stumbling into their wallows. In dry seasons alligators will traverse long distances overland to reach water, and travelers have come suddenly upon alligators crawling amid prairies or woods, in the most unexpected manner. The alligator as a rule is very wary, but at times sleeps quite soundly. I saw one struck twice with an oar before it woke.

There is a very prevalent[3] impression that the alligator differs from the crocodile in that one moves the upper jaw and the other the lower. Such, however, is not the case. Both animals move the lower jaw, though the raising of the head as the mouth opens sometimes gives the appearance of moving the upper jaw only. But alligators and crocodiles differ in the arrangement of the teeth, and the snout of the crocodile is more sharply pointed.

The hides are salted to preserve them and are shipped to dealers in Jacksonville, where those less than six feet long are worth a dollar, while for those which exceed this length twenty-five cents extra is allowed.[4] A fair estimate of the number of alligators killed for sale in Florida alone, and not counting those shot by tourists, would be ten thousand annually. One hears very conflicting reports as to the length of large alligators. A prominent dealer in Jacksonville said that out of ten thousand hides handled by him none were over twelve feet long. I am told that at the Centennial, side by side with a crocodile from the Nile, there was shown an alligator from Florida sixteen feet in length.

Years ago near a place called Enterprise, on a point jumping into Lake Monroe, during all bright days a certain big alligator used to lie basking in the sun. He was well known to the whole neighborhood. The entire coterie[5] of sportsmen at the only hotel used to call him "Big Ben," and proud hunters would talk, and even dream, of the time when a well-aimed rifle-shot would

---

[1] longer than they are wide
[2] cut down
[3] common
[4] This was the price back in Moore's day; it would be many times that today, of course!
[5] group

end his long career. But Big Ben was as cunning as a serpent, and whenever anyone, afoot or afloat, came unpleasantly near, he would slide off into the water—which meant "goodbye" for the rest of the day.

One fine morning one of these sportsmen, paddling up the lake, luckily with his rifle in his canoe, came upon Big Ben so sound asleep that he stole up within range and put a bullet through the alligator's brain. What to do next was a problem. He could not tow the monster all the way to Enterprise with his small canoe. A bright idea struck him. He put his visiting card in the beast's mouth and paddled swiftly back. A number of hunters were at the wharf, and the slayer of Big Ben hastened to inform them with apparent sincerity, that while out paddling he had come within easy range of the 'gator, who was, no doubt, still lying motionless on the point. A flotilla[6] of boats and canoes, manned by an army with rifles, instantly started for the point. To avoid confusion, it was unanimously agreed that all should go down together, and that the entire party, if they were lucky enough to find Big Ben still there, should fire a volley at the word of command. As they approached the point, the hearts of all beat quickly; and when, with straining eyes, they saw Big Ben apparently asleep and motionless upon the bank, even the coolest could scarcely control his feelings. The boats were silently drawn up within easy shot, and the word was given. Bang, bang! went a score of rifles and Big Ben, riddled with bullets, lay motionless upon the point! With a cheer of triumph, the excited sportsmen leaped ashore, and fastening a rope around the dead alligator, speedily towed him to Enterprise. There the original slayer awaited them upon the wharf. When Big Ben was

---

[6] fleet

laid upon the shore, opening the animal's mighty jaws he disclosed his visiting card, and thanked them most politely for their kindness in bringing his 'gator home for him.

I once met with a curious adventure. Man is rarely attacked by alligators in Florida, except by the female alligator called upon to defend her young. Some years ago, in a small steamer chartered for the purpose, I had gone up a branch of the St. John's beyond Salt Lake until we could proceed no farther, because the top of the river had become solid with floating vegetation under which the water flowed. We tied up for the night, and shortly after were boarded by two men who said that their camp was nearby and that they shot alligators and plume birds[7] for a living. One of the men carried his rifle, a muzzle-loader, and from its barrel projected the ramrod, which had become fast immediately above the ball while loading. He intended to draw it out after they should return to camp.

We went ashore with these men to look at an alligator's nest nearby, and were filling our pockets with baby alligators, when we heard a grunting sound and saw an alligator eight or nine feet long coming directly at us. With the exception of the man already referred to, we were all unarmed, and affairs began to look a little unpleasant, for the creature evidently meant mischief. When it was within a few feet, the man with the rifle, knowing that he alone had a weapon, took deliberate aim and fired bullet, ramrod, and all down the 'gator's throat. The animal turned over twice, and rolling off the bank, sank out of sight.

The alligators of the Amazon River in South America are very numerous, and owing to scarcity of hunters attain a very great size. In the upper waters apparently they are entirely unaccustomed to the report of firearms, and if not actually hit will lie still while shot after shot is fired. The largest I ever killed and measured was thirteen feet and four inches in length; but this was much smaller than many which I shot from dugouts and canoes too far away from shore to tow them in.

Buried an inch deep in one of these dead alligators I once found a piranha, that troublesome fish which makes swimming in some parts of the Amazon a risky matter. It bores into flesh very much after the manner of a circular punch, and when it starts, its habit is to go to the bone. The piranha, of course, could not penetrate the hide of the alligator, but entering by the bullet hole it had turned to one side and partially buried itself in the flesh. I have seen men bearing very ugly scars, the results of wounds inflicted by the piranha while they were bathing. If this fish is cut open after having bored its way into an animal a solid round mass of flesh will be found inside corresponding to the hole it has made, showing that the fish really bores its way in.

---

[7] Plume birds are birds with large, beautiful feathers used in decorations.

It is said that the alligator of the Amazon is more likely to attack man than its brother of our Southern States. The captain of a small steamer running between Iquitos and Para[8] told me that on the preceding trip he had carried to a doctor a boy who had lost his arm from the bite of an alligator, while allowing his arm to hang in the water from a raft. The same captain, however, also informed me that he had been treed by one of these animals and compelled to remain "up a tree" for some time; so that I have some hesitation in quoting him as an authority upon the nature and habits of these alligators. The flesh of young alligators is considered a delicacy in Brazil and is regularly sold in the markets.

Questions for Review

1. What is even more dangerous to the alligator population than man?

2. Give some characteristic of alligators that the author lists in the essay.

3. How does the author say alligators differ in the United States and the Amazon?

---

[8] Iquitos is in Peru, and Para is in Brazil.

Matthew 5:1-20

By The Apostle Matthew

This selection is known as the Beatitudes. The word beatitude *means "happiness" or "blessedness," and Jesus uses the word "blessed" many times. In the previous chapter, Jesus called several disciples to follow Him, traveled around Galilee teaching and healing the people of sickness and disease and demons, and attracted large crowds. He said these words to his disciples and the crowd; it is part of what is known as "The Sermon on the Mount."*

• • • • •

1 – And seeing the multitudes, he went up into a mountain: and when he was set, his disciples came unto him:

2 – And he opened his mouth, and taught them, saying,

3 – Blessed are the poor in spirit: for theirs is the kingdom of heaven.

4 – Blessed are they that mourn: for they shall be comforted.

5 – Blessed are the meek: for they shall inherit the earth.

6 – Blessed are they which do hunger and thirst after righteousness: for they shall be filled.

7 – Blessed are the merciful: for they shall obtain mercy.

8 – Blessed are the pure in heart: for they shall see God.

9 – Blessed are the peacemakers: for they shall be called the children of God.

10 – Blessed are they which are persecuted for righteousness' sake: for theirs is the kingdom of heaven.

11 – Blessed are ye, when men shall revile[1] you, and persecute you, and shall say all manner of evil against you falsely, for my sake.

12 – Rejoice, and be exceeding glad: for great is your reward in heaven: for so persecuted they the prophets which were before you.

---

[1] insult, criticize

13 – Ye are the salt of the earth: but if the salt have lost his savour, wherewith shall it be salted? it is thenceforth good for nothing, but to be cast out, and to be trodden under foot of men.

14 – Ye are the light of the world. A city that is set on an hill cannot be hid.

15 – Neither do men light a candle, and put it under a bushel, but on a candlestick; and it giveth light unto all that are in the house.

16 – Let your light so shine before men, that they may see your good works, and glorify your Father which is in heaven.

17 – Think not that I am come to destroy the law, or the prophets: I am not come to destroy, but to fulfil.

18 – For verily[2] I say unto you, Till heaven and earth pass, one jot or one tittle[3] shall in no wise pass from the law, till all be fulfilled.

19 – Whosoever therefore shall break one of these least commandments, and shall teach men so, he shall be called the least in the kingdom of heaven: but whosoever shall do and teach them, the same shall be called great in the kingdom of heaven.

20 – For I say unto you, That except your righteousness shall exceed the righteousness of the scribes and Pharisees, ye shall in no case enter into the kingdom of heaven.

Questions for Review

1. What do you think a "peacemaker" is? (See verse eight.) How can we be peacemakers?

2. How should Jesus followers feel if they are "persecuted for righteousness' sake? (See verses 10-12.)

3. Give an example of how Jesus followers can be "salt" and "light" in our world today.

---

[2] truly

[3] A jot and a tittle are tiny accent marks put on Hebrew words. The word *jot* is related to the word *iota*, or a tiny amount.

Uncle Remus: His Songs and His Sayings

By Joel Chandler Harris

One of the most beloved literary characters ever, the former slave Uncle Remus was created by Georgian Joel Chandler Harris (1848-1908). Uncle Remus is a master storyteller who mesmerizes those children to whom he tells tales about Brer (Brother) Fox, Brer Bear, Brer Rabbit, and other animals. Like Aesop's fables, these stories teach lessons on human nature. These tales come from the 1881 book Uncle Remus: His Songs and His Sayings.[1]

• • • • •

Uncle Remus Initiates the Little Boy

One evening recently, the lady whom Uncle Remus calls "Miss Sally" missed her little seven-year-old. Making search for him through the house and through the yard, she heard the sound of voices in the old man's cabin, and, looking through the window, saw the child sitting by Uncle Remus. His head rested against the old man's arm, and he was gazing with an expression of the most intense interest into the rough, weather-beaten face, that beamed so kindly upon him. This is what "Miss Sally" heard:

"Bimeby, one day, atter Brer Fox bin doin' all dat he could fer ter ketch Brer Rabbit, en Brer Rabbit bein doin' all he could fer ter keep 'im fum it, Brer Fox say to hisse'f dat he'd put up a game on Brer Rabbit, en he ain't mo'n got de wuds out'n his mouf twel Brer Rabbit came a lopin' up de big road, lookin' des ez plump, en ez fat, en ez sassy ez a Moggin hoss in a barley patch.

"'Hol' on dar, Brer Rabbit,' sez Brer Fox, sezee.

---

[1] Several Uncle Remus stories are told in the 1946 Disney film *Song of the South*, a wonderful movie that combines animation and live action (it won two Academy Awards).

"'I ain't got time, Brer Fox,' sez Brer Rabbit, sezee, sorter mendin' his licks.

"'I wanter have some confab wid you, Brer Rabbit,' sez Brer Fox, sezee.

"'All right, Brer Fox, but you better holler fum whar you stan'. I'm monstus full er fleas dis mawnin',' sez Brer Rabbit, sezee.

"'I seed Brer B'ar yistiddy, 'sez Brer Fox, sezee, 'en he sorter rake me over de coals kaze you en me ain't make frens en live naberly, en I tole 'im dat I'd see you.'

"Den Brer Rabbit scratch one year wid his off hinefoot sorter jub'usly, en den he ups en sez, sezee:

"'All a settin', Brer Fox. Spose'n you drap roun' ter-morrer en take dinner wid me. We ain't got no great doin's at our house, but I speck de ole 'oman en de chilluns kin sorter scramble roun' en git up sump'n fer ter stay yo' stummick.'

"'I'm 'gree'ble, Brer Rabbit,' sez Brer Fox, sezee.

"'Den I'll 'pen' on you,' sez Brer Rabbit, sezee.

"Nex' day, Mr. Rabbit an' Miss Rabbit got up soom, 'fo' day, en raided on a gyarden like Miss Sally's out dar, en got some cabbiges, en some roas'n—years, en some sparrer-grass, en dey fix up a smashin' dinner. Bimeby one er de little Rabbits, playin' out in de back-yard, come runnin' in hollerin', 'Oh, ma! oh, ma! I seed Mr. Fox a comin'!' En den Brer Rabbit he tuck de chilluns by der years en make um set down, en den him and Miss Rabbit sorter dally roun' waitin' for Brer Fox. En dey keep on waitin' for Brer Fox. En dey keep on waitin', but no Brer Fox ain't come. Atter 'while Brer Rabbit goes to de do', easy like, en peep out, en dar, stickin' fum behime de cornder, wuz de tip-een' er Brer Fox tail. Den Brer Rabbit shot de do' en sot down, en put his paws behime his years en begin fer ter sing:

"'De place wharbouts you spill de grease, Right dar you er boun' ter slide, An' whar you fin' a bunch er ha'r, You'll sholy fine de hide.'

"Nex' day, Brer Fox sont word by Mr. Mink, en skuze hisse'f kaze he wuz too sick fer ter come, en he ax Brer Rabbit fer ter come en take dinner wid him, en Brer Rabbit say he wuz 'gree'ble.

"Bimeby, w'en de shadders wuz at der shortes', Brer Rabbit he sorter brush up en sa'nter down ter Brer Fox's house, en w'en he got dar, he hear somebody groanin', en he look in de do' an dar he see Brer Fox settin' up in a rockin'-cheer all wrop up wid flannil, en he look mighty weak. Brer Rabbit look all roun', he did, but he ain't see no dinner. De dish-pan wuz settin' on de table, en close by wuz a kyarvin' knife.

"'Look like you gwineter have chicken fer dinner, Brer Fox,' sez Brer Rabbit, sezee.

"'Yes, Brer Rabbit, dey er nice, en fresh, en tender, 'sez Brer Fox, sezee.

"Den Brer Rabbit sorter pull his mustarsh, en say: 'You ain't got no calamus root, is you, Brer Fox? I done got so now dat I can't eat no chicken 'ceppin she's seasoned up wid calamus root.' En wid dat Brer Rabbit lipt out er de do' and dodge 'mong the bushes, en sot dar watchin' for Brer Fox; en he ain't watch long, nudder, kaze Brer Fox flung off de flannil en crope out er de house en got whar he could cloze in on Brer Rabbit, en bimeby Brer Rabbit holler out: 'Oh, Brer Fox! I'll des put yo' calamus root out yer on dish yer stump. Better come git it while hit's fresh,' and wid dat Brer Rabbit gallop off home. En Brer Fox ain't never kotch 'im yit, en w'at's mo', honey, he ain't gwineter."

The Wonderful Tar Baby Story

"Didn't the fox never catch the rabbit, Uncle Remus?" asked the little boy the next evening.

"He come mighty nigh it, honey, sho's you born—Brer Fox did. One day atter Brer Rabbit fool 'im wid dat calamus root, Brer Fox went ter wuk en got 'im some tar, en mix it wid some turkentime, en fix up a contrapshun w'at he call a Tar-Baby, en he tuck dish yer Tar-Baby en he sot 'er in de big road, en den he lay off in de bushes fer to see what de news wuz gwine ter be. En he didn't hatter wait long, nudder, kaze bimeby here come Brer Rabbit pacin' down de road—lippity-clippity, clippity-lippity—dez ez sassy ez a jay-bird. Brer Fox, he lay low. Brer Rabbit come prancin' 'long twel he spy de Tar-Baby, en den he fotch up on his behime legs like he wuz 'stonished. De Tar Baby, she sot dar, she did, en Brer Fox, he lay low.

"'Mawnin'!' sez Brer Rabbit, sezee—'nice wedder dis mawnin',' sezee.

"Tar-Baby ain't sayin' nuthin', en Brer Fox he lay low.

"'How duz yo' sym'tums seem ter segashuate?' sez Brer Rabbit, sezee.

"Brer Fox, he wink his eye slow, en lay low, en de Tar-Baby, she ain't sayin' nuthin'.

"'How you come on, den? Is you deaf?' sez Brer Rabbit, sezee. 'Kaze if you is, I kin holler louder,' sezee.

"Tar-Baby stay still, en Brer Fox, he lay low.

"'You er stuck up, dat's w'at you is,' says Brer Rabbit, sezee, 'en I'm gwine ter kyore you, dat's w'at I'm a gwine ter do,' sezee.

"Brer Fox, he sorter chuckle in his stummick, he did, but Tar-Baby ain't sayin' nothin'.

"'I'm gwine ter larn you how ter talk ter 'spectubble folks ef hit's de las' ack,' sez Brer Rabbit, sezee. 'Ef you don't take off dat hat en tell me howdy, I'm gwine ter bus' you wide open,' sezee.

"Tar-Baby stay still, en Brer Fox, he lay low.

"Brer Rabbit keep on axin' 'im, en de Tar-Baby, she keep on sayin' nothin', twel present'y Brer Rabbit draw back wid his fis', he did, en blip he tuck 'er side er de head. Right dar's whar he broke his merlasses jug. His fis' stuck, en he can't pull loose. De tar hilt 'im. But Tar-Baby, she stay still, en Brer Fox, he lay low.

"'Ef you don't lemme loose, I'll knock you agin,' sez Brer Rabbit, sezee, en wid dat he fotch 'er a wipe wid de udder han', en dat stuck. Tar-Baby, she ain't sayin' nuthin', en Brer Fox, he lay low.

"'Tu'n me loose, fo' I kick de natchul stuffin' outen you,' sez Brer Rabbit, sezee, but de Tar-Baby, she ain't sayin' nuthin'. She des hilt on, en de Brer Rabbit lose de use er his feet in de same way. Brer Fox, he lay low. Den Brer Rabbit squall out dat ef de Tar-Baby don't tu'n 'im loose he butt 'er cranksided. En den he butted, en his head got stuck. Den Brer Fox, he sa'ntered fort', lookin' dez ez innercent ez wunner yo' mammy's mockin'-birds.

"Howdy, Brer Rabbit,' sez Brer Fox, sezee. 'You look sorter stuck up dis mawnin',' sezee, en den he rolled on de groun', en laft en laft twel he couldn't laff no mo'. 'I speck you'll take dinner wid me dis time, Brer Rabbit. I done laid in some calamus root, en I ain't gwineter take no skuse,' sez Brer Fox, sezee."

Here Uncle Remus paused, and drew a two-pound yam out of the ashes.

"Did the fox eat the rabbit?" asked the little boy to whom the story had been told.

"Dat's all de fur de tale goes," replied the old man. "He mout, an den agin he moutent. Some say Judge B'ar come 'long en loosed 'im—some say he didn't. I hear Miss Sally callin'. You better run 'long."

Why Mr. Possum Loves Peace

"One night," said Uncle Remus—taking Miss Sally's little boy on his knee, and stroking the child's hair thoughtfully and caressingly—"one night Brer Possum call by fer Brer Coon, 'cordin' ter 'greement, en atter gobblin' up a dish er fried greens en smokin' a seegyar, dey rambled fort' fer ter see how de ballance er de settlement wuz gittin' long. Brer Coon, he wuz one er deze yer natchul pacers, en he racked 'long same ez Mars John's bay pony, en Brer Possum he went in a han'-gallup; en dey got over heap er groun, mon. Brer Possum, he got his belly full er 'simmons, en Brer Coon, he scoop up a 'bunnunce er frogs en tadpoles. Dey amble long, dey did, des ez sociable ez a basket er kittens, twel bimeby dey hear Mr. Dog talkin' ter hisse'f way off in de woods.

"'Spozen he runs up on us, Brer Possum, w'at you gwineter do?' sez Brer Coon, sezee. Brer Possum sorter laugh 'round de cornders un his mouf.

"'Oh, ef he come, Brer Coon, I'm gwineter stan' by you,' sez Brer Possum. 'W'at you gwineter do?' sezee.

"'Who? me?' sez Brer Coon. 'Ef he run up onter me, I lay I give 'im one twis',' sezee."

"Did the dog come?" asked the little boy.

"Go 'way, honey!" responded the old man, in an impressive tone. "Go way! Mr. Dog, he come en he come a zoonin'. En he ain't wait fer ter say howdy, nudder. He des sail inter de two un um. De ve'y fus pas he make Brer Possum fetch a grin fum year ter year, en keel over like he wuz dead. Den Mr. Dog, he sail inter Brer Coon, en right dar's whar he drap his money purse, kaze Brer Coon wuz cut out fer dat kinder bizness, en he fa'rly wipe up de face er de yeth wid 'im. You better b'leeve dat w'en Mr. Dog got a chance to make hisse'f skase he tuck it, en w'at der wuz lef' un him went skaddlin' thoo de woods like hit wuz shot outen a muskit. En Brer Coon, he sorter lick his cloze inter shape en rack off, en Brer Possum, he lay dar like he wuz dead, twel bimeby he raise up sorter keerful like, en w'en he fine de coas' cle'r he scramble up en scamper off like sumpin' was atter 'im."

Here Uncle Remus paused long enough to pick up a live coal of fire in his fingers, transfer it to the palm of his hand, and thence to his clay pipe, which he had been filling—a proceeding that was viewed by the little boy with undisguised admiration. The old man then proceeded:

"Nex' time Brer Possum met Brer Coon, Brer Coon 'fuse ter 'spon' ter his howdy, en dis make Brer Possum feel mighty bad, seein' ez how dey useter make so many 'scurshuns tergedder.

"'W'at make you hol' yo' head so high, Brer Coon?' sez Brer Possum, sezee.

"'I ain't runnin' wid cowerds deze days,' sez Brer Coon. 'W'en I wants you I'll sen' fer you,' sezee.

"Den Brer Possum git mighty mad.

"'Who's enny cowerd?' sezee.

"'You is,' sez Brer Coon, 'dat's who. I ain't soshatin' wid dem w'at lays down on de groun' en plays dead w'en dar's a free fight gwine on,' sezee.

"Den Brer Possum grin en laugh fit to kill hisse'f. "'Brer Coon, you don't speck I done dat kaze I wuz 'feared, duz you?' sezee. 'W'y I want no mo' 'feared dan you is dis minnit. W'at wuz dey fer ter be skeered un?' sezee. 'I know'd you'd git away wid Mr. Dog ef I didn't, en I des lay dar watchin' you shake him, waitin' fer ter put in w'en de time come,' sezee.

"Brer Coon tu'n up his nose.

"'Dat's a mighty likely tale,' sezee, 'w'en Mr. Dog ain't mo'n tech you 'fo' you keel over, en lay dar stiff,' sezee.

"'Dat's des w'at I wuz gwineter tell you 'bout; sez Brer Possum, sezee. 'I want no mo' skeer'd dan you is right now, en' I wuz fixin' fer ter give Mr. Dog a sample er my jaw,' sezee, 'but I'm de most ticklish chap w'at you ever laid eyes on, en no sooner did Mr. Dog put his nose down yer 'mong my ribs dan I got ter laughin', en I laughed twel I ain't had no use er my lim's,' sezee, 'en it's a mussy unto Mr. Dog dat I wuz ticklish, kaze a little mo' en I'd e't 'im up,' sezee. 'I don't mine fightin', Brer Coon, no mo' dan you duz,' sezee, 'but I declar' ter grashus ef I kin stan' ticklin'. Git me in a row whar dey ain't no ticklin' 'lowed, en I'm your man, sezee.

"En down ter dis day"—continued Uncle Remus, watching the smoke from his pipe curl upward over the little boy's head—"down ter dis day, Brer Possum's bound ter s'render w'en you tech him in de short ribs, en he'll laugh ef he knows he's gwineter be smashed fer it."

How Mr. Rabbit Was Too Sharp for Mr. Fox

"Uncle Remus," said the little boy one evening, when he had found the old man with little or nothing to do, "did the fox kill and eat the rabbit when he caught him with the Tar-Baby?"

"Law, honey, ain't I tell you 'bout dat?" replied the old man, chuckling slyly. "I 'clar ter grashus I ought er tole you dat, but old man Nod wuz ridin' on my eyeleds 'twel a leetle mo'n I'd a dis'member'd my own name, en den on to dat here come yo' mammy hollerin' atter you.

"W'at I tell you w'en I fus' begin? I tole you Brer Rabbit wuz a monstus soon creetur; leas'ways dat's w'at I laid out fer ter tell you. Well, den, honey, don't you go en make no udder calkalashuns, kaze in dem days Brer Rabbit en his fambly wuz at de head er de gang w'en enny racket wuz on han', en dar dey stayed. 'Fo' you begins fer ter wipe yo' eyes 'bout Brer Rabbit, you wait en see whar'bouts Brer Rabbit gwineter fetch up at. But dat's needer yer ner dar.

"W'en Brer Fox fine Brer Rabbit mixt up wid de Tar-Baby, he feel mighty good, en he roll on de groun' en laff. Bimeby he up'n say, sezee:

"'Well, I speck I got you dis time, Brer Rabbit, sezee; 'maybe I ain't, but I speck I is. You been runnin' roun' here sassin' atter me a mighty long time, but I speck you done come ter de een' er de row. You bin cuttin' up yo' capers en bouncin' 'roun' in dis neighberhood ontwel you come ter b'leeve yo'se'f de boss er de whole gang. En den you er allers somers whar you got no bizness,' sez Brer Fox, sezee. 'Who ax you fer ter come en strike up a 'quaintance wid dish yer Tar-Baby? En who stuck you up dar whar you iz? Nobody in de roun' worl'. You des tuck en jam yo'se'f on dat Tar-Baby widout waitin' fer enny invite,' sez Brer Fox, sezee, en dar you is, en dar you'll stay twel I fixes up a bresh-pile and fires her up, kaze I'm gwineter bobby-cue you dis day, sho,' sez Brer Fox, sezee.

"Den Brer Rabbit talk mighty 'umble.

"'I don't keer w'at you do wid me, Brer Fox,' sezee, 'so you don't fling me in dat brier-patch. Roas' me, Brer Fox' sezee, 'but don't fling me in dat brierpatch,' sezee.

"'Hit's so much trouble fer ter kindle a fier,' sez Brer Fox, sezee, 'dat I speck I'll hatter hang you,' sezee.

"'Hang me des ez high as you please, Brer Fox,' sez Brer Rabbit, sezee, 'but don't fling me in dat brier-patch,' sezee.

"'I ain't got no string,' sez Brer Fox, sezee, 'en now I speck I'll hatter drown you,' sezee.

"'Drown me des ez deep ez you please, Brer Fox,' sez Brer Rabbit, sezee, 'but do don't fling me in dat brier-patch,' sezee.

"'Dey ain't no water nigh,' sez Brer Fox, sezee, 'en now I speck I'll hatter skin you,' sezee.

"'Skin me, Brer Fox,' sez Brer Rabbit, sezee, 'snatch out my eyeballs, t'ar out my years by de roots, en cut off my legs,' sezee, 'but do please, Brer Fox, don't fling me in dat brier- patch,' sezee.

"Co'se Brer Fox wanter hurt Brer Rabbit bad ez he kin, so he cotch 'im by de behime legs en slung 'im right in de middle er de brier-patch. Dar wuz a considerbul flutter whar Brer Rabbit struck de bushes, en Brer Fox sorter hang 'roun' fer ter see w'at wuz gwineter happen. Bimeby he hear somebody call 'im, en way up de hill he see Brer Rabbit settin' crosslegged on a chinkapin log koamin' de pitch outen his har wid a chip. Den Brer Fox know dat he bin swop off mighty bad. Brer Rabbit wuz bleedzed fer ter fling back some er his sass, en he holler out:

"'Bred en bawn in a brier-patch, Brer Fox—bred en bawn in a brier-patch!' en wid dat he skip out des ez lively ez a cricket in de embers."

Questions for Review

1. What lessons about human nature are expressed in "The Wonderful Tar Baby Story" and "Why Mr. Possum Loves Peace"?

2. Look up the term *reverse psychology* and write down the definition. How does Brer Rabbit use reverse psychology in "How Mr. Rabbit Was Too Sharp for Mr. Fox"?

What a Friend We Have in Jesus

By Joseph Scriven

Ireland-born Joseph Scriven (1820-1886) wrote this poem, now a beloved hymn, in 1855. Shortly before his wedding day, Scriven's fiancée fell into a river and tragically drowned. He wrote the poem afterwards—reportedly to comfort his own mother—and American lawyer Charles Converse in 1868 composed music for it.

• • • • •

What a Friend we have in Jesus,
    All our sins and griefs to bear!
What a privilege to carry
    Everything to God in prayer!
O what peace we often forfeit,
    O what needless pain we bear,
All because we do not carry
    Everything to God in prayer!

Have we trials and temptations?
    Is there trouble anywhere?
We should never be discouraged—
    Take it to the Lord in prayer.
Can we find a friend so faithful
    Who will all our sorrows share?
Jesus knows our every weakness—
    Take it to the Lord in prayer.

Are we weak and heavy laden,
    Cumbered[1] with a load of care?
Precious Saviour, still our refuge—
    Take it to the Lord in prayer.
Do thy friends despise, forsake thee?
    Take it to the Lord in prayer;
In His arms He'll take and shield thee—
    Thou wilt find a solace[2] there.

---

[1] burdened
[2] comfort

Questions for Review

1. Look up and read Luke 11:5-13, Luke 18:1, and 1 Thessalonians 5:17. How do these passages compare to "What a Friend We Have in Jesus"?

2. Listen to a choir sing this poem/hymn.

3. Take a few minutes and pray to the Lord about something that's on your heart that you haven't brought to Him.

The Lumber Room

By Saki

Saki was the pen name of English short story writer Hector Hugh Munro (1870-1916). Munro was an expert at creating inventive, unusual short stories, and excelled at saying a lot using only a few words. His opening paragraphs to these short stories were memorable and sometimes startling. When Munro was a child, his mother died, and he was sent to live with his grandmother and aunts. Reportedly, these women were not too pleasant to live with....

• • • • •

The children were to be driven, as a special treat, to the sands at Jagborough. Nicholas was not to be of the party; he was in disgrace. Only that morning he had refused to eat his wholesome bread and milk on the seemingly frivolous ground[1] that there was a frog in it. Older and wiser and better people had told him that there could not possibly be a frog in his bread and milk, and that he was not to talk nonsense; he continued, nevertheless, to talk what seemed the veriest[2] nonsense, and described with much detail the coloration and markings of the alleged frog. The dramatic part of the incident was that there really was a frog in Nicholas's basin of bread and milk; he had put it there himself, so he felt entitled to know something about it. The sin of taking a frog from the garden and putting it into a bowl of wholesome bread and milk was enlarged on at great length, but the fact that stood out clearest in the whole affair, as it presented itself to the mind of Nicholas, was that the older, wiser, and better people had been proved to be profoundly in error in matters about which they had expressed the utmost assurance.

"You said there couldn't possibly be a frog in my bread and milk; there was a frog in my bread and milk," he repeated, with the insistence of a skilled tactician who does not intend to shift from favorable ground.

So his boy cousin and girl cousin and his quite uninteresting younger brother were to be taken to Jagborough sands that afternoon, and he was to stay at home. His cousins' aunt, who insisted, by an unwarranted[3] stretch of imagination, in styling herself his aunt also, had hastily invented the Jagborough expedition in order to impress on Nicholas the delights that he had

---

[1] "frivolous ground": silly excuse
[2] truest
[3] undeserved

justly forfeited by his disgraceful conduct at the breakfast table. It was her habit, whenever one of the children fell from grace, to improvise something of a festival nature from which the offender would be rigorously debarred;[4] if all the children sinned collectively they were suddenly informed of a circus in a neighboring town, a circus of unrivaled merit and uncounted elephants, to which, but for their depravity,[5] they would have been taken that very day.

A few decent tears were looked for on the part of Nicholas when the moment for the departure of the expedition arrived. As a matter of fact, however, all the crying was done by his girl cousin, who scraped her knee rather painfully against the step of the carriage as she was scrambling in.

"How she did howl," said Nicholas cheerfully, as the party drove off without any of the elation of high spirits that should have characterized it.

"She'll soon get over that," said the soidisant[6] aunt; "it will be a glorious afternoon for racing about over those beautiful sands. How they will enjoy themselves!"

"Bobby won't enjoy himself much, and he won't race much either," said Nicholas with a grim chuckle; "his boots are hurting him. They're too tight."

"Why didn't he tell me they were hurting?" asked the aunt with some asperity.[7]

"He told you twice, but you weren't listening. You often don't listen when we tell you important things."

"You are not to go into the gooseberry garden," said the aunt, changing the subject.

"Why not?" demanded Nicholas.

"Because you are in disgrace," said the aunt loftily.

Nicholas did not admit the flawlessness of the reasoning; he felt perfectly capable of being in disgrace and in a gooseberry garden at the same moment. His face took on an expression of considerable obstinacy.[8] It was clear to his aunt that he was determined to get into the gooseberry garden, "only," as she remarked to herself, "because I have told him he is not to."

Now the gooseberry garden had two doors by which it might be entered, and once a small person like Nicholas could slip in there he could effectually disappear from view amid the masking growth of artichokes, raspberry canes, and fruit bushes. The aunt had many other things to do that afternoon, but she spent an hour or two in trivial gardening operations among flower

---

[4] excluded

[5] wickedness

[6] so-called, supposed

[7] harshness

[8] stubbornness

beds and shrubberies, whence she could keep a watchful eye on the two doors that led to the forbidden paradise. She was a woman of few ideas, with immense powers of concentration.

Nicholas made one or two sorties[9] into the front garden, wriggling his way with obvious stealth[10] of purpose towards one or other of the doors, but never able for a moment to evade the aunt's watchful eye. As a matter of fact, he had no intention of trying to get into the gooseberry garden, but it was extremely convenient for him that his aunt should believe that he had; it was a belief that would keep her on self-imposed sentry duty for the greater part of the afternoon. Having thoroughly confirmed and fortified her suspicions, Nicholas slipped back into the house and rapidly put into execution a plan of action that had long germinated[11] in his brain. By standing on a chair in the library one could reach a shelf on which reposed[12] a fat, important-looking key. The key was as important as it looked; it was the instrument which kept the mysteries of the lumber room secure from unauthorized intrusion, which opened a way only for aunts and such-like privileged persons. Nicholas had not had much experience of the art of fitting keys into keyholes and turning locks, but for some days past he had practiced with the key of the schoolroom door; he did not believe in trusting too much to luck and accident. The key turned stiffly in the lock, but it turned. The door opened, and Nicholas was in an unknown land, compared with which the gooseberry garden was a stale delight, a mere material pleasure.

Often and often Nicholas had pictured to himself what the lumber room might be like, that region that was so carefully sealed from youthful eyes and concerning which no questions were ever answered. It came up to his expectations. In the first place it was large and dimly lit, one high window opening on to the forbidden garden being its only source of illumination. In the second place it was a storehouse of unimagined treasures. The aunt-by-assertion was one of those people who think that things spoil by use and consign them to dust and damp by way of preserving them. Such parts of the house as Nicholas knew best were rather bare and cheerless, but here there were wonderful things for the eye to feast on. First and foremost, there was a piece of framed tapestry that was evidently meant to be a fire screen. To Nicholas it was a living, breathing story; he sat down on a roll of Indian hangings, glowing in wonderful colors beneath a layer of dust, and took in all the details of the tapestry picture. A man, dressed in the hunting costume of some remote period, had just transfixed a stag with an arrow; it could not have been a difficult shot because the stag was only one or two paces away

---

[9] trips

[10] secrecy

[11] grown

[12] rested

from him; in the thickly-growing vegetation that the picture suggested it would not have been difficult to creep up to a feeding stag, and the two spotted dogs that were springing forward to join in the chase had evidently been trained to keep to heel till the arrow was discharged. That part of the picture was simple, if interesting, but did the huntsman see, what Nicholas saw, that four galloping wolves were coming in his direction through the wood? There might be more than four of them hidden behind the trees, and in any case would the man and his dogs be able to cope with the four wolves if they made an attack? The man had only two arrows left in his quiver, and he might miss with one or both of them; all one knew about his skill in shooting was that he could hit a large stag at a ridiculously short range. Nicholas sat for many golden minutes revolving the possibilities of the scene; he was inclined to think that there were more than four wolves and that the man and his dogs were in a tight corner.

But there were other objects of delight and interest claiming his instant attention: there were quaint twisted candlesticks in the shape of snakes, and a teapot fashioned like a china duck, out of whose open beak the tea was supposed to come. How dull and shapeless the nursery teapot seemed in comparison! And there was a carved sandalwood box packed tight with aromatic cottonwool, and between the layers of cottonwool were little brass figures, hump-necked bulls, and peacocks and goblins, delightful to see and to handle. Less promising in appearance was a large square book with plain black covers; Nicholas peeped into it, and, behold, it was full of colored pictures of birds. And such birds! In the garden, and in the lanes when he went for a walk, Nicholas came across a few birds, of which the largest were an occasional magpie or wood-pigeon; here were herons and bustards, kites, toucans, tiger-bitterns, brush turkeys, ibises, golden pheasants, a whole portrait gallery of undreamed-of creatures. And as he was admiring the coloring of the mandarin duck and assigning a life-history to it, the voice of his aunt in shrill vociferation[13] of his name came from the gooseberry garden without. She had grown suspicious at his long disappearance, and had leapt to the conclusion that he had climbed over the wall behind the sheltering screen of the lilac bushes; she was now engaged in energetic and rather hopeless search for him among the artichokes and raspberry canes.

"Nicholas, Nicholas!" she screamed, "you are to come out of this at once. It's no use trying to hide there; I can see you all the time."

It was probably the first time for twenty years that anyone had smiled in that lumber room.

Presently the angry repetitions of Nicholas's name gave way to a shriek, and a cry for somebody to come quickly. Nicholas shut the book, restored it carefully to its place in a corner, and shook some dust from a neighboring

---

[13] cry

pile of newspapers over it. Then he crept from the room, locked the door, and replaced the key exactly where he had found it. His aunt was still calling his name when he sauntered into the front garden.

"Who's calling?" he asked.

"Me," came the answer from the other side of the wall; "didn't you hear me? I've been looking for you in the gooseberry garden, and I've slipped into the rainwater tank. Luckily there's no water in it, but the sides are slippery, and I can't get out. Fetch the ladder from under the cherry tree—"

"I was told I wasn't to go into the gooseberry garden," said Nicholas promptly.

"I told you not to, and now I tell you that you may," came the voice from the rainwater tank, rather impatiently.

"Your voice doesn't sound like aunt's," objected Nicholas; "you may be the Evil One tempting me to be disobedient. Aunt often tells me that the Evil One tempts me and that I always yield. This time I'm not going to yield."

"Don't talk nonsense," said the prisoner in the tank; "go and fetch the ladder."

"Will there be strawberry jam for tea?" asked Nicholas innocently.

"Certainly there will be," said the aunt, privately resolving that Nicholas should have none of it.

"Now I know that you are the Evil One and not aunt," shouted Nicholas gleefully; "when we asked aunt for strawberry jam yesterday, she said there wasn't any. I know there are four jars of it in the store cupboard, because I looked, and of course you know it's there, but she doesn't, because she said there wasn't any. Oh, Devil, you have sold yourself!"

There was an unusual sense of luxury in being able to talk to an aunt as though one was talking to the Evil One, but Nicholas knew, with childish discernment, that such luxuries were not to be overindulged in. He walked noisily away, and it was a kitchenmaid, in search of parsley, who eventually rescued the aunt from the rainwater tank.

Tea that evening was partaken of in a fearsome silence. The tide had been at its highest when the children had arrived at Jagborough Cove, so there had been no sands to play on—a circumstance that the aunt had overlooked in the haste of organizing her punitive[14] expedition. The tightness of Bobby's boots had had disastrous effect on his temper the whole of the afternoon, and altogether the children could not have been said to have enjoyed themselves. The aunt maintained the frozen muteness of one who has suffered undignified and unmerited detention in a rainwater tank for thirty-five minutes. As for Nicholas, he, too, was silent, in the absorption of one who

---

[14] disciplinary

has much to think about; it was just possible, he considered, that the huntsman would escape with his hounds while the wolves feasted on the stricken
stag.

Questions for Review

1. What kind of kid is Nicholas? What makes him still somewhat likable?

2. How does Nicholas get in the lumber room? What does he find there?

3. Explain the trick Nicholas pulls on his "aunt." Why do you think he
   thinks about the huntsman's escape at the story's end?

A Safety Match

By W. W. Jacobs

English writer William Wymark Jacobs (1863-1943) specialized in writing humorous and offbeat short stories, often about the sea and sailors. Jacobs grew up near water (his father was a manager on a wharf on the Thames River in London), and he used what he saw there as inspiration for the stories he later wrote about men who worked on boats. The delightful "A Safety Match" was included in an 1899 collection of short stories titled Sea Urchins.

• • • • •

M
r. Boom, late of the mercantile marine,[1] had the last word, but only by the cowardly expedient[2] of getting out of earshot of his daughter first, and then hurling it at her with a voice trained to compete with hurricanes. Miss Boom avoided a complete defeat by leaning forward with her head on one side in the attitude of an eager but unsuccessful listener, a pose which she abandoned for one of innocent joy when her sire, having been deluded into twice repeating his remarks, was fain[3] to relieve his overstrained muscles by a fit of violent coughing.

"I b'lieve she heard it all along," said Mr. Boom sourly, as he continued his way down the winding lane to the little harbor below. "The only way to live at peace with wimmen is to always be at sea; then they make a fuss of you when you come home—if you don't stay too long, that is."

He reached the quay,[4] with its few tiny cottages, and brown nets spread about to dry in the sun, and walking up and down, grumbling, regarded with jaundiced[5] eye a few small smacks which lay in the harbor, and two or three crusted amphibians lounging aimlessly about.

"Mornin', Mr. Boom," said a stalwart[6] youth in sea boots, appearing suddenly over the edge of the quay from his boat.

"Mornin', Dick," said Mr. Boom affably; "just goin' off?"

"'Bout an hour's time," said the other: "Miss Boom well, sir?"

---

[1] previously with the navy
[2] method
[3] happy
[4] dock
[5] pessimistic
[6] strong

"She's a' right," said Mr. Boom; "me an' her 've just had a few words. She picked up something off the floor what she said was a cake o' mud off my heel. Said she wouldn't have it," continued Mr. Boom, his voice rising. "My own floor too. Swep' it up off the floor with a dustpan and brush, and held it in front of me to look at."

Dick Tarrell gave a grunt which might mean anything—Mr. Boom took it for sympathy.

"I called her old maid," he said with gusto; "'you're a fidgety old maid,' I said. You should ha' seen her look. Do you know what I think, Dick?"

"Not exactly," said Tarrell cautiously.

"I b'leeve she's that savage that she'd take the first man that asked her," said the other triumphantly; "she's sitting up there at the door of the cottage, all by herself."

Tarrell sighed.

"With not a soul to speak to," said Mr. Boom pointedly.

The other kicked at a small crab which was passing, and returned it to its native element in sections.

"I'll walk up there with you if you're going that way," he said at length.

"No, I'm just having a look round," said Mr. Boom, "but there's nothing to hinder you going, Dick, if you've a mind to."

"There's no little thing you want, as I'm going there, I s'pose?" suggested Tarrell. "It's awkward when you go there and say, 'Good morning,' and the girl says, 'Good morning,' and then you don't say any more and she don't say any more. If there was anything you wanted that I could help her look for, it 'ud make talk easier."

"Well—go for my baccy[7] pouch," said Mr. Boom, after a minute's thought. "It'll take you a long time to find that."

"Why?" inquired the other.

"'Cos I've got it here," said the unscrupulous[8] Mr. Boom, producing it, and placidly filling his pipe.

"You might spend—ah—the best part of an hour looking for that."

He turned away with a nod, and Tarrell, after looking about him in a hesitating fashion to make sure that his movements were not attracting the attention his conscience told him they deserved, set off in the hangdog[9] fashion peculiar to nervous lovers up the road to the cottage. Kate Boom was sitting at the door as her father had described, and, in apparent unconsciousness of his approach, did not raise her eyes from her book. "Good morning," said Tarrell, in a husky voice.

---

[7] tobacco
[8] deceitful
[9] intimidated, guilty

Miss Boom returned the salutation, and, marking the place in her book with her forefinger, looked over the hedge on the other side of the road to the sea beyond.

"Your father has left his pouch behind, and being as I was coming this way, asked me to call for it," faltered the young man.

Miss Boom turned her head, and, regarding him steadily, noted the rising color and the shuffling feet.

"Did he say where he had left it?" she inquired.

"No," said the other.

"Well, my time's too valuable to waste looking for pouches," said Kate, bending down to her book again, "but if you like to go in and look for it, you may!"

She moved aside to let him pass, and sat listening with a slight smile as she heard him moving about the room.

"I can't find it," he said, after a pretended search.

"Better try the kitchen now then," said Miss Boom, without looking up, "and then the scullery. It might be in the woodshed or even down the garden. You haven't half looked."

She heard the kitchen door close behind him, and then, taking her book with her, went upstairs to her room. The conscientious Tarrell, having duly searched all the above-mentioned places, returned to the parlor and waited. He waited a quarter of an hour, and then going out by the front door, stood irresolute.[10]

"I can't find it," he said at length, addressing himself to the bedroom window.

"No. I was coming down to tell you," said Miss Boom, glancing sedately at him from over the geraniums. "I remember seeing father take it out with him this morning."

Tarrell affected a clumsy surprise. "It doesn't matter," he said. "How nice your geraniums are."

"Yes, they're all right," said Miss Boom briefly.

"I can't think how you keep 'em so nice," said Tarrell.

"Well, don't try," said Miss Boom kindly. "You'd better go back and tell father about the pouch. Perhaps he's waiting for a smoke all this time."

"There's no hurry," said the young man; "perhaps he's found it."

"Well, I can't stop to talk," said the girl; "I'm busy reading."

With these heartless words she withdrew into the room, and the discomfited swain,[11] only too conscious of the sorry figure he cut, went slowly

---

[10] indecisive
[11] "discomfited swain": embarrassed admirer

back to the harbor, to be met by Mr. Boom with a wink of aggravating and portentous[12] dimensions.

"You've took a long time," he said slyly. "There's nothing like a little scheming in these things."

"It didn't lead to much," said the discomfited Tarrell.

"Don't be in a hurry, my lad," said the elder man, after listening to his experiences. "I've been thinking over this little affair for some time now, an' I think I've got a plan."

"If it's anything about baccy pouches—" began the young man ungratefully.

"It ain't," interrupted Mr. Boom, "it's quite diff'rent. Now, you'd best get aboard your craft and do your duty. There's more young men won girls' 'arts while doing of ther duty than—than—if they wasn't doing their duty. Do you understand me?"

It is inadvisable to quarrel with a prospective father-in-law, so that Tarrell said he did, and with a moody nod tumbled into his boat and put off to the smack. Mr. Boom having walked up and down a bit, and exchanged a few greetings, bent his steps in the direction of the "Jolly Sailor," and, ordering two mugs of ale, set them down on a small bench opposite his old friend Raggett.

"I see young Tarrell go off grumpy-like," said Raggett, drawing a mug towards him and gazing at the fast-receding boats.

"Ay, we'll have to do what we talked about," said Boom slowly. "It's opposition what that gal wants. She simply sits and mopes for the want of somebody to contradict her."

"Well, why don't you do it?" said Raggett. "That ain't much for a father to do surely."

"I hev," said the other slowly, "more than once. O' course, when I insist upon a thing, it's done; but a woman's a delikit creeter, Raggett, and the last row[13] we had she got that ill that she couldn't get up to get my breakfast ready, no, nor my dinner either. It made us both ill, that did."

"Are you going to tell Tarrell?" inquired Raggett.

"No," said his friend. "Like as not he'd tell her just to curry favor with her. I'm going to tell him he's not to come to the house no more. That'll make her want him to come, if anything will. Now there's no use wasting time. You begin today."

"I don't know what to say," murmured Raggett, nodding to him as he raised the beer to his lips.

"Just go now and call in—you might take her a nosegay."[14]

---

[12] important
[13] fight (pronounced to rhyme with "cow")
[14] bouquet of flowers

"I won't do nothing so silly," said Raggett shortly.

"Well, go without 'em," said Boom impatiently; "just go and get your-selves talked about, that's all—have everybody making game of both of you, talking about a good-looking young girl being sweet-hearted by an old chap with one foot in the grave and a face like a dried herring. That's what I want."

Mr. Raggett, who was just about to drink, put his mug down again and regarded his friend fixedly.

"Might, I ask who you're alloodin' to?" he inquired somewhat shortly.

Mr. Boom, brought up in mid-career, shuffled a little and laughed un-easily. "Them ain't my words, old chap," he said; "it was the way she was speaking of you the other day."

"Well, I won't have nothin' to do with it," said Raggett, rising.

"Well, nobody needn't know anything about it," said Boom, pulling him down to his seat again. "She won't tell, I'm sure—she wouldn't like the disgrace of it."

"Look here," said Raggett, getting up again.

"I mean from her point of view," said Mr. Boom querulously;[15] "you're very 'asty,[16] Raggett."

"Well, I don't care about it," said Raggett slowly; "it seemed all right when we was talking about it; but s'pose I have all my trouble for nothing, and she don't take Dick after all? What then?"

"Well, then there's no harm done," said his friend, "and it 'll be a bit o' sport for both of us. You go up and start, an' I'll have another pint of beer and a clean pipe waiting for you against you come back."

Sorely against his better sense Mr. Raggett rose and went off, grumbling. It was fatiguing work on a hot day, climbing the road up the cliff, but he took it quietly, and having gained the top, moved slowly towards the cottage.

"Morning, Mr. Raggett," said Kate cheerily, as he entered the cottage. "Dear, dear, the idea of an old man like you climbing about! It's wonder-ful."

"I'm sixty-seven," said Mr. Raggett viciously, "and I feel as young as ever I did."

"To be sure," said Kate soothingly; "and look as young as ever you did. Come in and sit down a bit."

Mr. Raggett with some trepidation[17] complied, and sitting in a very up-right position, wondered how he should begin. "I am just sixty-seven," he

---

[15] grouchily
[16] hasty
[17] nervousness

said slowly. "I'm not old and I'm not young, but I'm just old enough to begin to want somebody to look after me a bit."

"I shouldn't while I could get about if I were you," said the innocent Kate. "Why not wait until you're bedridden?"

"I don't mean that at all," said Mr. Raggett snappishly. "I mean I'm thinking of getting married."

"Good—gracious!" said Kate, open-mouthed.

"I may have one foot in the grave, and resemble a dried herring in the face," pursued Mr. Raggett with bitter sarcasm, "but—

"You can't help that," said Kate gently.

"But I'm going to get married," said Raggett savagely.

"Well, don't get in a way about it," said the girl. "Of course, if you want to, and—and—you can find somebody else who wants to, there's no reason why you shouldn't! Have you told father about it?"

"I have," said Mr. Raggett, "and he has given his consent."

He put such meaning into this remark, and so much more in the contortion of visage[18] which accompanied it, that the girl stood regarding him in blank astonishment.

"His consent?" she said in a strange voice.

Mr. Raggett nodded.

"I went to him first," he said, trying to speak confidently. "Now I've come to you—I want you to marry me!"

"Don't you be a silly old man, Mr. Raggett," said Kate, recovering her composure. "And as for my father, you go back and tell him I want to see him."

She drew aside and pointed to the door, and Mr. Raggett, thinking that he had done quite enough for one day, passed out and retraced his steps to the "Jolly Sailor." Mr. Boom met him halfway, and having received his message, spent the rest of the morning in fortifying[19] himself for the reception which awaited him.

It would be difficult to say which of the two young people was the more astonished at this sudden change of affairs. Miss Boom, pretending to think that her parent's reason was affected, treated him accordingly, a state of affairs not without its drawbacks, as Mr. Boom found to his cost. Tarrell, on the other hand, attributed it to greed, and being forbidden the house, spent all his time ashore on a stile[20] nearly opposite, sullenly watching events.

For three weeks Mr. Raggett called daily, and after staying to tea, usually wound up the evening by formally proposing for Kate's hand. Both

---

[18] twisting up of the face

[19] strengthening

[20] set steps over a wall

conspirators were surprised and disappointed at the quietness with which Miss Boom received these attacks, Mr. Raggett meeting with a politeness which was a source of much wonder to both of them.

His courting came to an end suddenly. He paused one evening with his hand on the door, and having proposed in the usual manner, was going out, when Miss Boom called him back.

"Sit down, Mr. Raggett," she said calmly. Mr. Raggett, wondering inwardly, resumed his seat.

"You have asked me a good many times to marry you," said Kate.

"I have," said Mr. Raggett, nodding.

"And I'm sure it's very kind of you," continued the girl, "and if I've hurt your feelings by refusing you, it is only because I have thought perhaps I was not good enough for you."

In the silence which followed this unexpected and undeserved tribute to Mr. Raggett's worth, the two old men eyed each other in silent consternation.[21]

"Still, if you've made up your mind," continued the girl, "I don't know that it's for me to object. You're not much to look at, but you've got the loveliest chest of drawers and the best furniture all round in Mastleigh. And I suppose you've got a little money?"

Mr. Raggett shook his head, and in a broken voice was understood to say: "A very little."

"I don't want any fuss or anything of that kind," said Miss Boom calmly. "No bridesmaids or anything of that sort; it wouldn't be suitable at your age."

Mr. Raggett withdrew his pipe, and holding it an inch or two from his mouth, listened like one in a dream.

"Just a few old friends, and a bit of cake," continued Miss Boom musingly. "And instead of spending a lot of money in foolish waste, we'll have three weeks in London."

Mr. Raggett made a gurgling noise in his throat, and suddenly, remembering himself, pretended to think that it was something wrong with his pipe, and removing it blew noisily through the mouthpiece.

"Perhaps," he said, in a trembling voice—"perhaps you'd better take a little longer to consider, my dear."

Kate shook her head. "I've quite made up my mind," she said, "quite. And now I want to marry you just as much as you want to marry me. Good night, father; good night—George."

Mr. Raggett started[22] violently, and collapsed in his chair.

"Raggett," said Mr. Boom huskily.

---

[21] concern

[22] jumped in surprise

"Don't talk to me," said the other, "I can't bear it."

Mr. Boom, respecting his friend's trouble, relapsed into silence again, and for a long time not a word was spoken.

"My 'ed's in a whirl," said Mr. Raggett at length.

"It 'ud be a wonder if it wasn't," said Mr. Boom sympathetically.

"To think," continued the other miserably, "how I've been let in for this. The plots an' the plans and the artfulness what's been goin' on round me, an' I've never seen it."

"What d'ye mean?" demanded Mr. Boom, with sudden violence.

"I know what I mean," said Mr. Raggett darkly.

"P'raps you'll tell me then," said the other.

"Who thought of it first?" demanded Mr. Raggett ferociously. "Who came to me and asked me to court his slip of a girl?"

"Don't you be a old fool," said Mr. Boom heatedly. "It's done now, and what's done can't be undone. I never thought to have a son-in-law seven or eight years older than what I am, and what's more, I don't want it."

"Said I wasn't much to look at, but she liked my chest o' drawers," repeated Raggett mechanically.

"Don't ask me where she gets her natur' from, cos I couldn't tell you," said the unhappy parent; "she don't get it from me."

Mr. Raggett allowed this reflection upon the late Mrs. Boom to pass unnoticed, and taking his hat from the table fixed it firmly upon his head, and gazing with scornful indignation[23] upon his host, stepped slowly out of the door without going through the formality of bidding him good night.

"George," said a voice from above him.

Mr. Raggett started, and glanced up at somebody leaning from the window.

"Come in to tea tomorrow early," said the voice pressingly; "good night, dear."

Mr. Raggett turned and fled into the night, dimly conscious that a dark figure had detached itself from the stile opposite, and was walking beside him.

"That you, Dick?" he inquired nervously, after an oppressive silence.

"That's me," said Dick. "I heard her call you 'dear.'" Mr. Raggett, his face suffused[24] with blushes, hung his head.

"Called you 'dear,'" repeated Dick; "I heard her say it. I'm going to pitch you in the harbor. I'll learn you to go courting a young girl. What are you stopping for?"

---

[23] anger
[24] covered

Mr. Raggett delicately intimated[25] that he was stopping because he preferred, all things considered, to be alone. Finding the young man, however, bent upon accompanying him, he divulged[26] the plot of which he had been the victim, and bitterly lamented his share in it.

"You don't want to marry her then?" said the astonished Dick.

"Course I don't," snarled Mr. Raggett; "I can't afford it. I'm too old; besides which, she'll turn my little place topsy-turvy. Look here, Dick, I done this all for you. Now, it's evident she only wants my furniture: if I give all the best of it to you, she'll take you instead."

"No, she won't," said Dick grimly; "I wouldn't have her now, not if she asked me on her bended knee."

"Why not?" said Raggett.

"I don't want to marry that sort o' girl," said the other scornfully; "it's cured me."

"What about me then?" said the unfortunate Raggett.

"Well, so far as I can see it serves you right for mixing in other people's business," said Dick shortly. "Well, good night, and good luck to you."

To Mr. Raggett's sore disappointment he kept to his resolution, and being approached by Mr. Boom on his elderly friend's behalf, was rudely frank to him.

"I'm a free man again," he said blithely,[27] "and I feel better than I've felt for ever so long. More manly."

"You ought to think of other people," said Mr. Boom severely; "think of poor old Raggett."

"Well, he's got a young wife out of it," said Dick. "I daresay he'll be happy enough. He wants somebody to help him spend his money."

In this happy frame of mind he resumed his ordinary life, and when he encountered his former idol, met her with a heartiness and unconcern which the lady regarded with secret disapproval. He was now so sure of himself that, despite a suspicion of ulterior design[28] on the part of Mr. Boom, he even accepted an invitation to tea.

The presence of Mr. Raggett made it a slow and solemn function. Nobody with any feelings could eat with an appetite with that afflicted man at the table, and the meal passed almost in silence. Kate cleared the meal away, and the men sat at the open door with their pipes while she washed up in the kitchen.

"Me an' Raggett thought o' stepping down to the 'Sailor,'" said Mr. Boom, after a third application of his friend's elbow.

---

[25] hinted

[26] revealed

[27] happily

[28] secret goal

"I'll come with you," said Dick.

"Well, we've got a little business to talk about," said Boom confidentially; "but we sha'n't be long. If you wait here, Dick, we'll see you when we come back."

"All right," said Tarrell.

He watched the two old men down the road, and then, moving his chair back into the room, silently regarded the busy Kate.

"Make yourself useful," said she brightly; "shake the tablecloth."

Tarrell took it to the door, and having shaken it, folded it with much gravity, and handed it back.

"Not so bad for a beginner," said Kate, taking it and putting it in a drawer. She took some needlework from another drawer, and, sitting down, began busily stitching.

"Wedding dress?" inquired Tarrell, with an assumption of great ease.

"No, tablecloth!" said the girl, with a laugh.

"You'll want to know a little more before you get married."

"Plenty o' time for me," said Tarrell; "I'm in no hurry."

The girl put her work down and looked up at him.

"That's right," she said staidly.[29] "I suppose you were rather surprised to hear I was going to get married?"

"A little," said Tarrell; "there's been so many after old Raggett, I didn't think he'd ever be caught."

"Oh!" said Kate.

"I daresay he'll make a very good husband," said Tarrell patronizingly. "I think you'll make a nice couple. He's got a nice home."

"That's why I'm going to marry him," said Kate. "Do you think it's wrong to marry a man for that?"

"That's your business," said Tarrell coldly. "Speaking for myself, and not wishing to hurt your feelings, I shouldn't like to marry a girl like that."

"You mean you wouldn't like to marry me?" said Kate softly.

She leaned forward as she spoke, until her breath fanned his face.

"That's what I do mean," said Tarrell, with a suspicion of doggedness in his voice.

"Not even if I asked you on my bended knees?" said Kate. "Aren't you glad you're cured?"

"Yes," said Tarrell manfully.

"So am I," said the girl; "and now that you are happy, just go down to the 'Jolly Sailor,' and make poor old Raggett happy too."

"How?" asked Tarrell.

"Tell him that I have only been having a joke with him," said Kate, surveying him with a steady smile. "Tell him that I overheard him and father

---

[29] seriously

talking one night, and that I resolved to give them both a lesson. And tell them that I didn't think anybody could have been so stupid as they have been to believe in it."

She leaned back in her chair, and, regarding the dumbfounded Tarrell with a smile of wicked triumph, waited for him to speak. "Raggett, indeed!" she said disdainfully.

"I suppose," said Tarrell at length, speaking very slowly, "my being stupid was no surprise to you?"

"Not a bit," said the girl cheerfully.

"I'll ask you to tell Raggett yourself," said Tarrell, rising and moving towards the door. "I sha'n't see him. Good night."

"Good night," said she. "Where are you going, then?"

There was no reply.

"Where are you going?" she repeated. Then a suspicion of his purpose flashed across her. "You're not foolish enough to be going away?" she cried in dismay.

"Why not?" said Tarrell slowly.

"Because," said Kate, looking down—"oh, because—well, it's ridiculous. I'd sooner have you stay here and feel what a stupid you've been making of yourself. I want to remind you of it sometimes."

"I don't want reminding," said Tarrell, taking Raggett's chair; "I know it now."

Questions for Review

1. What does Mr. Boom claim to Dick Tarrell about Kate's state of mind at the story's opening? How does Dick's attempt at speaking with her privately go?

2. How does Boom try to use Raggett? What does *he* think of the plan?

3. What is Kate's surprising answer to Raggett's proposal? How does he react?

4. Describe the conversation between Kate and Dick after her father and Raggett leave.

5. Look up the term "safety match." What does it mean? Why do you think the story is titled "Safety Match"?

On Raising Questions

By Charles Spurgeon

English preacher Charles Spurgeon (1834-1892) be-gan preaching as a young man, quickly gaining atten-tion for his booming voice (he could be heard—with no microphone, of course—by 20,000 persons at a time!). More importantly, he gave outspoken, plain messages about Jesus aimed at the ordinary person. This mes-sage comes from an 1890 book titled Around the Wic-ket Gate: Or, a Friendly Talk with Seekers Concerning Faith in the Lord Jesus Christ.

• • • • •

In these days, a simple, childlike faith is very rare; but the usual thing is to believe nothing, and question everything. Doubts are as plentiful as blackberries, and all hands and lips are stained with them. To me it seems very strange that men should hunt up difficulties as to their own sal-vation. If I were doomed to die, and I had a hint of mercy, I am sure I should not set my wits to work to find out reasons why I should *not* be pardoned. I could leave my enemies to do that: I should be on the lookout in a very different direction.

If I were drowning, I should sooner catch at a straw than push a life-belt away from me. To reason against one's own life is a sort of constructive suicide of which only a drunken man would be guilty. To argue against your only hope is like a foolish man sitting on a bough, and chopping it away so as to let himself down.

Who but an idiot would do that?

Yet many appear to be special pleaders for their own ruin. They hunt the Bible through for threatening texts; and when they have done with that, they turn to reason, and philosophy, and skepticism,[1] in order to shut the door in their own faces. Surely this is poor employment for a sensible man.

Many nowadays who cannot quite get away from religious thought are able to stave off the inconvenient pressure of conscience by quibbling over the great truths of revelation.[2] Great mysteries are in the Book of God of necessity; for how can the infinite God so speak that all his thoughts can be grasped by finite man? But it is the height of folly to get discussing these deep things, and to leave plain, soul-saving truths in abeyance.[3] It reminds one of the two philosophers who debated about food, and went away empty from the table, while the common countryman in the corner asked no question, but used his knife and fork with great diligence, and went on his way rejoicing.

Thousands are now happy in the Lord through receiving the gospel like little children; while others, who can always see difficulties, or invent them, are as far off as ever from any comfortable hope of salvation....The fact is, that we most of us *know* quite enough already, and the real want with us is not light in the head, but truth in the heart; not help over difficulties, but grace to make us hate sin and seek reconciliation.

Here let me add a warning against tampering with the Word of God. No habit can be more ruinous to the soul. It is cool, contemptuous imperti-

---

[1] distrust, disbelief
[2] the revealed Word of God (the Bible)
[3] suspension, or putting off thinking about it

nence[4] to sit down and correct your Maker, and it tends to make the heart harder than the millstone. We remember one who used a penknife on his Bible,[5] and it was not long before he had given up all his former beliefs. The spirit of reverence is healthy, but the impertinence of criticizing the inspired Word is destructive of all proper feeling towards God.

If ever a man does feel his need of a Savior after treating Scripture with a proud, critical spirit, he is very apt to find his conscience standing in the way, and hindering him from comfort by reminding him of ill-treatment of the sacred Word. It comes hard to him to draw consolation[6] out of passages of the Bible which he has treated cavalierly,[7] or even set aside altogether, as unworthy of consideration. In his distress the sacred texts seem to laugh at his calamity.[8] When the time of need comes, the wells which he stopped with stones yield no water for his thirst. Beware, when you despise a Scripture, lest you cast away the only friend that can help you in the hour of agony.

A certain German duke was accustomed to call upon his servant to read a chapter of the Bible to him every morning. When anything did not square with his judgment he would sternly cry, "Hans, strike that out." At length Hans was a long time before he began to read. He fumbled over the Book, till his master called out, "Hans, why do you not read?" Then Hans answered, "Sir, there is hardly anything left. It is all struck out!" One day his master's objections had run one way, and another day they had taken another turn, and another set of passages had been blotted, till nothing was left to instruct or comfort him. Let us not, by carping[9] criticism, destroy our own mercies. We may yet need those promises which appear needless; and those portions of Holy Writ which have been most assailed[10] by skeptics may yet prove essential to our very life: wherefore let us guard the priceless treasure of the Bible, and determine never to resign a single line of it.

What have we to do with recondite[11] questions while our souls are in peril? The way to escape from sin is plain enough. The wayfaring man, though a fool, shall not err therein. God has not mocked us with a salvation which we cannot understand. BELIEVE AND LIVE is a command which a babe may comprehend and obey.

> Doubt no more, but now believe;
> Question not, but just receive.

---

[4] "contemptuous impertinence": mocking arrogance
[5] that is, to cut out all the teachings he thought were wrong
[6] comfort, relief
[7] casually, disrespectfully
[8] misfortune
[9] grouching, complaining
[10] attacked
[11] complicated, hard to understand

Artful doubts and reasonings be
Nailed with Jesus to the tree.

Instead of caviling[12] at Scripture, the man who is led of the Spirit of God will close in with the Lord Jesus at once. Seeing that thousands of decent, common-sense people—people, too, of the best character—are trusting their all with Jesus, he will do the same, and have done with further delays. Then has he begun a life worth living, and he may have done with further fear. He may at once advance to that higher and better way of living, which grows out of love to Jesus, the Savior. Why should not the reader do so at once? Oh, that he would!

A Newark, New Jersey butcher received a letter from his old home in Germany, notifying that he had, by the death of a relative, fallen heir to a considerable amount of money. He was cutting up a pig at the time. After reading the letter, he hastily tore off his dirty apron, and did not stop to see the pork cut up into sausages, but left the shop to make preparations for going home to Germany. Do you blame him, or would you have had him stop in Newark with his block and his cleaver?

See here the operation of faith. The butcher believed what was told him, and acted on it at once. Sensible fellow, too!

God has sent his messages to man, telling him the good news of salvation. When a man believes the good news to be true, he accepts the blessing announced to him, and hastens to lay hold upon it. If he truly believes, he will at once take Christ, with all he has to bestow, turn from his present evil ways, and set out for the Heavenly City, where the full blessing is to be enjoyed. He cannot be holy too soon, or too early quit the ways of sin. If a

---

[12] nitpicking

man could really see what sin is, he would flee from it as from a deadly serpent, and rejoice to be freed from it by Christ Jesus.

Questions for Review

1. What would you say is the author's main point in "On Raising Questions"?

2. Explain the "two philosophers and a countryman" illustration.

3. Why does the author say it's dangerous for someone to cut out or disbelieve this or that part of the Bible as just a fairy tale, or incorrect?

Thankfulness

By Adelaide Procter

The following poem by English poet Adelaide Procter (1825-1864), is unusual. But then, Adelaide Procter was an unusual poet. Famous and well-liked in her day, Procter was said to be Queen Victoria's favorite, but she played down any claims to being famous. "Thankfulness" shows gratitude to God for some curious blessings.

• • • • •

My God, I thank Thee who hast made
The Earth so bright;
So full of splendor and of joy,
Beauty and light;
So many glorious things are here,
Noble and right!

I thank Thee, too, that Thou hast made
Joy to abound:[1]
So many gentle thoughts and deeds
Circling us round,
That in the darkest spot of Earth
Some love is found.

I thank Thee more than all our joy
Is touched with pain;
That shadows fall on brightest hours;
That thorns remain;
So that Earth's bliss may be our guide,
And not our chain.

For Thou who knowest, Lord, how soon
Our weak heart clings,
Hast given us joys, tender and true,
Yet all with wings,
So that we see, gleaming on high,
Diviner[2] things!

---

[1] overflow (Romans 15:13: "Now the God of hope fill you with all **joy** and peace in believing, that ye may abound in hope, through the power of the Holy Ghost.")
[2] more heavenly

I thank Thee, Lord, that Thou hast kept
The best in store;
We have enough, yet not too much
To long for more:
A yearning for a deeper peace,
Not known before.

I thank Thee, Lord, that here our souls,
Though amply[3] blest,
Can never find, although they seek,
A perfect rest—
Nor ever shall, until they lean
On Jesus' breast!

Questions for Review

1. Why does the author, interestingly, thank God that "our joy is touched with pain"? (See the third stanza.)

2. How does it affect a Christians' life to know that—as it says in the fifth stanza—"the best [is] in store"?

3. Write a six-line "seventh stanza" to "Thankfulness" in which you express your thankfulness to God for something else He's done for you.

---

[3] fully

The Pimientia Pancakes

By O. Henry

"O. Henry" was the pen name of William Sidney Porter (1862-1910). Porter has as much right as anybody to be called the greatest short story writer that America ever produced. He churned out hundreds of these wonderful little tales, filled with unforgettable characters, witty dialogue, unique plots, and striking endings. "The Pimientia Pancakes," which first appeared in a 1903 issue of McCall's *magazine, perfectly illustrates O. Henry's exceptional talents.*

• • • • •

While we were rounding up a bunch of the Triangle-O cattle in the Frio bottoms,[1] a projecting branch of a dead mesquite caught my wooden stirrup and gave my ankle a wrench that laid me up in camp for a week.

On the third day of my compulsory idleness,[2] I crawled out near the grub wagon, and reclined helpless under the conversational fire of Judson Odom, the camp cook. Jud was a monologist[3] by nature, whom Destiny, with customary blundering, had set in a profession wherein he was bereaved,[4] for the greater portion of his time, of an audience.

---

[1] The Frio is a river in Texas.
[2] "compulsory idleness": forced rest
[3] public speaker
[4] deprived

Therefore, I was manna in the desert of Jud's obmutescence.[5]

Betimes I was stirred by invalid longings for something to eat that did not come under the caption of "grub." I had visions of the maternal pantry[6] "deep as first love, and wild with all regret," and then I asked:

"Jud, can you make pancakes?"

Jud laid down his six-shooter, with which he was preparing to pound an antelope steak, and stood over me in what I felt to be a menacing attitude. He further endorsed my impression that his pose was resentful by fixing upon me with his light blue eyes a look of cold suspicion.

"Say, you," he said, with candid, though not excessive, choler,[7] "did you mean that straight, or was you trying to throw the gaff into me? Some of the boys been telling you about me and that pancake racket?"

"No, Jud," I said, sincerely, "I meant it. It seems to me I'd swap my pony and saddle for a stack of buttered brown pancakes with some first crop, open kettle, New Orleans sweetening. Was there a story about pancakes?"

Jud was mollified[8] at once when he saw that I had not been dealing in allusions. He brought some mysterious bags and tin boxes from the grub wagon and set them in the shade of the hackberry where I lay reclined. I watched him as he began to arrange them leisurely and untie their many strings.

"No, not a story," said Jud, as he worked, "but just the logical disclosures in the case of me and that pink-eyed snoozer[9] from Mired Mule Canada and Miss Willella Learight. I don't mind telling you.

"I was punching[10] then for old Bill Toomey, on the San Miguel.[11] One day I gets all ensnared up in aspirations for to eat some canned grub that hasn't ever mooed or baaed or grunted or been in peck measures. So, I gets on my bronc and pushes the wind for Uncle Emsley Telfair's store at the Pimienta Crossing on the Nueces.

"About three in the afternoon I threw my bridle rein over a mesquite limb and walked the last twenty yards into Uncle Emsley's store. I got up on the counter and told Uncle Emsley that the signs pointed to the devastation of the fruit crop of the world. In a minute I had a bag of crackers and a long-handled spoon, with an open can each of apricots and pineapples and cherries and greengages beside of me with Uncle Emsley busy chopping away with the hatchet at the yellow clings. I was feeling like Adam before the apple stampede, and was digging my spurs into the side of the counter

---

[5] silence

[6] "maternal pantry": cooking Mom used to do

[7] anger

[8] calmed

[9] sheep rancher

[10] herding cattle

[11] a river in Colorado

and working with my twenty-four-inch spoon when I happened to look out of the window into the yard of Uncle Emsley's house, which was next to the store.

"There was a girl standing there—an imported girl with fixings on—philandering with a croquet maul and amusing herself by watching my style of encouraging the fruit canning industry.

"I slid off the counter and delivered up my shovel to Uncle Emsley.

"'That's my niece,' says he; 'Miss Willella Learight, down from Palestine[12] on a visit. Do you want that I should make you acquainted?'

"'The Holy Land,' I says to myself, my thoughts milling some as I tried to run 'em into the corral. 'Why not? There was sure angels in Pales—why, yes, Uncle Emsley,' I says out loud, 'I'd be awful edified to meet Miss Learight.'

"So Uncle Emsley took me out in the yard and gave us each other's entitlements.

"I never was shy about women. I never could understand why some men who can break a mustang before

breakfast and shave in the dark, get all left-handed and full of perspiration and excuses when they see a bold of calico draped around what belongs to it. Inside of eight minutes me and Miss Willella was aggravating the croquet balls around as amiable[13] as second cousins. She gave me a dig about the quantity of canned fruit I had eaten, and I got back at her, flat-footed, about how a certain lady named Eve started the fruit trouble in the first free-grass pasture— 'Over in Palestine, wasn't it?' says I, as easy and pat as roping a one-year-old.

"That was how I acquired cordiality for the proximities of Miss Willella Learight; and the disposition grew larger as time passed. She was stopping at Pimienta Crossing for her health, which was very good, and for the climate, which was forty percent hotter than Palestine. I rode over to see her

---

[12] a city in Texas
[13] friendly

once every week for a while; and then I figured it out that if I doubled the number of trips I would see her twice as often.

"One week I slipped in a third trip; and that's where the pancakes and the pink-eyed snoozer busted into the game.

"That evening, while I set on the counter with a peach and two damsons[14] in my mouth, I asked Uncle Emsley how Miss Willella was.

"'Why,' says Uncle Emsley, 'she's gone riding with Jackson Bird, the sheep man from over at Mired Mule Canada.'

"I swallowed the peach seed and the two damson seeds. I guess somebody held the counter by the bridle while I got off; and then I walked out straight ahead till I butted against the mesquite where my roan was tied.

"'She's gone riding,' I whisper in my bronc's ear, 'with Birdstone Jack, the hired mule from Sheep Man's Canada. Did you get that, old Leather-and-Gallops?'

"That bronc of mine wept, in his way. He'd been raised a cow pony and he didn't care for snoozers.

"I went back and said to Uncle Emsley: 'Did you say a sheep man?'

"'I said a sheep man,' says Uncle Emsley again. 'You must have heard tell of Jackson Bird. He's got eight sections of grazing and four thousand head of the finest Merinos south of the Arctic Circle.'

"I went out and sat on the ground in the shade of the store and leaned against a prickly pear. I sifted sand into my boots with unthinking hands while I soliloquized[15] a quantity about this bird with the Jackson plumage to his name.

"I never had believed in harming sheep men. I see one, one day, reading a Latin grammar on hossback, and I never touched him! They never irritated me like they do most cowmen. You wouldn't go to work now, and impair and disfigure snoozers, would you, that eat on tables and wear little shoes and speak to you on subjects? I had always let 'em pass, just as you would a jackrabbit; with a polite word and a guess about the weather, but no stopping to swap canteens. I never thought it was worthwhile to be hostile with a snoozer. And because I'd been lenient, and let 'em live, here was one going around riding with Miss Willella Learight!

"An hour by sun they come loping back, and stopped at Uncle Emsley's gate. The sheep person helped her off; and they stood throwing each other sentences all sprightful and sagacious[16] for a while. And then this feathered Jackson flies up in his saddle and raises his little stewpot of a hat, and trots off in the direction of his mutton ranch. By this time I had turned the sand

---

[14] plums
[15] talked to himself
[16] intelligent

out of my boots and unpinned myself from the prickly pear; and by the time he gets half a mile out of Pimienta, I singlefoots up beside him on my bronc.

"I said that snoozer was pink-eyed, but he wasn't. His seeing arrangement was grey enough, but his eyelashes was pink and his hair was sandy, and that gave you the idea. Sheep man?—he wasn't more than a lamb man, anyhow—a little thing with his neck involved in a yellow silk handkerchief, and shoes tied up in bowknots.

"'Afternoon!' says I to him. 'You now ride with a equestrian who is commonly called Dead-Moral-Certainty Judson, on account of the way I shoot. When I want a stranger to know me I always introduce myself before the draw, for I never did like to shake hands with ghosts.'

"'Ah,' says he, just like that—'Ah, I'm glad to know you, Mr. Judson. I'm Jackson Bird, from over at Mired Mule Ranch.'

"Just then one of my eyes saw a roadrunner skipping down the hill with a young tarantula in his bill, and the other eye noticed a rabbit-hawk sitting on a dead limb in a water elm. I popped over one after the other with my forty-five, just to show him. 'Two out of three,' says I. 'Birds just naturally seem to draw my fire wherever I go.'[17]

"'Nice shooting,' says the sheep man, without a flutter. 'But don't you sometimes ever miss the third shot? Elegant fine rain that was last week for the young grass, Mr. Judson?' says he.

"'Willie,' says I, riding over close to his palfrey, 'your infatuated[18] parents may have denounced you by the name of Jackson, but you sure molted into a twittering Willie—let us slough off this here analysis of rain and the elements, and get down to talk that is outside the vocabulary of parrots. That is a bad habit you have got of riding with young ladies over at Pimienta. I've known birds,' says I, 'to be served on toast for less than that.

---

[17] Do you get Judson's joke/threat there?
[18] in love

Miss Willella,' says I, 'don't ever want any nest made out of sheep's wool by a bird of the Jacksonian branch of ornithology. Now, are you going to quit, or do you wish for to gallop up against this Dead-Moral-Certainty attachment to my name, which is good for two hyphens and at least one set of funeral obsequies?'[19]

"Jackson Bird flushed up some, and then he laughed.

"'Why, Mr. Judson,' says he, 'you've got the wrong idea. I've called on Miss Learight a few times; but not for the purpose you imagine. My object is purely a gastronomical[20] one.'

"I reached for my gun.

"'Any coyote,' says I, 'that would boast of dishonorable—'

"'Wait a minute,' says this Bird, 'till I explain. What would I do with a wife? If you ever saw that ranch of mine! I do my own cooking and mending. Eating—that's all the pleasure I get out of sheep raising. Mr. Judson, did you ever taste the pancakes that Miss Learight makes?'

"'Me? No,' I told him. 'I never was advised that she was up to any culinary maneuvers.'

"'They're golden sunshine,' says he, 'honey-browned by the ambrosial fires of Epicurus. I'd give two years of my life to get the recipe for making them pancakes. That's what I went to see Miss Learight for,' says Jackson Bird, 'but I haven't been able to get it from her. It's an old recipe that's been in the family for seventy-five years. They hand it down from one generation to another, but they don't give it away to outsiders. If I could get that recipe, so I could make them pancakes for myself on my ranch, I'd be a happy man,' says Bird.

"'Are you sure,' I says to him, 'that it ain't the hand that mixes the pancakes that you're after?'

"'Sure,' says Jackson. 'Miss Learight is a mighty nice girl, but I can assure you my intentions go no further than the gastro—' but he seen my hand going down to my holster and he changed his similitude—'than the desire to procure a copy of the pancake recipe,' he finishes.

"'You ain't such a bad little man,' says I, trying to be fair. 'I was thinking some of making orphans of your sheep, but I'll let you fly away this time. But you stick to pancakes,' says I, 'as close as the middle one of a stack; and don't go and mistake sentiments for syrup, or there'll be singing at your ranch, and you won't hear it.'

"'To convince you that I am sincere,' says the sheep man, 'I'll ask you to help me. Miss Learight and you being closer friends, maybe she would do for you what she wouldn't for me. If you will get me a copy of that pancake recipe, I give you my word that I'll never call upon her again.'

---

[19] services
[20] having to do with the stomach or eating

"'That's fair,' I says, and I shook hands with Jackson Bird. 'I'll get it for you if I can, and glad to oblige.' And he turned off down the big pear flat on the Piedra, in the direction of Mired Mule; and I steered northwest for old Bill Toomey's ranch.

"It was five days afterward when I got another chance to ride over to pimienta. Miss Willella and me passed a gratifying evening at Uncle Emsley's. She sang some, and exasperated the piano quite a lot with quotations from the operas. I gave imitations of a rattlesnake, and told her about Snaky McFee's new way of skinning cows, and described the trip I made to Saint Louis once. We was getting along in one another's estimations fine. Thinks I, if Jackson Bird can now be persuaded to migrate, I win. I recollect his promise about the pancake receipt, and I thinks I will persuade it from Miss Willella and give it to him; and then if I catches Birdie off of Mired Mule again, I'll make him hop the twig.

"So, along about ten o'clock, I put on a wheedling[21] smile and says to Miss Willella: 'Now, if there's anything I do like better than the sight of a red steer on green grass it's the taste of a nice hot pancake smothered in sugar-house molasses.'

"Miss Willella gives a little jump on the piano stool, and looked at me curious.

"'Yes,' says she, 'they're real nice. What did you say was the name of that street in Saint Louis, Mr. Odom, where you lost your hat?'

---

[21] charming

"'Pancake Avenue,' says I, with a wink, to show her that I was on about the family receipt, and couldn't be side-corralled off of the subject. 'Come, now, Miss Willella,' I says; 'let's hear how you make 'em. Pancakes is just whirling in my head like wagon wheels. Start her off, now—pound of flour, eight dozen eggs, and so on. How does the catalogue of constituents run?'

"'Excuse me for a moment, please,' says Miss Willella, and she gives me a quick kind of sideways look, and slides off the stool. She ambled out into the other room, and directly Uncle Emsley comes in in his shirt sleeves, with a pitcher of water. He turns around to get a glass on the table, and I see a forty-five in his hip pocket. 'Great post-holes!' thinks I, 'but here's a family thinks a heap of cooking receipts, protecting it with firearms. I've known outfits that wouldn't do that much by a family feud.'

"'Drink this here down,' says Uncle Emsley, handing me the glass of water. 'You've rid too far today, Jud, and got yourself over-excited. Try to think about something else now.'

"'Do you know how to make them pancakes, Uncle Emsley?' I asked.

"'Well, I'm not as apprised in the anatomy of them as some,' says Uncle Emsley, 'but I reckon you take a sifter of plaster of Paris and a little dough and saleratus[22] and corn meal, and mix 'em with eggs and buttermilk as usual. Is old Bill going to ship beeves to Kansas City again this spring, Jud?'

"That was all the pancake specifications I could get that night. I didn't wonder that Jackson Bird found it uphill work. So I dropped the subject and talked with Uncle Emsley for a while about hollow-horn and cyclones. And

---

[22] baking soda

then Miss Willella came and said 'Good night,' and I hit the breeze for the ranch.

"About a week afterward I met Jackson Bird riding out of Pimienta as I rode in, and we stopped on the road for a few frivolous[23] remarks.

"'Got the bill of particulars for them flapjacks yet?' I asked him.

"'Well, no,' says Jackson. 'I don't seem to have any success in getting hold of it. Did you try?'

"'I did,' says I, 'and 'twas like trying to dig a prairie dog out of his hole with a peanut hull. That pancake receipt must be a jookalorum,[24] the way they hold on to it.'

"'I'm most ready to give it up,' says Jackson, so discouraged in his pronunciations that I felt sorry for him; 'but I did want to know how to make them pancakes to eat on my lonely ranch,' says he. 'I lie awake at nights thinking how good they are.'

"'You keep on trying for it,' I tells him, 'and I'll do the same. One of us is bound to get a rope over its horns before long. Well, so long, Jacksy.'

"You see, by this time we were on the peacefulest of terms. When I saw that he wasn't after Miss Willella, I had more endurable contemplations[25] of that sandy-haired snoozer. In order to help out the ambitions of his appetite I kept on trying to get that receipt from Miss Willella. But every time I would say 'pancakes' she would get sort of remote and fidgety about the eye, and try to change the subject. If I held her to it she would slide out and round up Uncle Emsley with his pitcher of water and hip-pocket howitzer.[26]

"One day I galloped over to the store with a fine bunch of blue verbenas that I cut out of a herd of wildflowers over on Poisoned Dog Prairie. Uncle Emsley looked at 'em with one eye shut and says:

"'Haven't ye heard the news?'

"'Cattle up?' I asks.

"'Willella and Jackson Bird was married in Palestine yesterday,' says he. 'Just got a letter this morning.'

"I dropped them flowers in a cracker-barrel, and let the news trickle in my ears and down toward my upper left-hand shirt pocket until it got to my feet.

"'Would you mind saying that over again once more, Uncle Emsley?' says I. 'Maybe my hearing has got wrong, and you only said that prime heifers was $4.80 on the hoof, or something like that.'

"'Married yesterday,' says Uncle Emsley, 'and gone to Waco and Niagara Falls on a wedding tour. Why, didn't you see none of the signs all

---

[23] silly, trivial

[24] a real puzzle or problem (O. Henry made this word up himself)

[25] thoughts

[26] "hip-pocket howitzer": gun

along? Jackson Bird has been courting Willella ever since that day he took her out riding.'

"'Then,' says I, in a kind of yell, 'what was all this zizzaparoola he gives me about pancakes? Tell me that.'

"When I said 'pancakes' Uncle Emsley sort of dodged and stepped back.

"'Somebody's been dealing me pancakes from the bottom of the deck,' I says, 'and I'll find out. I believe you know. Talk up,' says I, 'or we'll mix a panful of batter right here.'

"I slid over the counter after Uncle Emsley. He grabbed at his gun, but it was in a drawer, and he missed it two inches. I got him by the front of his shirt and shoved him in a corner.

"'Talk pancakes,' says I, 'or be made into one. Does Miss Willella make 'em?'

"'She never made one in her life, and I never saw one,' says Uncle Emsley, soothing. 'Calm down now, Jud—calm down. You've got excited, and that wound in your head is contaminating your sense of intelligence. Try not to think about pancakes.'

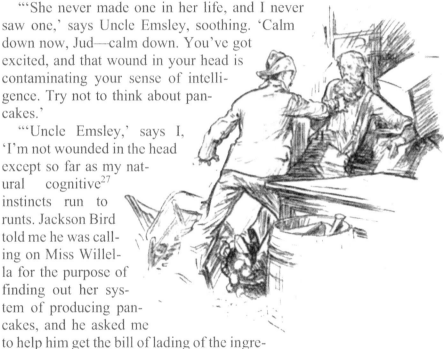

"'Uncle Emsley,' says I, 'I'm not wounded in the head except so far as my natural cognitive[27] instincts run to runts. Jackson Bird told me he was calling on Miss Willella for the purpose of finding out her system of producing pancakes, and he asked me to help him get the bill of lading of the ingredients. I done so, with the results as you see. Have I been sodded down with Johnson grass by a pink-eyed snoozer, or what?'

"'Slack up your grip in my dress shirt,' says Uncle Emsley, 'and I'll tell you. Yes, it looks like Jackson Bird has gone and humbugged you some. The day after he went riding with Willella he came back and told me and her to watch out for you whenever you got to talking about pancakes. He said you was in camp once where they was cooking flapjacks, and one of the fellows cut you over the head with a frying pan. Jackson said that when-

---

[27] mental

ever you got overhot or excited that wound hurt you and made you kind of crazy, and you went raving about pancakes. He told us to just get you worked off of the subject and soothed down, and you wouldn't be danger-ous. So, me and Willella done the best by you we knew how. Well, well,' says Uncle Emsley, 'that Jackson Bird is sure a seldom kind of a snoozer.'"

During the progress of Jud's story he had been slowly but deftly com-bining certain portions of the contents of his sacks and cans. Toward the close of it he set before me the finished product—a pair of red-hot, rich-hued pancakes on a tin plate. From some secret hoarding he also brought a lump of excellent butter and a bottle of golden syrup.

"How long ago did these things happen?" I asked him.

"Three years," said Jud. "They're living on the Mired Mule Ranch now. But I haven't seen either of 'em since. They say Jackson Bird was fixing his ranch up fine with rocking chairs and window curtains all the time he was putting me up the pancake tree. Oh, I got over it after a while. But the boys kept the racket up."

"Did you make these cakes by the famous recipe?" I asked.

"Didn't I tell you there wasn't no recipe?" said Jud. "The boys hollered pancakes till they got pancake hungry, and I cut this recipe out of a news-paper. How does the truck taste?"

"They're delicious," I answered. "Why don't you have some, too, Jud?" I was sure I heard a sigh.

"Me?" said Jud. "I don't ever eat 'em."

Questions for Review

1. How does Judson's often fancy way of talking contrast with his beha-vior toward Willella Learight and Jackson Bird?

2. What is the basic gag that Jackson Bird uses to fool Jud? In what fun-ny ways do Willella and Uncle Emsley act when Jud asks about pan-cakes?

3. What common elements of a tale set in the American West does this story contain? How is the gunfighting element different?

My First Christmas Tree

By Hamlin Garland

This charming essay, from Wisconsin native Hamlin Garland (1860-1940) was written in 1911. Garland lived in different areas of the Midwest as a boy, from Iowa to the Dakotas, and experienced hard farm labor, freezing winters, and other hardships. Many of his novels and short stories included the hardworking farmers and small-town residents of the Midwest. "My First Christmas Tree" is a magical remembrance of a special Christmas Eve in his childhood.

· · · · ·

I will begin by saying that we never had a Christmas tree in our house in the Wisconsin coulee;[1] indeed, my father never saw one in a family circle till he saw that which I set up for my own children last year. But we celebrated Christmas in those days, always, and I cannot remember a time when we did not all hang up our stockings for "Sandy Claws" to fill. As I look back upon those days it seems as if the snows were always deep, the night skies crystal clear, and the stars especially lustrous[2] with frosty sparkles of blue and yellow fire, and probably this was so, for we lived in a northern land where winter was usually stern and always long.

I recall one Christmas when "Sandy" brought me a sled and a horse that stood on rollers—a wonderful tin horse, which I very shortly split in two in order to see what his insides were. Father traded a cord of wood for the sled, and the horse cost twenty cents, but they made the day wonderful.

Another notable Christmas Day, as I stood in our front yard, mid-leg-deep in snow, a neighbor drove by closely muffled in furs, while behind his seat his son, a lad of twelve or fifteen, stood beside a barrel of apples, and as he passed, he hurled a glorious big one at me. It missed me, but bored a deep, round hole in the soft snow. I thrill yet with the remembered joy of burrowing for that delicious bomb. Nothing will ever smell quite as good as that Winesap or Northern Spy or whatever it was. It was wayward[3] impulse on the part of the boy in the sleigh, but it warms my heart after more than forty years.

We had no chimney in our home, but the stocking hanging was a ceremony nevertheless. My parents, and especially my mother, entered into it

---

[1] valley
[2] shiny
[3] naughty

with the best of humor. They always put up their own stockings or permitted us to do it for them, and they always laughed the next morning when they found potatoes or ears of corn in them. I can see now that my mother's laugh had a tear in it, for she loved pretty things and seldom got any during the years that we lived in the coulee.

When I was ten years old, we moved to Mitchell County, an Iowa prairie land, and there we prospered in such ways that our stocking always held toys of some sort, and even my mother's stocking occasionally sagged with a simple piece of jewelry or a new comb or brush. But the thought of a family tree remained the luxury of millionaire city dwellers; indeed, it was not till my fifteenth or sixteenth year that our Sunday school rose to the extravagance of a tree and it is of this wondrous festival that I write.

The land about us was only partly cultivated at this time, and our district schoolhouse, a bare little box, was set bleakly on the prairie; but the Burr Oak schoolhouse was not only larger, but it stood beneath great oaks as well and possessed the charm of a forest background through which a stream ran silently. It was our chief social center. There on a Sunday a regular preacher held "divine service" with Sunday school as a sequence. At night—usually on Friday nights—the young people met in "lyceums," as we called them, to debate great questions or to "speak pieces" and read essays, and here it was that I saw my first Christmas tree.

I walked to that tree across four miles of moonlit snow. Snow? No, it was a floor of diamond, a magical world, so beautiful that my heart still aches with the wonder of it and with the regret that it has all gone—gone with the keen eyes and the bounding pulses of the boy.

Our home at the time was a small frame house on the prairie almost directly west of the Burr Oak grove, and as it was too cold to take the horses out, my brother and I, with our tall boots, our visored caps, and our long woolen mufflers, started forth afoot defiant of the cold. We left the gate on the trot, bound for a sight of the glittering unknown. The snow was deep, and we moved side by side in the grooves made by the hoofs of the horses, setting our feet in the shine left by the broad shoes of the wood sleighs whose going had smoothed the way for us. Our breaths rose like smoke in the still air. It must have been ten below zero, but that did not trouble us in those days, and at last we came in sight of the lights, in sound of the singing, the laughter, the bells of the feast.

It was a poor little building without tower or bell, and its low walls had but three windows on a side, and yet it seemed very imposing to me that night as I crossed the threshold and faced the strange people who packed it to the door. I say "strange people," for though I had seen most of them many times, they all seemed somehow alien to me that night; therefore I stood against the wall and gazed with open-eyed marveling at the shining pine which stood where the pulpit was wont to be. I was made to feel the more embarrassed by reason of the remark of a boy who accused me of having forgotten to comb my hair.

This was not true, but the cap I wore always matted my hair down over my brow, and then, when I lifted it off, invariably[4] disarranged it completely. Nevertheless, I felt guilty—and hot. I don't suppose my hair was artistically barbered that night—I rather guess Mother had used the shears—and I can believe that I looked the half-wild colt that I was; but there was no call for that youth to direct attention to my unavoidable shagginess.

I don't think the tree had many candles, and I don't remember that it glittered with golden apples. But it was loaded with presents, and the girls coming and going clothed in bright garments made me forget my own looks—I think they made me forget to remove my overcoat, which was a sodden[5] thing of poor cut and worse quality. I think I must have stood agape[6] for nearly two hours listening to the songs, noting every motion of Adoniram Burtsch and Asa Walker as they directed the ceremonies and prepared the way for the great event—that is to say, for the coming of Santa Claus himself.

A furious jingling of bells, a loud voice outside, the lifting of a window, the nearer clash of bells, and the dear old saint appeared (in the person of Stephen Bartle) clothed in a red robe, a belt of sleigh bells, and a long white beard. The children cried out, "Oh!" The girls tittered and shrieked with excitement, and the boys laughed and clapped their hands. Then "Sandy" made a little speech about being glad to see us all, but as he had many other places to visit, and as there were a great many presents to distribute, he guessed he'd have to ask some of the many pretty girls to help him. So he called upon Betty Burtsch and Hattie Knapp—and I for one admired his tastes, for they were the most popular maids of the school.

---

[4] always ("without varying")
[5] soaking wet
[6] amazed (maybe to the point of having his mouth hanging wide open)

They came up blushing, and a little bewildered by the publicity thus blown upon them. But their native dignity asserted itself, and the distribution of the presents began. I have a notion now that the fruit upon the tree was mostly bags of popcorn and "corny copias"[7] of candy, but as my brother and I stood there that night and saw everybody, even the rowdiest boy, getting something, we felt aggrieved and rebellious. We forgot that we had come from afar—we only knew that we were being left out.

But suddenly, in the midst of our gloom, my brother's name was called, and a lovely with a gentle smile handed him a bag of popcorn. My heart glowed with gratitude. Somebody had thought of us, and when she came to me, saying sweetly, "Here's something for you," I had not words to thank her. This happened nearly forty years ago, but her smile, her outstretched hand, her sympathetic eyes are vividly before me as I write. She was sorry for the shock-headed boy who stood against the wall, and her pity made the little box of candy a casket of pearls. The fact that I swallowed the jewels on the road home does not take from the reality of my adoration.[8]

At last I had to take my final glimpse of that wondrous tree, and I well remember that walk home. My brother and I traveled in wordless companionship. The moon was sinking toward the west, and the snow crust gleamed with a million fairy lamps. The sentinel watchdogs barked from lonely farmhouses, and the wolves answered from the ridges. Now and then sleighs passed us with lovers sitting two and two, and the bells on their horses had the remote music of romance to us whose boots drummed like clogs of wood upon the icy road.

Our house was dark as we approached and entered it, but how deliciously warm it seemed after the pitiless wind! I confess we made straight for the cupboard for a mince pie, a doughnut, and a bowl of milk.

As I write this there stands in my library a thick-branched, beautifully tapering fir tree covered with the gold and purple apples of Hesperides,[9] together with crystal ice points, green and red and yellow candles, clusters of gilded grapes, wreaths of metallic frost, and glittering angels swinging in ecstasy; but I doubt if my children will ever know the keen pleasure (that is almost pain) which came to my brother and to me in those Christmas days when an orange was not a breakfast fruit, but a casket of incense and of spice, a message from the sunlands of the South.

That was our compensation—we brought to our Christmas time a keen appetite and empty hands. And the lesson of it all is, if we are seeking a

---

[7] cornucopias (those horn-shaped baskets with goodies filling them up and overflowing out)
[8] love
[9] Greek mythological female figures who were said to tend a garden with a tree that grew golden apples

lesson, that it is better to give to those who want[10] than to those from whom "we ought to do something because they did something for us last year."

---

[10] lack, need

A Christmas Inspiration

By L. M. Montgomery

Lucy Maud Montgomery (1874-1942) might be Canada's most beloved writer, best known for her Anne of Green Gables *novels. She was a skilled short story writer, producing hundreds over her career. In these stories, Montgomery often included an uplifting little lesson for the reader or a heartwarming event—and often, both! The setting for "A Christmas Inspiration" is a boarding school for girls—and boarding schools are not usually fun places to be during Christmas....*

• • • • •

"Well, I really think Santa Claus has been very good to us all," said Jean Lawrence, pulling the pins out of her heavy coil of fair hair and letting it ripple over her shoulders.

"So do I," said Nellie Preston as well as she could with a mouthful of chocolates. "Those blessed home folks of mine seem to have divined[1] by instinct the very things I most wanted."

It was the dusk of Christmas Eve, and they were all in Jean Lawrence's room at No. 16 Chestnut Terrace. No. 16 was a boarding house, and boarding houses are not proverbially cheerful places in which to spend Christmas, but Jean's room, at least, was a pleasant spot, and all the girls had brought their Christmas presents in to show each other. Christmas came on Sunday that year and the Saturday evening mail at Chestnut Terrace had been an exciting one.

Jean had lighted the pink-globed lamp on her table, and the mellow light fell over merry faces as the girls chatted about their gifts. On the table was a big white box heaped with roses that betokened a bit of Christmas extravagance on somebody's part. Jean's brother had sent them to her from Montreal, and all the girls were enjoying them in common.

No. 16 Chestnut Terrace was overrun with girls generally. But just now only five were left; all the others had gone home for Christmas, but these five could not go and were bent on making the best of it.

Belle and Olive Reynolds, who were sitting on the bed—Jean could never keep them off it—were High School girls; they were said to be always laughing, and even the fact that they could not go home for Christmas because a young brother had measles did not dampen their spirits.

---

[1] discovered, guessed

Beth Hamilton, who was hovering over the roses, and Nellie Preston, who was eating candy, were art students, and their homes were too far away to visit. As for Jean Lawrence, she was an orphan, and had no home of her own. She worked on the staff of one of the big city newspapers, and the other girls were a little in awe of her cleverness, but her nature was a "chummy" one and her room was a favorite rendezvous.[2] Everybody liked frank, open-handed and hearted Jean.

"It was so funny to see the postman when he came this evening," said Olive. "He just bulged with parcels. They were sticking out in every direction."

"We all got our share of them," said Jean with a sigh of content.

"Even the cook got six—I counted."

"Miss Allen didn't get a thing—not even a letter," said Beth quickly. Beth had a trick of seeing things that other girls didn't.

"I forgot Miss Allen. No, I don't believe she did," answered Jean thoughtfully as she twisted up her pretty hair. "How dismal it must be to be so forlorn as that on Christmas Eve of all times. Ugh! I'm glad I have friends."

"I saw Miss Allen watching us as we opened our parcels and letters," Beth went on. "I happened to look up once, and such an expression as was on her face, girls! It was pathetic and sad and envious all at once. It really made me feel bad—for five minutes," she concluded honestly.

"Hasn't Miss Allen any friends at all?" asked Beth.

"No, I don't think she has," answered Jean. "She has lived here for fourteen years, so Mrs. Pickrell says. Think of that, girls! Fourteen years at Chestnut Terrace! Is it any wonder that she is thin and dried-up and snappy?"

"Nobody ever comes to see her, and she never goes anywhere," said Beth. "Dear me! She must feel lonely now when everybody else is being remembered by their friends. I can't forget her face tonight; it actually haunts me. Girls, how would you feel if you hadn't anyone belonging to you, and if nobody thought about you at Christmas?"

"Ow!" said Olive, as if the mere idea made her shiver.

A little silence followed. To tell the truth, none of them liked Miss Allen. They knew that she did not like them either, but considered them frivolous and pert,[3] and complained when they made a racket.

"The skeleton at the feast," Jean called her, and certainly the presence of the pale, silent, discontented-looking woman at the No. 16 table did not tend to heighten its festivity.

---

[2] meeting place
[3] sassy

Presently Jean said with a dramatic flourish, "Girls, I have an inspiration—a Christmas inspiration!"

"What is it?" cried four voices.

"Just this. Let us give Miss Allen a Christmas surprise. She has not received a single present, and I'm sure she feels lonely. Just think how we would feel if we were in her place."

"That is true," said Olive thoughtfully. "Do you know, girls, this evening I went to her room with a message from Mrs. Pickrell, and I do believe she had been crying. Her room looked dreadfully bare and cheerless, too. I think she is very poor. What are we to do, Jean?"

"Let us each give her something nice. We can put the things just outside of her door so that she will see them whenever she opens it. I'll give her some of Fred's roses too, and I'll write a Christmassy letter in my very best style to go with them," said Jean, warming up to her ideas as she talked.

The other girls caught her spirit and entered into the plan with enthusiasm.

"Splendid!" cried Beth. "Jean, it is an inspiration, sure enough. Haven't we been horribly selfish—thinking of nothing but our own gifts and fun and pleasure? I really feel ashamed."

"Let us do the thing up the very best way we can," said Nellie, forgetting even her beloved chocolates in her eagerness. "The shops are open yet. Let us go up town and invest."

Five minutes later five capped and jacketed figures were scurrying up the street in the frosty, starlit December dusk. Miss Allen in her cold little room heard their gay voices and sighed. She was crying by herself in the dark. It was Christmas for everybody but her, she thought drearily.

In an hour the girls came back with their purchases.

"Now, let's hold a council of war," said Jean jubilantly.[4] "I hadn't the faintest idea what Miss Allen would like, so I just guessed wildly. I got her a lace handkerchief and a big bottle of perfume and a painted photograph frame—and I'll stick my own photo in it for fun. That was really all I could afford. Christmas purchases have left my purse dreadfully lean."

"I got her a glove-box and a pin tray," said Belle, "and Olive got her a calendar and Whittier's poems. And besides we are going to give her half of that big plummy fruitcake Mother sent us from home. I'm sure she hasn't tasted anything so delicious for years, for fruitcakes don't grow on Chestnut Terrace, and she never goes anywhere else for a meal."

Beth had bought a pretty cup and saucer and said she meant to give one of her pretty watercolors[5] too. Nellie, true to her reputation, had invested in a big box of chocolate creams, a gorgeously striped candy cane, a bag of

---

[4] delightedly
[5] paintings

oranges, and a brilliant lampshade of rose-colored crepe paper to top off with.

"It makes such a lot of show for the money," she explained. "I am bankrupt, like Jean."

"Well, we've got a lot of pretty things," said Jean in a tone of satisfaction. "Now we must do them up nicely. Will you wrap them in tissue paper, girls, and tie them with baby ribbon—here's a box of it—while I write that letter?"

While the others chatted over their parcels Jean wrote her letter, and Jean could write delightful letters. She had a decided talent in that respect, and her correspondents all declared her letters to be things of beauty and joy forever. She put her best into Miss Allen's Christmas letter. Since then she has written many bright and clever things, but I do not believe she ever in her life wrote anything more genuinely original and delightful than that letter. Besides, it breathed the very spirit of Christmas, and all the girls declared that it was splendid.

"You must all sign it now," said Jean, "and I'll put it in one of those big envelopes; and, Nellie, won't you write her name on it in fancy letters?"

Which Nellie proceeded to do, and furthermore embellished the envelope by a border of chubby cherubs, dancing hand in hand around it and a sketch of No. 16 Chestnut Terrace in the corner in lieu of a stamp. Not content with this, she hunted out a huge sheet of drawing paper and drew upon it an original pen-and-ink design after her own heart. A dudish cat— Miss Allen was fond of the No. 16 cat if she could be said to be fond of anything—was portrayed seated on a rocker arrayed in smoking jacket and cap with a cigar waved airily aloft in one paw while the other held out a placard bearing the legend "Merry Christmas." A second cat in full street costume bowed politely, hat in paw, and waved a banner inscribed with "Happy New Year," while faintly suggested kittens gamboled[6] around the border. The girls laughed until they cried over it and voted it to be the best thing Nellie had yet done in original work.

All this had taken time and it was past eleven o'clock. Miss Allen had cried herself to sleep long ago and everybody else in Chestnut Terrace was abed when five figures cautiously crept down the hall, headed by Jean with a dim lamp. Outside of Miss Allen's door the procession halted and the girls silently arranged their gifts on the floor.

"That's done," whispered Jean in a tone of satisfaction as they tiptoed back. "And now let us go to bed or Mrs. Pickrell, bless her heart, will be down on us for burning so much midnight oil. Oil has gone up, you know, girls."

---

[6] frolicked

It was in the early morning that Miss Allen opened her door. But early as it was, another door down the hall was half open too, and five rosy faces were peering cautiously out. The girls had been up for an hour for fear they would miss the sight and were all in Nellie's room, which commanded a view of Miss Allen's door.

That lady's face was a study. Amazement, incredulity,[7] wonder, chased each other over it, succeeded by a glow of pleasure. On the floor before her was a snug little pyramid of parcels topped by Jean's letter. On a chair behind it was a bowl of delicious hot-house roses and Nellie's placard.

Miss Allen looked down the hall but saw nothing, for Jean had slammed the door just in time. Half an hour later when they were going down to breakfast Miss Allen came along the hall with outstretched hands to meet them. She had been crying again, but I think her tears were happy ones; and she was smiling now. A cluster of Jean's roses were pinned on her breast.

"Oh, girls, girls," she said, with a little tremble in her voice, "I can never thank you enough. It was so kind and sweet of you. You don't know how much good you have done me."

Breakfast was an unusually cheerful affair at No. 16 that morning. There was no skeleton at the feast, and everybody was beaming. Miss Allen laughed and talked like a girl herself.

"Oh, how surprised I was!" she said. "The roses were like a bit of summer, and those cats of Nellie's were so funny and delightful. And your letter too, Jean! I cried and laughed over it. I shall read it every day for a year."

After breakfast everyone went to Christmas service. The girls went uptown to the church they attended. The city was very beautiful in the morning sunshine. There had been a white frost in the night and the tree-lined avenues and public squares seemed like glimpses of fairyland.

"How lovely the world is," said Jean.

"This is really the very happiest Christmas morning I have ever known," declared Nellie. "I never felt so really Christmassy in my inmost soul before."

"I suppose," said Beth thoughtfully, "that it is because we have discovered for ourselves the old truth that it is more blessed to give than to receive. I've always known it, in a way, but I never realized it before."

"Blessing on Jean's Christmas inspiration," said Nellie. "But, girls, let us try to make it an all-the-year-round inspiration, I say. We can bring a little of our own sunshine into Miss Allen's life as long as we live with her."

"Amen to that!" said Jean heartily. "Oh, listen, girls—the Christmas chimes!"

And over all the beautiful city was wafted the grand old message of peace on earth and good will to all the world.

---

[7] amazement

Christmas Bells

By Henry Wadsworth Longfellow

Well-known American poet Henry Wadsworth Longfellow (1807-1882) wrote this poem in 1863, in the middle year of the North/South War (1861-1865). Later, others wrote music to accompany the poem; it's known today as the Christmas carol "I Heard the Bells on Christmas Day"—one of the most beautiful Christmas songs of all.[1]

* * * * *

I heard the bells on Christmas Day—
Their old, familiar carols play,
    And wild and sweet
    The words repeat
Of peace on earth, good-will to men!

And thought how, as the day had come,
The belfries[2] of all Christendom
    Had rolled along
    The unbroken song
Of peace on earth, good-will to men!

Till, ringing, singing on its way,
The world revolved from night to day,
    A voice, a chime,
    A chant sublime
Of peace on earth, good-will to men!

It was as if an earthquake rent
The hearth-stones of a continent,
    And made forlorn
    The households born
Of peace on earth, good-will to men!

And in despair I bowed my head;
"There is no peace on earth," I said:

---

[1] Popular singer Andy Williams, who also has a well-known and beautiful version of the Christmas song "It's the Most Wonderful Time of the Year," sings a magnificent and moving version of this song.
[2] tops of church towers where bells are rung

"For hate is strong,
  And mocks the song
Of peace on earth, good-will to men!"

Then pealed the bells more loud and deep:
"God is not dead; nor doth he sleep!
  The Wrong shall fail,
  The Right prevail,
With peace on earth, good-will to men!"

Luke, Chapter 2

By Luke, the Physician

One of the most incredible Bible prophecies, the birth of Jesus Christ in Bethlehem was predicted hundreds of years before in Micah 5:2. And it's amazing that participators in this event acted without even knowing that they were fulfilling prophecy! The Roman ruler Caesar Augustus ordered all Roman citizens back to the cities of their birth. Joseph, from the line of David, took himself and his expectant wife back to Bethlehem, his hometown.

· · · · ·

1 – And it came to pass in those days, that there went out a decree[1] from Caesar Augustus that all the world should be taxed.

2 – (And this taxing was first made when Cyrenius was governor of Syria.)

3 – And all went to be taxed, every one into his own city.

4 – And Joseph also went up from Galilee, out of the city of Nazareth, into Judaea, unto the city of David, which is called Bethlehem;[2] (because he was of the house and lineage[3] of David:)

5 – To be taxed with Mary his espoused wife, being great with child.

6 – And so it was, that, while they were there, the days were accomplished that she should be delivered.

7 – And she brought forth her firstborn son, and wrapped him in swaddling clothes, and laid him in a manger; because there was no room for them in the inn.

8 – And there were in the same country shepherds abiding in the field, keeping watch over their flock by night.

---

[1] order

[2] The word "Bethlehem" in Hebrew means "house of bread." Jesus later said, "I am the bread of life: he that cometh to me shall never hunger; and he that believeth on me shall never thirst" (John 6:35).

[3] family

9 – And, lo, the angel of the Lord came upon them, and the glory of the Lord shone round about them: and they were sore afraid.

10 – And the angel said unto them, Fear not: for, behold, I bring you good tidings[4] of great joy, which shall be to all people.

11 – For unto you is born this day in the city of David a Saviour, which is Christ the Lord.

12 – And this shall be a sign unto you; Ye shall find the babe wrapped in swaddling clothes, lying in a manger.

13 – And suddenly there was with the angel a multitude of the heavenly host praising God, and saying,

14 – Glory to God in the highest, and on earth peace, good will toward men.

15 – And it came to pass, as the angels were gone away from them into heaven, the shepherds said one to another, Let us now go even unto Beth-lehem, and see this thing which is come to pass, which the Lord hath made known unto us.

16 – And they came with haste, and found Mary, and Joseph, and the babe lying in a manger.

17 – And when they had seen it, they made known abroad the saying which was told them concerning this child.

18 – And all they that heard it wondered at those things which were told them by the shepherds.

19 – But Mary kept all these things, and pondered them in her heart.

20 – And the shepherds returned, glorifying and praising God for all the things that they had heard and seen, as it was told unto them.

---

[4] news

Have You Done Your Best?

By Booker T. Washington

"Have You Done Your Best?" is the title of a short talk given at Tuskegee Institute by principal Booker T. Washington. Each Sunday evening, Washington spoke at the Tuskegee Chapel (pictured below) to the students to encourage them for the upcoming week of studies and work. Many of these talks were collected in a 1902 collection titled Character Building.

• • • • •

I f you have not already done so—and I hope you have—I think that you will find this a convenient season[1] for each one of you to stop and to consider your school year very carefully; to consider your life in school from every point of view; to place yourselves, as it were, in the presence of your parents, or your friends at home; to place yourselves in the presence of those who stand by and support this institution; to place yourselves in the presence of your teachers and of all who are in any way interested in you.

Now, suppose you were tonight sitting down by your parents' side, by their fireside, looking them in the face, or by the side of your nearest and dearest friends, those who have done the most for you, those who have stood by you most closely. Suppose you were in that position. I want to ask you to answer this question, In considering your school life—in your studies, for example—during the year, thus far, have you done your best?

---

[1] See Acts 24:24-25.

Have you been really honest with your parents, who have struggled, who have sacrificed, who have toiled for years, in ways you do not know of, in order that you might come here, and in order that you might remain here? Have you really been interested in them? Have you really been honest with your teachers? Have you been honest with those who support this institution? Have you really, in a word, in the preparation and recitation of your lessons, done your level best? Right out from your hearts, have you done your best? I fear that a great many of you, when you look your conscience squarely in the face, when you get right down to your real selves, at the bottom of your lives, must answer that you have not done your best. There have been precious minutes, there have been precious hours, that you have completely thrown away, hours for which you cannot show a single return.

Now, if you have not done your level best, right out straight from your heart, in the preparation and recitation of your lessons, and in all your work, it is not too late for you to make amends. I should be very sorry if I waited until the end of the term to remind you of this, because it would then be too late. There would be many of you with long faces, who would say, if you were reminded then, that you could have done so much better, would have been so much more honest with your parents and friends, if you had only been reminded earlier; and that in every way you would have made your lives so different from what they had been. Now, it isn't too late.

Grant, as I know that numbers of you will grant, that you have thrown away precious time, that you have been indifferent to the advice of your teachers, that you really haven't been honest with yourselves in the preparation of your lessons, that you have been careless in your recitations. I want you to be really honest with yourselves and say, from tonight on, "I am going to take charge of myself. I am not going to drift in this respect. I am going to row up the stream; and my life, as a schoolboy or a school-girl, is going to be different from what it has been."

Now place yourselves again in the presence of your parents, of those who are dearest to you, and answer this question, In your work, in your industrial work here, have you done your real best? In the field and in the shop, with the plough, the trowel, the hammer, the saw, have you done your level best? Have you done your best in the sewing room and in the cooking classes? Have you justified your parents in the sacrifice of time and money which they have made in order to allow you to come here? If you haven't done your best in these respects—and many of you haven't—there is still time for you to become a different man or woman. It isn't too late. You can turn yourselves completely around. Those of you who have been indifferent and slow, those of you who have been thoughtless and slovenly,[2] those of you who have tried to find out how little effort of body or mind you could put

---

[2] careless, sloppy

into your industrial work here—it isn't too late for you to turn yourselves completely around in that respect, and to say that from tonight you are going to be a different man or woman.

Have you done your level best in making your surroundings what the school requires, what your school life should be, in learning how to take care of your bodies, in learning how to keep your bodies clean and pure, in the conscientious, systematic use of the toothbrush? Have you done your best? Have you been downright honest in that respect, alone? Have you used the toothbrush just because you felt it was a requirement of the school, or because you felt that you could not be clean or honest with your roommates, that you could not be yourself in the sight of God, unless you used the toothbrush? Have you used it in the dark, as well as in the light? Have you learned that, even if your room was not going to be inspected on a certain day, it was just as important that you learn the lesson of being conscientious about keeping it in order as if you knew it was going to be inspected? Have you been careful in this respect? Have you shifted this duty, or neglected that duty? Have you thrown some task off on to your roommates? Have you tried to "slide out" of it, or, as it were, "to get by," as the slang phrase goes, without doing really honest, straightforward work, as regards the cleanliness of your room, the improvement of it, the making of it more attractive?

Have you been really honest with yourselves and your parents, and with those who spend so much money for the support of this institution? Above all, have you been really true to your parents and to your best selves in growing in strength of character, in strength of purpose, in being downright honest? Those of you who came here, for instance, with the habit of telling falsehoods, of deceiving in one way or another; those of you who came here with the temptation, perhaps, in too many cases, overshadowing you and overpowering you, to take property which does not belong to you; have you been really honest in overcoming habits of this kind? Are you building character? Are you less willing to yield to temptation? Are you more able to overcome temptation now than you were? If you are not more able, you have not grown in this respect.

But it is not too late. If there are some of you who have been unfortunate enough to allow little mean[3] habits, mean dispositions,[4] mean acts, mean thoughts, mean words, to get the uppermost of you—in a word, if your life thus far has been a little, dried-up, narrow life, get rid of that life. Throw open your heart. Say now, "I am not going to be conquered by little, mean thoughts, words and acts any longer. Hereafter all my thoughts, all my words, all my acts, shall be large, generous, high, pure."

In a word, I want you to get hold of this idea, that you can make the future of your lives just what you want to make it. You can make it bright, happy, useful, if you learn this fundamental lesson, and stick to it while in school, or after you go away from here, that it doesn't pay any individual to do any less than his very best. It doesn't pay to be anything else but downright hon-

---

[3] poor
[4] moods

est in heart. Any person who is not honest, who is not trying to do his very best in the classroom or in the shop, no matter where he may be, will find out that it does not pay in the long run. You may think it best for a little while, but permanently it does not pay any man or woman to be anything but really, downright honest, and to do his or her level best.

Now I want you to think about these things, not only here in the chapel tonight, but tomorrow in your classrooms, and with reference to everything you touch. I want to see you let it shine out, even at the very ends of your fingers, that you are doing your best in everything. Do this, and you will find at the end of the year that you are growing stronger, purer, and brighter, that you are making your parents and those interested in you happier, and that you are preparing yourselves to do what this institution and the country expect you to do.

Questions for Review

1. Which things said by Booker T. Washington spoke to you or prompted you to think about the quality of your work, or your attitude toward it?

2. Look up and read Colossians 3:22-24, a passage Paul wrote to Christian *slaves*. What are Christian slaves commanded to do? If that's true, what does God expect of those of us who *aren't* slaves?

3. Write down several things you can start doing this week—today, if possible—to help your Mom and Dad, either around the house, or maybe by taking charge of your own homeschooling. Pray about your attitude, and commit to the Lord to make it better!

"Billy" Sunday: The Man and His Message

By William T. Ellis

The below excerpts are from "Billy" Sunday: The Man and His Message, *a 1914 book written by former U. S. representative William T. Ellis (1845-1925). The book collected many of the sermons and sayings of preacher—and former professional baseball player—Billy Sunday (1862-1935). Sunday left pro baseball, and a huge salary, to become a minister, taking a modest, low-paying YMCA job at first. The below selections show his lively, energetic preaching style.*

· · · · ·

The Battle with Death

"Just one thing divides you people. You are either across the line of safety, or you are outside the kingdom of God. Old or young, rich or poor, high or low, ignorant or educated, white or colored, each of you is upon one side or upon the other.

"The young man who talked to Jesus didn't let an infidel[1] persuade him, and neither should you.

"The time will come when his head will lie on his pillow and his fevered head will toss from side to side.

"The time will come when there will be a rap on the door.

"'Who are you?'

"'Death.'

"'I didn't send for you. Why do you come here?'

"'Nobody sends for me. I choose my own time. If I waited for people to send for me I would never come.'

"'But don't come in now, Death.'

"'I am coming in. I have waited for a long time. I have held a mortgage on you for fifty years, and I've come to foreclose.'

"'But, ah, Death, I'm not ready.'

"'Hush! Hush! I've come to take you. You must come.'

"'Death! Death! Go get my pocketbook, there! Go get my bankbook! Go get the key to my safety deposit box! Take my gold watch, my jewelry, my lands, my home, everything I've got, I'll give all to you if you'll only go.'

---

[1] unbeliever

But Death says, 'I've come for you. I don't want your money or your land or anything that you have. You must come with me.'

"'Death! Death! Don't blow that icy breath upon me. Don't crowd me against the wall!'

"'You must come! You have a week—you have five days—you have one day—you have twelve hours—you have one hour—you have thirty minutes—you have ten minutes—you have one minute—you have thirty seconds— you have ten seconds! I'll count them—one—two—three—four—five—six—ha! ha!—seven—eight—nine—ten!'

"He's gone. Telephone for the undertaker. Carry him to the graveyard. Lay him beside his mother. She died saying, 'I'm sweeping through the gates, washed in the blood of the Lamb.' He died shrieking, 'Don't blow that cold breath in my face! Don't crowd me against the wall!' Oh! God, don't let that old infidel keep you out of the kingdom of God.

"Who'll come into the kingdom of God? Come quick—quick—quick!"

Salvation a Personal Matter

The first thing to remember about being saved is that salvation is a personal matter. "Seek ye the Lord"—that means every one must seek for himself. It won't do for the parent to seek for the children; it won't do for the children to seek for the parent. If you were sick, all the medicine I might take wouldn't do you any good. Salvation is a personal matter that no one else can do for you; you must attend to it yourself.

Some persons have lived manly or womanly lives, and they lack but one thing—open confession of the Lord Jesus Christ. Some men think that they must come to him in a certain way—that they must be stirred by emotion or something like that.

Some people have a deeper conviction of sin before they are converted than after they are converted. With some it is the other way. Some know when they are converted, and others don't.

Some people are emotional. Some are demonstrative. Some will cry easily. Some are cold and can't be moved to emotion. A man jumped up in a meeting and asked whether he could be saved when he hadn't shed a tear in forty years. Even as he spoke he began to shed tears. It's all a matter of how you're constituted.[2] I am vehement,[3] and I serve God with the same vehemence that I served the devil when I went down the line.

Some of you say that in order to accept Jesus you must have different surroundings. You think you could do it better in some other place. You can be saved where you are as well as any place on earth. I say, "My watch doesn't run. It needs new surroundings. I'll put it in this other pocket, or I'll put it here, or here on these flowers." It doesn't need new surroundings. It needs a new mainspring; and that's what the sinner needs. You need a new heart, not a new suit.

What can I do to keep out of hell? "Believe on the Lord Jesus Christ and thou shalt be saved."

The Philippian jailer was converted. He had put the disciples into the stocks when they came to the prison, but after his conversion he stooped down and washed the blood from their stripes.

Now, leave God out of the proposition for a minute. Never mind about the new birth—that's his business. Jesus Christ became a man, bone of our bone, flesh of our flesh. He died on the cross for us, so that we might escape the penalty pronounced on us. Now, never mind about anything but our part in salvation. Here it is: "Believe on the Lord Jesus Christ, and thou shalt be saved."

You say, "Mr. Sunday, the Church is full of hypocrites."

So's hell.

I say to you if you don't want to go to hell and live with that whole bunch forever, come into the Church, where you won't have to associate with them very long. There are no hypocrites in heaven.

You say, "It's so mysterious. I don't understand." You'll be surprised to find out how little you know. You plant a seed in the ground—that's your

---

[2] made, created
[3] intense, passionate

part. You don't understand how it grows. How God makes that seed grow is mysterious to you.

Some people think that they can't be converted unless they go down on their knees in the straw at a camp meeting, unless they pray all hours of the night, and all nights of the week, while some old brother storms heaven in prayer. Some think a man must lose sleep, must come down the aisle with a haggard look, and he must froth at the mouth and dance and shout. Some get it that way, and they don't think that the work I do is genuine unless conversions are made in the same way that they have got religion.

I want you to see what God put in black and white; that there can be a sound, thorough conversion in an instant; that man can be converted as quietly as the coming of day and never

backslide. I do not find fault with the way other people get religion. What I want and preach is the fact that a man can be converted without any fuss.

If a man wants to shout and clap his hands in joy over his wife's conversion, or if a wife wants to cry when her husband is converted, I am not going to turn the hose on them, or put them in a strait-jacket. When a man turns to God truly in conversion, I don't care what form his conversion takes. I wasn't converted that way, but I do not rush around and say, with gall and bitterness, that you are not saved because you did not get religion the way I did. If we all got religion in the same way, the devil might go to sleep with a regular Rip Van Winkle snooze and still be on the job.

Look at Nicodemus. You could never get a man with the temperament of Nicodemus near a camp meeting, to kneel down in the straw, or to shout and sing. He was a quiet, thoughtful, honest, sincere and cautious man. He wanted to know the truth and he was willing to walk in the light when he found it.

Look at the man at the pool of Bethesda. He was a big sinner and was in a lot of trouble which his sins had made for him. He had been in that condition for a long time. It didn't take him three minutes to say "Yes," when the Lord spoke to him. See how quietly he was converted.

Derelicts in the Church

In the Church of God today you know there are a lot of people who are nothing but derelicts[4] and nothing but driftwood.

By power I do not mean wealth. We are the richest people on the earth; nineteen-twentieths of all the wealth or all the money in the United States today is in the hands of professing Christians. That ought to mean that it is in God's hands; but it doesn't. They are robbing God. I was in a church in Iowa that had three members who were worth $200,000 each and they paid their preacher the measly salary of $600 a year, and I will be hornswaggled if they did not owe him $400 then. If I ever skinned any old fellows I did those old stingy coots. A man who doesn't pay to the church is as big a swindler as a man who doesn't pay his grocery bill, and he is dead-beating his way to hell. You let somebody else pay your bills, you old deadbeat. God hasn't any more use today for a deadbeat in the church than he has for the man who doesn't pay his grocery bill—not a bit!

By power I do not mean culture. There never was a time when the people of America were better informed than they are today; they have newspapers, telephones, telegraphs, rural delivery, fast trains. You can leave home and in five days you are in Europe. If something happens in China or Japan tonight you can read it before you go to bed. The islands of the sea are our neighbors.

A stranger once asked: "What is the most powerful and influential church in this town?"

"That big stone church on the hill."

"How many members has it?"

"I don't know; my wife is a member."

"How many Sunday school members?"

"I don't know; my children go."

"How many go to prayer meetings?"

"I don't know; I have never been there."

"How many go to communion?"

"I don't know, I never go; my wife goes."

Then the stranger said: "Will you please tell me why you said it was the most powerful and influential church in the community?"

"Yes, sir; it is the only church in the town that has three millionaires in the church." That was why he thought it was a great church. The Church in America would die of dry rot and sink forty-nine fathoms in hell if all members were multimillionaires and college graduates. That ought not to be a barrier to spiritual power. By power I do not mean influence.

---

[4] worthless-acting, lazy, immoral persons

I'd hate to have to walk back nineteen hundred years to Pentecost. There were 120 at Pentecost who saved 3,000 souls.

Some of the most powerful churches I have ever worked with were not the churches that had the largest number or the richest members. Out in a town in Iowa there were three women who used to pray all night every Thursday night. People used to come under [one woman's] windows at night and listen to her pray. She murdered the king's English five times in every sentence, but oh, she knew God. They had 500 names on their list for prayer, and when the meetings closed they had checked off 397 of them. Every Friday I would be called over the telephone or receive a letter or meet those women and they would tell me what assurances God gave them as to who would be saved. I have never met three women that were stronger in faith than those three. That town was Fairfield, Iowa, one of the brightest, cleanest, snappiest little towns I ever went into.

Men Believe in God

Most men believe in God. Now and then you find a man who doesn't, and he's a fool, for "The fool hath said in his heart, there is no God." Most men have sense. Occasionally you will find a fool, or an infidel, who doesn't believe in God. Most men believe in a God that will reward the right and punish the wrong; therefore it is clear what attitude you ought to assume toward my message tonight, for the message I bring to you is not from human reason or intelligence, but from God's Book.

"What shall the end be of them that obey not the gospel of God?" Now listen, and I will try to help you. Israel's condition was desperate. Peter told them that if they continued to break God's law, they would merit his wrath. I can imagine him crying out in the words of Jeremiah: "What will you do in the swelling of the Jordan?" I hear him cry in the words of Solomon: "The way of the transgressor is hard." That seems to have moved him, and I can hear him cry in the words of my text: "What shall the end be of them that obey not the gospel of God?"

There are those who did obey. Peter knew what their end would be—blessings here and eternal life hereafter—but he said, "What shall the end be of them that obey not?"

A man said, "I cannot be a Christian. I cannot obey God." That is not true. That would make God out a demon and a wretch. God says if you are not a Christian you will be doomed. If God asked mankind to do something, and he knew when he asked them that they could not do it, and he told them he would damn them if they didn't do it, it would make God out a demon and a wretch, and I will not allow you or any other man to stand up and insult my God. You can be a Christian if you want to, and it is your cussedness[55] that you are unwilling to give up that keeps you away from God.

Supposing I should go on top of a building and say to my little baby boy, "Fly up to me." If he could talk, he would say, "I can't." And supposing I would say, "But you can; if you don't, I'll whip you to death." When I asked him to do it, I knew he couldn't, yet I told him I would whip him to death if he didn't, and in saying that I would, as an earthly father, be just as reasonable as God would be if he should ask you to do something you couldn't do, and though he knew when he asked you that you couldn't do it, nevertheless would damn you if you didn't do it.

Don't tell God you can't. Just say you don't want to be a Christian, that's the way to be a man. Just say, "I don't want to be decent; I don't want to quit cussing; I don't want to quit booze-fighting; I don't want to quit lying; I don't want to quit committing adultery. If I should be a Christian I would have to quit all these things, and I don't want to do it." Tell God you are not man enough to be a Christian. Don't try to saddle it off on the Lord. You don't want to do it, that's all; that's the trouble with you.

The Judgment of God

What is your life? A hand's breadth—yes, a hair's breadth—yes, one single heartbeat, and you are gone, and yet you sit with the judgment of God hovering over you. "What shall the end be?"

I never met any man or woman in my life who disbelieved in Christianity but could not be classified under one of these two headings.

First—They who, because of an utter disregard of God's claims upon their lives, have, by and through that disregard, become poltroons, marplots, or degenerate scoundrels, and have thrown themselves beyond the pale of God's mercy.

Second—Men and women with splendid, noble and magnificent abilities, which they have allowed to become absorbed in other matters, and they do not give to the subjects of religion so much as passing attention. They

---

[55] stubbornness

have the audacity[6] to claim for themselves an intellectual superiority to those who believe the Bible, which they sneeringly term 'that superstition.'

But, listen! I will challenge you. If you will bring to religion or to the divinity of Jesus, or the salvation of your soul, the same honest inquiry you demand of yourself in other matters, you will know God is God; you will know the Bible is the Word of God, and you will know that Jesus Christ is the Son of God. You will know that you are a sinner on the road to hell, and you will turn from your sins. But you don't give to religion, you don't demand of yourself, the same amount of research that you would demand of yourself if you were going to buy a piece of property, to find out whether or not the title was perfect. You wouldn't buy it if you didn't know the title was without a flaw, and yet you will pass the Bible by and claim you have more sense than the person who does investigate and finds out, accepts, and is saved.

Questions for Review

1. How does Billy Sunday's speaking style differ from many preachers you've probably heard?

2. Write down one or two plain-spoken or interesting sentences from the sermon excerpts in this selection.

3. How is Billy Sunday tough on both non-Christians *and* those who call themselves Christians?

---

[6] nerve, boldness

Jim, Who Ran Away from His Nurse, and Was Eaten by a Lion

By Hilaire Belloc

He was Hilaire Belloc (1870-1953), and he was hilar...ious. "Jim, Who Ran Away from His Nurse" comes from Belloc's 1907 book Cautionary Tales for Children, *a group of amusing tales and poems that **parodied**—or poked fun at—the lesson-teaching tales that writers like T. S. Arthur made so popular (see Week 4, Day 3).*

• • • • •

There was a Boy whose name was Jim;
His Friends were very good to him.
They gave him Tea, and Cakes, and Jam,
And slices of delicious Ham,
And Chocolate with pink inside,
And little Tricycles to ride,
And

read him Stories through and through,
And even took him to the Zoo—
But there it was the dreadful Fate
Befell him, which I now relate.

You know—at least you *ought* to know.
For I have often told you so—
That Children never are allowed
To leave their Nurses in a Crowd;

Now this was Jim's especial Foible,[1]
He ran away when he was able,
And on this inauspicious[2] day
He slipped his hand and ran away!
He hadn't gone a yard when—

Bang!
With open Jaws, a Lion sprang,
And hungrily began to eat
The Boy: beginning at his feet.

Now just imagine how it feels
When first your toes and then your heels,
And then by gradual degrees,
Your shins and ankles, calves and knees,
Are slowly eaten, bit by bit.
No wonder Jim detested it!

---

[1] fault
[2] unfavorable, ill-fated

No wonder that he shouted "Hi!"
The Honest Keeper heard his cry,
Though very fat he almost ran
To help the little gentleman.
"Ponto!" he ordered as he came
(For Ponto was the Lion's name),
"Ponto!" he cried, with angry Frown.
"Let go, Sir! Down, Sir! Put it down!"

The Lion made a sudden Stop,
He let the Dainty Morsel drop,
And slunk reluctant to his Cage,
Snarling with Disappointed Rage.
But when he bent him over Jim,
The Honest Keeper's Eyes were dim.
The Lion having reached his Head,
The Miserable Boy was dead!

When Nurse informed his Parents, they
Were more Concerned than I can say:
His Mother, as She dried her eyes,
Said, "Well—it gives me no surprise,
He would not do as he was told!"
His Father, who was self-controlled,
Bade all the children round attend
To James's miserable end,
And always keep ahold of Nurse
For fear of finding something worse.

Questions for Review

1. Look up the definition of *parody*. Compare T. S. Arthur's "Temptation Resisted" (see page 63) to "Jim, Who Ran Away from His Nurse." How does today's poem qualify as a parody?

2. Read another selection or two from Hilaire Belloc's *Cautionary Tales for Children*. What "lesson" did what you read offer to children?

The Adventure of the Norwood Builder

By Sir Arthur Conan Doyle

Physician Arthur Conan Doyle (1859-1930) began to write stories about his creation, the great detective Sherlock Holmes—and his doctor sidekick John Watson—in 1887. Doyle wrote 56 short stories featuring Holmes, and four full-length novels. "The Adventure of the Norwood Builder" was first published in 1903. The illustrations here are the original ones that English artist Sidney Paget drew for the Strand *magazine, where the story was published.*

• • • • •

"From the point of view of the criminal expert," said Mr. Sherlock Holmes, "London has become a singularly uninteresting city since the death of the late lamented Professor Moriarty."

"I can hardly think that you would find many decent citizens to agree with you," I answered.

"Well, well, I must not be selfish," said he, with a smile, as he pushed back his chair from the breakfast-table. "The community is certainly the gainer, and no one the loser, save the poor out-of-work specialist, whose occupation has gone. With that man in the field, one's morning paper presented infinite possibilities. Often it was only the smallest trace, Watson, the faintest indication, and yet it was enough to tell me that the great malignant[1] brain was there, as the gentlest tremors of the edges of the web remind one of the foul spider which lurks in the center. Petty thefts, wanton assaults, purposeless outrage—to the man who held the clue all could be worked into one connected whole. To the scientific student of the higher criminal world, no capital in Europe offered the advantages which London then possessed. But now—" He shrugged his shoulders in humorous deprecation[2] of the state of things which he had himself done so much to produce.

At the time of which I speak, Holmes had been back for some months, and I at his request had sold my practice and returned to share the old quarters in Baker Street. A young doctor, named Verner, had purchased my small Kensington practice, and given with astonishingly little demur[3] the highest price that I ventured to ask—an incident which only explained itself

---

[1] evil, cruel
[2] modesty
[3] protest

some years later, when I found that Verner was a distant relation of Holmes, and that it was my friend who had really found the money.

Our months of partnership had not been so uneventful as he had stated, for I find, on looking over my notes, that this period includes the case of the papers of ex-President Murillo, and also the shocking affair of the Dutch steamship *Friesland*, which so nearly cost us both our lives. His cold and proud nature was always averse, however, from anything in the shape of public applause, and he bound me in the most stringent[4] terms to

say no further word of himself, his methods, or his successes—a prohibition which, as I have explained, has only now been removed.

Mr. Sherlock Holmes was leaning back in his chair after his whimsical protest, and was unfolding his morning paper in a leisurely fashion, when our attention was arrested by a tremendous ring at the bell, followed immediately by a hollow drumming sound, as if someone were beating on the outer door with his fist. As it opened there came a tumultuous rush into the hall, rapid feet clattered up the stair, and an instant later a wild-eyed and frantic young man, pale, disheveled, and palpitating,[5] burst into the room. He looked from one to the other of us, and under our gaze of inquiry he became conscious that some apology was needed for this unceremonious entry.

"I'm sorry, Mr. Holmes," he cried. "You mustn't blame me. I am nearly mad. Mr. Holmes, I am the unhappy John Hector McFarlane."

He made the announcement as if the name alone would explain both his visit and its manner, but I could see, by my companion's unresponsive face, that it meant no more to him than to me.

"Have a cigarette, Mr. McFarlane," said he, pushing his case across. "I am sure that, with your symptoms, my friend Dr. Watson here would prescribe a sedative.[6] The weather has been so very warm these last few days. Now, if you feel a little more composed, I should be glad if you would sit down in that chair, and tell us very slowly and quietly who you are, and

---

[4] strict

[5] shaking

[6] a drug to calm someone

what it is that you want. You mentioned your name, as if I should recognize it, but I assure you that, beyond the obvious facts that you are a bachelor, a solicitor, a Freemason, and an asthmatic, I know nothing whatever about you."

Familiar as I was with my friend's methods, it was not difficult for me to follow his deductions, and to observe the untidiness of attire, the sheaf of legal papers, the watch-charm, and the breathing which had prompted them. Our client, however, stared in amazement.

"Yes, I am all that, Mr. Holmes; and, in addition, I am the most unfortunate man at this moment in London. For heaven's sake, don't abandon me, Mr. Holmes! If they come to arrest me before I have finished my story, make them give me time, so that I may tell you the whole truth. I could go to jail happy if I knew that you were working for me outside."

"Arrest you!" said Holmes. "This is really most grati—most interesting. On what charge do you expect to be arrested?"

"Upon the charge of murdering Mr. Jonas Oldacre, of Lower Norwood."

My companion's expressive face showed a sympathy which was not, I am afraid, entirely unmixed with satisfaction.

"Dear me," said he, "it was only this moment at breakfast that I was saying to my friend, Dr. Watson, that sensational cases had disappeared out of our papers."

Our visitor stretched forward a quivering hand and picked up the *Daily Telegraph*, which still lay upon Holmes's knee.

"If you had looked at it, sir, you would have seen at a glance what the errand is on which I have come to you this morning. I feel as if my name and my misfortune must be in every man's mouth." He turned it over to expose the central page. "Here it is, and with your permission I will read it to you. Listen to this, Mr. Holmes. The headlines are: 'Mysterious Affair at Lower Norwood. Disappearance of a Well-known Builder. Suspicion of Murder and Arson. A Clue to the Criminal.' That is the clue which they are already following, Mr. Holmes, and I know that it leads infallibly to me. I have been followed from London Bridge Station, and I am sure that they are only waiting for the warrant to arrest me. It will break my mother's heart—it will break her heart!" He wrung his hands in an agony of apprehension, and swayed backward and forward in his chair.

I looked with interest upon this man, who was accused of being the perpetrator of a crime of violence. He was flaxen-haired[7] and handsome, in a washed-out negative fashion, with frightened blue eyes, and a clean-shaven face, with a weak, sensitive mouth. His age may have been about twenty-seven, his dress and bearing that of a gentleman. From the pocket of his

---

[7] blonde

light summer overcoat protruded the bundle of indorsed papers which proclaimed his profession.

"We must use what time we have," said Holmes. "Watson, would you have the kindness to take the paper and to read the paragraph in question?"

Underneath the vigorous headlines which our client had quoted, I read the following suggestive narrative:

> Late last night, or early this morning, an incident occurred at Lower Norwood which points, it is feared, to a serious crime. Mr. Jonas Oldacre is a well-known resident of that suburb, where he has carried on his business as a builder for many years. Mr. Oldacre is a bachelor, fifty-two years of age, and lives in Deep Dene House, at the Sydenham end of the road of that name. He has had the reputation of being a man of eccentric habits, secretive and retiring. For some years he has practically withdrawn from the business, in which he is said to have massed considerable wealth. A small timber-yard still exists, however, at the back of the house, and last night, about twelve o'clock, an alarm was given that one of the stacks was on fire. The engines were soon upon the spot, but the dry wood burned with great fury, and it was impossible to arrest the conflagration[8] until the stack had been entirely consumed. Up to this point the incident bore the appearance of an ordinary accident, but fresh indications seem to point to serious crime. Surprise was expressed at the absence of the master of the establishment from the scene of the fire, and an inquiry followed, which showed that he had disappeared from the house. An examination of his room revealed that the bed had not been slept in, that a safe which stood in it was open, that a number of important papers were scattered about the room, and finally, that there were signs of a murderous struggle, slight traces of blood being found within the room, and an oaken walking-stick, which also showed stains of blood upon the handle. It is known that Mr. Jonas Oldacre had received a late visitor in his bedroom upon that night, and the stick found has been identified as the property of this person, who is a young London solicitor[9] named John Hector McFarlane, junior partner of Graham and McFarlane, of 426, Gresham Buildings, E.C. The police believe that they have evidence in their possession which supplies a very convincing motive for the crime, and altogether it cannot be doubted that sensational developments will follow.

> "LATER.—It is rumoured as we go to press that Mr. John Hector McFarlane has actually been arrested on the charge of the murder of Mr. Jonas Oldacre. It is at least certain that a warrant has been is-

---

[8] "arrest the conflagration": put out the fire
[9] lawyer

sued. There have been further and sinister developments in the investigation at Norwood. Besides the signs of a struggle in the room of the unfortunate builder it is now known that the French windows of his bedroom (which is on the ground floor) were found to be open, that there were marks as if some bulky object had been dragged across to the wood-pile, and, finally, it is asserted that charred remains have been found among the charcoal ashes of the fire. The police theory is that a most sensational crime has been committed, that the victim was clubbed to death in his own bed-room, his papers rifled, and his dead body dragged across to the wood-stack, which was then ignited so as to hide all traces of the crime. The conduct of the criminal investigation has been left in the experienced hands of Inspector Lestrade, of Scotland Yard, who is following up the clues with his accustomed energy and sagacity.

Sherlock Holmes listened with closed eyes and fingertips together to this remarkable account.

"The case has certainly some points of interest," said he, in his languid[10] fashion. "May I ask, in the first place, Mr. McFarlane, how it is that you are still at liberty, since there appears to be enough evidence to justify your arrest?"

"I live at Torrington Lodge, Blackheath, with my parents, Mr. Holmes, but last night, having to do business very late with Mr. Jonas Oldacre, I stayed at an hotel in Norwood, and came to my business from there. I knew nothing of this affair until I was in the train, when I read what you have just heard. I at once saw the horrible danger of my position, and I hurried to put the case into your hands. I have no doubt that I should have been arrested either at my city office or at my home. A man followed me from London Bridge Station, and I have no doubt—great heaven! what is that?"

It was a clang of the bell, followed instantly by heavy steps upon the stair. A moment later, our old friend Lestrade appeared in the doorway. Over his shoulder I caught a glimpse of one or two uniformed policemen outside.

"Mr. John Hector McFarlane?" said Lestrade.

Our unfortunate client rose with a ghastly face.

---

[10] relaxed, laid-back

"I arrest you for the willful murder of Mr. Jonas Oldacre, of Lower Norwood."

McFarlane turned to us with a gesture of despair, and sank into his chair once more like one who is crushed.

"One moment, Lestrade," said Holmes. "Half an hour more or less can make no difference to you, and the gentleman was about to give us an account of this very interesting affair, which might aid us in clearing it up."

"I think there will be no difficulty in clearing it up," said Lestrade, grimly.

"Nonetheless, with your permission, I should be much interested to hear his account."

"Well, Mr. Holmes, it is difficult for me to refuse you anything, for you have been of use to the force once or twice in the past, and we owe you a good turn at Scotland Yard," said Lestrade. "At the same time I must remain with my prisoner, and I am bound to warn him that anything he may say will appear in evidence against him."

"I wish nothing better," said our client. "All I ask is that you should hear and recognize the absolute truth."

Lestrade looked at his watch. "I'll give you half an hour," said he.

"I must explain first," said McFarlane, "that I knew nothing of Mr. Jonas Oldacre. His name was familiar to me, for many years ago my parents were acquainted with him, but they drifted apart. I was very much surprised therefore, when yesterday, about three o'clock in the afternoon, he walked into my office in the city. But I was still more astonished when he told me the object of his visit. He had in his hand several sheets of a notebook, covered with scribbled writing—here they are—and he laid them on my table.

"'Here is my will,' said he. 'I want you, Mr. McFarlane, to cast it into proper legal shape. I will sit here while you do so.'

"I set myself to copy it, and you can imagine my astonishment when I found that, with some reservations, he had left all his property to me. He was a strange little ferret-like man, with white eyelashes, and when I looked up at him I found his keen grey eyes fixed upon me with an amused expression. I could hardly believe my own as I read the terms of the will; but he explained that he was a bachelor with hardly any living relation, that he had known my parents in his youth, and that he had always heard of me as a very deserving young man, and was assured that his money would be in worthy hands. Of course, I could only stammer out my thanks. The will was duly finished, signed, and witnessed by my clerk. This is it on the blue paper, and these slips, as I have explained, are the rough draft. Mr. Jonas Oldacre then informed me that there were a number of documents—building leases, title-deeds, mortgages, scrip,[11] and so forth—which it was necessary that I should see and understand. He said that his mind would not be easy until the whole thing was settled, and he begged me to come out to his house at Norwood that night, bringing the will with me, and to arrange matters. 'Remember, my boy, not one word to your parents about the affair until everything is settled. We will keep it as a little surprise for them.' He was very insistent upon this point, and made me promise it faithfully.

"You can imagine, Mr. Holmes, that I was not in a humor to refuse him anything that he might ask. He was my benefactor, and all my desire was to carry out his wishes in every particular. I sent a telegram home, therefore, to say that I had important business on hand, and that it was impossible for me to say how late I might be. Mr. Oldacre had told me that he would like me to have supper with him at nine, as he might not be home before that hour. I had some difficulty in finding his house, however, and it was nearly half-past before I reached it. I found him—"

"One moment!" said Holmes. "Who opened the door?"

"A middle-aged woman, who was, I suppose, his housekeeper."

"And it was she, I presume, who mentioned your name?"

"Exactly," said McFarlane.

"Pray proceed."

McFarlane wiped his damp brow, and then continued his narrative:

"I was shown by this woman into a sitting room, where a frugal supper was laid out. Afterwards, Mr. Jonas Oldacre led me into his bedroom, in which there stood a heavy safe. This he opened and took out a mass of documents, which we went over together. It was between eleven and twelve when we finished. He remarked that we must not disturb the housekeeper. He showed me out through his own French window, which had been open all this time."

"Was the blind down?" asked Holmes.

"I will not be sure, but I believe that it was only half down. Yes, I remember how he pulled it up in order to swing open the window. I could not find my stick, and he said, 'Never mind, my boy, I shall see a good deal of you now, I hope, and I will keep your stick until you come back to claim it.' I left him there, the safe open, and the papers made up in packets upon the table. It was so late that I could not get back to Blackheath, so I spent the night at the Anerley Arms, and I knew nothing more until I read of this horrible affair in the morning."

"Anything more that you would like to ask, Mr. Holmes?" said Lestrade, whose eyebrows had gone up once or twice during this remarkable explanation.

"Not until I have been to Blackheath."

---

[11] legal claims to land

"You mean to Norwood," said Lestrade.

"Oh, yes, no doubt that is what I must have meant," said Holmes, with his enigmatical[12] smile. Lestrade had learned by more experiences than he would care to acknowledge that that brain could cut through that which was impenetrable to him. I saw him look curiously at my companion.

"I think I should like to have a word with you presently, Mr. Sherlock Holmes," said he. "Now, Mr. McFarlane, two of my constables are at the door, and there is a four-wheeler waiting." The wretched young man arose, and with a last beseeching glance at us walked from the room. The officers conducted him to the cab, but Lestrade remained.

Holmes had picked up the pages which formed the rough draft of the will, and was looking at them with the keenest interest upon his face.

"There are some points about that document, Lestrade, are there not?" said he, pushing them over.

The official looked at them with a puzzled expression.

"I can read the first few lines and these in the middle of the second page, and one or two at the end. Those are as clear as print," said he, "but the writing in between is very bad, and there are three places where I cannot read it at all."

"What do you make of that?" said Holmes.

"Well, what do *you* make of it?"

"That it was written in a train. The good writing represents stations, the bad writing movement, and the very bad writing passing over points. A scientific expert would pronounce at once that this was drawn up on a suburban line, since nowhere save in the immediate vicinity[13] of a great city could there be so quick a succession of points. Granting that his whole journey was occupied in drawing up the will, then the train was an express, only stopping once between Norwood and London Bridge."

Lestrade began to laugh.

"You are too many for me when you begin to get on your theories, Mr. Holmes," said he. "How does this bear on the case?"

"Well, it corroborates[14] the young man's story to the extent that the will was drawn up by Jonas Oldacre in his journey yesterday. It is curious—is it not?—that a man should draw up so important a document in so haphazard a fashion. It suggests that he did not think it was going to be of much practical importance. If a man drew up a will which he did not intend ever to be effective, he might do it so."

"Well, he drew up his own death warrant at the same time," said Lestrade.

---

[12] mysterious
[13] area
[14] backs up

"Oh, you think so?"

"Don't you?"

"Well, it is quite possible, but the case is not clear to me yet."

"Not clear? Well, if that isn't clear, what *could* be clearer? Here is a young man who learns suddenly that, if a certain older man dies, he will succeed to a fortune. What does he do? He says nothing to anyone, but he arranges that he shall go out on some pretext[15] to see his client that night. He waits until the only other person in the house is in bed, and then in the solitude of a man's room he murders him, burns his body in the wood-pile, and departs to a neighboring hotel. The bloodstains in the room and also on the stick are very slight. It is probable that he imagined his crime to be a bloodless one, and hoped that if the body were consumed it would hide all traces of the method of his death—traces which, for some reason, must have pointed to him. Is not all this obvious?"

"It strikes me, my good Lestrade, as being just a trifle too obvious," said Holmes. "You do not add imagination to your other great qualities, but if you could for one moment put yourself in the place of this young man, would you choose the very night after the will had been made to commit your crime? Would it not seem dangerous to you to make so very close a relation between the two incidents? Again, would you choose an occasion when you are known to be in the house, when a servant has let you in? And, finally, would you take the great pains to conceal the body, and yet leave your own stick as a sign that you were the criminal? Confess, Lestrade, that all this is very unlikely."

"As to the stick, Mr. Holmes, you know as well as I do that a criminal is often flurried, and does such things, which a cool man would avoid. He was very likely afraid to go back to the room. Give me another theory that would fit the facts."

"I could very easily give you half a dozen," said Holmes. "Here for example, is a very possible and even probable one. I make you a free present of it. The older man is showing documents which are of evident value. A passing tramp sees them through the window, the blind of which is only half down. Exit the solicitor. Enter the tramp! He seizes a stick, which he observes there, kills Oldacre, and departs after burning the body."

"Why should the tramp burn the body?"

"For the matter of that, why should McFarlane?"

"To hide some evidence."

"Possibly the tramp wanted to hide that any murder at all had been committed."

"And why did the tramp take nothing?"

"Because they were papers that he could not negotiate."

---

[15] excuse

Lestrade shook his head, though it seemed to me that his manner was less absolutely assured than before.

"Well, Mr. Sherlock Holmes, you may look for your tramp, and while you are finding him we will hold on to our man. The future will show which is right. Just notice this point, Mr. Holmes: that so far as we know, none of the papers were removed, and that the prisoner is the one man in the world who had no reason for removing them, since he was heir-at-law, and would come into them in any case."

My friend seemed struck by this remark.

"I don't mean to deny that the evidence is in some ways very strongly in favor of your theory," said he. "I only wish to point out that there are other theories possible. As you say, the future will decide. Good morning! I dare say that in the course of the day I shall drop in at Norwood and see how you are getting on."

When the detective departed, my friend rose and made his preparations for the day's work with the alert air of a man who has a congenial[16] task before him.

"My first movement Watson," said he, as he bustled into his frockcoat, "must, as I said, be in the direction of Blackheath."

"And why not Norwood?"

"Because we have in this case one singular incident coming close to the heels of another singular incident. The police are making the mistake of concentrating their attention upon the second, because it happens to be the one which is actually criminal. But it is evident to me that the logical way to approach the case is to begin by trying to throw some light upon the first incident—the curious will, so suddenly made, and to so unexpected an heir. It may do something to simplify what followed. No, my dear fellow, I don't think you can help me. There is no prospect of danger, or I should not dream of stirring out without you. I trust that when I see you in the evening, I will be able to report that I have been able to do something for this unfortunate youngster, who has thrown himself upon my protection."

It was late when my friend returned, and I could see, by a glance at his haggard and anxious face, that the high hopes with which he had started had not been fulfilled. For an hour he droned away upon his violin, endeavoring to soothe his own ruffled spirits. At last he flung down the instrument, and plunged into a detailed account of his misadventures.

"It's all going wrong, Watson—all as wrong as it can go. I kept a bold face before Lestrade, but, upon my soul, I believe that for once the fellow is on the right track and we are on the wrong. All my instincts are one way, and all the facts are the other, and I much fear that British juries have not

---

[16] welcome, pleasant

yet attained that pitch of intelligence when they will give the preference to my theories over Lestrade's facts."

"Did you go to Blackheath?"

"Yes, Watson, I went there, and I found very quickly that the late lamented Oldacre was a pretty considerable blackguard.[17] The father was away in search of his son. The mother was at home—a little, fluffy, blue-eyed person, in a tremor of fear and indignation. Of course, she would not admit even the possibility of his guilt. But she would not express either surprise or regret over the fate of Oldacre. On the contrary, she spoke of him with such bitterness that she was unconsciously considerably strengthening the case of the police for, of course, if her son had heard her speak of the man in this fashion, it would predispose him towards hatred and violence. 'He was more like a malignant and cunning ape than a human being,' said she, 'and he always was, ever since he was a young man.'

"'You knew him at that time?' said I.

"'Yes, I knew him well, in fact, he was an old suitor of mine. Thank heaven that I had the sense to turn away from him and to marry a better, if poorer, man. I was engaged to him, Mr. Holmes, when I heard a shocking story of how he had turned a cat loose in an aviary,[18] and I was so horrified at his brutal cruelty that I would have nothing more to do with him.' She rummaged in a bureau,[19] and presently she produced a photograph of a woman, shamefully defaced and mutilated with a knife. 'That is my own photograph,' she said. 'He sent it to me in that state, with his curse, upon my wedding morning.'

"'Well,' said I, 'at least he has forgiven you now, since he has left all his property to your son.'

"'Neither my son nor I want anything from Jonas Oldacre, dead or alive!' she cried, with a proper spirit. 'There is a God in heaven, Mr. Holmes, and

---

[17] villain

[18] birdhouse

[19] dresser

that same God who has punished that wicked man will show, in His own good time, that my son's hands are guiltless of his blood.'

"Well, I tried one or two leads, but could get at nothing which would help our hypothesis,[20] and several points which would make against it. I gave it up at last and off I went to Norwood.

"This place, Deep Dene House, is a big modern villa of staring brick, standing back in its own grounds, with a laurel-clumped lawn in front of it. To the right and some distance back from the road was the timber-yard which had been the scene of the fire. Here's a rough plan on a leaf of my notebook. This window on the left is the one which opens into Oldacre's room. You can look into it from the road, you see. That is about the only bit of consolation I have had today. Lestrade was not there, but his head constable did the honors. They had just found a great treasure trove. They had spent the morning raking among the ashes of the burned wood-pile, and besides the charred organic remains they had secured several discolored metal discs. I examined them with care, and there was no doubt that they were trouser buttons. I even distinguished that one of them was marked with the name of 'Hyams,' who was Oldacre's tailor. I then worked the lawn very carefully for signs and traces, but this drought has made everything as hard as iron. Nothing was to be seen save that some body or bundle had been dragged through a low privet hedge which is in a line with the wood-pile. All that, of course, fits in with the official theory. I crawled about the lawn with an August sun on my back, but I got up at the end of an hour no wiser than before.

"Well, after this fiasco I went into the bedroom and examined that also. The bloodstains were very slight, mere smears and discolorations, but un-doubtedly fresh. The stick had been removed, but there also the marks were slight. There is no doubt about the stick belonging to our client. He admits it. Footmarks of both men could be made out on the carpet, but none of any third person, which again is a trick for the other side. They were piling up their score all the time and we were at a standstill.

"Only one little gleam of hope did I get—and yet it amounted to noth-ing. I examined the contents of the safe, most of which had been taken out and left on the table. The papers had been made up into sealed envelopes, one or two of which had been opened by the police. They were not, so far as I could judge, of any great value, nor did the bankbook show that Mr. Oldacre was in such very affluent[21] circumstances. But it seemed to me that all the papers were not there. There were allusions to some deeds—possibly the more valuable—which I could not find. This, of course, if we could def-

---

[20] theory
[21] wealthy

initely prove it, would turn Lestrade's argument against himself, for who would steal a thing if he knew that he would shortly inherit it?

"Finally, having drawn every other cover and picked up no scent, I tried my luck with the housekeeper. Mrs. Lexington is her name—a little, dark, silent person, with suspicious and sidelong eyes. She could tell us something if she would—I am convinced of it. But she was as close as wax. Yes, she had let Mr. McFarlane in at half-past nine. She wished her hand had withered before she had done so. She had gone to bed at half-past ten. Her room was at the other end of the house, and she could hear nothing of what had passed. Mr. McFarlane had left his hat, and to the best of her belief his stick, in the hall. She had been awakened by the alarm of fire. Her poor, dear master had certainly been murdered. Had he any enemies? Well, every man had enemies, but Mr. Oldacre kept himself very much to himself, and only met people in the way of business. She had seen the buttons, and was sure that they belonged to the clothes which he had worn last night. The wood-pile was very dry, for it had not rained for a month. It burned like tinder, and by the time she reached the spot, nothing could be seen but flames. She and all the firemen smelled the burned flesh from inside it. She knew nothing of the papers, nor of Mr. Oldacre's private affairs.

"So, my dear Watson, there's my report of a failure. And yet—and yet—" he clenched his thin hands in a paroxysm of conviction—"I *know* it's all wrong. I feel it in my bones. There is something that has not come out, and that housekeeper knows it. There was a sort of sulky defiance in her eyes, which only goes with guilty knowledge. However, there's no good talking any more about it, Watson; but unless some lucky chance comes our way I fear that the Norwood Disappearance Case will not figure in that chronicle of our successes which I foresee that a patient public will sooner or later have to endure."

"Surely," said I, "the man's appearance would go far with any jury?"

"That is a dangerous argument my dear Watson. You remember that terrible murderer, Bert Stevens, who wanted us to get him off in '87? Was there ever a more mild-mannered, Sunday-school young man?"

"It is true."

"Unless we succeed in establishing an alternative theory, this man is lost. You can hardly find a flaw in the case which can now be presented against him, and all further investigation has served to strengthen it. By the way, there is one curious little point about those papers which may serve us as the starting point for an inquiry. On looking over the bankbook I found that the low state of the balance was principally due to large checks which have been made out during the last year to Mr. Cornelius. I confess that I should be interested to know who this Mr. Cornelius may be with whom a retired builder has such very large transactions. Is it possible that he has had a hand in the affair? Cornelius might be a broker, but we have found no scrip to correspond with these large payments. Failing any other indication, my researches must now take the direction of an inquiry at the bank for the gentleman who has cashed these checks. But I fear, my dear fellow, that our case will end ingloriously by Lestrade hanging our client, which will certainly be a triumph for Scotland Yard."

I do not know how far Sherlock Holmes took any sleep that night, but when I came down to breakfast I found him pale and harassed, his bright eyes the brighter for the dark shadows round them. The carpet round his chair was littered with cigarette ends and with the early editions of the morning papers. An open telegram lay upon the table.

"What do you think of this, Watson?" he asked, tossing it across.

It was from Norwood, and ran as follows:

> Important fresh evidence to hand. McFarlane's guilt definitely established. Advise you to abandon case.—LESTRADE.

"This sounds serious," said I.

"It is Lestrade's little cock-a-doodle of victory," Holmes answered, with a bitter smile. "And yet it may be premature to abandon the case. After all, important fresh evidence is a two-edged thing, and may possibly cut in a very different direction to that which Lestrade imagines. Take your breakfast, Watson, and we will go out together and see what we can do. I feel as if I shall need your company and your moral support today."

My friend had no breakfast himself, for it was one of his peculiarities that in his more intense moments he would permit himself no food, and I have known him presume upon his iron strength until he has fainted from pure inanition.[22] "At present I cannot spare energy and nerve force for digestion," he would say in answer to my medical remonstrances.[23] I was not surprised, therefore, when this morning he left his untouched meal behind him, and started with me for Norwood. A crowd of morbid sight-seers were still gathered round Deep Dene House, which was just such a suburban villa as I had pictured. Within the gates Lestrade met us, his face flushed with victory, his manner grossly triumphant.

"Well, Mr. Holmes, have you proved us to be wrong yet? Have you found your tramp?" he cried.

"I have formed no conclusion whatever," my companion answered.

"But we formed ours yesterday, and now it proves to be correct, so you must acknowledge that we have been a little in front of you this time, Mr. Holmes."

"You certainly have the air of something unusual having occurred," said Holmes.

---

[22] lack of food
[23] protests

Lestrade laughed loudly.

"You don't like being beaten any more than the rest of us do," said he. "A man can't expect always to have it his own way, can he, Dr. Watson? Step this way, if you please, gentlemen, and I think I can convince you once for all that it was John McFarlane who did this crime."

He led us through the passage and out into a dark hall beyond.

"This is where young McFarlane must have come out to get his hat after the crime was done," said he. "Now look at this." With dramatic suddenness he struck a match, and by its light exposed a stain of blood upon the whitewashed wall. As he held the match nearer, I saw that it was more than a stain. It was the well-marked print of a thumb.

"Look at that with your magnifying glass, Mr. Holmes."

"Yes, I am doing so."

"You are aware that no two thumb-marks are alike?"

"I have heard something of the kind."

"Well, then, will you please compare that print with this wax impression of young McFarlane's right thumb, taken by my orders this morning?"

As he held the waxen print close to the bloodstain, it did not take a magnifying glass to see that the two were undoubtedly from the same thumb. It was evident to me that our unfortunate client was lost.

"That is final," said Lestrade.

"Yes, that is final," I involuntarily echoed.

"It is final," said Holmes.

Something in his tone caught my ear, and I turned to look at him. An extraordinary change had come over his face. It was writhing with inward merriment. His two eyes were shining like stars. It seemed to me that he was making desperate efforts to restrain a convulsive attack of laughter.

"Dear me! Dear me!" he said at last. "Well, now, who would have thought it? And how deceptive appearances may be, to be sure! Such a nice young man to look at! It is a lesson to us not to trust our own judgment, is it not, Lestrade?"

"Yes, some of us are a little too much inclined to be cock-sure, Mr. Holmes," said Lestrade. The man's insolence[24] was maddening, but we could not resent it.

"What a providential thing that this young man should press his right thumb against the wall in taking his hat from the peg! Such a very natural action, too, if you come to think of it." Holmes was outwardly calm, but his whole body gave a wriggle of suppressed excitement as he spoke.

"By the way, Lestrade, who made this remarkable discovery?"

"It was the housekeeper, Mrs. Lexington, who drew the night constable's attention to it."

"Where was the night constable?"

"He remained on guard in the bedroom where the crime was committed, so as to see that nothing was touched."

"But why didn't the police see this mark yesterday?"

"Well, we had no particular reason to make a careful examination of the hall. Besides, it's not in a very prominent place, as you see."

"No, no—of course not. I suppose there is no doubt that the mark was there yesterday?"

Lestrade looked at Holmes as if he thought he was going out of his mind. I confess that I was myself surprised both at his hilarious manner and at his rather wild observation.

"I don't know whether you think that McFarlane came out of jail in the dead of the night in order to strengthen the evidence against himself," said Lestrade. "I leave it to any expert in the world whether that is not the mark of his thumb."

"It is unquestionably the mark of his thumb."

"There, that's enough," said Lestrade. "I am a practical man, Mr. Holmes, and when I have got my evidence I come to my conclusions. If you have anything to say, you will find me writing my report in the sitting room."

Holmes had recovered his equanimity,[25] though I still seemed to detect gleams of amusement in his expression.

"Dear me, this is a very sad development, Watson, is it not?" said he. "And yet there are singular points about it which hold out some hopes for our client."

"I am delighted to hear it," said I, heartily. "I was afraid it was all up with him."

"I would hardly go so far as to say that, my dear Watson. The fact is that there is one really serious flaw in this evidence to which our friend attaches so much importance."

---

[24] gall, disrespect
[25] calmness, self-control

"Indeed, Holmes! What is it?"

"Only this: that I *know* that that mark was not there when I examined the hall yesterday. And now, Watson, let us have a little stroll round in the sunshine."

With a confused brain, but with a heart into which some warmth of hope was returning, I accompanied my friend in a walk round the garden. Holmes took each face of the house in turn, and examined it with great interest. He then led the way inside, and went over the whole building from basement to attic. Most of the rooms were unfurnished, but none the less Holmes inspected them all minutely. Finally, on the top corridor, which ran outside three untenanted bedrooms, he again was seized with a spasm of merriment.

"There are really some very unique features about this case, Watson," said he. "I think it is time now that we took our friend Lestrade into our confidence. He has had his little smile at our expense, and perhaps we may do as much by him, if my reading of this problem proves to be correct. Yes, yes, I think I see how we should approach it."

The Scotland Yard inspector was still writing in the parlour when Holmes interrupted him.

"I understood that you were writing a report of this case," said he.

"So I am."

"Don't you think it may be a little premature? I can't help thinking that your evidence is not complete."

Lestrade knew my friend too well to disregard his words. He laid down his pen and looked curiously at him.

"What do you mean, Mr. Holmes?"

"Only that there is an important witness whom you have not seen."

"Can you produce him?"

"I think I can."

"Then do so."

"I will do my best. How many constables have you?"

"There are three within call."

"Excellent!" said Holmes. "May I ask if they are all large, able-bodied men with powerful voices?"

"I have no doubt they are, though I fail to see what their voices have to do with it."

"Perhaps I can help you to see that and one or two other things as well," said Holmes. "Kindly summon your men, and I will try."

Five minutes later, three policemen had assembled in the hall.

"In the outhouse you will find a considerable quantity of straw," said Holmes. "I will ask you to carry in two bundles of it. I think it will be of the greatest assistance in producing the witness whom I require. Thank you very much. I believe you have some matches in your pocket Watson. Now, Mr. Lestrade, I will ask you all to accompany me to the top landing."

As I have said, there was a broad corridor there, which ran outside three empty bedrooms. At one end of the corridor we were all marshalled by Sherlock Holmes, the constables grinning and Lestrade staring at my friend with amazement, expectation, and derision[26] chasing each other across his features. Holmes stood before us with the air of a conjurer who is performing a trick.

"Would you kindly send one of your constables for two buckets of water? Put the straw on the floor here, free from the wall on either side. Now I think that we are all ready."

Lestrade's face had begun to grow red and angry. "I don't know whether you are playing a game with us, Mr. Sherlock Holmes," said he. "If you know anything, you can surely say it without all this tomfoolery."

"I assure you, my good Lestrade, that I have an excellent reason for everything that I do. You may possibly remember that you chaffed me a little, some hours ago, when the sun seemed on your side of the hedge, so you must not grudge me a little pomp and ceremony now. Might I ask you, Watson, to open that window, and then to put a match to the edge of the straw?"

I did so, and driven by the draught a coil of grey smoke swirled down the corridor, while the dry straw crackled and flamed.

"Now we must see if we can find this witness for you, Lestrade. Might I ask you all to join in the cry of 'Fire!'? Now then; one, two, three—"

"Fire!" we all yelled.

"Thank you. I will trouble you once again."

"Fire!"

"Just once more, gentlemen, and all together."

"Fire!" The shout must have rung over Norwood.

It had hardly died away when an amazing thing happened. A door suddenly flew open out of what appeared to be solid wall at the end of the corridor, and a little, wizened[27] man darted out of it, like a rabbit out of its burrow.

"Capital!" said Holmes, calmly. "Watson, a bucket of water over the straw. That will do! Lestrade, allow me to present you with your principal missing witness, Mr. Jonas Oldacre."

The detective stared at the newcomer with blank amazement. The latter was blinking in the bright light of the corridor, and peering at us and at the smouldering fire. It was an odious face—crafty, vicious, malignant, with shifty, light-grey eyes and white lashes.

"What's this, then?" said Lestrade, at last. "What have you been doing all this time, eh?"

---

[26] scorn
[27] wrinkly

Oldacre gave an uneasy laugh, shrinking back from the furious red face of the angry detective.

"I have done no harm."

"No harm? You have done your best to get an innocent man hanged. If it wasn't for this gentleman here, I am not sure that you would not have succeeded."

The wretched creature began to whimper.

"I am sure, sir, it was only my practical joke."

"Oh! a joke, was it? You won't find the laugh on your side, I promise you. Take him down, and keep him in the sitting room until I come. Mr. Holmes," he continued, when they had gone, "I could not speak before the constables, but I don't mind say-

ing, in the presence of Dr. Watson, that this is the brightest thing that you have done yet, though it is a mystery to me how you did it. You have saved an innocent man's life, and you have prevented a very grave scandal, which would have ruined my reputation in the Force."

Holmes smiled, and clapped Lestrade upon the shoulder.

"Instead of being ruined, my good sir, you will find that your reputation has been enormously enhanced. Just make a few alterations in that report which you were writing, and they will understand how hard it is to throw dust in the eyes of Inspector Lestrade."

"And you don't want your name to appear?"

"Not at all. The work is its own reward. Perhaps I shall get the credit also at some distant day, when I permit my zealous historian to lay out his foolscap[28] once more—eh, Watson? Well, now, let us see where this rat has been lurking."

A lath-and-plaster partition had been run across the passage six feet from the end, with a door cunningly concealed in it. It was lit within by slits under the eaves. A few articles of furniture and a supply of food and water were within, together with a number of books and papers.

"There's the advantage of being a builder," said Holmes, as we came out. "He was able to fix up his own little hiding place without any confeder-

---

[28] writing paper

ate[29]—save, of course, that precious housekeeper of his, whom I should lose no time in adding to your bag, Lestrade."

"I'll take your advice. But how did you know of this place, Mr. Holmes?"

"I made up my mind that the fellow was in hiding in the house. When I paced one corridor and found it six feet shorter than the corresponding one below, it was pretty clear where he was. I thought he had not the nerve to lie quiet before an alarm of fire. We could, of course, have gone in and taken him, but it amused me to make him reveal himself. Besides, I owed you a little mystification, Lestrade, for your chaff in the morning."

"Well, sir, you certainly got equal with me on that. But how in the world did you know that he was in the house at all?"

"The thumb-mark, Lestrade. You said it was final; and so it was, in a very different sense. I knew it had not been there the day before. I pay a good deal of attention to matters of detail, as you may have observed, and I had examined the hall, and was sure that the wall was clear. Therefore, it had been put on during the night."

"But how?"

"Very simply. When those packets were sealed up, Jonas Oldacre got McFarlane to secure one of the seals by putting his thumb upon the soft wax. It would be done so quickly and so naturally, that I daresay the young man himself has no recollection of it. Very likely it just so happened, and Oldacre had himself no notion of the use he would put it to. Brooding over the case in that den of his, it suddenly struck him what evidence he could make against McFarlane by using that thumb-mark. It was the simplest thing in the world for him to take a wax impression from the seal, to moisten it in as much blood as he could get from a pin-prick, and to put the mark upon the wall during the night, either with his own hand or with that of his housekeeper. If you examine among those documents which he took with him into his retreat, I will lay you a wager that you find the seal with the thumb-mark upon it."

"Wonderful!" said Lestrade. "Wonderful! It's all as clear as crystal, as you put it. But what is the object of this deep deception, Mr. Holmes?"

It was amusing to me to see how the detective's overbearing manner had changed suddenly to that of a child asking questions of its teacher.

"Well, I don't think that is very hard to explain. A very deep, malicious, vindictive[30] person is the gentleman who is now waiting us downstairs. You know that he was once refused by McFarlane's mother? You don't! I told you that you should go to Blackheath first and Norwood afterwards. Well, this injury, as he would consider it, has rankled in his wicked, scheming brain, and all his life he has longed for vengeance, but never seen his

---

[29] partner
[30] vengeful

chance. During the last year or two, things have gone against him—secret speculation, I think—and he finds himself in a bad way. He determines to swindle his creditors, and for this purpose he pays large checks to a certain Mr. Cornelius, who is, I imagine, himself under another name. I have not traced these checks yet, but I have no doubt that they were banked under that name at some provincial town where Oldacre from time to time led a double existence. He intended to change his name altogether, draw this money, and vanish, starting life again elsewhere."

"Well, that's likely enough."

"It would strike him that in disappearing he might throw all pursuit off his track, and at the same time have an ample and crushing revenge upon his old sweetheart, if he could give the impression that he had been murdered by her only child. It was a masterpiece of villainy, and he carried it out like a master. The idea of the will, which would give an obvious motive for the crime, the secret visit unknown to his own parents, the retention of the stick, the blood, and the animal remains and buttons in the woodpile, all were admirable. It was a net from which it seemed to me, a few hours ago, that there was no possible escape. But he had not that supreme gift of the artist, the knowledge of when to stop. He wished to improve that which was already perfect—to draw the rope tighter yet round the neck of his unfortunate victim—and so he ruined all. Let us descend, Lestrade. There are just one or two questions that I would ask him."

The malignant creature was seated in his own parlor, with a policeman upon each side of him.

"It was a joke, my good sir—a practical joke, nothing more," he whined incessantly. "I assure you, sir, that I simply concealed myself in order to see the effect of my disappearance, and I am sure that you would not be so unjust as to imagine that I would have allowed any harm to befall poor young Mr. McFarlane."

"That's for a jury to decide," said Lestrade. "Anyhow, we shall have you on a charge of conspiracy, if not for attempted murder."

"And you'll probably find that your creditors will impound the banking account of Mr. Cornelius," said Holmes.

The little man started, and turned his malignant eyes upon my friend.

"I have to thank you for a good deal," said he. "Perhaps I'll pay my debt some day."

Holmes smiled indulgently.

"I fancy that, for some few years, you will find your time very fully occupied," said he. "By the way, what was it you put into the wood-pile besides your old trousers? A dead dog, or rabbits, or what? You won't tell? Dear me, how very unkind of you! Well, well, I daresay that a couple of rabbits would account both for the blood and for the charred ashes. If ever you write an account, Watson, you can make rabbits serve your turn."

Questions for Review

1. What evidence is there at the "scene of the crime" that points to McFarlane's guilt?

2. Why does Oldacre tell McFarlane to keep his inheritance from him a secret from anyone?

3. Why does Holmes doubt McFarlane's guilt after hearing his story?

4. How is the thumbprint an important piece of evidence?

5. What is the motive of the criminal?

The Eagle

By Alfred, Lord Tennyson

*Alfred, Lord Tennyson (1809-1882) was one of England's greatest and most honored poets. In "The Eagle," which he wrote in 1851, Tennyson uses a poetic technique called **alliteration**, which is a repeating of consonant sounds. He also uses a technique called **simile**, which is a comparison using the word "like" or "as."*

• • • • •

He clasps the crag[1] with crooked hands;
Close to the sun in lonely lands,
Ring'd with the azure[2] world, he stands.

The wrinkled sea beneath him crawls;
He watches from his mountain walls,
And like a thunderbolt he falls.

Questions for Review

1. Where is the *alliteration* and the *simile* in this poem?

2. What's the poem's rhyme scheme and number of syllables in each line?

3. How is the eagle "ring'd with the azure world"? (That is, what blue things is the eagle surrounded by?)

4. Think of an animal you admire or are interested in. Write a six-line poem about that animal in the same style (i.e., same number of syllables per line, same rhyme scheme).

---

[1] cliff, mountaintop
[2] blue

Ingratitude (Blow, Blow, Thou Winter Wind)

By William Shakespeare

 *William Shakespeare (1564-1616) was best known for his plays like* Julius Caesar *and* Romeo and Juliet. *But he also wrote much poetry. "Ingratitude" comes from one of his plays called* As You Like It. *The poem can be classified as an* **apostrophe**—*a piece of writing that addresses someone, an animal, or something else that cannot respond.*

• • • • •

Blow, blow, thou winter wind;
Thou are not so unkind
As man's ingratitude;
Thy tooth is not so keen[1]
Because thou are not seen,
Although thy breath be rude.

Freeze, freeze, thou bitter sky,
Thou dost not bite so nigh[2]
As benefits forgot;
Though thou the waters warp,
Thy sting is not so sharp
As friend remembered not.

Questions for Review

1. Define the word *ingratitude*.

2. What does the poet speak to?

3. What does the poet say is worse than a cold winter wind and a bitter, frozen sky?

4. What does God's Word say about ingratitude in Luke 6:35 and 2 Timothy 3:1-2? Take a minute to thank God for His blessings!

---

[1] sharp
[2] near

The Golden Windows

By Laura E. Richards

Have you ever noticed someone else your age who seemed to have everything—things you didn't have? If so, you're not alone! God has blessed different families (and allowed them to have more) in various ways. This 1881 story by Laura E. Richards (1850-1943) expresses that feeling through the eyes of a boy. Richards wrote "The Golden Windows" in the style of a fairy tale or a fable—an interesting choice that makes this tale even more effective.

• • • • •

All day long the little boy worked hard, in field and barn and shed, for his people were poor farmers, and could not pay a workman; but at sunset there came an hour that was all his own, for his father had given it to him. Then the boy would go up to the top of a hill and look across at another hill that rose some miles away. On this far hill stood a house with windows of clear gold and diamonds. They shone and blazed so that it made the boy wink to look at them: but after a while the people in the house put up shutters, as it seemed, and then it looked like any common farmhouse. The boy supposed they did this because it was suppertime; and then he would go into the house and have his supper of bread and milk, and so to bed.

One day the boy's father called him and said: "You have been a good boy, and have earned a holiday. Take this day for your own; but remember that God gave it, and try to learn some good thing."

The boy thanked his father and kissed his mother; then he put a piece of bread in his pocket, and started off to find the house with the golden windows.

It was pleasant walking. His bare feet made marks in the white dust, and when he looked back, the footprints seemed to be following him, and making company for him. His shadow, too, kept beside him, and would dance or run with him as he pleased; so it was very cheerful.

By and by he felt hungry; and he sat down by a brown brook that ran through the alder hedge by the roadside, and ate his bread, and drank the clear water. Then he scattered the crumbs for the birds, as his mother had taught him to do, and went on his way.

After a long time he came to a high green hill; and when he had climbed the hill, there was the house on the top; but it seemed that the shutters were up, for he could not see the golden windows. He came up to the house, and then he could well have wept, for the windows were of clear glass, like any others, and there was no gold anywhere about them.

A woman came to the door, and looked kindly at the boy, and asked him what he wanted.

"I saw the golden windows from our hilltop," he said, "and I came to see them, but now they are only glass."

The woman shook her head and laughed.

"We are poor farming people," she said, "and are not likely to have gold about our windows; but glass is better to see through."

She bade the boy sit down on the broad stone step at the door, and brought him a cup of milk and a cake, and bade him rest; then she called her daughter, a child of his own age, and nodded kindly at the two, and went back to her work.

The little girl was barefooted like himself, and wore a brown cotton gown, but her hair was golden like the windows he had seen, and her eyes were blue like the sky at noon. She led the boy about the farm, and showed him her black calf with the white star on its forehead, and he told her about his own at home, which was red like a chestnut, with four white feet. Then when they had eaten an apple together, and so had become friends, the boy asked her about the golden windows. The little girl nodded, and said she knew all about them, only he had mistaken the house.

"You have come quite the wrong way!" she said. "Come with me, and I will show you the house with the golden windows, and then you will see for yourself."

They went to a knoll[1] that rose behind the farmhouse, and as they went the little girl told him that the golden windows could only be seen at a certain hour, about sunset.

"Yes, I know that!" said the boy.

When they reached the top of the knoll, the girl turned and pointed; and there on a hill far away stood a house with windows of clear gold and diamond, just as he had seen them. And when they looked again, the boy saw that it was his own home.

Then he told the little girl that he must go; and he gave her his best pebble, the white one with the red band, that he had carried for a year in his pocket; and she gave him three horse-chestnuts, one red like satin, one spotted, and one white like milk. He kissed her, and promised to come again, but he did not tell her what he had learned; and so he went back down the hill, and the little girl stood in the sunset light and watched him.

The way home was long, and it was dark before the boy reached his father's house; but the lamplight and firelight shone through the windows,

---

[1] hill

making them almost as bright as he had seen them from the hilltop; and when he opened the door, his mother came to kiss him, and his little sister ran to throw her arms about his neck, and his father looked up and smiled from his seat by the fire.

"Have you had a good day?" asked his mother.

Yes, the boy had had a very good day.

"And have you learned anything?" asked his father.

"Yes!" said the boy. "I have learned that our house has windows of gold and diamond."

Questions for Review

1. What about this story makes it read like a fairy tale or a fable?

2. What lesson does the boy say he learns? What does he mean by it?

3. Have you ever envied someone else's home or possessions? What have you been blessed with that you wouldn't trade for anything?

A Dilemma

By S. Weir Mitchell

A dilemma *is a situation in which someone must make a choice between two alternatives, both of which are unpleasant. This story by Silas Weir Mitchell (1829-1914) describes a dilemma, no question! Mitchell was a neurologist: a doctor who worked on the brain, spinal cord, and nervous system.*[1] *He was also a poet and short story writer, and he came up with this interesting piece in 1902. What would* you *do if you were faced with the following dilemma?*

•••••

I was just thirty-seven when my Uncle Philip died. A week before that event he sent for me; and here let me say that I had never set eyes on him. He hated my mother, but I do not know why. She told me long before his last illness that I need expect nothing from my father's brother. He was an inventor, an able and ingenious mechanical engineer, and had made much money by his improvement in turbine wheels. He was a bachelor; lived alone, cooked his own meals, and collected precious stones, especially rubies and pearls. From the time he made his first money he had this mania.[2] As he grew richer, the desire to possess rare and costly gems became stronger. When he bought a new stone, he carried it in his pocket for a month and now and then took it out and looked at it. Then it was added to the collection in his safe at the trust company.

At the time he sent for me I was a clerk, and poor enough. Remembering my mother's words, his message gave me, his sole relative, no new hopes; but I thought it best to go.

When I sat down by his bedside, he began, with a malicious[3] grin:

"I suppose you think me queer. I will explain." What he said was certainly queer enough. "I have been living on an annuity[4] into which I put my fortune. In other words, I have been, as to money, concentric[5] half of my life to enable me to be as eccentric as I pleased the rest of it. Now I re-pent of my wickedness to you all, and desire to live in the memory of at least

---

[1] And trying to figure out the dilemma in this story might just work on *your* brain (and maybe your spinal cord and nervous system, too).
[2] obsession
[3] hateful, nasty
[4] yearly income
[5] acting regularly or normally

one of my family. You think I am poor and have only my annuity. You will be profitably surprised. I have never parted with my precious stones; they will be yours. You are my sole heir. I shall carry with me to the other world the satisfaction of making one man happy.

"No doubt you have always had expectations, and I desire that you should continue to expect. My jewels are in my safe. There is nothing else left."

When I thanked him he grinned all over his lean face, and said:

"You will have to pay for my funeral."

I must say that I never looked forward to any expenditure with more pleasure than to what it would cost me to put him away in the earth. As I rose to go, he said:

"The rubies are valuable. They are in my safe at the trust company. Before you unlock the box, be very careful to read a letter which lies on top of it; and be sure not to shake the box." I thought this odd. "Don't come back. It won't hasten things."

He died that day week, and was handsomely buried. The day after, his will was found, leaving me his heir. I opened his safe and found in it nothing but an iron box, evidently of his own making, for he was a skilled workman and very ingenious. The box was heavy and strong, about ten inches long, eight inches wide, and ten inches high. On it lay a letter to me. It ran thus:

"DEAR TOM: This box contains a large number of very fine pigeon-blood rubies and a fair lot of diamonds; one is blue—a beauty. There are hundreds of pearls—one the famous green pearl and a necklace of blue pearls, for which any woman would sell her soul—or her affections." I thought of Susan. "I wish you to continue to have expectations and continuously to remember your dear uncle. I would have left these stones to some charity, but I hate the poor as much as I hate your mother's son—yes, rather more.

"The box contains an interesting mechanism, which will act with certainty as you unlock it, and explode ten ounces of my improved, supersensitive dynamite—no, to be accurate, there are only nine and a half ounces. Doubt me, and open it, and you will be blown to atoms. Believe me, and you will continue to nourish expectations which will never be fulfilled. As a considerate man, I counsel extreme care in handling the box. Don't forget your affectionate "UNCLE."

I stood appalled, the key in my hand. Was it true? Was it a lie? I had spent all my savings on the funeral, and was poorer than ever.

Remembering the old man's oddity, his malice, his cleverness in mechanic arts, and the patent explosive which had helped to make him rich, I began to feel how very likely it was that he had told the truth in this cruel letter.

I carried the iron box away to my lodgings, set it down with care in a closet, laid the key on it, and locked the closet.

Then I sat down, as yet hopeful, and began to exert my ingenuity[6] upon ways of opening the box without being killed. There must be a way.

After a week of vain[7] thinking I bethought me, one day, that it would be easy to explode the box by unlocking it at a safe distance, and I arranged a plan with wires, which seemed as if it would answer. But when I reflected on what would happen when the dynamite scattered the rubies, I knew that I should be none the richer. For hours at a time I sat looking at that box and handling the key.

At last I hung the key on my watch-guard; but then it occurred to me that it might be lost or stolen. Dreading this, I hid it, fearful that some one might use it to open the box. This state of doubt and fear lasted for weeks, until I became nervous and began to dread that some accident might happen to that box. A burglar might come and boldly carry it away and force it open and find it was a wicked fraud of my uncle's. Even the rumble and vibration caused by the heavy vans in the street became at last a terror.

Worst of all, my salary was reduced, and I saw that marriage was out of the question.

In my despair I consulted Professor Clinch about my dilemma, and as to some safe way of getting at the rubies. He said that, if my uncle had not lied, there was none that would not ruin the stones, especially the pearls, but that it was a silly tale and altogether incredible. I offered him the biggest ruby if he wished to test his opinion. He did not desire to do so.

Dr. Schaff, my uncle's doctor, believed the old man's letter, and added a caution, which was entirely useless, for by this time I was afraid to be in the room with that terrible box.

At last the doctor kindly warned me that I was in danger of losing my mind with too much thought about my rubies. In fact, I did nothing else but contrive wild plans to get at them safely. I spent all my spare hours at one of the great libraries reading about dynamite. Indeed, I talked of it until the library attendants, believing me a lunatic or a dynamite fiend, declined to humor me, and spoke to the police. I suspect that for a while I was "shadowed" as a suspicious, and possibly criminal, character. I gave up the libraries, and, becoming more and more fearful, set my precious box on a down pillow, for fear of its being shaken; for at this time even the absurd possibility of its being disturbed by an earthquake troubled me. I tried to calculate the amount of shake needful to explode my box.

The old doctor, when I saw him again, begged me to give up all thought of the matter, and, as I felt how completely I was the slave of one despotic[8] idea, I tried to take the good advice thus given me.

---

[6] imagination
[7] hopeless, unsuccessful
[8] cruel

Unhappily, I found, soon after, between the leaves of my uncle's Bible, a numbered list of the stones with their cost and much beside. It was dated two years before my uncle's death. Many of the stones were well known, and their enormous value amazed me.

Several of the rubies were described with care, and curious histories of them were given in detail. One was said to be the famous "Sunset ruby," which had belonged to the Empress-Queen Maria Theresa. One was called the "Blood ruby," not, as was explained, because of the color, but on account of the murders it had occasioned. Now, as I read, it seemed again to threaten death.

The pearls were described with care as an unequaled collection. Concerning two of them my uncle had written what I might call biographies—for, indeed, they seemed to have done much evil and some good. One, a black pearl, was mentioned in an old bill of sale as—She—which seemed queer to me.

It was maddening. Here, guarded by a vision of sudden death, was wealth "beyond the dreams of avarice."[9] I am not a clever or ingenious man; I know little beyond how to keep a ledger, and so I was, and am, no doubt, absurd about many of my notions as to how to solve this riddle.

At one time I thought of finding a man who would take the risk of unlocking the box, but what right had I to subject any one else to the trial I dared not face? I could easily drop the box from a height somewhere, and if it did not explode could then safely unlock it; but if it did blow up when it fell, goodbye to my rubies. *Mine*, indeed! I was rich, and I was not....

Two years have gone by, and I am one of the richest men in the city, and have no more money than will keep me alive.

Susan said I was half cracked like Uncle Philip, and broke off her engagement. In my despair I have advertised in the *Journal of Science*, and have had absurd schemes sent me by the dozen. At last, as I talked too much about it, the thing became so well known that when I put the horror in a safe, in bank, I was promptly desired to withdraw it. I was in constant fear of burglars, and my landlady gave me notice to leave, because no one would stay in the house with that box. I am now advised to print my story and await advice from the ingenuity of the American mind.

I have moved into the suburbs and hidden the box and changed my name and my occupation. This I did to escape the curiosity of the reporters. I ought to say that when the government officials came to hear of my inheritance, they very reasonably desired to collect the succession tax on my uncle's estate.

I was delighted to assist them. I told the collector my story, and showed him Uncle Philip's letter. Then I offered him the key, and asked for time to

---

[9] greed

get half a mile away. That man said he would think it over and come back later.

This is all I have to say....If any man thinks this account a joke or an invention, let him coldly imagine the situation:

Given an iron box, known to contain wealth, said to contain dynamite, arranged to explode when the key is used to unlock it—what would any sane man do? What would he advise?

Questions for Review

1. What is ironic about the uncle's saying to the narrator that he (the uncle) wants his nephew "continuously to remember [his] dear uncle"?

2. Do you find it strange that the nephew finds a list of the stones and their value "between the leaves of [his] uncle's Bible"? If so, why?

3. Well, what *would* you do if you were faced with this dilemma?

Inscriptions on a Sun-Dial

By John Greenleaf Whittier

You've no doubt seen a picture of a sun-dial, a device that tells the time of day by the position that a shadow is cast on its face. (As the sun travels across the sky, the shadow on the sun-dial indicates the time.) Massachusetts-born poet and editor John Greenleaf Whittier (1807-1892) expresses an interesting observation about the sun-dial.

• • • • •

With warning hand I mark Time's rapid flight
From life's glad morning to its solemn night;
Yet through thee dear God's love, I also show
There's Light above me by the shade below.

Questions for Review

1. Who is narrating the above poem?

2. In what other way could the reader interpret the poem's last two lines?

3. Find and listen to the song "Road to Zion" by the Christian band Petra. (The song provides a similar message to "Inscriptions on a Sun-Dial.")

Four Things

By Henry Van Dyke

Proverbs 6:16-19 says that the Lord hates seven things: "a proud look, a lying tongue, and hands that shed innocent blood, an heart that deviseth wicked imaginations, feet that be swift in running to mischief, a false witness that speaketh lies, and he that soweth discord among brethren." Henry Van Dyke (1852-1933) thought of another list.

• • • • •

Four things a man must learn to do
If he would make his record true:
To think without confusion clearly;
To love his fellow man sincerely;
To act from honest motives purely;
To trust in God and Heaven securely.

Question for Review

Think of four different things that a person *should* do. Then write your own, original last four lines to the above poem.

The Revolt of "Mother"

By Mary E. Wilkins Freeman

*Mary E. Wilkins Freeman (1852-1930) was born in Massachusetts and lived there and in Vermont nearly all her life. She gained popularity as a writer partly because of her reputation as a **regionalist**. That is, Freeman often wrote stories that were set in a specific region—in her case, the northeast United States, since that's what she was quite familiar with. "The Revolt of 'Mother,'" first published in 1890, has always been one of her most popular short stories.*

• • • • •

"**F**ATHER!"

"What is it?"

"What are them men diggin' over there in the field for?"

There was a sudden dropping and enlarging of the lower part of the old man's face, as if some heavy weight had settled therein; he shut his mouth tight, and went on harnessing the great bay mare. He hustled the collar on to her neck with a jerk.

"Father!"

The old man slapped the saddle upon the mare's back.

"Look here, father, I want to know what them men are diggin' over in the field for, an' I'm goin' to know."

"I wish you'd go into the house, mother, an' 'tend to your own affairs," the old man said then. He ran his words together, and his speech was almost as inarticulate[1] as a growl.

But the woman understood; it was her most native tongue. "I ain't goin' into the house till you tell me what them men are doin' over there in the field," said she.

Then she stood waiting. She was a small woman, short and straight-waisted like a child in her brown cotton gown. Her forehead was mild and benevolent[2] between the smooth curves of gray hair; there were meek downward lines about her nose and mouth; but her eyes, fixed upon the old man, looked as if the meekness had been the result of her own will, never of the will of another.

---

[1] unclear, mumbling
[2] kindly

They were in the barn, standing before the wide-open doors. The spring air, full of the smell of growing grass and unseen blossoms, came in their faces. The deep yard in front was littered with farm wagons and piles of wood; on the edges, close to the fence and the house, the grass was a vivid green, and there were some dandelions.

The old man glanced doggedly[3] at his wife as he tightened the last buckles on the harness. She looked as immovable to him as one of the rocks in his pastureland, bound to the earth with generations of blackberry vines. He slapped the reins over the horse, and started forth from the barn.

"Father!" said she.

The old man pulled up. "What is it?"

"I want to know what them men are diggin' over there in that field for."

"They're diggin' a cellar, I s'pose, if you've got to know."

"A cellar for what?"

"A barn."

"A barn? You ain't goin' to build a barn over there where we was goin' to have a house, father?"

The old man said not another word. He hurried the horse into the farm wagon, and clattered out of the yard, jouncing as sturdily on his seat as a boy.

The woman stood a moment looking after him, then she went out of the barn across a corner of the yard to the house. The house, standing at right angles with the great barn and a long reach of sheds and out-buildings, was infinitesimal[4] compared with them. It was scarcely as commodious[5] for people as the little boxes under the barn eaves were for doves.

A pretty girl's face, pink and delicate as a flower, was looking out of one of the house windows. She was watching three men who were digging over in the field which bounded the yard near the road line. She turned quietly when the woman entered.

"What are they diggin' for, mother?" said she. "Did he tell you?"

"They're diggin' for—a cellar for a new barn."

"Oh, mother, he ain't goin' to build another barn?"

"That's what he says."

A boy stood before the kitchen glass combing his hair. He combed slowly and painstakingly, arranging his brown hair in a smooth hillock over his forehead. He did not seem to pay any attention to the conversation.

"Sammy, did you know father was goin' to build a new barn?" asked the girl.

---

[3] stubbornly
[4] tiny
[5] roomy

The boy combed assiduously.[6]

"Sammy!"

He turned, and showed a face like his father's under his smooth crest of hair. "Yes, I s'pose I did," he said, reluctantly.

"How long have you known it?" asked his mother.

"'Bout three months, I guess."

"Why didn't you tell of it?"

"Didn't think 'twould do no good."

"I don't see what father wants another barn for," said the girl, in her sweet slow voice. She turned again to the window, and stared out at the digging men in the field. Her tender sweet face was full of a gentle distress. Her forehead was as bald and innocent as a baby's, with the light hair strained back from it in a row of curl-papers. She was quite large, but her soft curves did not look as if they covered muscles.

Her mother looked sternly at the boy. "Is he goin' to buy more cows?" said she.

The boy did not reply; he was tying his shoes.

"Sammy, I want you to tell me if he's goin' to buy more cows."

"I s'pose he is."

"How many?"

"Four, I guess."

His mother said nothing more. She went into the pantry, and there was a clatter of dishes. The boy got his cap from a nail behind the door, took an old arithmetic from the shelf, and started for school. He was lightly built, but clumsy. He went out of the yard with a curious spring in the hips that made his loose homemade jacket tilt up in the rear.

The girl went to the sink, and began to wash the dishes that were piled up there. Her mother came promptly out of the pantry, and shoved her aside. "You wipe 'em," said she; "I'll wash. There's a good many this mornin'."

The mother plunged her hands vigorously into the water, the girl wiped the plates slowly and dreamily. "Mother," said she, "don't you think it's too bad father's goin' to build that new barn, much as we need a decent house to live in?"

Her mother scrubbed a dish fiercely. "You ain't found out yet we're women-folks, Nanny Penn," said she. "You ain't seen enough of men-folks yet to. One of these days you'll find it out, an' then you'll know that we know only what men-folks think we do, so far as any use of it goes, an' how we'd ought to reckon men-folks in with Providence an' not complain of what they do any more than we do of the weather."

---

[6] diligently

"I don't care; I don't believe George is anything like that, anyhow," said Nanny. Her delicate face flushed pink, her lips pouted softly, as if she were going to cry.

"You wait an' see. I guess George Eastman ain't no better than other men. You hadn't ought to judge father, though. He can't help it, 'cause he don't look at things jest the way we do. An' we've been pretty comfortable here, after all. The roof don't leak—ain't never but once—that's one thing. Father kept it shingled right up."

"I do wish we had a parlor."

"I guess it won't hurt George Eastman any to come to see you in a nice clean kitchen. I guess a good many girls don't have as good a place as this. Nobody's ever heard me complain."

"I ain't complained either, mother."

"Well, I don't think you'd better, a good father an' a good home as you've got. S'pose your father made you go out an' work for your livin'? Lots of girls have to that ain't no stronger an' better able to than you be."

Sarah Penn washed the frying pan with a conclusive air. She scrubbed the outside of it as faithfully as the inside. She was a masterly keeper of her box of a house. Her one living room never seemed to have in it any of the dust which the friction of life with inanimate[7] matter produces. She swept, and there seemed to be no dirt to go before the broom; she cleaned, and one could see no difference. She was like an artist so perfect that he has apparently no art. Today she got out a mixing bowl and a board, and rolled some pies, and there was no more flour upon her than upon her daughter who was doing finer work. Nanny was to be married in the fall, and she was sewing on some white cambric[8] and embroidery. She sewed industriously while her mother cooked, her soft milk-white hands and wrists showed whiter than her delicate work.

"We must have the stove moved out in the shed before long," said Mrs. Penn. "Talk about not havin' things, it's been a real blessin' to be able to put a stove up in that shed in hot weather. Father did one good thing when he fixed that stovepipe out there."

Sarah Penn's face as she rolled her pies had that expression of meek vigor which might have characterized one of the New Testament saints. She was making mince-pies. Her husband, Adoniram Penn, liked them better than any other kind. She baked twice a week. Adoniram often liked a piece of pie between meals. She hurried this morning. It had been later than usual when she began, and she wanted to have a pie baked for dinner. However

---

[7] non-living
[8] fabric

deep a resentment she might be forced to hold against her husband, she would never fail in sedulous[9] attention to his wants.

Nobility of character manifests itself at loop-holes when it is not provided with large doors. Sarah Penn's showed itself today in flaky dishes of pastry. So she made the pies faithfully, while across the table she could see, when she glanced up from her work, the sight that rankled in her patient and steadfast soul—the digging of the cellar of the new barn in the place where Adoniram forty years ago had promised her their new house should stand.

The pies were done for dinner. Adoniram and Sammy were home a few minutes after twelve o'clock. The dinner was eaten with serious haste. There was never much conversation at the table in the Penn family. Adoniram asked a blessing, and they ate promptly, then rose up and went about their work.

Sammy went back to school, taking soft sly lopes out of the yard like a rabbit. He wanted a game of marbles before school, and feared his father would give him some chores to do. Adoniram hastened to the door and called after him, but he was out of sight.

"I don't see what you let him go for, mother," said he. "I wanted him to help me unload that wood."

Adoniram went to work out in the yard unloading wood from the wagon. Sarah put away the dinner dishes, while Nanny took down her curl-papers and changed her dress. She was going down to the store to buy some more embroidery and thread.

When Nanny was gone, Mrs. Penn went to the door. "Father!" she called. "Well, what is it?"

"I want to see you jest a minute, father."

"I can't leave this wood nohow. I've got to git it unloaded an' go for a load of gravel afore two o'clock. Sammy had ought to helped me. You hadn't ought to let him go to school so early."

"I want to see you jest a minute."

"I tell ye I can't, nohow, mother."

"Father, you come here." Sarah Penn stood in the door like a queen; she held her head as if it bore a crown; there was that patience which makes authority royal in her voice. Adoniram went.

Mrs. Penn led the way into the kitchen, and pointed to a chair. "Sit down, father," said she; "I've got somethin' I want to say to you."

He sat down heavily; his face was quite stolid,[10] but he looked at her with restive eyes. "Well, what is it, mother?"

"I want to know what you're buildin' that new barn for, father?"

"I ain't got nothin' to say about it."

---

[9] hard-working
[10] emotionless, dull

"It can't be you think you need another barn?"

"I tell ye I ain't got nothin' to say about it, mother; an' I ain't goin' to say nothin'."

"Be you goin' to buy more cows?"

Adoniram did not reply; he shut his mouth tight.

"I know you be, as well as I want to. Now, father, look here"—Sarah Penn had not sat down; she stood before her husband in the humble fashion of a Scripture woman—"I'm goin' to talk real plain to you: I never have sence I married you, but I'm goin' to now. I ain't never complained, an' I ain't goin' to complain now, but I'm goin' to talk plain. You see this room here, father; you look at it well. You see there ain't no carpet on the floor, an' you see the paper is all dirty, an' droppin' off the walls. We ain't had no new paper on it for ten year, an' then I put it on myself, an' it didn't cost but nine-pence a roll. You see this room, father; it's all the one I've had to work in an' eat in an' sit in sence we was married. There ain't another woman in the whole town whose husband ain't got half the means you have but what's got better. It's all the room Nanny's got to have her company in; an' there ain't one of her mates but what's got better, an' their fathers not so able as hers is. It's all the room she'll have to be married in. What would you have thought, father, if we had had our weddin' in a room no better than this? I was married in my mother's parlor, with a carpet on the floor, an' stuffed furniture, an' a mahogany card table. An' this is all the room my daughter will have to be married in. Look here, father!"

Sarah Penn went across the room as though it were a tragic stage. She flung open a door and disclosed a tiny bedroom, only large enough for a bed and bureau, with a path between. "There, father," said she—"there's all the room I've had to sleep in for forty year. All my children were born there—the two that died, an' the two that's livin'. I was sick with a fever there."

She stepped to another door and opened it. It led into the small, ill-lighted pantry. "Here," said she, "is all the buttery I've got—every place I've got for my dishes to set away my victuals[11] in, an' to keep my milk-pans in. Father, I've been takin' care of the milk of six cows in this place, an' now you're goin' to build a new barn, an' keep more cows, an' give me more to do in it."

She threw open another door. A narrow crooked flight of stairs wound upward from it. "There, father!" said she; "I want you to look at the stairs that go up to them two unfinished chambers that are all the places our son an' daughter have had to sleep in all their lives. There ain't a prettier girl in town nor a more ladylike one than Nanny, an' that's the place she has to sleep in. It ain't so good as your horse's stall; it ain't so warm an' tight."

---

[11] food (pronounced *vittles*)

Sarah Penn went back and stood before her husband. "Now, father," said she, "I want to know if you think you're doin' right an' accordin' to what you profess. Here, when we was married, forty year ago, you promised me faithful that we should have a new house built in that lot over in the field before the year was out. You said you had money enough, an' you wouldn't ask me to live in no such place as this. It is forty year now, an' you've been makin' more money, an' I've been savin' of it for you ever since, an' you ain't built no house yet. You've built sheds, an' cow-houses an' one new barn, an' now you're goin' to build another. Father, I want to know if you think it's right. You're lodgin' your dumb beasts better than you are your own flesh an' blood. I want to know if you think it's right."

"I ain't got nothin' to say."

"You can't say nothin' without ownin' it ain't right, father. An' there's another thing—I ain't complained; I've got along forty year, an' I s'pose I should forty more, if it wa'n't for that—if we don't have another house, Nanny she can't live with us after she's married. She'll have to go some-wheres else to live away from us, an' it don't seem as if I could have it so, noways, father. She wa'n't ever strong. She's got considerable color, but there wa'n't never any backbone to her. I've always took the heft of everything off her, an' she ain't fit to keep house an' do everything herself. She'll be all worn out inside of a year. Think of her doin' all the washin' an' ironin' an' bakin' with them soft white hands an' arms, an' sweepin'! I can't have it so, noways, father."

Mrs. Penn's face was burning; her mild eyes gleamed. She had pleaded her little cause like a Webster;[12] she had ranged from severity to pathos;[13]

<hr />

[12] Daniel Webster (1782-1852) was an American congressman noted for his passionate speeches.
[13] sorrow

but her opponent employed that obstinate[14] silence which makes eloquence futile with mocking echoes. Adoniram arose clumsily.

"Father, ain't you got nothin' to say?" said Mrs. Penn.

"I've got to go off after that load of gravel. I can't stan' here talkin' all day."

"Father, won't you think it over, an' have a house built there instead of a barn?"

"I ain't got nothin' to say."

Adoniram shuffled out. Mrs. Penn went into her bedroom. When she came out, her eyes were red. She had a roll of unbleached cotton cloth. She spread it out on the kitchen table, and began cutting out some shirts for her husband. The men over in the field had a team to help them this afternoon; she could hear their halloos. She had a scanty pattern for the shirts; she had to plan and piece the sleeves.

Nanny came home with her embroidery, and sat down with her needle-work. She had taken down her curl-papers, and there was a soft roll of fair hair like an aureole[15] over her forehead; her face was as delicately fine and clear as porcelain. Suddenly she looked up, and the tender red flamed all over her face and neck. "Mother," said she.

"What say?"

"I've been thinkin'—I don't see how we're goin' to have any—weddin' in this room. I'd be ashamed to have his folks come if we didn't have anybody else."

"Mebbe we can have some new paper before then; I can put it on. I guess you won't have no call to be ashamed of your belongin's."

"We might have the weddin' in the new barn," said Nanny, with gentle pettishness. "Why, mother, what makes you look so?"

Mrs. Penn had started,[16] and was staring at her with a curious expression. She turned again to her work, and spread out a pattern carefully on the cloth. "Nothin'," said she.

Presently Adoniram clattered out of the yard in his two-wheeled dump cart, standing as proudly upright as a Roman charioteer. Mrs. Penn opened the door and stood there a minute looking out; the halloos of the men sounded louder.

It seemed to her all through the spring months that she heard nothing but the halloos and the noises of saws and hammers. The new barn grew fast. It was a fine edifice[17] for this little village. Men came on pleasant Sundays, in their meeting suits and clean shirt bosoms, and stood around it admiringly.

---

[14] stubborn
[15] halo
[16] jumped in surprise or shock
[17] building

Mrs. Penn did not speak of it, and Adoniram did not mention it to her, although sometimes, upon a return from inspecting it, he bore himself with injured dignity.

"It's a strange thing how your mother feels about the new barn," he said, confidentially, to Sammy one day.

Sammy only grunted after an odd fashion for a boy: he had learned it from his father.

The barn was all completed ready for use by the third week in July. Adoniram had planned to move his stock in on Wednesday; on Tuesday he received a letter which changed his plans. He came in with it early in the morning. "Sammy's been to the post office," said he, "an' I've got a letter from Hiram." Hiram was Mrs. Penn's brother, who lived in Vermont.

"Well," said Mrs. Penn, "what does he say about the folks?"

"I guess they're all right. He says he thinks if I come up country right off there's a chance to buy jest the kind of a horse I want." He stared reflectively out of the window at the new barn.

Mrs. Penn was making pies. She went on clapping the rolling-pin into the crust, although she was very pale, and her heart beat loudly.

"I dunno' but what I'd better go," said Adoniram. "I hate to go off jest now, right in the midst of hayin', but the ten-acre lot's cut, an' I guess Rufus an' the others can git along without me three or four days. I can't get a horse round here to suit me, nohow, an' I've got to have another for all that wood-haulin' in the fall. I told Hiram to watch out, an' if he got wind of a good horse to let me know. I guess I'd better go."

"I'll get out your clean shirt an' collar," said Mrs. Penn, calmly.

She laid out Adoniram's Sunday suit and his clean clothes on the bed in the little bedroom. She got his shaving water and razor ready. At last she buttoned on his collar and fastened his black cravat.[18]

Adoniram never wore his collar and cravat except on extra occasions. He held his head high, with a rasped dignity. When he was all ready, with his coat and hat brushed, and a lunch of pie and cheese in a paper bag, he hesitated on the threshold of the door. He looked at his wife, and his manner was defiantly apologetic. "If them cows come today, Sammy can drive 'em into the new barn," said he; "an' when they bring the hay up, they can pitch it in there."

"Well," replied Mrs. Penn.

Adoniram set his shaven face ahead and started. When he had cleared the doorstep, he turned and looked back with a kind of nervous solemnity.[19] "I shall be back by Saturday if nothin' happens," said he.

"Do be careful, father," returned his wife.

---

[18] necktie
[19] seriousness

She stood in the door with Nanny at her elbow and watched him out of sight. Her eyes had a strange, doubtful expression in them; her peaceful forehead was contracted. She went in, and about her baking again. Nanny sat sewing. Her wedding day was drawing nearer, and she was getting pale and thin with her steady sewing. Her mother kept glancing at her.

"Have you got that pain in your side this mornin'?" she asked.

"A little."

Mrs. Penn's face, as she worked, changed, her perplexed forehead smoothed, her eyes were steady, her lips firmly set. She formed a maxim[20] for herself, although incoherently with her unlettered thoughts. "Unsolicited[21] opportunities are the guideposts of the Lord to the new roads of life," she repeated in effect, and she made up her mind to her course of action.

"S'posin' I had wrote to Hiram," she muttered once, when she was in the pantry—"s'posin' I had wrote, an' asked him if he knew of any horse? But I didn't, an' father's goin' wa'n't none of my doin'. It looks like a Providence."[22] Her voice rang out quite loud at the last.

"What you talkin' about, mother?" called Nanny.

"Nothin'."

Mrs. Penn hurried her baking; at eleven o'clock it was all done. The load of hay from the west field came slowly down the cart track, and drew up at the new barn. Mrs. Penn ran out. "Stop!" she screamed—"stop!"

The men stopped and looked; Sammy upreared from the top of the load, and stared at his mother.

"Stop!" she cried out again. "Don't you put the hay in that barn; put it in the old one."

"Why, he said to put it in here," returned one of the haymakers, wonderingly. He was a young man, a neighbor's son, whom Adoniram hired by the year to help on the farm.

"Don't you put the hay in the new barn; there's room enough in the old one, ain't there?" said Mrs. Penn.

"Room enough," returned the hired man, in his thick, rustic tones. "Didn't need the new barn, nohow, far as room's concerned. Well, I s'pose he changed his mind." He took hold of the horses' bridles.

Mrs. Penn went back to the house. Soon the kitchen windows were darkened, and a fragrance like warm honey came into the room.

Nanny laid down her work. "I thought father wanted them to put the hay into the new barn?" she said, wonderingly.

"It's all right," replied her mother.

---

[20] proverb, saying
[21] not asked for
[22] a work of God

Sammy slid down from the load of hay and came in to see if dinner was ready.

"I ain't goin' to get a regular dinner today, as long as father's gone," said his mother. "I've let the fire go out. You can have some bread an' milk an' pie. I thought we could get along." She set out some bowls of milk, some bread, and a pie on the kitchen table. "You'd better eat your dinner now," said she. "You might jest as well get through with it. I want you to help me afterward."

Nanny and Sammy stared at each other. There was something strange in their mother's manner. Mrs. Penn did not eat anything herself. She went into the pantry, and they heard her moving dishes while they ate. Presently she came out with a pile of plates. She got the clothes basket out of the shed, and packed them in it. Nanny and Sammy watched. She brought out cups and saucers, and put them in with the plates.

"What you goin' to do, mother?" inquired Nanny, in a timid voice. A sense of something unusual made her tremble, as if it were a ghost. Sammy rolled his eyes over his pie.

"You'll see what I'm goin' to do," replied Mrs. Penn. "If you're through, Nanny, I want you to go up stairs an' pack up your things; an' I want you, Sammy, to help me take down the bed in the bedroom."

"Oh, mother, what for?" gasped Nanny.

"You'll see."

During the next few hours a feat was performed by this simple, pious New England mother which was equal in its way to Wolfe's storming of the Heights of Abraham.[23] It took no more genius and audacity[24] of bravery for Wolfe to cheer his wondering soldiers up those steep precipices,[25] under the sleeping eyes of the enemy, than for Sarah Penn, at the head of her children, to move all her little household goods into the new barn while her husband was away.

Nanny and Sammy followed their mother's instructions without a murmur; indeed, they were overawed. There is a certain uncanny and superhuman quality about all such purely original undertakings as their mother's was to them. Nanny went back and forth with her light loads, and Sammy tugged with sober energy.

At five o'clock in the afternoon the little house in which the Penns had lived for forty years had emptied itself into the new barn.

Every builder builds somewhat for unknown purposes, and is in a measure a prophet. The architect of Adoniram Penn's barn, while he designed

---

[23] In the Battle of the Plains of Abraham, British general James Wolfe (1727-1759) won a victory over the French in Quebec, Canada.

[24] daring

[25] cliffs

it for the comfort of four-footed animals, had planned better than he knew for the comfort of humans. Sarah Penn saw at a glance its possibilities. Those great box-stalls, with quilts hung before them, would make better bedrooms than the one she had occupied for forty years, and there was a tight carriage room. The harness room, with its chimney and shelves, would make a kitchen of her dreams. The great middle space would make a parlor, by-and-by, fit for a palace. Upstairs there was as much room as down. With partitions and windows, what a house would there be! Sarah looked at the row of stanchions[26] before the allotted space for cows, and reflected that she would have her front entry there.

At six o'clock the stove was up in the harness room, the kettle was boiling, and the table set for tea. It looked almost as home-like as the abandoned house across the yard had ever done. The young hired man milked, and Sarah directed him calmly to bring the milk to the new barn. He came gaping,[27] dropping little blots of foam from the brimming pails on the grass. Before the next morning he had spread the story of Adoniram Penn's wife moving into the new barn all over the little village. Men assembled in the store and talked it over, women with shawls over their heads scuttled into each other's houses before their work was done. Any deviation[28] from the ordinary course of life in this quiet town was enough to stop all progress in it. Everybody paused to look at the staid,[29] independent figure on the side track. There was a difference of opinion with regard to her. Some held her to be insane; some, of a lawless and rebellious spirit.

Friday the minister went to see her. It was in the forenoon, and she was at the barn door shelling peas for dinner. She looked up and returned his salutation with dignity, then she went on with her work. She did not invite him in. The saintly expression of her face remained fixed, but there was an angry flush over it.

The minister stood awkwardly before her and talked. She handled the peas as if they were bullets. At last she looked up, and her eyes showed the spirit that her meek front had covered for a lifetime.

"There ain't no use talkin', Mr. Hersey," said she. "I've thought it all over an' over, an' I believe I'm doin' what's right. I've made it the subject of prayer, an' it's betwixt me an' the Lord an' Adoniram. There ain't no call for nobody else to worry about it."

"Well, of course if you have brought it to the Lord in prayer, and feel satisfied that you are doing right, Mrs. Penn," said the minister, helplessly.

---

[26] vertical posts

[27] in shock (with his mouth hanging open)

[28] change

[29] calm, solid

His thin, gray-bearded face was pathetic. He was a sickly man; his youthful confidence had cooled....

"I think it's right jest as much as I think it was right for our forefathers to come over from the old country 'cause they didn't have what belonged to 'em," said Mrs. Penn. She arose. The barn threshold might have been Plymouth Rock from her bearing. "I don't doubt you mean well, Mr. Hersey," said she, "but there are things people hadn't ought to interfere with. I've been a member of the church for over forty year. I've got my own mind an' my own feet, an' I'm goin' to think my own thoughts an' go my own ways, an' nobody but the Lord is goin' to dictate to me unless I've a mind to have him. Won't you come in an' set down? How is Mis' Hersey?"

"She is well, I thank you," replied the minister. He added some more perplexed apologetic remarks; then he retreated.

He could expound the intricacies of every character study in the Scriptures, he was competent to grasp the Pilgrim Fathers and all historical innovators, but Sarah Penn was beyond him....But, after all, although it was aside from his province, he wondered more how Adoniram Penn would deal with his wife than how the Lord would. Everybody shared the wonder. When Adoniram's four new cows arrived, Sarah ordered three to be put in the old barn, the other in the house shed where the cooking stove had stood. That added to the excitement. It was whispered that all four cows were domiciled in the house.

Toward sunset on Saturday, when Adoniram was expected home, there was a knot of men in the road near the new barn. The hired man had milked, but he still hung around the premises. Sarah Penn had supper all ready. There were brown bread and baked beans and a custard pie; it was the supper that Adoniram loved on a Saturday night. She had on a clean calico, and she bore herself imperturbably.[30] Nanny and Sammy kept close at her heels. Their eyes were large, and Nanny was full of nervous tremors. Still there was to them more pleasant excitement than anything else. An inborn confidence in their mother over their father asserted itself.

Sammy looked out of the harness room window. "There he is," he announced, in an awed whisper. He and Nanny peeped around the casing. Mrs. Penn kept on about her work. The children watched Adoniram leave the new horse standing in the drive while he went to the house door. It was fastened. Then he went around to the shed. That door was seldom locked, even when the family was away. The thought how her father would be confronted by the cow flashed upon Nanny. There was a hysterical sob in her throat. Adoniram emerged from the shed and stood looking about in a dazed fashion. His lips moved; he was saying something, but they could not

---

[30] calmly, unflappably

hear what it was. The hired man was peeping around a corner of the old barn, but nobody saw him.

Adoniram took the new horse by the bridle and led him across the yard to the new barn. Nanny and Sammy slunk close to their mother. The barn doors rolled back, and there stood Adoniram, with the long mild face of the great Canadian farm horse looking over his shoulder.

Nanny kept behind her mother, but Sammy stepped suddenly forward, and stood in front of her.

Adoniram stared at the group. "What on airth you all down here for?" said he. "What's the matter over to the house?"

"We've come here to live, father," said Sammy. His shrill voice quavered out bravely.

"What"—Adoniram sniffed—"what is it smells like cookin'?" said he. He stepped forward and looked in the open door of the harness room. Then he turned to his wife. His old bristling face was pale and frightened. "What on airth does this mean, mother?" he gasped.

"You come in here, father," said Sarah. She led the way into the harness room and shut the door. "Now, father," said she, "you needn't be scared. I ain't crazy. There ain't nothin' to be upset over. But we've come here to live, an' we're goin' to live here. We've got jest as good a right here as new horses an' cows. The house wa'n't fit for us to live in any longer, an' I made up my mind I wa'n't goin' to stay there. I've done my duty by you forty year, an' I'm goin' to do it now; but I'm goin' to live here. You've got to put in some windows and partitions; an' you'll have to buy some furniture."

"Why, mother!" the old man gasped.

"You'd better take your coat off an' get washed—there's the washbasin—an' then we'll have supper."

"Why, mother!"

Sammy went past the window, leading the new horse to the old barn. The old man saw him, and shook his head speechlessly. He tried to take off his coat, but his arms seemed to lack the power. His wife helped him. She poured some water into the tin basin, and put in a piece of soap. She got the comb and brush, and smoothed his thin gray hair after he had washed. Then she put the beans, hot bread, and tea on the table. Sammy came in, and the family drew up. Adoniram sat looking dazedly at his plate, and they waited.

"Ain't you goin' to ask a blessin', father?" said Sarah.

And the old man bent his head and mumbled.

All through the meal he stopped eating at intervals, and stared furtively[31] at his wife; but he ate well. The home food tasted good to him, and his old frame was too sturdily healthy to be affected by his mind. But after supper he went out and sat down on the step of the smaller door at the right of the

---

[31] secretly

barn, through which he had meant his Jerseys to pass in stately file, but which Sarah designed for her front house door, and he leaned his head on his hands.

After the supper dishes were cleared away and the milk pans washed, Sarah came out to him. The twilight was deepening. There was a clear green glow in the sky. Before them stretched the smooth level of field; in the distance was a cluster of haystacks like the huts of a village; the air was very cool and calm and sweet. The landscape might have been an ideal one of peace.

Sarah bent over and touched her husband on one of his thin, sinewy shoulders. "Father!"

The old man's shoulders heaved: he was weeping.

"Why, don't do so, father," said Sarah.

"I'll—put up the—partitions, an'—everything you—want, mother."

Sarah put her apron up to her face; she was overcome by her own triumph.

Adoniram was like a fortress whose walls had no active resistance, and went down the instant the right besieging tools were used. "Why, mother," he said, hoarsely, "I hadn't no idee you was so set on't as all this comes to."

Questions for Review

1. What kind of people are Sarah and Adoniram Penn?

2. Why is Sarah upset at the digging of the barn?

3. What does Nanny say to Sarah that shocks her into action?

4. What does the town think of what Sarah has done? What do they do when Adoniram is due back?

5. Why do you think Adoniram weeps at the story's end?

What Can I Do?

By T. S. Arthur

The productive and enlightening storyteller T. S. Arthur comes up with another winning tale, this time from 1868.

• • • • •

He was a poor cripple—with fingers twisted out of all useful shape, and lower limbs paralyzed so that he had to drag them after him wearily when he moved through the short distances that limited his sphere of locomotion[1]—a poor, unhappy, murmuring, and, at times, ill-natured cripple, eating the bread which a mother's hard labor procured for him. For hours every fair day, during spring, summer, and autumn, he might be seen in front of the little house where he lived leaning upon the gate, or sitting on an old bench looking with a sober face at the romping village children, or dreamily regarding the passengers who moved with such strong limbs up and down the street. How often bitter envy stung the poor cripple's heart! How often, as the thoughtless village children taunted him cruelly with his misfortune, would he fling harsh maledictions[2] after them. Many pitied the poor cripple; many looked upon him with feelings of disgust and repulsion; but few, if any, sought to do him good.

Not far from where the cripple lived was a man who had been bedridden for years, and who was likely to remain so to the end of his days. He was supported by the patient industry of a wife.

"If good works are the only passport to heaven," he said to a neighbor one day, "I fear my chances will be small."

"'Well done, good and faithful servant'[3] is the language of welcome," was replied; and the neighbor looked at the sick man in a way that made him feel a little uncomfortable.

"I am sick and bedridden—what can I do?" he spoke, fretfully.

"When little is given, little is required. But if there be only a single talent it must be improved."

"I have no talent," said the invalid.

"Are you sure of that?"

"What can I do? Look at me! No health, no strength, no power to rise from this bed. A poor, helpless creature, burdening my wife. Better for me, and for all, if I were in my grave."

---

[1] movement
[2] curses
[3] See Matthew 25:14-23.

"If that were so you would be in your grave. But God knows best. There is something for you to do, or you would be no longer permitted to live," said the neighbor.

The sick man shook his head.

"As I came along just now," continued the neighbor, "I stopped to say a word to poor Tom Hicks, the cripple, as he stood swinging on the gate before his mother's house, looking so unhappy that I pitied him in my heart. 'What do you do with yourself all through these long days, Tom?' I asked. 'Nothing,' he replied, moodily. 'Don't you read sometimes?' I queried. 'Can't read,' was his sullen answer. 'Were you never at school?' I went on. 'No: how can I get to school?' 'Why don't your mother teach you?' 'Because she can't read herself,' replied Tom. 'It isn't too late to begin now,' said I, encouragingly; 'suppose I were to find some one willing to teach you, what would you say?' The poor lad's face brightened as if the sunshine had fallen upon it; and he answered, 'I would say that nothing could please me better.' I promised to find him a teacher; and, as I promised, the thought of you, friend Croft, came into my mind. Now, here is something that you can do; a good work in which you can employ your one talent."

The sick man did not respond warmly to this proposition. He had been so long a mere recipient of good offices—had so long felt himself the object towards which pity and service must tend—that he had nearly lost the relish for good deeds. Idle dependence had made him selfish.

"Give this poor cripple a lesson every day," went on the neighbor, pressing home the subject, "and talk and read to him. Take him in charge as one of God's children, who needs to be instructed and led up to a higher life than the one he is now living. Is not this a good and a great work? It is, my friend, one that God has brought to your hand, and in the doing of which there will be great reward. What can you do? Much! Think of that poor boy's weary life, and of the sadder years that lie still before him. What will become of him when his mother dies? The almshouse[4] alone will open its doors for the helpless one. But who can tell what resources may open before him if stimulated by thought? Take him, then, and unlock the doors of a mind that now sits in darkness, that sunlight may come in. To you it will give a few hours of pleasant work each day; to him it will be a lifelong benefit. Will you do it?"

"Yes."

The sick man could not say "No," though in uttering that half-extorted assent[5] he manifested no warm interest in the case of poor Tom Hicks.

---

[4] poorhouse

[5] agreement, acceptance

On the next day the cripple came to the sick man, and received his first lesson; and every day, at an appointed hour, he was in Mr. Croft's room, eager for the instruction he received. Quickly he mastered the alphabet, and as quickly learned to construct small words, preparatory to combining them in a reading lesson.

After the first three or four days the sick man, who, had undertaken this work with reluctance, began to find his heart going down into it. Tom was so ready a scholar, so interested, and so grateful, that Mr. Croft found the task of instructing him a real pleasure. The neighbor, who had suggested this useful employment of the invalid's time, looked in now and then to see how matters were progressing, and to speak words of encouragement.

Poor Tom was seen less frequently than before hanging on the gate, or sitting idly on the bench before his mother's dwelling; and when you did find him there, as of old, you saw a different expression on his face. Soon the children, who had only looked at him, half in fear, from a distance, or come closer to the gate where he stood gazing with his strange eyes out into the street, in order to worry him, began to have a different feelings for the cripple, and one and another stopped occasionally to speak with him; for Tom no longer made queer faces, or looked at them wickedly, as if he would harm them if in his power, nor retorted angrily if they said things to worry him. And now it often happened that a little boy or girl, who had pitied the poor cripple, and feared him at the same time, would offer him a flower, or an apple, or at handful of nuts in passing to school; and he would take these gifts thankfully, and feel better all day in remembrance of the kindness with which they had been bestowed. Sometimes he would risk to see their books, and his eyes would run eagerly over the pages so far in advance of his comprehension, yet with the hope in his heart of one day mastering them; for he had grown all athirst for knowledge.

As soon as Tom could read, the children in the neighborhood, who had grown to like him, and always gathered around him at the gate, when they happened to find him there, supplied him with books; so that he had an abundance of mental food, and now began to repay his benefactor, the bed-ridden man, by reading to him for hours every day.

The mind of Tom had some of this qualities of a sponge: it absorbed a great deal, and, like a sponge, gave out freely at every pressure.

Whenever his mind came in contact with another mind, it must either absorb or impart.[6] So he was always talking or always listening when he had anybody who would talk or listen.

There was something about him that strongly attracted the boys in the neighborhood, and he usually had three or four of them around him and often a dozen, late in the afternoon, when the schools were out. As Tom had

---

[6] teach

entered a new world—the world of books—and was interested in all he found there, the subjects on which he talked with the boys who sought his company were always instructive. There, was no nonsense about the cripple: suffering of body and mind had long ago made him serious; and all nonsense, or low, sensual talk, to which boys are sometimes addicted, found no encouragement in his presence. His influence over these boys was therefore of the best kind. The parents of some of the children, when they found their sons going so often to the house of Tom Hicks, felt doubts as to the safety of such intimate intercourse with the cripple, towards whom few were prepossessed,[7] as he bore in the village the reputation of being ill-tempered and depraved,[8] and questioned them very closely in regard to the nature of their intercourse. The report of these boys took their parents by surprise; but, on investigation, it proved to be true, and Tom's character soon rose in the public estimation.

Then came, as a natural consequence, inquiry as to the cause of such a change in the unfortunate lad; and the neighbor of the sick man who had instructed Tom told the story of Mr. Croft's agency in the matter. This interested the whole town in both the cripple and his bedridden instructor. The people were taken by surprise at such a notable interest of the great good which may sometimes be done where the means look discouragingly small. Mr. Croft was praised for his generous conduct, and not only praised, but helped by many who had, until now, felt indifferent, towards his case—for his good work rebuked them for neglected opportunities.

The cripple's eagerness to learn, and rapid progress under the most limited advantages, becoming generally known, a gentleman, whose son had been one of Tom's visitors, and who had grown to be a better boy under his influence, offered to send him in his wagon every day to the schoolhouse, which stood half a mile distant, and have him brought back in the afternoon.

It was the happiest day in Tom's life when he was helped down from the wagon, and went hobbling into the schoolroom.

Before leaving home on that morning he had made his way up to the sick room of Mr. Croft.

"I owe it all to you," he said, as he brought the white, thin hand of his benefactor to his lips. It was damp with more than a kiss when he laid it back gently on the bed. "And our Father in heaven will reward you."

"You have done a good work," said the neighbor, who had urged Mr. Croft to improve his one talent, as he sat talking with him on that evening about the poor cripple and his opening prospects; "and it will serve you in that day when the record of life is opened. Not because of the work itself, but for the true charity which prompted the work. It was begun, I know, in

---

[7] inclined
[8] wicked

some self-denial, but that self-denial was for another's good; and because you put away love of ease, and indifference, and forced yourself to do kind offices, seeing that it was right to help others, God will send a heavenly love of doing good into your soul, which always includes a great reward, and is the passport to eternal felicities.

"You said," continued the neighbor, "only a few months ago, 'What can I do?' and spoke as a man who felt that he was deprived of all the means of accomplishing good; and yet you have, with but little effort, lifted a human soul out of the dark valley of ignorance, where it was groping ill self-torture, and placed it on an ascending mountain path. The light of hope has fallen, through your aid, with sunny warmth upon a heart that was cold and barren a little while ago, but is now green with verdure, and blossoming in the sweet promise of fruit. The infinite years to come alone can reveal the blessings that will flow from this one act of a bedridden man, who felt that in him was no capacity[9] for good deeds."

The advantages of a school being placed within the reach of Tom Hicks, he gave up every thought to the acquirement of knowledge. And now came a serious difficulty. His bent, stiff fingers could not be made to hold either pen or pencil in the right position, or to use them in such a way as to make intelligible[10] signs. But Tom was too much in earnest to give up on the first, or second, or third effort. He found, after a great many trials, that he could hold a pencil more firmly than at first, and guide his hand in some obedience to his will. This was sufficient to encourage him to daily long-continued efforts, the result of which was a gradual yielding of the rigid muscles, which became in time so flexible that he could make quite passable figures, and write a fair hand. This did not satisfy him, however. He was ambitious to do better; and so kept on trying and trying, until few boys in the school could give a fairer copy.

"Have you heard the news?" said a neighbor to Mr. Croft, the poor bed-ridden man. It was five years from the day he gave the poor cripple, Tom Hicks, his first lesson.

"What news?" the sick man asked, in a feeble voice, not even turning his head towards the speaker. Life's pulses were running very low. The long struggle with disease was nearly over.

"Tom Hicks has received the appointment of teacher to our public school."

"Are you in earnest?" There was a mingling of surprise and doubt in the low tones that crept out upon the air.

"Yes. It is true what I say. You know that after Mr. Wilson died, the directors got Tom, who was a favorite with all the scholars, to keep the school

---

[9] ability
[10] understandable, readable

together for a few weeks until a successor could be appointed. He managed so well, kept such good order, and showed himself so capable as an instructor, that, when the election took place today, he received a large majority of votes over a number of highly-recommended teachers, and this without his having made application for the situation, or even dreaming of such a thing."

At this moment the cripple's well-known shuffling tread and the rattle of crutches was heard on the stairs. He came up with more than his usual hurry. Croft turned with an effort, so as to get a sight of him as he entered the room.

"I have heard the good news," he said, as he reached a hand feebly towards Tom, "and it has made my heart glad."

"I owe it all to you," replied the cripple, in a voice that trembled with feeling. "God will reward you."

And he caught the shadowy hand, touched it with his lips, and wet it with grateful tears, as once before. Even as he held that thin, white hand the low-moving pulse took an lower beat—lower and lower—until the long-suffering heart grew still, and the freed spirit went up to its reward.

"My benefactor!" sobbed the cripple, as he stood by the wasted form shrouded in grave clothes, and looked upon it for the last time ere[11] the coffin lid closed over it. "What would I have been except for you?"

Are your opportunities for doing good few, and limited in range, to all appearances, reader? Have you often said, like the bedridden man, "What can I do?" Are you poor, weak, ignorant, obscure,[12] or even sick as he was, and shut out from contact with the busy outside world? No matter. If you have a willing heart, good work will come to your hands. Is there no poor, unhappy neglected one to whom you can speak words of encouragement, or lift out of the vale of ignorance? Think! Cast around you. You may, by a single sentence, spoken in the right time and in the right spirit, awaken thoughts in some dull mind that may grow into giant powers in after times, wielded for the world's good. While you may never be able to act directly on society to any great purpose, in consequence of mental or physical disabilities, you may, by instruction and guidance, prepare some other mind for useful work, which, but for your agency, might have wasted its powers in ignorance or crime. All around us are human souls that may be influenced. The nurse, who ministers to you in sickness, may be hurt or helped by you; the children, who look into your face and read it daily, who listen to your speech, and remember what you say, will grow better or worse, according to the spirit of your life, as it flows into them; the neglected son of a neighbor may find in you the wise counselor who holds him back from

---

[11] before
[12] unknown, not famous

vice.[13] Indeed, you cannot pass a single day, whether your sphere be large or small, your place exalted or lowly, without abundant opportunities for doing good. Only the willing heart is required. As for the harvest, that is nodding, ripe for the sickle, in every man's field. What of that time when the Lord of the Harvest comes, and you bind up your sheaves and lay them at his feet?

Questions for Review

1. Croft says he can't earn his way into heaven because he's not able. What does the Bible say about earning our way into heaven?

2. What happens as Croft goes to work? How does this work end up blessing both him and Tom's friends?

3. What is some talent *you* have that you could use to help someone around you like Croft helped Tom?

---

[13] wicked deeds

A Pioneer Mother

By Hamlin Garland

We previously read Hamlin Garland's touching remembrance of the time when he was a boy, and he (and his brother) attended a Christmas Eve service with a beautiful Christmas tree. Below is Garland's tribute to his mother, Charlotte, which he wrote when he was more than 60 years old.

· · · · ·

She was neither witty, nor learned in books, nor wise in the ways of the world, but I contend that her life was noble. There was something in her unconscious heroism which transcends[1] wisdom and the deeds of those who dwell in the rose-golden light of romance. Now that her life is rounded into the silence whence[2] it came, its significance appears.

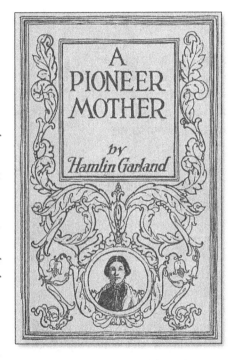

To me she was never young, for I am her son, and as I first remember her she was a large, handsome, smiling woman—deft[3] and powerful of movement, sweet and cheery of smile and voice. She played the violin then, and I recall how she used to lull me to sleep at night with simple tunes like "Money Musk" and "Dan Tucker." She sang, too, and I remember her clear soprano rising out of the singing of the Sunday congregation at the schoolhouse with thrilling sweetness and charm. Her hair was dark, her eyes brown, her skin fair and her lips rested in lines of laughter.

Her first home was in Greene's Coolly, in La Crosse County, Wisconsin, and was only a rude[4] little cabin with three rooms and a garret.[5] The windows of the house overlooked a meadow and a low range of wooded

---

[1] rises above
[2] from where
[3] skillful
[4] simple, basic
[5] attic

hills to the east. In this house she lived alone during two years of the Civil War while my father went as a volunteer into the Army of the Tennessee. My memory of these times is vague but inset with charm. Though my mother worked hard, she had time to visit with her neighbors and often took her children with her to quilting bees, which they enjoyed, for they could play beneath the quilt as if it were a tent, and run under it for shelter from imaginary storms. I feel again her strong, soft, warm arms as she shielded me at nightfall from menacing wolves and other terrible creatures. When the world grew mysterious and vast and thick-peopled with yawning monsters eager for little men and women, she gathered us to her bosom and sang us through the gates of sleep into a golden land of dreams. We never knew how she longed for the return of her blue-coated soldier.

Our stove was a high-stepper, with long bent legs, and bore its oven on its back as a dromedary[6] his hump. Under its arch I loved to lie watching my mother as she trod to and fro about her work in the kitchen. She taught me to read while working thus—for I was constantly interrupting her by asking the meaning of words in the newspaper which I had smuggled under the stove beneath me.

• • • • •

My father's return from the war brought solace[7] and happiness, but increased her labors, for he set to work with new zeal to widen his acres of plow-land.

I have the sweetest recollections of my mother's desire to make us happy each Christmas-time, and to this end she planned jokes for herself and little surprises for us. We were desperately poor in those days, for my father was breaking the tough sod of the natural meadows and grubbing away trees from the hillside, "opening a farm," as he called it, and there was hardly enough extra money to fill three stockings with presents. So it came about that mother's stocking often held more rags and potatoes than silks or silverware. But she always laughed, and we considered it all very good fun then. Its pathos[8] makes my heart ache now.

She was a neighborly woman. She had no enemies. I don't believe any one ever spoke an unkind word of Belle Garland as she was called—she was always sunny—her little petulances[9] passed quickly like small summer showers, and then she laughed—shook with laughter while the tears shone on her face. I can see now that she was only a big, handsome girl, but she was my mother, and as such seemed an "old person."

---

[6] camel
[7] comfort
[8] sadness
[9] irritations

Her physical strength was very great. I have heard my father say that at the time he went away to war she was his equal in many contests, and I know she was very deft and skillful in her work. She could cut and fit and finish the calico dress purchased in the morning of the same day. She cooked with the same adroitness, and though her means were meager,[10] everything she made tasted good. She liked nothing better than to have her neighbors drop in to tea or dinner.

After all, I do not remember very much of her life while we lived in this Coolly—nor while in Winnesheik County, Iowa, whereto we moved in 1869. She remained of the same physical dignity to me, and though she grew rapidly heavier and older, I did not realize it. My second sister Jessie came to us while living in an old log house in a beautiful wood just west of Hesper, and I now know that my mother never recovered from the travail[11] of this birth—though she returned to her domestic duties as before and was to her children the jolly personality she had always been. While living on this farm, smallpox came to our family, and we were all smitten with this much-dreaded disease, but mother not only nursed her baby and took care of us all, but she also smiled down into our faces without apparent anxiety—though some of us lay at death's door for weeks. Shortly after we recovered from this we moved again to the newer West.

· · · · ·

I don't know what her feelings were about these constant removals to the border, but I suspect now that each new migration was a greater hardship than those which preceded it. My father's adventurous and restless spirit was never satisfied. The sunset land always allured him, and my mother, being of those who follow their husbands' feet without complaining word, seemed always ready to take up the trail. With the blindness of youth and the spirit of seeking which I inherited, I saw no tear on my mother's face. I inferred that she, too, was eager and exalted at the thought of "going West." I now see that she must have suffered each time the bitter pangs of doubt and unrest which strike through the woman's heart when called upon to leave her snug, safe fire for a ruder cabin in strange lands.

· · · · ·

She had four children at this time, and I fear her boys gave her considerable trouble, but her eldest daughter was of growing service in working about the house as well as in tending the fair-haired baby, but work grew harder and harder. My father purchased some wild land in Mitchell County, Iowa,

---

[10] skimpy, not enough
[11] labor, struggle

and we all set to work to break the sod for the third time. A large part of the hardship involved in this fell upon my mother, for the farm required a great many "hands," and these "hands" had enormous appetites, and the household duties grew more unrelenting from year to year.

Our new house was a small one with but three rooms below and two above, but it had a little lean-to which served as a summer kitchen. It was a bare home, with no touch of grace other than that given by my mother's cheery presence. Her own room was small and crowded, but as she never found time to occupy it save to sleep, I hope it did not trouble her as it does me now as I look back to it.

Each year, as our tilled acres grew, churning and washing and cooking became harder, until at last it was borne in upon my boyish mind that my mother was condemned to never-remitting labor. She was up in the morning before the light cooking breakfast for us all, and she seldom went to bed before my father. She was not always well, and yet the work had to be done. We all worked in those days; even my little sister ran on errands, and perhaps this was the reason why we did not realize more fully the grinding weight of drudgery[12] which fell on this pioneer's wife. But Harriet was growing into a big girl and began to materially aid my mother, though she brought an added expense in clothing and schooling. We had plenty of good wholesome things to eat in those days, but our furniture remained poor. Our little sitting room was covered with a rag carpet which we children helped to make, tearing, sewing and winding rags during the winter nights. I remember helping mother to dye them also, and in the spring she made her own soap. This also I helped to do.

Churning and milking we boys did for her, and the old up and down churn was a dreaded beast to us as it was to all the boys of the countryside; and yet I knew mother ought not to do such work, and I went to the dasher regularly, but with a wry face. Father was not niggardly[13] of labor-saving implements, and a clotheswringer and washer and a barrel churn came along, and they helped a little, but work never "lets up" on a farm. There are always three meals to get and the dishes to wash, and each day is like another so far as duties are concerned. Sunday brings little rest for housewives, even in winter.

$$\bullet \ \bullet \ \bullet \ \bullet \ \bullet$$

But into those monotonous days some pleasure came. The neighbors dropped in of a summer evening, and each Sunday we drove away to church. In winter we attended all the "lyceums" and church "sociables," and took part in occasional "surprise parties." In all these neighborhood jollities

---

[12] hard work
[13] cheap, stingy

my mother had a generous hand. Her coming always added to the fun. "Here comes Mrs. Garland!" some one would say, and every face shone brighter because of her smile. She was ever ready to help on the gayety in any way, and was always in voice to sing, provided some one else started the song to give her courage. She loved games, practical jokes, and jesting of all kinds. Her natural gayety was almost unquenchable; not even unending work and poverty could entirely subdue her or embitter her.

Death touching her eldest daughter threw the first enduring shadow over her life. She never entirely returned to the jollity of her former years, though she regained a cheerfulness inseparable from her life. She had been youthful to that moment; after that she was middle-aged—even to her sons.

Her two boys and her baby Jessie comforted her, and she had no time for unavailing grief. As she had sent her daughter to school, so now she urged her sons to study, for though a woman of little schooling herself, she had a firm belief in the value of learning. She took strong ground in my behalf, and I have many dear recollections of her quiet support of my plans for an education. In this I owe her much. My father felt the need of my services too keenly to instantly grant me leave of absence, but together they made sacrifices to send me to school as they had sent my sister before me, and as they were willing to send those who came after me. At sixteen I began to attend a seminary in the town, six miles away.

These were my happiest days, and I hope I carried something of my larger outlook back to my mother. I boarded myself for several terms in a fashion common among the boys of the school, and mother's pies and doughnuts and "self-rising" bread enabled me to sustain life joyously from Monday morning till Friday night. She never seemed to tire of doing little things for my comfort, and I took them, I fear, with the carelessness of youth, never thinking of the pain they cost. I did not even perceive how swiftly she was growing old. She still shook with laughter over my tales of school life and sent me away each week with the products of her loving labor.

She heard my graduation address with how much of pride or interest I do not know, for she never expressed her deeper feelings. She seldom kissed her children, and after we grew to be boys of twelve or fourteen, too large to snuggle in her arms, she never embraced us, though I think she liked to have us come and lay our heads in her lap. She still continued to threaten to "trounce" us, a menace which always provoked us to laughter. "Mother's whippings don't last long," we used to say.

Our home remained unchanged. The expense of opening a farm, of buying machinery and building barns, made it seem necessary to live in the same little story-and-a-half house. The furniture grew shabbier, but was not replaced. My mother's dresses were always cheap and badly made, but so were the coats my father wore. Money seemed hard to hold, even when the crops were good. I cannot recall a single beautiful thing about our house, not one. The sunlight and the songs of birds, the flame of winter snow, the blaze of snow-crystals, I clearly call to mind, but the house I remember only as a warm shelter, where my mother strove to feed and clothe us. But as nearly all other homes of the neighborhood were of like character I don't suppose she realized her own poverty.

· · · · ·

At last a great change came to us all. The country was fairly filled with settlers and my father's pioneer heart began to stir again, and once more he planned a flight into the wilder West, and in the fall of 1881, when I was twenty-one years of age, we parted company. My parents and my sister and brother journeyed westward into South Dakota and settled in the little town of Ordway, on a treeless plain, while I turned eastward, intent on further education.

I mention this going especially because, when it became certain that my people were leaving never to return, the neighbors thronged about the house one August day to say goodbye, and with appropriate speeches presented mother with some silver and glassware. These were the first nice dishes she had ever owned, and she was too deeply touched to speak a word of thanks. But the givers did not take so much virtue to themselves. Some of them were women who had known the touch of my mother's hand in sickness and travail. Others had seen her close the eyes of their dead—for she had come to be a mother to everyone who suffered. Those who brought the richest gifts considered them a poor return for her own unstinting helpfulness.

I shall always remember that day. I was about to "go forth into the world," as our graduating orations had declared we should do. My people were again adventuring into strange lands—leaving the house they had built, the trees they had planted, and the friends they had drawn around them. The vivid autumnal sun was shining over all the lanes we had learned to love and sifting through the leaves of the trees that had grown up around us. The familiar faces of the bronzed and wrinkled old farmers were tremulous[14] with emotion. The women frankly wept on each other's bosoms—and in the hush of that golden day I heard the sound of wings—the wings of the death-angel whose other name is Time. I knew we would never return to this place: that the separation of friends there beginning would last forever. The future was luminous[15] before me, but its forms were too vague to be delineated.[16] I turned my face eastward with a thought in my brain

---

[14] quivering
[15] bright
[16] explained, defined

beating like the clock of the ages. In such moments the past becomes beautiful, the future a menace.

• • • • •

This story does not concern itself with my wanderings, but with the life of my mother. When I saw her again she was living in a small house beside my father's store in Ordway, South Dakota. She had not changed perceptibly,[17] and she had won a new and wide circle of friends. She was "Mrs. Garland" now, and not Belle—but she was the life of every social, and her voice was still marvelously clear and vibrant in song. She was a little heavier, a little older, but her face had the same sweet curves about the mouth and chin. Life was a little easier for her, too. She was clear of the farm and its terrible drudgery at last. She could sleep like a human being till daylight came, for she had no one to cook for save her own small family. She saw and was a part of the village life, which was exceedingly jolly and of good report. Her son Franklin and her little daughter were still with her, and she did not much miss her eldest—who had gone far seeking fair cities in intellectual seas. The home was still poor and shabby of furniture, but it was not lonely. Mother missed, but no longer mourned, her vanished friends.

I did not see her again for nearly four years, and my heart contracted with a sudden pain at sight of her. She was growing old. Her hair was gray, and as she spoke, her voice was weak and tremulous. She was again on the farm and working as of old—like one on a treadmill. My father, too, was old. He had not prospered. A drought had swept over the fair valley, and men on all sides were dropping away into despair. Jessie was at home—the only one of all the children. The house was a little better than any my mother had owned before, but it was a poor, barren place for all that.

Old as she was, and suffering constantly from pain in her feet and ankles, she was still mother to every one who suffered. Even while I was there she got up on two demands in the middle of the night and rode away across the plain in answer to some suffering woman's call for help. She knew death intimately. She had closed the eyes of many a world-weary wife or suffering child, and more than once a poor outcast woman of the town, sick and alone, felt the pitying touch of her lips.

• • • • •

I saw with greater clearness than ever before the lack of beauty in her life. She had a few new things, but they were all cheap and poor. She now had one silk dress—which her son had sent her. All else was calico. But worse

---

[17] noticeably

than all was the bleak, burning, wind-swept plain—treeless, scorched, and silent save for the song of the prairie lark. I felt the monotony of her surroundings with greater keenness than ever before.

I was living in Boston at that time, and having heard many of the great singers I was eager to test my mother's voice with the added knowledge I had of such things. Even then, weakened as she was and without training or practice, she still possessed a compass of three octaves and one note, and was able to sing one complete octave above the ordinary soprano voice with every note sweet and musical. I have always believed that a great singer was lost to the world in this pioneer's wife.

One day as I sat writing in the sitting room I heard a strange cry outside—a cry for help. I rushed out into the yard, and there just outside the door in the vivid sunlight stood my mother, unable to move—a look of fear and horror on her face. The black-winged angel had sent her his first warning. She was paralyzed in the lower limbs. I carried her to her bed with a feeling that her life was ended there on the lonely plain, and my heart was bitter and rebellious and my mind filled with self-accusations. If she died now—here—what would she know of the great world outside? Her life had been always on the border—she knew nothing of civilization's splendor of song and story. She would go away from the feast without a crumb. All her toilsome, monotonous days rushed through my mind with a roar, like a file of gray birds in the night—how little—how tragically small her joys, and how black her sorrows, her toil, her tedium.[18]

It chanced that a physician friend was visiting us at the time, and his skill reassured me a little. The bursting of a minute blood vessel in the brain had done the mischief. A small clot had formed, he said, which must either grow or be reabsorbed. He thought it would be reabsorbed and that she would slowly recover.

This diagnosis proved to be correct, and in a few days she was able to sit up, and before I returned to Boston she could walk a little, though she could not lift her feet from the floor.

• • • • •

Our parting at this time was the most painful moment of my life. I had my work to do in Boston. I could earn nothing out on the plain, so I must go, but I promised it would not be for long. In my heart I determined that the remainder of her life should be freer from care and fuller of joy. I resolved to make a home for her in some more hospitable land, but the cling of her arms to my neck remained with me many days.

She gained slowly, and a year later was able to revisit the scenes of her girlhood in Wisconsin. In two years she was able to go to California with

---

[18] boredom

me. She visited the World's Fair in Chicago, and her sons wheeled her about the grounds as if to say: "Mother, you have pioneered enough; henceforth fold your hands and rest and be happy."

She entered now upon another joy—the quiet joy of reminiscence, for the old hard days of pioneering on the Iowa prairie grew mellow with re-membered sunshine—the storms grew faint and vague. She loved to sit and dream of the past. She loved to recall old faces, and to hear us tell of old times and old neighbors. Beside the glow of her fire, she had a keen delight in the soughing[19] of the winds in the grim pines of Wisconsin, the flame of lightning in the cyclonic nights in Iowa, and the howling blasts of stern blizzards on the wide Dakota sod. She came back to old friends in "the Coolly Country of Wisconsin," and there her sons built a roomy house about her. They put nice rugs under her feet and new silver on her table. It was all on a very humble scale, but it made her eyes misty with happy tears. For eleven years after her first stroke she lived with us in this way—or we with her. And my father was glad of the shelter and the comfort, for he, too, admitted growing age and joined with his sons in making the wife happy.

• • • • •

I have a purpose in this frank disclosure of my mother's life. It is not from any self-complacency,[20] For I did so little and it came so late—I write in the hope of making some other work-weary mother happy. There is nothing more appealing to me than neglected age. To see an old father or mother sitting in loneliness and poverty dreaming of an absent son who never comes, of a daughter who never writes, is to me more moving than *Hamlet* or *Othello*. If we are false to those who gave us birth, we are false indeed.

Most of us in America are the children of working people, and the toil-worn hands of our parents should be heaped to overflowing with whatever good things success brings to us. They bent to the plow and the washboard when we were helpless. They clothed us when clothing was bought with blood, and we should be glad to return this warmth, this protection, an hundredfold. Fill their rooms with sunshine and the odor of flowers—you sons and daughters of the pioneers of America. Gather them around you, let them share in your success, and when some one looks askance[21] at them, stand beside them and say: "These gray old heads, these gnarled limbs, sheltered me in days when I was weak and life was stern."

Then will the debt be lessened—for in such coin alone can the wistful hearts be paid.

---

[19] rustling

[20] smug satisfaction with one's accomplishments

[21] doubtfully or mockingly

Questions for Review

1. List some of the qualities of the author's mother. Which of these are especially touching to you?

2. How does the death of her eldest daughter affect Mrs. Garland?

3. When the family goes west, and they part with Hamlin, how do their neighbors send Mrs. Garland off? How does she respond?

4. Why does the author say he wrote this account of his mother?

5. Find online a video of a violinist/fiddler playing "Money Musk" and "Old Dan Tucker" (like the author's mother used to play).

6. The author mentions his mother's highly beautiful singing voice, and believes that the world lost a great singer because his mother worked the farm and home instead. What talent does *your* mother have that might have made her well-known or appreciated by others—one that she gave up or focused less upon in order to stay home and teach you? Can you express your thanks to her right now for loving you and homeschooling you?

Up Hill

By Christina Rossetti

English poet Christina Rossetti (1830-1894) had a talent for poetry, composing her first when she was only 11. She was also a Christian who attempted to honor the Lord with her writing. Rossetti was well-liked and praised, publishing several books of her verse. "Up Hill" is an example of how she wrote to encourage readers through poetry.

• • • • •

Does the road wind up hill all the way?
Yes, to the very end.
Will the day's journey take the whole long day?
From morn to night, my friend.
But is there for the night a resting-place?
A roof for when the slow dark hours begin.
May not the darkness hide it from my face?
You cannot miss that inn.
Shall I meet other wayfarers[1] at night?
Those who have gone before.
Then must I knock, or call when just in sight?
They will not keep you standing at that door.
Shall I find comfort, travel-sore and weak?
Of labor you shall find the sum.
Will there be beds for me and all who seek?
Yea, beds for all who come.

Questions for Review

1. Why does the poet use italics for every other line?

2. What do you think "the road" in this poem really stands for, other than an actual road? Why?

3. Compare lines five and thirteen to Matthew 11:28-30.

---

[1] travelers, wanderers

Quality

By John Galsworthy

*This story, published in 1912 by English author John Galsworthy (1867-1933), is a remembrance of a man who meets two German shoemaker brothers as a boy, and continues to keep in contact with them for many years. In "Quality," Galsworthy uses **dialect**, which means that he spells some words said by characters (in this case, the German brothers) exactly as they pronounced them. The brothers' pronunciation isn't perfect, but their shoes come close!*

•••••

I knew him from the days of my extreme youth, because he made my father's boots; inhabiting with his elder brother two little shops let into one, in a small by-street-now no more, but then most fashionably placed in the West End.

That tenement[1] had a certain quiet distinction; there was no sign upon its face that he made for any of the Royal Family—merely his own German name of Gessler Brothers; and in the window a few pairs of boots. I remember that it always troubled me to account for those unvarying boots in the window, for he made only what was ordered, reaching nothing down, and it seemed so inconceivable that what he made could ever have failed to fit. Had he bought them to put there? That, too, seemed inconceivable. He would never have tolerated in his house leather on which he had not worked himself. Besides, they were too beautiful—the pair of pumps, so inexpressibly slim, the patent leathers with cloth tops, making water come into one's mouth, the tall brown riding boots with marvelous sooty glow, as if, though new, they had been worn a hundred years. Those pairs could only have been made by one who saw before him the Soul of Boot—so truly were they prototypes[2] incarnating[3] the very spirit of all foot-gear. These thoughts, of course, came to me later, though even when I was promoted to him, at the age of perhaps fourteen, some inkling haunted me of the dignity of himself and brother. For to make boots—such boots as he made—seemed to me then, and still seems to me, mysterious and wonderful.

I remember well my shy remark, one day, while stretching out to him my youthful foot:

---

[1] apartment building
[2] originals, patterns
[3] representing

"Isn't it awfully hard to do, Mr. Gessler?"

And his answer, given with a sudden smile from out of the sardonic[4] redness of his beard: "Id is an Ardt!"

Himself, he was a little as if made from leather, with his yellow crinkly face, and crinkly reddish hair and beard; and neat folds slanting down his cheeks to the corners of his mouth, and his guttural[5] and one-toned voice; for leather is a sardonic substance, and stiff and slow of purpose. And that was the character of his face, save that his eyes, which were grey-blue, had in them the simple gravity of one secretly possessed by the Ideal. His elder brother was so very like him—though watery, paler in every way, with a great industry[6]—that sometimes in early days I was not quite sure of him until the interview was over. Then I knew that it was he, if the words, "I will ask my brudder," had not been spoken; and that, if they had, it was his elder brother.

When one grew old and wild and ran up bills, one somehow never ran them up with Gessler Brothers. It would not have seemed becoming to go in there and stretch out one's foot to that blue iron-spectacled glance, owing him for more than—say—two pairs, just the comfortable reassurance that one was still his client.

For it was not possible to go to him very often—his boots lasted terribly, having something beyond the temporary—some, as it were, essence of boot stitched into them.

One went in, not as into most shops, in the mood of: "Please serve me, and let me go!" but restfully, as one enters a church; and, sitting on the single wooden chair, waited—for there was never anybody there. Soon, over the top edge of that sort of well—rather dark, and smelling soothingly of leather—which formed the shop, there would be seen his face, or that of his elder brother, peering down. A guttural sound, and the tip-tap of bast slippers[7] beating the narrow wooden stairs, and he would stand before one without coat, a little bent, in leather apron, with sleeves turned back, blinking—as if awakened from some dream of boots, or like an owl surprised in daylight and annoyed at this interruption.

And I would say: "How do you do, Mr. Gessler? Could you make me a pair of Russia leather boots?"

Without a word he would leave me, retiring whence he came, or into the other portion of the shop, and I would, continue to rest in the wooden chair, inhaling the incense of his trade. Soon he would come back, holding in his thin, veined hand a piece of gold-brown leather. With eyes fixed on it, he

---

[4] mocking
[5] deep
[6] diligence
[7] shoes made from tree bark

would remark: "What a beaudiful biece!" When I, too, had admired it, he would speak again. "When do you wand dem?" And I would answer: "Oh! As soon as you conveniently can." And he would say: "Tomorrow ford-nighd?" Or if he were his elder brother: "I will ask my brudder!"

Then I would murmur: "Thank you! Good-morning, Mr. Gessler." "Goot-morning!" he would reply, still looking at the leather in his hand. And as I moved to the door, I would hear the tip-tap of his bast slippers restoring him, up the stairs, to his dream of boots. But if it were some new kind of foot-gear that he had not yet made me, then indeed he would observe ceremony—divesting me of my boot and holding it long in his hand, looking at it with eyes at once critical and loving, as if recalling the glow with which he had created it, and rebuking the way in which one had disorganized this masterpiece. Then, placing my foot on a piece of paper, he would two or three times tickle the outer edges with a pencil and pass his nervous fingers over my toes, feeling himself into the heart of my requirements.

I cannot forget that day on which I had occasion to say to him; "Mr. Gessler, that last pair of town walking-boots creaked, you know."

He looked at me for a time without replying, as if expecting me to withdraw or qualify the statement, then said:

"Id shouldn'd 'ave greaked."

"It did, I'm afraid."

"You goddem wed before dey found demselves?"

"I don't think so."

At that he lowered his eyes, as if hunting for memory of those boots, and I felt sorry I had mentioned this grave thing.

"Zend dem back!" he said; "I will look at dem."

A feeling of compassion for my creaking boots surged up in me, so well could I imagine the sorrowful long curiosity of regard which he would bend on them.

"Zome boods," he said slowly, "are bad from birdt. If I can do noding wid dem, I dake dem off your bill."

Once (once only) I went absent-mindedly into his shop in a pair of boots bought in an emergency at some large firm's. He took my order without showing me any leather, and I could feel his eyes penetrating the inferior integument[8] of my foot. At last he said:

"Dose are nod my boods."

The tone was not one of anger, nor of sorrow, not even of contempt, but there was in it something quiet that froze the blood. He put his hand down and pressed a finger on the place where the left boot, endeavoring to be fashionable, was not quite comfortable.

"Id 'urds you dere,", he said. "Dose big virms 'ave no self-respect. Drash!" And then, as if something had given way within him, he spoke long and bitterly. It was the only time I ever heard him discuss the conditions and hardships of his trade.

"Dey get id all," he said, "dey get id by adverdisement, nod by work. Dey dake it away from us, who lofe our boods. Id gomes to this—presently I haf no work. Every year id gets less; you will see." And looking at his lined face, I saw things I had never noticed before, bitter things and bitter struggle—and what a lot of grey hairs there seemed suddenly in his red beard!

As best I could, I explained the circumstances of the purchase of those ill-omened boots. But his face and voice made so deep impression that during the next few minutes I ordered many pairs. Nemesis[9] fell! They lasted more terribly than ever. And I was not able conscientiously to go to him for nearly two years.

When at last I went I was surprised to find that outside one of the two little windows of his shop another name was painted, also that of a boot-maker-making, of course, for the Royal Family. The old familiar boots, no longer in dignified isolation, were huddled in the single window. Inside, the now contracted well of the one little shop was more scented and darker than ever. And it was longer than usual, too, before a face peered down, and the tip-tap of the bast slippers began. At last he stood before me, and, gazing through those rusty iron spectacles, said:

"Mr.—, isn'd it?"

"Ah! Mr. Gessler," I stammered, "but your boots are really too good, you know! See, these are quite decent still!" And I stretched out to him my foot. He looked at it.

"Yes," he said, "beople do nod wand good hoods, id seems."

---

[8] covering
[9] Punishment, revenge

To get away from his reproachful[10] eyes and voice I hastily remarked: "What have you done to your shop?"

He answered quietly: "Id was too exbensif. Do you wand some boods?"

I ordered three pairs, though I had only wanted two, and quickly left. I had, I do not know quite what feeling of being part, in his mind, of a conspiracy against him; or not perhaps so much against him as against his idea of boot. One does not, I suppose, care to feel like that; for it was again many months before my next visit to his shop, paid, I remember, with the feeling: "Oh! well, I can't leave the old boy—so here goes! Perhaps it'll be his elder brother!"

For his elder brother, I knew, had not character enough to reproach me, even dumbly.[11]

And, to my relief, in the shop there did appear to be his elder brother, handling a piece of leather.

"Well, Mr. Gessler," I said, "how are you?"

He came close, and peered at me.

"I am breddy well," he said slowly "but my elder brudder is dead."

And I saw that it was indeed himself—but how aged and wan![12] And never before had I heard him mention his brother. Much shocked; I murmured: "Oh! I am sorry!"

"Yes," he answered, "he was a good man, he made a good bood; but he is dead." And he touched the top of his head, where the hair had suddenly gone as thin as it had been on that of his poor brother, to indicate, I suppose, the cause of death. "He could nod ged over losing de oder shop. Do you wand any hoods?" And he held up the leather in his hand: "Id's a beaudiful biece."

I ordered several pairs. It was very long before they came—but they were better than ever. One simply could not wear them out. And soon after that I went abroad.

It was over a year before I was again in London. And the first shop I went to was my old friend's. I had left a man of sixty, I came back to one of seventy-five, pinched and worn and tremulous, who genuinely, this time, did not at first know me.

"Oh! Mr. Gessler," I said, sick at heart; "how splendid your boots are! See, I've been wearing this pair nearly all the time I've been abroad; and they're not half worn out, are they?"

He looked long at my boots—a pair of Russia leather, and his face seemed to regain steadiness. Putting his hand on my instep, he said:

"Do dey vid you here? I 'ad drouble wid dat bair, I remember."

---

[10] accusing, disapproving
[11] without speaking
[12] pale, feeble

I assured him that they had fitted beautifully.

"Do you wand any boods?" he said. "I can make dem quickly; id is a slack dime."

I answered: "Please, please! I want boots all round—every kind!"

"I will make a vresh model. Your food must be bigger." And with utter slowness, he traced round my foot, and felt my toes, only once looking up to say:

"Did I dell you my brudder was dead?"

To watch him was painful, so feeble had he grown; I was glad to get away.

I had given those boots up, when one evening they came. Opening the parcel, I set the four pairs out in a row. Then one by one I tried them on. There was no doubt about it. In shape and fit, in finish and quality of leather, they were the best he had ever made me. And in the mouth of one of the Town walking-boots I found his bill.

The amount was the same as usual, but it gave me quite a shock. He had never before sent it in till quarter day.[13] I flew downstairs, and wrote a check, and posted it at once with my own hand.

A week later, passing the little street, I thought I would go in and tell him how splendidly the new boots fitted. But when I came to where his shop had been, his name was gone. Still there, in the window, were the slim pumps, the patent leathers with cloth tops, the sooty riding boots.

I went in, very much disturbed. In the two little shops—again made into one—was a young man with an English face.

"Mr. Gessler in?" I said.

He gave me a strange, ingratiating[14] look.

"No, sir," he said, "no. But we can attend to anything with pleasure. We've taken the shop over. You've seen our name, no doubt, next door. We make for some very good people."

"Yes, Yes," I said; "but Mr. Gessler?"

"Oh!" he answered; "dead."

"Dead! But I only received these boots from him last Wednesday week."

"Ah!" he said; "a shockin' go. Poor old man starved 'imself."

"Good heavens!"

"Slow starvation, the doctor called it! You see he went to work in such a way! Would keep the shop on; wouldn't have a soul touch his boots except himself. When he got an order, it took him such a time. People won't wait. He lost everybody. And there he'd sit, goin' on and on—I will say that for him not a man in London made a better boot! But look at the competition!

---

[13] every third month (but this time he sent the bill immediately, which indicated he needed the money right away)

[14] slimy, creepy

He never advertised! Would 'ave the best leather, too, and do it all 'imself. Well, there it is. What could you expect with his ideas?"

"But starvation—!"

"That may be a bit flowery, as the sayin' is—but I know myself he was sittin' over his boots day and night, to the very last. You see I used to watch him. Never gave 'imself time to eat; never had a penny in the house. All went in rent and leather. How he lived so long I don't know. He regular let his fire go out. He was a character. But he made good boots."

"Yes," I said, "he made good boots."

And I turned and went out quickly, for I did not want that youth to know that I could hardly see.

Questions for Review

1. What kind of men are the Gessler brothers? What are their shoes like?

2. What does the author learn about the Gesslers and their business when he brings his new walking boots back to them? How does the author soothe his guilt?

3. What discovery does the author make one day as he enters the Gesslers' shop? Why has this happened? What could the Gesslers done to have avoided it?

4. Why do you think the story is titled "Quality"?

Proverbs 13

By King Solomon

After coming to Solomon in a dream, God granted him any wish he wanted, and Solomon asked for wisdom. Well, he got it: 1 Kings 4:29-32 says, "God gave Solomon wisdom and understanding...as the sand that is on the sea shore. And Solomon's wisdom excelled the wisdom of all the children of the east country, and all the wisdom of Egypt. For he was wiser than all men...And he spake three thousand proverbs...." Here is one chapter of Proverbs.

• • • • •

1 – A wise son heareth his father's instruction: but a scorner heareth not rebuke.

2 – A man shall eat good by the fruit of his mouth: but the soul of the transgressors[1] shall eat violence.

3 – He that keepeth his mouth keepeth his life: but he that openeth wide his lips shall have destruction.

4 – The soul of the sluggard[2] desireth, and hath nothing: but the soul of the diligent shall be made fat.

5 – A righteous man hateth lying: but a wicked man is loathsome,[3] and cometh to shame.

6 – Righteousness keepeth him that is upright in the way: but wickedness overthroweth the sinner.

7 – There is that maketh himself rich, yet hath nothing: there is that maketh himself poor, yet hath great riches.

8 – The ransom of a man's life are his riches: but the poor heareth not rebuke.

9 – The light of the righteous rejoiceth: but the lamp of the wicked shall be put out.

---

[1] sinners, offenders, deceitful persons

[2] lazy person

[3] disgusting, nasty

10 – Only by pride cometh contention:[4] but with the well advised is wisdom.

11 – Wealth gotten by vanity shall be diminished: but he that gathereth by labour shall increase.

12 – Hope deferred maketh the heart sick: but when the desire cometh, it is a tree of life.

13 – Whoso despiseth the word shall be destroyed: but he that feareth the commandment shall be rewarded.

14 – The law of the wise is a fountain of life, to depart from the snares of death.

15 – Good understanding giveth favour: but the way of transgressors is hard.

16 – Every prudent man dealeth with knowledge: but a fool layeth open his folly.

17 – A wicked messenger falleth into mischief: but a faithful ambassador is health.

18 – Poverty and shame shall be to him that refuseth instruction: but he that regardeth reproof[5] shall be honoured.

19 – The desire accomplished is sweet to the soul: but it is abomination[6] to fools to depart from evil.

20 – He that walketh with wise men shall be wise: but a companion of fools shall be destroyed.

21 – Evil pursueth sinners: but to the righteous good shall be repayed.

22 – A good man leaveth an inheritance to his children's children: and the wealth of the sinner is laid up for the just.

23 – Much food is in the tillage[7] of the poor: but there is that is destroyed for want of judgment.

24 – He that spareth his rod hateth his son: but he that loveth him chasteneth him betimes.[8]

---

[4] conflict, disagreement
[5] "regardeth reproof": listens to correction
[6] hateful
[7] planting crops
[8] early (as a young child)

25 – The righteous eateth to the satisfying of his soul: but the belly of the wicked shall want.[9]

Questions for Review

1. Put into your own words the main ideas expressed by verses three, seven, thirteen, and twenty-four.

2. Which ones of the other verses' main ideas have *you* seen come true in your experience and observation?

---

[9] lack

Bears of High and Low Degree

By Ernest Thompson Seton

Ernest Thompson Seton (1860-1946) had some skills. Not only did he write interesting tales about animals and the outdoors, he also created wonderful artwork of them, and he could make realistic imitations of animal sounds and bird calls! His love of the outdoors led him to help start up the Boy Scouts of America. This selection is taken from Seton's 1923 book Wild Animals at Home, *which includes stories about animals from bats to skunks to rabbits to elk.*

• • • • •

W hy is snoring a crime at night and a joke by day? It seems to be so, and the common sense of the public mind so views it.

In the September of 1912 I went with a good guide and a party of friends to the region southeast of Yellowstone Lake.[1] This is quite the wildest part of the Park; it is the farthest possible from human dwellings, and in it the animals are wild and quite unchanged by daily association with man....

Our party was carefully selected, a lot of choice spirits, and yet there was one with a sad and unpardonable weakness—he always snored a dreadful snore as soon as he fell asleep. That is why he was usually put in a tent by himself, and sent to sleep with a twenty-five foot deadening space between him and us of gentler somnolence.[2]

He had been bad the night before, and now, by request, was sleeping *fifty* feet away. But what is fifty feet of midnight silence to a forty-inch chest and a pair of tuneful nostrils? About 2 AM I was awakened as before, but worse than ever, by the most terrific, measured snorts, and so loud that they seemed just next me. Sitting up, I bawled in wrath, "Oh, Jack, shut up, and let some one else have a chance to sleep."

The answer was a louder snort, a crashing of brush, and a silence that, so far as I know, continued until sunrise.

Then I arose and learned that the snorts and the racket were made, not by my friend, but by a huge grizzly that had come prowling about the camp, and had awakened me by snorting into my tent.

---

[1] a 136-square-mile lake in Wyoming
[2] sleep

But he had fled in fear at my yell; and this behavior exactly shows the attitude of the grizzlies in the west today. They are afraid of man, they fly at whiff or sound of him, and if in the Yellowstone you run across a grizzly that seems aggressive, rest assured he has been taught such bad manners by association with our own species around the hotels.

The Different Kinds of Bears

Some guides of unsound information will tell the traveler that there are half a dozen different kinds of bears in or near the Yellowstone Park—black bear, little cinnamon, big cinnamon, grizzlies, silver-tip, and roach-backs. This is sure; however, there are but two species, namely, the black bear and the grizzly.

The black bear is known by its short front claws, flat profile and black color, with or without a tan-colored muzzle.[1] Sometimes in a family of black bears there appears a redheaded youngster, just as with ourselves; he is much like his brethren, but "all over red complected," as they say in Canada. This is known to hunters as a "little cinnamon."

The grizzly is known by its great size, its long foreclaws, its hollow profile, and its silver-sprinkled coat. Sometimes a grizzly has an excessive amount of silver; this makes a silver-tip. Sometimes the silver is nearly absent, in which case the Bear is called a "big cinnamon." Sometimes the short mane over his humped shoulders is exaggerated; this makes a "roach-back." Any or all of these are to be looked for in the park, yet remember: They form only two species. All of the black bear group are good climbers; none of the grizzly group climb after they are fully grown.

Bear-Trees

There is a curious habit of bears that is well known without being well understood; it is common to all these mentioned. In traveling along some familiar trail they will stop at a certain tree, claw it, tear it with their teeth, and rub their back and head up against it as high as they can reach, even with the tip of the snout, and standing on tiptoes. There can be no doubt that a bear coming to a tree can tell by scent whether another bear has been there recently, and whether that bear is a male or female, a friend, a foe, or a stranger. Thus the tree serves as a sort of news depot; and there is one every few hundred yards in country with a large bear population.

---

[1] nose, mouth, and jaws

These trees, of course, abound in the park. Any good guide will point out some examples. In the country south of the lake, I found them so common that it seemed as if the Bears had made many of them for mere sport.

A Peep into Bear Family Life

When we went to the Yellowstone in 1897 to spend the season studying wild animal life, we lived in a small shanty that stood near Yancey's, and had many pleasant meetings with antelope, beaver, etc., but were disappointed in not seeing any bears. One of my reasons for coming was the promise of "as many bears as I liked." But some tracks on the trail a mile away were the only proofs that I found of bears being in the region.

One day General Young, then in charge of the park, came to see how we were getting along. And I told him that although I had been promised as many bears as I liked, and I had been there investigating for six weeks already, I hadn't seen any. He replied, "You are not in the right place. Go over to the Fountain Hotel, and there you will see as many bears as you wish." That was impossible, for there were not bears enough in the west to satisfy me, I thought. But I went at once to the Fountain Hotel, and without loss of time stepped out the back door.

I had not gone fifty feet before I walked onto a big black bear her two roly-poly black cubs. The latter were having a boxing match, while the mother sat by to see fair play. As soon as they saw me they stopped their boxing, and as soon as I saw them I stopped walking. The old bear gave a peculiar "*Koff koff*," I suppose of warning, for the young ones ran to a tree, and up that they shinned with alacrity[2] that amazed me. When safely aloft, they sat like small boys, holding on with their hands, while their little black legs dangled in the air, and waited to see what was to happen down below.

The mother bear, still on her hind legs, came slowly toward me, and I began to feel very uncomfortable indeed, for she stood about six feet high in her stocking feet, and I had not even a stick to defend myself with. I began backing slowly toward the hotel, and by way of my best defense, *I* turned on her all the power of my magnetic eye. We have all of us heard of the wonderful power of the magnetic human eye. Yes, *we* have, but apparently this old bear had not, for she came on just the same. She gave a low woof, and I was about to abandon all attempts at dignity, and run for

---

[2] speed

the hotel; but just at this turning-point the old bear stopped, and gazed at me calmly.

Then she faced about and waddled over to the tree, up which were the cubs. Underneath she stood, looking first at me, then at her family. I realized that she wasn't going to bother me; in fact, she never seemed very serious about it, so I plucked up courage. I remembered what I came for and got down my camera. But when I glanced at the sky, and gauged the light— near sundown in the woods—I knew the camera would not serve me; so I got out my sketch book instead....

Meanwhile the old bear had been sizing me up, and evidently made up her mind that, "although that human being might be all right, she would take no chances for her little ones."

She looked up to her two hopefuls, and gave a peculiar whining "*Er-r-r er-r,*" whereupon, like obedient children, they jumped as at the word of command. There was nothing about them heavy or bear-like as commonly understood; lightly they swung from bough to bough till they dropped to the ground, and all went off together into the woods.

I was much tickled by the prompt obedience of these little bears. As soon as their mother told them to do something they did it. They did not even offer a suggestion. But I also found out that there was a good reason back of it, for, had they not done as she had told them, they would have got such a spanking as would have made them howl. Yes, it is quite the usual thing, I find, for an old black bear to spank her little ones when in her opinion they need it, and she lays it on well. She has a good strong paw, and does not stop for their squealing;[3] so that one correction lasts a long time.

This was a delightful peep into bear home-life, and would have been well worth coming for, if the insight had ended there. But my friends in the hotel said that that was not the best place for bears. I should go to the garbage-heap, a quarter-mile off in the forest. There, they said, I surely could see as many bears as I wished, which was absurd of them.

The Day at the Garbage Pile

Early next morning I equipped myself with pencils, paper and a camera, and set out for the garbage pile. At first I watched from the bushes, some seventy-five yards away, but later I made a hole in the odorous pile itself, and stayed there all day long, sketching and snapshotting the bears which came and went in greater numbers as the day was closing.

---

[3] "Chasten thy son while there is hope, and let not thy soul spare for his crying" (Proverbs 19:18).

A sample of my notes made on the spot will illustrate the continuity of the bear procession, yet I am told that there are far more of these animals there today than at the time of my visit.

Those readers who would follow my adventures in detail will find them fully and exactly set forth in the story of Johnny Bear, which appears in *Lives of the Hunted*, so I shall not further enlarge on them here, except to relate one part which was omitted, as it dealt with a photographic experience.

In the story I told how, backed by a mounted cowboy, I sat on the garbage pile while the great grizzly that had worsted Old Grumpy came striding nearer, and looming larger.

He had not quite forgotten the recent battle, his whole air was menacing, and I had all the appropriate sensations as he approached. At forty yards I snapped him, and again at twenty. Still he was coming, but at fifteen feet he stopped and turned his head, giving me the side view I wanted, and I snapped the camera again. The effect was startling. That insolent,[4] nagging little click brought the wrath of the grizzly onto myself. He turned on me with a savage growl. I was feeling just as I should be feeling; wondering, indeed, if my last moment had not come, but I found guidance in the old adage: "When you don't know a thing to do, don't do a thing." For a minute or two the grizzly glared, and I remained still; then calmly ignoring me he set about his feast.

All of this I tell in detail in my story. But there was one thing I did not dare to do then; that was show the snaps I made.

Surely it would be a wonderful evidence of my courage and coolness if I could show a photograph of that big grizzly when he was coming on— maybe to kill me—I did not know, but I had a dim vision of my sorrowing relatives developing the plate to see how it happened, for I pressed the button at the right time....I was so calm and cool and collected that I quite forgot to focus the camera.

Lonesome Johnny

During all this time Johnny had been bemoaning his sad lot, at the top of the tree; there I left him, still lamenting. That was the last I ever saw of him.

---

[4] rude

In my story of Johnny Bear, I relate many other adventures that were ascribed[5] to him, but these were told me by the men who lived in the park, and knew the lame cub much better than I did. My own acquaintance with him was all within the compass of the one day I spent in the garbage pile.

It is worthy of note that although Johnny died that autumn, they have had him every year ever since; and some years they have had two for the satisfaction of visitors who have read up properly before coming to the park. Indeed, when I went back to the Fountain Hotel fifteen years afterward, a little bear came and whined under my window about dawn, and the hotel folk assured me it was Little Johnny calling on his creator.

Further Annals of the Sanctuary

All of this was fifteen years ago. Since then there have been some interesting changes, but they are in the line of growth. Thirteen bears in view at one time was my highest record, and that after sundown; but I am told that as many as twenty or twenty-five bears are now to be seen there at once in June and July, when the wildwood foods are scarce. Most of them are black bears, but there are always a few grizzlies about.

In view of their reputation, their numbers and the gradual removal of the restraining fear of men, one wonders whether these creatures are not a serious menace to the human dwellers of the park. The fundamental peacefulness of the unhungry animal world is wonderfully brought out by the groups of huge shaggy monsters about the hotels.

At one time, and for long it was said, and truthfully, that the bears in the park had never abused the confidence man had placed in them. But one or two encounters have taken place to prove the exception.

An enthusiastic camera-hunter, after hearing of my experiences at the garbage pile, went there some years later, duly equipped to profit by the opportunity.

A large she bear with a couple of cubs appeared, but they hovered at a distance and did not give the artist a fair chance. He waited a long time, then seeing that they would not come to him, he decided to go to them. Quitting that sheltering hole, he sneaked along; crouching low and holding the camera ready, he rapidly approached the family group. When the young ones saw this strange two-legged beast coming threateningly near them, they took alarm and ran whin-

---

[5] credited

ing to their mother. All her maternal wrath was aroused to see this smallish, two-legged, one-eyed creature, evidently chasing her cubs to harm them. A less combination than that would have made her take the warpath, and now she charged. She struck him but once; that was enough. His camera was wrecked, and for two weeks afterward he was in the hospital, nursing three broken ribs, as well as a body suffering from shock.

There was another, an old grizzly that became a nuisance about the hotels, as he did not hesitate to walk into the kitchens and help himself to food. Around the tents of campers he became a terror, as he soon realized that these folk carried food, and white canvas walls rising in the woods were merely invitations to a dinner ready and waiting. It is not recorded that he hurt anyone in his numerous raids for food. But he stampeded horses and broke the camp equipments, as well as pillaged many larders.[6]

One of my guides described a lively scene in which the bear, in spite of blazing brands, ran into the cook's quarters and secured a ham. The cook pursued with a stick of firewood. At each whack the Bear let off a "whoof," but he did not drop the ham, and the party had to return to Fort Yellowstone for supplies.

Incidents of this kind multiplied, and finally Buffalo Jones, who was then the chief scout of the park, was permitted to punish the old sinner. Mounted on his trained saddlehorse, swinging the lasso that has caught so many different kinds of beasts in so many different lands, the Colonel gave chase. Old Grizzly dodged among the pines for a while, but the pony was good to follow; and when the culprit[7] took to open ground, the unerring lasso whistled in the air and seized him by the hind paw. It takes a good rope to stand the jerk of half a ton of savage muscle, but the rope was strong; it stood, and there was some pretty maneuvering, after which the lasso was found over a high branch, with a couple of horses on the "Jones end," and they hauled the bear aloft where, through the medium of a stout club, he received a drubbing that has become famous in the moving-picture world.

Another of these big, spoiled babies was sent to Washington Zoo, where he is now doing duty as an exhibition grizzly.

---

[6] "pillaged many larders": stole from many pantries
[7] guilty person/animal

The comedy element is far from lacking in this life; in fact, it is probably the dominant one. But the most grotesque story of all was told me by a friend who chummed with the bears about ten years ago.

One day, it seems, a black bear more tame than usual went right into the barroom of one of the hotels. The timid floating population moved out; the bar-keep was cornered, but somewhat protected by his bar; and when the bear reared up with both paws on the mahogany, the wily "dispenser" pushed a glass of beer across, saying nervously, "Is that what you are after?"

The bear liked the smell of the offering, and, stooping down, lapped up the whole glassful, and what was spilt he carefully licked up afterward, to the unmeasured joy of the loafers who peeped in at doors and windows, and jeered at the bar-keep and his new customer.

"Say, bar-keep, who's to pay?" "If I come in a fur coat, will you treat me?" "No! you got to scare him to drink free," etc. were examples of their remarks.

Whatever that bear came for, she seemed satisfied with what she got, for she went off peaceably to the woods, and was seen later lying asleep under a tree. Next day, however, she was back again. The scene in the bar-room was repeated with less intensity.

On the third and fourth days she came as before, but on the fifth day she seemed to want something else. Prompted by a kindred feeling, one of the loafers suggested that "She wants another round." His guess was right, and having got it, that abandoned old bear began to reel, but she was quite good-natured about it, and at length lay down under a table, where her loud snores proclaimed to all that she was asleep—beastly drunk, and asleep—just like one of the lords of creation.

From that time on she became a habitual frequenter of the bar-room. Her potations[8] were increased each month. There was a time when one glass of beer made her happy, but now it takes three or four, and sometimes even a little drop of something stronger. But whatever it is, it has the desired effect, and "Swizzling Jinnie" lurches over to the table, under which she sprawls at length, and tuning up her nasophone[9] she sleeps aloud, and unpeacefully, demonstrating to all the world that after all a "bear is jest a kind o' a man in a fur coat." Who can doubt it that reads this tale, for it is true; at least it

---

[8] drinks
[9] nose

was told me for the truth, by no less an authority than one of Jennie's intimate associates at the bar-room.

The Grizzly and the Can

When one remembers the grizzly bear as the monarch of the mountains, the king of the plains, and the one of matchless might and unquestioned sway[10] among the wild things of the West, it gives one a shock to think of him being conquered and cowed by a little tin can. Yet he was, and this is how it came about.

A grand old grizzly, that was among the summer retinue[11] of a park hotel, was working with two claws to get out the very last morsel of some exceptionally delicious canned stuff. The can was extra strong, its ragged edges were turned in, and presently both toes of the bear were wedged firmly in the clutch of that impossible, horrid little tin trap. The monster shook his paw and battered the enemy, but it was as sharp within as it was smooth without, and it gripped his paw with the fell clutch of a disease. His toes began to swell with all this effort and violence, till they filled the inner space completely. The trouble was made worse, and the paw became painfully inflamed.

All day long that old grizzly was heard clumping around with that dreadful little tin pot wedged on his foot. Sometimes there was a loud succession of *clamp, clamp, clamps* which told that the enraged monarch with canned toes was venting his rage on some of the neighboring black bears.

The next day and the next that shiny tin maintained its frightful grip on the grizzly, who, limping noisily around, was known and recognized as "Can-foot." His comings and goings to and from the garbage heap, by day and by night, were plainly announced to all by the clamp, clamp, clamp of that maddening, galling tin. Some weeks went by, and still the implacable[12] meat box held on.

The officer in charge of the park came riding by one day; he heard the strange tale of

---

[10] power, authority
[11] group of visitors
[12] unyielding, stubborn

trouble, and saw with his own eyes the limping grizzly, with his muzzled foot. At a wave of his hand two of the trusty scouts of the park patrol set out with their ponies and whistling lassoes on the strangest errand that they, or any of their kind, had ever known. In a few minutes those wonderful raw-hide ropes had seized him, and the monarch of the mountains was a prisoner bound. Strong shears were at hand. That vicious little can was ripped open. It was completely filled now with the swollen toes. The surgeon dressed the wounds, and the grizzly was set free. His first blind animal impulse was to attack his seeming tormenters, but they were wise and the ponies were bear-broken; they easily avoided the charge, and he hastened to the woods to recover, finally, both his health and his good temper, and continue about the park, the only full-grown grizzly bear, probably, that man ever captured to help in time of trouble, and then set loose again to live his life in peace.

Questions for Review

1. How does the author's descriptions of the bears make them seem almost human?

2. What do you think the author's lighthearted approach and sense of humor do for his bear tales?

3. Look up the grizzly bear, and find out a few facts about the animal that you weren't aware of.

The Children's Hour

By Henry Wadsworth Longfellow

Longfellow wrote the following poem in 1860 about his three daughters: Alice, Allegra, and Edith.

• • • • •

Between the dark and the daylight,
When the night is beginning to lower,
Comes a pause in the day's occupations
That is known as the Children's Hour.
I hear in the chamber above me
The patter of little feet,
The sound of a door that is opened,
And voices soft and sweet.
From my study I see in the lamplight,
Descending the broad hall stair,
Grave Alice, and laughing Allegra,
And Edith with golden hair.
A whisper, and then a silence:
Yet I know by their merry eyes
They are plotting and planning together
To take me by surprise.
A sudden rush from the stairway,
A sudden raid from the hall!
By three doors left unguarded
They enter my castle wall!
They climb up into my turret[1]
O'er the arms and back of my chair;
If I try to escape, they surround me;
They seem to be everywhere.
They almost devour me with kisses,
Their arms about me entwine,[2]
Till I think of the Bishop of Bingen
In his Mouse-Tower on the Rhine!
Do you think, O blue-eyed banditti,[3]
Because you have scaled the wall,

---

[1] a tower on a castle
[2] wrap around
[3] robbers, outlaws

Such an old mustache as I am
Is not a match for you all!
I have you fast in my fortress,
And will not let you depart,
But put you down into the dungeon
In the round-tower of my heart.
And there will I keep you forever,
Yes, forever and a day,
Till the walls shall crumble to ruin,
And molder in dust away!

Questions for Review

1. Name some of the strong nouns and verbs that Longfellow uses in this poem to create images in the reader's mind.

2. Do you have younger brothers or sisters that you enjoy playing with? What are some funny or cute things you love about them?

3. Look up the Mouse Tower and the legend of Bishop Hatto. Now go back and read the four lines beginning with "They almost devour me with kisses...." How is this picture the poet paints a little clearer now?

I Like To See It Lap the Miles

By Emily Dickinson

American poet Emily Dickinson (1830-1886) never gained fame in her lifetime for her poems. Her sister found a bundle of around 1800 poems after Emily's death, and these were published and have been greatly praised since. Dickinson's poems were offbeat, with unusual rhymes and subjects. Can you guess what the "it" refers to in this poem?

• • • • •

I like to see it lap the miles,
And lick the valleys up,
And stop to feed itself at tanks;
And then, prodigious,[1] step

Around a pile of Mountains,
And, supercilious,[2] peer
In shanties by the sides of roads;
And then a quarry pare[3]

To fit its sides, and crawl between,
Complaining all the while
In horrid, hooting stanza;
Then chase itself down hill

And neigh like Boanerges;[4]
Then, punctual as a star,
Stop—docile and omnipotent—[5]
At its own stable door.

Questions for Review

1. Well, what *is* the "it" referred to in this poem's first line?

2. Sum up what happens in each stanza.

---

[1] enormous

[2] pompous, arrogant

[3] cut down

[4] "And James the son of Zebedee, and John the brother of James; and [Jesus] surnamed them Boanerges, which is, The sons of thunder" (Mark 3:17).

[5] "docile and omnipotent": tame and all-powerful

The Doctor's Cow

By Emma S. Allen

Proverbs 12:10 says, "A righteous man regardeth the life of his beast...." That is, when God gave man authority over the animals, He also included the responsibility to take care of them. But the worth of a human's life is much more than an animal's! Jesus said in Matthew 12:12, "How much then is a man better than a sheep?" In Luke 12:6-7 He says, "Are not five sparrows sold for two farthings, and not one of them is forgotten before God? But even the very hairs of your head are all numbered. Fear not therefore: ye are of more value than many sparrows." And in Luke He says, "Consider the ravens: for they neither sow nor reap; which neither have storehouse nor barn; and God feedeth them: how much more are ye better than the fowls?" In "The Doctor's Cow," a wise judgement is made about the life of a cow and the life of a boy.

• • • • •

"I am afraid she is done for," said the veterinary surgeon as he came out of the barn with Dr. Layton, after working for an hour over Brindle, who had broken into the feed bins, and devoured bran and middlings[1] until she could eat no more. "But keep up the treatment faithfully, and if she lives through the night, she will stand some show of getting well."

The doctor walked down the driveway with the surgeon, and stood for a few minutes at the gate under the maple trees that lined the sidewalk, talking earnestly. Then he went back into the house by the kitchen door. His wife met him, with the oft-repeated words, "I told you so; I said that boy would turn out of no earthly account."

"But he has turned out of some account," contradicted the doctor mildly. "In spite of this carelessness, he has been a great help to me during the last month. It was boyish ignorance more than mere carelessness that brought about this disaster. To be sure, I have cautioned him not to leave the door of the feed room unfastened. But he had no idea how a cow would make a glutton of herself if she had a chance at the bins. You cannot expect a boy who was reared in a city tenement[2] to learn all about the country, and the habits and weaknesses of cattle, in one short month. No, I shall not send him adrift again—not even if poor Brindle dies."

---

[1] wheat mixed with bran
[2] apartment

"You mean to say you are going to keep him just the same, John Layton?" cried the doctor's wife. "Well, if you are not the meekest man! Moses was not anything to you! He did lose his temper once."[3]

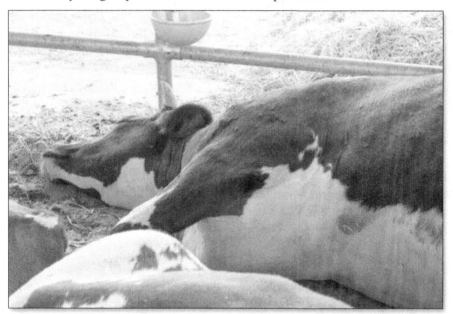

The doctor smiled, and said quietly: "Yes, and missed entering the promised land on account of it.[4] Perhaps I should have done the same thing in his place; but I am sure that Moses, if he were in my place today, would feel just as I do about discharging Harry. It is pretty safe to assume that he, even if he did lose his temper at the continual grumbling of the croakers who were sighing for the flesh-pots of Egypt, never ordered a young Israelite boy whose father and mother had been bitten by the fiery serpents and died in the wilderness, to clear out of camp for not putting a halter on one of the cows."

"John Layton, you are talking Scripture!" remonstrated[5] the perturbed housewife, looking up reprovingly as she sadly skimmed the cream from the very last pan of milk poor Brindle would ever give her.

"I certainly am, and I am going to act Scripture, too," declared the doctor, with the air of gentle firmness that always ended any controversy between him and his excellent, though somewhat exacting,[6] wife. "Harry is a good boy, and he had a good mother, too, he says, but he has had a hard life, ill-treated by a father who was bitten by the fiery serpent of drink. Now

---

[3] "Now the man Moses was very meek, above all the men which were upon the face of the earth" (Numbers 12:3).

[4] See Numbers 20:7-12.

[5] protested

[6] demanding

because of his first act of negligence[7] I am not going to send him adrift in the world again."

"Not if it costs you a cow!" remarked the woman.

"No, my dear, not if it costs me two cows," reasserted the doctor. "A cow is less than a boy, and it might cost the world a man if I sent Harry away in a fit of displeasure, disgraced by my discharge so that he could not find another place in town to work for his board, and go to school. Besides, Brindle will die anyway, and discharging the boy will not save her."

"No, of course not. But it was your taking the boy in, a penniless, unknown fellow, that has cost you a cow," persisted the wife. "I told you at the time you would be sorry for it."

"I have not intimated[8] that I am sorry I took the boy in," remarked the doctor, not perversely, but with steadfast kindness. "If our own little boy had lived, and had done this thing accidentally, would I have been sorry he had ever been born? Or if little Ted had grown to be thirteen, and you and I had died in the wilderness of poverty, leaving him to wander out of the city to seek for a home in God's fair country, where his little peaked[9] face could fill out and grow rosy, as Harry's has, would you think it just to have him sent away because he had made a boyish mistake? Of course you would not. Your heart is in the right place, even if it does get covered up sometimes. And I guess, to come right down to it, you would not send Harry away any more than I would, when the poor boy is almost heart-broken over this unfortunate affair. Now, let us have supper, for I must be off. We cannot neglect sick people for a poor, dying cow. Harry will look after Brindle. He will not eat a bite, I am afraid, so it is no use to call him in now. By and by you would better take a plate of something out to him; but do not say a harsh word to the poor fellow, to make it any harder for him than it is."

The doctor ate his supper hurriedly, for the sick cow had engaged every moment of his spare hours that day, and he had postponed until his evening round of visits a number of calls that were not pressing. When he came out to his buggy, Harry Aldis stood at the horse's head, at the carriage steps beside the driveway, his chin sunk on his breast, in an attitude of hopeless misery.

"Keep up the treatment, Harry, and make her as easy as possible," said the doctor as he stepped into his buggy.

"Yes, sir; I'll sit up all night with her, Dr. Layton, if I can only save her," was the choking answer, as the boy carefully spread the lap robe over the doctor's knees.

---

[7] carelessness

[8] suggested

[9] pale, sickly

"I know you will, Harry; but I am afraid nothing can save the poor creature. About all we can do is to relieve her suffering until morning, giving her a last chance; and if she is no better then, the veterinary surgeon says we would better shoot her, and put her out of her misery."

The boy groaned. "Oh, Dr. Layton, why do you not scold me? I could bear it better if you would say just one cross word!" he sobbed. "You have been kinder to me than my own father ever was, and I have tried so hard to be useful to you. Now this dreadful thing has taken place, all because of my carelessness. I wish you would take that buggy whip to me; I deserve it."

The doctor took the whip, and gently dropped its lash across the drooping shoulders bowed on the horse's neck as the boy hid his face in the silken mane he loved to comb. Indeed, Dandy's black satin coat had never shone with such a luster from excessive currying as in the month past, since the advent[10] of this new little groom, who slept in the little back bedroom of the doctor's big white house, and thought it a nook in paradise.

"There's no use in scolding or thrashing a fellow who is all broken up, anyway, over an accident, as you are," the doctor said, kindly. "Of course, it is a pretty costly accident for me, but I think I know where I can get a heifer—one of Brindle's own calves, that I sold to a farmer two years ago—that will make as fine a cow as her mother."

"But the money, Dr. Layton! How can I ever earn that to make good your loss?" implored the boy, looking up.

"The money? Oh, well, some day when you are a rich man, you can pay me for the cow!" laughed the doctor, taking up the reins. "In the meantime, make a good, trustworthy, honest man of yourself, no matter whether you get rich or not, and keep your thinking cap on a little better."

"You had better eat some supper," said a voice in the doorway a little later, as Mrs. Layton came noiselessly to the barn, and surprised the boy kneeling on the hay in the horse's stall adjoining the one where Brindle lay groaning, his face buried in his arms, which were flung out over the manger.

The lad scrambled to his feet in deep confusion.

"Thank you, Mrs. Layton, but I cannot eat a bite!" he protested. "It is ever so good of you to think of me, but I cannot eat anything."

"You must," said the doctor's wife, firmly. "Come outside and wash in the trough if you do not want to leave Brindle. You can sit nearby and watch her, if you think you must, though it will not do a particle of good, for she is bound to die anyway. What were you doing in there on your knees—praying?"

The woman's voice softened perceptibly as the question passed her lips, and she looked half-pityingly into the pale, haggard young face, thinking of

---

[10] arrival

little Ted's, and wondering how it would have looked at thirteen if he had done this thing.

"Yes," muttered Harry, plunging his hands into the water of the trough, and splashing it over the red flame of a sudden burning blush that kindled in his ash-pale cheeks. "Isn't it all right to pray for a cow to get well? It almost kills me to see her suffer so."

Mrs. Layton smiled unwillingly; for the value of her pet cow's products touched her more deeply than a boy's penitent[11] tears, particularly when that boy was not her own. "There is no use of your staying in there and watching her suffer, you cannot do her any good," she insisted. "Stay out here in the fresh air. Do you hear?"

"Yes, ma'am," choked Harry, drying his face on the sleeve of his gingham shirt. He sat down on a box before the door, the plate of food in his lap, and made an attempt to eat the daintily cooked meal, but every mouthful almost choked him.

At about midnight, the sleepless young watcher, lying on the edge of the hay just above the empty manger over which a lantern swung, lifted himself on his elbow at the sound of a long, low, shuddering groan, and in another moment, Harry knew that poor Brindle had ceased to suffer the effects of her gluttonous appetite. Creeping down into the stall, he saw at a glance that the cow was dead, and for a moment, alone there in the stillness and darkness of the spring night, he felt as if he were the principal actor in some terrible crime.

"Poor old boss!" he sobbed, kneeling down, and putting his arm over the still warm neck. "I—I have killed you—after all the rich milk and butter you have given me, that have made me grow strong and fat—just by my carelessness!"

In after-years the memory of that hour came back to Harry Aldis as the dominant note in some real tragedy, and he never again smelled the fragrance of new hay, mingled with the warm breath of sleeping cattle, without recalling the misery and self-condemnation of that long night's watch.

In the early dawn, Dr. Layton found the boy lying beside the quiet form in the stall, fast asleep from exhaustion and grief, his head pillowed on the soft, tawny coat he had loved to brush until it gleamed like silk.

"Child alive!" he gasped, bending over and taking the lad in his arms, and carrying him out into the sweet morning air. "Harry, why did you not come and tell me, and then go to bed?" he cried, setting the bewildered boy on his feet, and leading him to the house. "Now, my boy, no more of this grieving. The thing is done, and you cannot help it now. There is no more use in crying for a dead cow than for spilled milk. Now come in and go to bed, and stay there until tonight; and when you wake up, the new heifer,

[11] repentant, regretful

Brindle's daughter, will be in the barn waiting for you to milk her. I am going to buy her this morning."

• • • • •

Five years after that eventful night, Harry Aldis stood on the doctor's front porch, a youth of eighteen, bidding goodbye to the two who had been more to him than father and mother. He was going to college in the West, where he could work his way, and in his trunk was a high school diploma, and in his pocket a "gilt-edge recommendation" from Dr. Layton.

"God bless you, my boy! Don't forget us," said the doctor, his voice husky with unshed tears as he wrung the strong young hand that had been so helpful to him in the busy years flown by.

"Forget you, my more than father!" murmured the young man, not even trying to keep the tears out of his eyes. "No matter how many years it may be before I see you again, I shall always remember your unfailing kindness to me. And can I ever forget how you saved me for a higher life than I could possibly have lived if you had set me adrift in the world again for leaving that barn door unfastened, and killing your cow? As long as I live, I shall remember that great kindness, and shall try to deserve it by my life."

"Pshaw, Harry," said the doctor, "that was nothing but common humanity!"

"Uncommon humanity," corrected the youth. "Goodbye, Mrs. Layton. I shall always remember your kindness, too, and that you never gave me any less butter or cream from poor Brindle's daughter for my grave offense. You have been like an own mother to me."

"You have deserved it all, Harry," said the doctor's wife, and there was a tear in her eye, too, which was an unusual sight, for she was not an emotional woman. "I do not know as it was such a great calamity, after all, to lose Brindle just as we did, for Daisy is a finer cow than her mother was, and there has not been another chance since to get as good a heifer."

"So it was a blessing in disguise, after all, Harry," laughed the doctor. "As for you, you have been a blessing undisguised from that day to this. May the Lord bless and prosper you! Write to us often."

• • • • •

Four years passed, and in one of the Western States a young college graduate stepped from his pedestal of oratorical[12] honors to take a place among the rising young lawyers of a prosperous new town that was fast developing into a commercial center.

---

[12] speechmaking

"I am doing well, splendidly," he wrote Dr. Layton after two years of hard work, "and one of these days I am coming back to make that promised visit."

But the years came and went, and still the West held him in its powerful clutch. Success smiled upon his pathway, and into his life entered the sweet, new joy of a woman's love and devotion, and into his home came the happy music of children's voices. When his eldest boy was eight years old, his district elected him to the State senate, and four years later sent him to Congress—an honest, uncompromising adherent[13] to principle and duty.

"And now, at last," he wrote Dr. Layton, "I am coming East, and I shall run down from Washington for that long-promised visit. Why do you write so seldom, when I have never yet failed to inform you of my advancement into the world of politics? It is not fair. And how is the family cow? Surely Madam Daisy sleeps with her poor mother ere[14] this, or has been cut up into roasts and steaks."

And to this letter the doctor replied briefly but gladly:

So you are coming at last, my boy! Well, you will find us in the same old house—a little the worse for wear, perhaps—and leading the same quiet life. No, not the same, though it is quiet enough, for I am growing old, and the town is running after the new young doctors, leaving us old ones in the rear, to trudge along as best we can.

There isn't any 'family cow' now, Harry. Daisy was sold long ago for beef, poor thing! We never got another, for I am getting too old to milk, and there never seemed to come along another boy like the old Harry, who would take all the barnyard responsibility on his shoulders. Besides, mother is crippled with rheumatism, and can hardly get around to do her housework, let alone to make butter. We are not any too well off since the Union Bank failed; for, besides losing all my stock, I have had to help pay the depositors' claims. But we have enough to keep us comfortable, and much to be thankful for, most of all that our famous son is coming home for a visit. Bring your wife, too, Harry, if she thinks it will not be too much of a drop from Washington society to our humble home; and the children, all five of those bright boys and girls—bring them all! I want to show them the old stall in the barn, where, twenty-five years ago, I picked their father up in my arms early one spring morning as he lay fast asleep on the neck of the old cow over whose expiring breath he had nearly broken his poor little heart."

● ● ● ● ●

---

[13] supporter
[14] before

"Yes, father, of course it has paid to come down here. I would not have missed it for all the unanimous votes of the third ballot that sent me East," declared the United States senator at the end of his three days' visit. Long ago, the Hon. Henry Aldis had fallen into the habit of addressing Dr. Layton, in his letters, by the paternal[15] title.

"It does not seem possible that it is twenty years since I stood here, saying goodbye when I started West. By the way, do you remember what you told me that memorable night when the lamented Brindle laid down her life because of my carelessness, and her own gluttony? I was standing at the horse's head, and you were sitting in your buggy, there at the carriage steps, and I said I wished you would horsewhip me, instead of treating me so kindly. I remember you reached over and tickled my neck with the lash playfully, and told me there was no use in thrashing a fellow who was all broken up, anyway, over an accident."

The doctor laughed as he held his arms more closely about the shoulders of Senator Aladis's two eldest boys; while "Grandmother Layton," with little Ted in her lap, was dreaming again of the little form that had long, long ago been laid in the graveyard on the hillside.

"Yes, yes," said the doctor, "I remember. What a blessed thing it was I did not send you off that day to the tune the old cow died on," and he laughed through his tears.

"Blessed!" echoed Mrs. Layton, putting down the wriggling Ted. "It was providential. You know, Harry, I was not so kindhearted as John in those days and I thought he ought to send you off. But he declared he would not, even if you had cost him two cows. He said that if he did it might cost the world a man. And so it would have, if all they say you are doing out West for clean government is true."

Senator Aldis laughed, and kissed the old lady.

"I do not know about that," he said modestly. "I am of the opinion that he might have saved more of a man for the world; but certain it is, he saved whatever manhood there was in that boy from going to waste by his noble act of kindness. But what I remember most, father, is what you told me, there at the carriage step, that when I became a rich man, I could pay you for that cow. Well, I am not exactly a rich man, for I am not in politics for all the money I can get out of it, but I am getting a better income than my leaving that barn door open would justify any one in believing I ever could get by my brains; so now I can pay that long-standing debt without inconvenience. It may come handy for you to have a little fund laid by, since the Union Bank went to smash, and all your stock with it, and so much of your other funds went to pay the poor depositors of that defunct[16] institution. It

---

[15] fatherly
[16] out of business

was just like you, father, not to dodge the assessments, as so many of the stockholders did, by putting all your property in your wife's name. So, since you made one investment twenty-five years ago that has not seemed to depreciate[17] in value very much—an investment in a raw young boy who did not have enough gumption[18] to fasten a barn door—here is the interest on what the investment was worth to the boy, at least a little of it; for I can never begin to pay it all. Goodbye, both of you, and may God bless you! Here comes our carriage, Helen."

When the dust of the departing hack had filtered through the morning sunlight, two pairs of tear-dimmed eyes gazed at the slip of blue paper in Dr. Layton's hand—a check for five thousand dollars.[19]

"We saved a man that time, sure enough!" murmured the old doctor softly.

Questions for Review

1. Give several reasons why Dr. Layton refuses to get rid of Harry.

2. How does the Dr.'s investment in Harry reap many dividends?

3. How does this story compare to God's treatment of mankind? (See, for example, 2 Peter 3:9.)

---

[17] reduce

[18] sense

[19] This is roughly $100,000-$200,000 today.

The Right to What I Consider a Normal Standard of Living

By Mabel R. Williamson

We Americans often talk about our "rights." But what are the rights of Christian missionaries living overseas? In 1957 Mabel R. Williamson of the China Inland Mission wrote a book titled Have We No Rights?, *which attempts to answer that question. Chapter 1 is titled "Rights." In that chapter, she says, "Rights—your rights, my rights. Just what are rights, anyway?" Here is Chapter 2.*

· · · · ·

"Have we no right to eat and to drink?"[1] The white-haired mission secretary looked at me quizzically. "Well," he said, "it's all in your point of view. We find that these days in the tropics people may look upon the missionary's American refrigerator as a normal and necessary thing; but the cheap print curtains hanging at his windows may be to them unjustifiable extravagance!"

My mind goes back to a simple missionary home in China, with a cheap rug on the painted boards of the living room floor. I can see country women carefully skirting that rug, trying to get to the chairs indicated for them without stepping on it. Rugs, to them, belonged on beds, not on floors, and they would no more think of walking on my rug than you would on my best blanket! I think of our dining table set for a meal, and visitors examining with amazement the silver implements instead of bamboo chopsticks; and white cloth instead of a bare table. I think of having overheard our cook say proudly to a chance comer, "Oh, of course they have lots of money! Why, they always eat white bread; and they have meat every day, nearly; and as for sugar—why, you just can't imagine the amount of sugar they use!"

· · · · ·

English service was over, and we went home with a lady doctor and nurse of another mission. They had invited us to Sunday night supper. The sermon, delivered by a missionary of still another mission, who was stationed in the city, had been striking and thought-provoking. The text had been Luke 8:14: "And that which fell among thorns are they, which, when they

---

[1] 1 Corinthians 9:4

have heard, go forth, and are choked with cares and riches and pleasures of this life, and bring no fruit to perfection."

"This verse must refer to missionaries," the speaker had begun, "because it says that when they have heard, they go forth."

He had gone on to describe a picture he would like to paint. All around the border were to be the "cares" and "riches" and "pleasures" that hindered the real work of the missionary. Subjects that hit home were mentioned—there would be a big account book that tied the missionary down so that he had no time for a spiritual ministry; a teacup, symbolizing the round of entertaining that may develop in a city where there is a relatively large missionary community; a house and its furnishings, needing constant attention; and so on. The conclusion of the sermon had been very solemnizing, because of all these cares and pleasures and things that are second to God's best, it is tragically possible that the missionary may "bring no fruit to perfection."

At the supper table we had an interesting discussion of the sermon and its implications. Then the lady doctor made a remark that I have never forgotten.

"When my coworker and I set up this house," she said, "we agreed that one principle must never be violated. We would have nothing in our house—its furnishings, its arrangement—nothing that would keep the ordinary poor people among whom we work from coming in, or that would make them feel strange here."

• • • • •

A standard of living—what does it amount to? How important is it? Does it matter whether we missionaries sleep on spring beds, or those made of boards (I prefer the latter myself!), whether we eat with chopsticks, or fingers, or forks; whether we wear silk or homespun; whether we sit on chairs or on the floor? Does it matter whether we are poor or rich? Does it matter whether we eat rice or potatoes? Does it matter whether we live in the way to which we are accustomed, or adopt the way of living of those to whom we go?

It may matter quite a lot to ourselves. Most of us like potatoes better than rice. That is to say, most of us like things the way we are used to having them, rather than some other way. What is to be our attitude on the mission field? Are we free to try to have things the way we would like them, and to live, as much as possible, as we would at home? Or ought we to attempt, as far as we can, to conform to the way of life of the people among whom we live? This, of course, brings us to other questions: Does it matter to the people to whom we go whether we conform or not? And, more importantly, does it matter insofar as the progress of the Gospel is concerned? Will our conforming help to win souls to Christ?

The first thing to be said in answer to these questions is that the standards of missionary living necessarily must vary with local conditions. In some places there is a mixture of races and peoples, each in general keeping with its own customs and dress, and yet mixing freely with the others. In such places there may be many Westerners, and Western ways may not only be familiar, but even adopted to a certain extent by the local people. In situations like this there may be little or no need for the missionary to change his ordinary way of life.

Most missionaries go to places where the way of life is different from their own, and to people to whom their way of life is strange and by whom it is not understood. It is natural for us to like people who do things in the way in which we like them done. We are attracted to those who seem the same as ourselves, and turn (perhaps unconsciously) from those who seem queer and different. People of other lands are the same. When we see someone whose complexion, features, clothing, language, manners, and customs are different from our own, our natural reaction is to stare, or laugh, or both. It is not natural to be attracted to those who live differently from ourselves. The missionary wants to attract people. People must be attracted to him before they can be attracted to his message. They must accept him before they will accept his message. The more we can conform to their way of life, the easier and more natural and more rapid their acceptance of us will be.

The report of a China Inland Mission conference of missionaries held in England a few years ago includes as one of the lessons learned from past experience of missionary work in China, "the will to conform as nearly as possible to the social and living conditions of the people to whom we went." This means, of course, that different missionaries will live according to different standards. For example, my sister Frances and I are both members of the China Inland Mission. During the past few years I have been living in the modern and wealthy city of Singapore. I lived according to an ordinary middle-class standard—which meant running water, electricity, gas, and modern plumbing. I was conforming to the social standards and living conditions of the people to whom I went. During the same time my sister was in the Philippines, living in a palm-leaf hut in a clearing in the jungle, carrying her own water and sleeping on the floor. She was con-forming to the social standards and living conditions of the people to whom she went. Paul says: "I am become all things to all men, that I may by all means save some."[2] He found what the present-day missionary finds, that to some ex-

---

[2] 1 Corinthians 9:22

tent he must adopt the way of life and the standard of living of the people to whom he was sent.

Now, in what measure will it be desirable to adopt the local way of life? What principles will guide us? Well, in the first place we will certainly want to become familiar enough with it so that we feel at home in their homes. If we find their way of sitting uncomfortable, and their food unpleasant, they are not going to enjoy having us as guests. I may think it disgusting to eat my rice off a banana leaf with my fingers, but if I show that disgust, I probably will not be invited again. And my hostess may decide that I am merely an unmannerly foreigner, and that there is no profit in pursuing my acquaintance, or in listening to the strange stories of Someone called Jesus that I am so fond of telling. It is also in their homes that we may become really acquainted with them, and learn to know their needs. When we have become familiar with how they eat, how they sleep, how they work, how they play, what they like, what they dislike, what they hope, what they fear, how they think, how they feel—when we really understand them, then, and only then, will we be able to present the Gospel to them in an adequate way.

In the second place, we will want to live in our own homes on the mission field in such a way as to make our neighbors feel at home when they come to call on us. The fundamental attraction will not be externalities and material things. Even though I live in a little hut that is identical with their own, if in my heart I just do not like to have them around, they will know it, and they will not be attracted to me. But if not only the love and the welcome are there, but also a way of life that corresponds to their own, the approach will be made still easier.

This does not mean, of course, that I will unthinkingly accept all local standards. If I go to Central Africa, I probably will not decide that wearing clothes is an unjustifiable luxury. There is no need for me to neglect to sweep the floor of my palm-leaf hut just because my neighbors do not sweep theirs. The fact that everyone else chews betel nut,[3] or gambles with mah-jongg,[4] does not mean that I will take up these practices. But I will want, as far as possible, to live the sort of life that it would be suitable for a native Christian to imitate.

Another point must also be considered here. We missionaries might voice it like this: "I would love to live as the native peoples do, if I only could; but I just can't take it!" It is true that we may not be able to live entirely as they do and keep our health. The man who was born and bred in the tropics finds the climate just what he likes. The same climate takes all the energy out of the missionary who has come from the temperate zone. Foreigners are more susceptible to local diseases than natives. If the mis-

---

[3] similar to chewing tobacco
[4] a Chinese board game

sionary eats only what the local people do, his health may break down. If he himself does all the household chores in a land in which there are no modern conveniences, he may find that he has very little time left in which to study the language or preach the Gospel. On most mission fields it is found that a certain amount of variation from the local mode of life is necessary if the missionaries are to continue in good physical and mental health.

We can, however, gradually get used to unfamiliar things. I remember once, after I had been in China a few years, visiting a neighboring mission station. New workers had arrived there, a young couple fresh from language school. I was eager to meet them, but they did not appear. In answer to my inquiry, the reply was, "Oh, they were invited out to a feast last night, and it's upset them both! They are both in bed!"

My heart sank. Whatever use will these young workers be, I thought, if they can't eat Chinese food? They won't be able to go to the country and minister in all the little country churches that are so much in need of help—they can't get Western food there! They had better have stayed at home!

After a few years had passed, however, the young man mentioned above did start to do country work, and he did it very acceptably. What is more, he even came to prefer an ordinary country meal of local food to the best Western dishes that his wife could give him at home! Seeing that, I began to realize a thing that should be a comfort to all young workers who find the food or the living conditions difficult. Over a period of time familiarity not only turns difficulty to ease, but often even removes the "dis" from dislike!

The young worker goes with an older one to make a call or two. Everything is new. Everything is strange. Everything is nerve-wearing. If a seat is offered, it is uncomfortable. If food or drink is offered, either may be unpleasant. Even if he understands more or less of what is being said, the conversations are tiring. And by the time he reaches home he is utterly worn out. As far as he is concerned, however, that is not the worst. He looks at the older worker who has taken him out—someone getting on in years, perhaps a bit stooped, and obviously not in the pink of health. This missionary has done all the younger one did, and more. He has also preached a few times to crowds that gathered, and carried on endless conversations, but just listening made the younger worker tired. Yet this older man somehow has arrived home as fresh as a daisy!

The new worker, in his first station, often has to go through a stage in which he finds everything uncomfortable, unattractive, and difficult, but there is no need for him to become discouraged. Even that older worker probably did too, although he may have forgotten it! The change comes slowly, and the young missionary may not be able to see it for a long time, but if he everlastingly keeps at it, he will surely find that, after a few years, familiarity has made the difficult easy. Most people will find, as well, that it has even made the distasteful pleasant!

• • • • •

A mother was coaxing her little daughter to eat her vegetables. "But I don't like it!" the child objected.

"But you will," encouraged the mother. "Just eat it a few times and you will get used to it. It won't be long before you really like it!"

The child sat stock-still for a moment, considering. Then she burst out, "But I don't *want* to like the horrid stuff!"

Other people's ways, other people's customs, other people's standards—do we *want* to like them? Or do we cling tenaciously[5] to our own, insisting that we deserve them or that they are the only good and right ones? It is the attitude of mind and heart that matters. If we are willing to give up our own standard of living, willing to live as far as possible according to someone else's standards, then surely it is the business of our Master to make that possible in such degree as He sees is needed and best. Before we go to the field then, let us give up all right to our own standard of living, and be ready contentedly to embrace, as far as He makes possible, that of the people to whom He sends us.

Questions for Review

1. What one principle does the lady doctor say about her house? Why?

2. The author says that missionaries should adjust their living standards to fit into their surroundings in a new land, but shouldn't always adopt *all* customs or practices. What *principle* should missionaries follow to help them decide whether they should adopt a new custom or practice?

3. How can advice from a foreign missionary about what new missionaries should and shouldn't do apply to *your* life as a young person today?

---

[5] stubbornly

Shandon Waters

By Kathleen Norris

Popular American writer Kathleen Norris (1880-1966) wrote this story in 1912, one year after she wrote her first novel, titled Mother. *In that novel, Norris put a positive spin on large families during a time where they were being criticized. (Sound familiar?) "Shandon Waters" also places a high value on family and community. We've all known somebody like Shandon Waters. The question is: What do we* do *about her?*

· · · · ·

"Ror mercy's sakes, here comes Shandon Waters!" said Jane Dinwoodie, of the post office, leaving her pigeonholes[1] to peer through the one small window of that unpretentious[2] building. "Mother, here's Shandon Waters driving into town with the baby!" breathed pretty Mary Dickey, putting an awed face into the sitting room. "I declare that looks terrible like Shandon!" ejaculated Johnnie Larabee, straightening up at her washtubs and shading her eyes with her hand. "Well, what on earth brought her up to town!" said all Deaneville, crowding to the windows and doorways and halting the march of the busy Monday morning to watch a mud-spattered cart come bumping up and down over the holes in the little main street.

The woman—or girl, rather, for she was but twenty—who sat in the cart was in no way remarkable to the eye. She had a serious, even sullen face, and a magnificent figure, buttoned just now into a tan ulster[3] that looked curiously out of keeping with her close, heavy widow's bonnet and hanging veil. Sprawled luxuriously in her lap, with one fat, idle little hand playing above her own gauntleted[4] one on the reins, was a splendid child something less than a year old, snugly coated and capped against the cool air of a California February. She watched him closely as she drove, not moving her eyes from his little face even for a glance at the village street.

Poor Dan Waters had been six months in his grave, now, and this was the first glimpse Deaneville had had of his widow. For an unbroken half year she had not once left the solitude of the big ranch down by the marsh,

---

[1] mailbox compartments
[2] modest, simple
[3] overcoat
[4] gloved

or spoken to anyone except her old Indian woman servant and the various "hands" in her employ.

She had been, in the words of Deaneville, "sorta nutty" since her husband's death. Indeed, poor Shandon had been "sorta nutty" all her life. Motherless at six, and allowed by her big, half civilized father to grow up as wild as the pink mallow[5] that fringed the home marshes, she was regarded with mingled horror and pity by the well-ordered Deaneville matrons.[6] Jane Dinwoodie and Mary Dickey could well remember the day she was brought into the district school, her mutinous[7] black eyes gleaming under a shock of rough hair, her clumsy little apron tripping her with its unaccustomed strings. The lonely child had been frantic for companionship, and her direct, even forceful attempts at friendship had repelled and then amused the Deaneville children. As unfortunate chance would have it, it was shy, spoiled, adored little Mary Dickey that Shandon instantly selected for especial worship, and Mary, already bored by admiration, did not like it. But the little people would have adjusted matters in their own simple fashion presently had they been allowed to do so. It was the well-meant interference of the teacher that went amiss. Miss Larks explained to the trembling little newcomer that she mustn't smile at Mary, that she mustn't leave her seat to sit with Mary: it was making poor Mary cry.

Shandon listened to her with rising emotion, a youthful titter or two from different parts of the room pointing the moral. When the teacher had finished, she rose with a sudden scream of rage, flung her new slate violently in one direction, her books in another, and departed, kicking the stove over with a well-directed foot as she left. Thus she became a byword[8] to virtuous infancy, and as the years went by, and her wild beauty and her father's wealth grew apace,[9] Deaneville grew less and less charitable in its judgment of her. Shandon lived in a houseful of men, her father's adored companion and greatly admired by the rough cattlemen who came yearly to buy his famous stock.

When her father died, a little wave of pity swept over Deaneville, and more than one kindhearted woman took the five-mile drive down to the Bell Ranch ready to console and sympathize. But no one saw her. The girl, eighteen now, clung more to her solitude than ever, spending whole days and nights in lonely roaming over the marsh and the low meadows, like some frantic sick animal.

---

[5] a flower
[6] women
[7] rebellious
[8] perfect example
[9] quickly

Only Johnnie Larabee, the warmhearted little wife of the village hotel keeper, persevered and was rewarded by Shandon's bitter confidence, given while they rode up to the ridge to look up some roaming steer, perhaps, or down by the peach-cutting sheds, while Shandon supervised a hundred "hands." Shandon laughed now when she recounted the events of those old unhappy childish days, but Johnnie did not like the laughter. The girl always asked particularly for Mary Dickey, her admirers, her clothes, her good times.

"No wonder she acts as if there wasn't anybody else on earth but her!" would be Shandon's dry comment.

It was Johnnie who "talked straight" to Shandon when big Dan Waters began to haunt the Bell Ranch, and who was the only witness of their little wedding, and the only woman to kiss the unbride-like bride.

After that even, Johnnie lost sight of her for the twelve happy months that Big Dan was spared to her. Little Dan came, welcomed by no more skillful hands than the gentle big ones of his wondering father and the practiced ones of the old Indian. And Shandon bought hats that were laughed at by all Deaneville, and was tremulously happy in a clumsy, unused fashion.

And then came the accident that cost Big Dan his life. It was all a hideous blur to Shandon—a blur that enclosed the terrible, swift trip to Sacramento, with the blinking little baby in the hollow of her arm, and the long wait at the strange hospital. It was young Doctor Lowell, of Deaneville, who decided that only an operation could save Dan, and Doctor Lowell who performed it. And it was through him that Shandon learned, in the chill dawn, that the gallant[10] fight was lost. She did not speak again, but, moving like a sleepwalker, reached blindly for the baby, pushed aside the hands that would have detained her, and went stumbling out into the street. And since that day no one in Deaneville had been able to get close enough to speak to her. She did not go to Dan's funeral, and such sympathizers as tried to find her were rewarded by only desolate[11] glimpses of the tall figure flitting along the edge of the marshes like a hunted bird. A month old, little Danny accompanied his mother on these restless wanderings, and many a time his little mottled[12] hand was strong enough to bring her safely home when no other would have availed.

Her old Chinese "boy" came into the village once a week, and paid certain bills punctiliously[13] from a little canvas bag that was stuffed full of gold pieces; but Fong was not a communicative person, and Deaneville lan-

---

[10] heroic, brave
[11] miserable, lonely
[12] spotted, blotchy
[13] carefully

guished[14] for direct news. Johnnie, discouraged by fruitless attempts to have a talk with the forlorn young creature, had to content herself with sending occasional delicacies from her own kitchen and garden to Shandon, and only a week before this bright February morning had ventured a note, pinned to the napkin that wrapped a bowl of cream cheese. The note read:

> *Don't shorten Danny too early, Shandy. Awful easy for babies to ketch cold this weather.*

Of all the loitering curious men and women at doors and windows and in the street, Johnnie was the only one who dared speak to her today. Mrs. Larabee was dressed in the overalls and jersey that simplified both the dressing and the labor of busy Monday mornings; her sleek black hair arranged fashionably in a "turban swirl." She ran out to the cart with a little cry of welcome, a smile on her thin, brown face that well concealed the trepidation[15] this unheard-of circumstance caused her. "Lord, make me say the right thing!" prayed Johnnie, fervently. Mrs. Waters saw her coming, stopped the big horse, and sat waiting. Her eyes were wild with a sort of savage terror, and she was trembling violently.

"Well, how do, Shandon?" said Mrs. Larabee, cheerfully. Then her eyes fell on the child, and she gave a dramatic start. "Never you tell me this is Danny!" said she, sure of her ground now. "Well, you—old—buster—you! He's IMMENSE, ain't he, Shandon?"

"Isn't he?" stammered Shandon, nervously.

"He's about the biggest feller for nine months I ever saw," said Mrs. Larabee, generously. "He could eat Thelma for breakfast!"

"Johnnie—and he ain't quite seven yet!" protested Shandon, eagerly.

Mrs. Larabee gave her an astonished look, puckered up her forehead, nodded profoundly.

"That's right," she said. Then she dragged the wriggling small body from Shandon's lap and held the wondering, soft little face against her own.

"You come to Aunt Johnnie a minute," said she, "you fat old muggins! Look at him, Shandon. He knows I'm strange. Yes, 'course you do! He wants to go back to you, Shandy. Well, what do you know about that? Say, dearie," continued Mrs. Larabee, in a lower tone, "you've got a terrible handsome boy, and what's more, he's Dan's image."

Mrs. Waters gathered the child close to her heart. "He's awful like Dan when he smiles," said she, simply. And for the first time their eyes met. "Say, thank you, for the redishes and the custard pie and that cheese, Johnnie," said Shandon, awkwardly, but her eyes thanked this one friend for much more.

---

[14] longed, ached
[15] anxiety, fear

"Aw, shucks!" said Johnnie, gently, as she dislodged a drying clod of mud from the buggy robe. There was a moment's constrained silence, then Shandon said suddenly:

"Johnnie, what d'you mean by 'shortening' him?"

"Puttin' him in short clothes, dearie. Thelma's been short since Gran'-ma Larabee come down at Christmas," explained the other, briskly.

"I never knew about that," said Mrs. Waters, humbly. "Danny's the first little kid I ever touched. Lizzie Tom tells me what the Indians do, and for the rest I just watch him. I toast his feet good at the fire every night, becuz Dan said his mother useter toast his; and whenever the sun comes out, I take his clothes off and leave him sprawl in it, but I guess I miss a good deal." She finished with a wistful, half-questioning inflection, and Mrs. Larabee did not fail her.

"Don't ask me, when he's as big and husky as any two of mine!" said she, reassuringly. "I guess you do jest about right. But, Shandy, you've got to shorten him."

"Well, what'll I get?" asked Shandon.

Mrs. Larabee, in her element, considered.

"You'll want about eight good, strong calico rompers," she began authoritatively. Then suddenly she interrupted herself. "Say, why don't you come over to the hotel with me now," she suggested enthusiastically. "I'm just finishing my wash, and while I wrench out the last few things you can feed the baby; than I'll show you Thelma's things, and we can have lunch. Then him and Thel can take their naps, and you 'n' me'll go over to Miss Bates's and see what we can git. You'll want shoes for him, an' a good, strong hat—"

"Oh, honest, Johnnie—" Shandon began to protest hurriedly, in her hunted manner, and with a miserable glance toward the home road. "Maybe I'll come up next week, now I know what you meant—"

"Shucks! Next week nobody can talk anything but wedding," said Johnnie, off guard.

"Whose wedding?" Shandon asked, and Johnnie, who would have preferred to bite her tongue out, had to answer, "Mary Dickey's."

"Who to?" said Shandon, her face darkening. Johnnie's voice was very low.

"To the doc', Shandy; to Arnold Lowell."

"Oh!" said Shandon, quietly. "Big wedding, I suppose, and white dresses, and all the rest?"

"Sure," said Johnnie, relieved at her pleasant interest, and warming to the subject. "There'll be five generations there. Parker's making the cake in Sacramento. Five of the girls'll be bridesmaids—Mary Bell and Carrie and Jane and the two Powell girls. Poor Mrs. Dickey, she feels real bad. She—"

"She don't want to give Mary up?" said Shandon, in a hard voice. She began to twist the whip about in its socket. "Well, some people have everything, it seems. They're pretty, and their folks are crazy about 'em, and they can stand up and make a fuss over marrying a man who as good as killed some other woman's husband—a woman who didn't have any one else either."

"Shandy," said Johnnie, sharply, "ain't you got Danny?"

Something like shame softened the girl's stern eyes. She dropped her face until her lips rested upon the little fluffy fringe that marked the dividing line between Danny's cap and Danny's forehead.

"Sure I have," she said huskily. "But I've—I've always sort of had it in for Mary Dickey, Johnnie, I suppose becuz she IS so perfect, and so cool, and treats me like I was dirt—jest barely sees me, that's all!"

Johnnie answered at random, for she was suddenly horrified to see Dr. Lowell and Mary Dickey themselves come out of the post office. Before she could send them a frantic signal of warning, the doctor came toward the cart.

"How do you do, Mrs. Waters?" said he, holding out his hand.

Shandon brought her startled eyes from little Danny's face. The child, with little eager grunts and frowning concentration, was busy with the clasp of her pocketbook, and her big, gentle hand had been guarding it from his little, wild ones. The sight of the doctor's face brought back her bitterest memories with a sick rush, at a moment when her endurance was strained to the utmost. HE had decreed that Dan should be operated on, HE had decided that she should not be with him, HE had come to tell her that the big, protecting arm and heart were gone forever—and now he had an early buttercup in his buttonhole, and on his lips the last of the laughter that he had just been sharing with Mary Dickey! And Mary, the picture of complacent daintiness, was sauntering on, waiting for him.

Shandon was not a reasonable creature. With a sound between a snarl and a sob she caught the light driving whip from its socket and brought the lash fairly across the doctor's smiling face. As he started[16] back, stung with intolerable pain, she lashed in turn the nervous horse, and in another moment the cart and its occupants were racketing down the home road again.

"And now we never WILL git no closer to Shandon Waters!" said Johnnie Larabee, regretfully, for the hundredth time. It was ten days later, and Mrs. Larabee and Mrs. Cass Dinwoodie were high up on the wet hills, gathering cream-colored wild iris for the Dickey wedding that night.

"And serve her right, too!" said Mrs. Dinwoodie, severely. "A great girl like that lettin' fly like a child."

"She's—she's jest the kind to go crazy, brooding as she does," Mrs. Larabee submitted, almost timidly. She had been subtly pleading Shandon's cause for the past week, but it was no use. The last outrage had apparently sealed her fate so far as Deaneville was concerned. Now, straightening her cramped back and looking off toward the valleys below them, Mrs. Larabee said suddenly:

"That looks like Shandon down there now."

Mrs. Dinwoodie's eyes followed the pointing finger. She could distinguish a woman's moving figure, a mere speck on the road far below.

"Sure it is," said she. "Carryin' Dan, too."

"My goo'ness," said Johnnie, uneasily, "I wish she wouldn't take them crazy walks. I don't suppose she's walking up to town?"

---

[16] jumped

"I don't know why she should," said Mrs. Dinwoodie, dryly, "with the horses she's got. I don't suppose even Shandon would attempt to carry that great child that far, cracked as she seems to be!"

"I don't suppose we could drive home down by the marsh road?" Johnnie asked. Mrs. Dinwoodie looked horrified.

"Johnnie, are you crazy yourself?" she demanded. "Why, child, Mary's going to be married at half-past seven, and there's the five-o'clock train now."

The older matron made all haste to "hitch up," sending not even another look into the already shadowy valley. But Johnnie's thoughts were there all through the drive home, and even when she started with her beaming husband and her four young children to the wedding she was still thinking of Shandon Waters.

The Dickey home was all warmth, merriment, and joyous confusion. Three or four young matrons went busily in and out of the dining room. In the double parlors guests were gathering with the laughter and kissing that marked any coming together of these hardworking folk. Starched and awed little children sat on the laps of mothers and aunts, blinking at the lamps; the very small babies were upstairs, some drowsily enjoying a late supper in their mothers' arms, others already deep in sleep in Mrs. Dickey's bed. The downstairs rooms and the stairway were decorated with wilting smilax and early fruit blossoms.

To Deaneville it seemed quite natural that Dr. Lowell, across whose face the scar of Shandon Waters' whip still showed a dull crimson, should wait for his bride at the foot of the hall stairway, and that Mary's attendants should keep up a continual coming and going between the room where she was dressing and the top of the stairs, and should have a great many remarks to make to the young men below. Presently a little stir announced the clergyman, and a moment later everyone could hear Mary Dickey's thrilling young voice from the upper hallway:

"Arnold, mother says was that Dr. Lacey?"

And everyone could hear Dr. Lowell's honest, "Yes, dear, it was," and Mary's fluttered, diminishing, "All right!"

Rain began to beat noisily on the roof and the porches. Johnnie Larabee came downstairs with Grandpa and Grandma Arnold, and Rosamund Dinwoodie at the piano said audibly, "Now, Johnnie?"

There was expectant silence in the parlors. The whole house was so silent in that waiting moment that the sound of sudden feet on the porch and the rough opening of the hall door were a startlingly loud interruption.

It was Shandon Waters, who came in with a bitter rush of storm and wet air. She had little Dan in her arms. Drops of rain glittered on her hanging braids and on the shawl with which the child was wrapped, and beyond her the wind snarled and screamed like a disappointed animal. She went straight through the frightened, parting group to Mrs. Larabee, and held out the child.

"Johnnie," she said in a voice of agony, utterly oblivious of her surroundings, "Johnnie, you've always been my friend! Danny's sick!"

"Shandon—for pity's sake!" ejaculated little Mrs. Larabee, reaching out her arms for Danny, her face shocked and protesting and pitying all at once, "Why, Shandy, you should have waited for me over at the hotel," she said, in a lower tone, with a glance at the incongruous[17] scene. Then pity for the anguished face gained mastery, and she added tenderly, "Well, you poor child, you, was this where you was walking this afternoon? My stars, if I'd only known! Why on earth didn't you drive?"

"I couldn't wait!" said Shandon, hoarsely. "We were out in the woods, and Lizzie she gave Danny some mushrooms. And when I looked he—his little mouth—" she choked. "And then he began to have sorta cramps, and kinda doubled up, Johnnie, and he cried so queer, and I jest started up here on a run. He—JOHNNIE!" terror shook her voice when she saw the other's face, "Johnnie, is he going to die?" she said.

"Mushrooms!" echoed Mrs. Larabee, gravely, shaking her head. And a score[18] of other women looking over her shoulder at the child, who lay breathing heavily with his eyes shut, shook their heads, too.

"You'd better take him right home with me, dearie," Mrs. Larabee said gently, with a significant glance at the watching circle. "We oughtn't to lose any time."

Dr. Lowell stepped out beside her and gently took Danny in his arms.

"I hope you'll let me carry him over there for you, Mrs. Waters," said he. "There's no question that he's pretty sick. We've got a hard fight ahead."

There was a little sensation in the room, but Shandon only looked at him uncomprehendingly. In her eyes there was the dumb thankfulness of the dog who knows himself safe with friends. She wet her lips and tried to

---

[17] inappropriate

[18] twenty or so

speak. But before she could do so, the doctor's mother touched his arm half timidly and said:

"Arnold, you can't very well—surely, it's hardly fair to Mary—"

"Mary—?" he answered her quickly. He raised his eyes to where his wife-to-be, in a startled group of white-clad attendants, was standing halfway down the stairway.

She looked straight at Shandon, and perhaps at no moment in their lives did the two women show a more marked contrast; Shandon muddy, exhausted, haggard, her somber[19] eyes sick with dread, Mary's always fragile beauty more ethereal[20] than ever under the veil her mother had just caught back with orange blossoms. Shandon involuntarily flung out her hand toward her in desperate appeal.

"Couldn't you—could you jest wait till he sees Danny?" she faltered.

Mary ran down the remaining steps and laid her white hand on Shandon's.

"If it was ten weddings, we'd wait, Shandon!" said she, her voice thrilling with the fellowship of wifehood and motherhood to come. "Don't worry, Shandon. Arnold will fix him. Poor little Danny!" said Mary, bending over him. "He's not awful sick, is he, Arnold? Mother," she said, turning, royally flushed, to her stupefied mother, "every one'll have to wait. Johnnie and Arnold are going to fix up Shandon's baby."

"I don't see the slightest need of traipsing over to the hotel," said Mrs. Dickey, almost offended, as at a slight upon her hospitality. "Take him right up to the spare room, Arnold. There ain't no noise there, it's in the wing. And one of you chil'ren run and tell Aggie we want hot water, and—what else? Well, go ahead and tell her that, anyway."

"Leave me carry him up," said one big, gentle father, who had tucked his own baby up only an hour ago. "I've got a kimmoner[21] in my bag," old Mrs. Lowell said to Shandon. "It's a-plenty big enough for you. You git dry and comfortable before you hold him." "Shucks! Lloydy ate a green cherry when he wasn't but four months old," said one consoling voice to Shandon. "He's got a lot of fight in him," said another. "My Olive got an inch screw in her throat," contributed a third. Mrs. Larabee said in a low tone, with her hand tight upon Shandon's shaking one, "He'll be jest about fagged out[22] when the doctor's done with him, dearie, and as hungry as a hunter. Don't YOU git excited, or he'll be sick all over again."

---

[19] dark, sad

[20] fragile

[21] kimono (a long robe)

[22] tired out

Crowding solicitously[23] about her, the women got her upstairs and into dry clothing. This was barely accomplished when Mary Dickey came into the room, in a little blue cotton gown, to take her to Danny.

"Arnold says he's got him crying, and that's a good sign, Shandon," said Mary. "And he says that rough walk pro'bly saved him."

Shandon tried to speak again, but failed again, and the two girls went out together. Mary presently came back alone, and the lessened but not uncheerful group downstairs settled down to a vigil. Various reports drifted from the sick-room, but it was almost midnight before Mrs. Larabee came down with definite news.

"How is he?" echoed Johnnie, sinking into a chair. "Give me a cup of that coffee, Mary. That's a good girl. Well, say, it looks like you can't kill no Deaneville child with mushrooms. He's asleep now. But say, he was a pretty sick kid! Doc' looks like something the cat brought home, and I'm about dead, but Danny seems to feel real chipper. And EAT! And of course that poor girl looks like she'd inherited the earth, as the Scriptures say.[24] The ice is what you might call broken between the whole crowd of us and Shandon Waters. She's sitting there holding Danny and smiling softly at anyone who peeks in!" And, her voice thickening suddenly with tears on the last words, Mrs. Larabee burst out crying and fumbled in her unaccustomed grandeur for a handkerchief.

Mary Dickey and Arnold Lowell were married just twenty-four hours later than they had planned, the guests laughing joyously at the wilted decorations and stale sandwiches. After the ceremony the bride and bridegroom went softly upstairs, and the doctor had a last approving look at the convalescent[25] Danny.

Mary, almost oppressed by the sense of her own blessedness on this day of good wishes and affectionate demonstration, would have gently detached her husband's arm from her waist as they went to the door, that Shandon might not be reminded of her own loss and aloneness.

But the doctor, glancing back, knew that in Shandon's thoughts today there was no room for sorrow. Her whole body was curved about the child as he lay in her lap, and her adoring look was intent upon him. Danny was smiling up at his mother in a blissful interval, his soft little hand lying upon her contented heart.

---

[23] anxiously

[24] "Blessed are the meek: for they shall inherit the earth" (Matthew 5:5).

[25] recovering

Questions for Review

1. Sum up Shandon Waters's background, and why the townspeople are stunned to see her in town.

2. How does Dan's death affect Shandon?

3. How does Shandon react to the news about Mary's wedding, and Mary and the doctor's appearance?

4. How does the town rally around Shandon Waters when Danny needs help? If you had to predict what happens the next few years after this tale, what would you predict?

Old Aunt Mary's

By James Whitcomb Riley

Americans loved the poems of James Whitcomb Riley (1849-1916), because they brought back to their childhood days and the fond memories that went along with them. Riley, in fact, drew large crowds by performing his own poems! Almost everybody has a favorite relative like Old Aunt Mary, who loves and spoils you.

• • • • •

Wasn't it pleasant, O brother mine,
In those old days of the lost sunshine
Of youth—when the Saturday's chores were through,
And the "Sunday's wood" in the kitchen, too,[1]
And we went visiting, "me and you,"
      Out to Old Aunt Mary's?

"Me and you"—and the morning fair,
With the dewdrops twinkling everywhere;
The scent of the cherry-blossoms blown
After us, in the roadway lone,
Our capering[2] shadows onward thrown—
      Out to Old Aunt Mary's.

It all comes back so clear today!
Though I am as bald as you are gray—
Out by the barn-lot and down the lane,
We patter along in the dust again,
As light as the tips of the drops of rain,
      Out to Old Aunt Mary's

The last few houses of the town;
Then on, up the high creek bluffs and down;
Past the squat toll-gate with its well-sweep poll;
The bridge, "the old 'baptizin'-hole',"
Loitering,[3] awed, o'er pool and shoal,
      Out to Old Aunt Mary's.

---

[1] The kids would bring in extra wood for Sunday so they didn't have to do it that day.
[2] jumping, frolicking
[3] hanging around

We cross the pasture, and through the wood,
Where the old gray snag of the poplar stood,
Where the hammering "red-heads" hopped awry,[4]
And the buzzard "raised" in the "clearing"-sky
And lolled and circled as we went by,
      Out to Old Aunt Mary's.

Or, stayed[5] by the glint of the redbird's wings,
Or the glitter of the song that the bluebird sings,
All hushed we feign[6] to strike strange trails,
As the "big braves" do in the Indian tales,
Till again our real quest lags and fails—
      Out to Old Aunt Mary's.

And the woodland echoes with yells of mirth[7]
That make old war-whoops of minor worth!...
Where such heroes of war as we?
With bows and arrows of fantasy,
Chasing each other from tree to tree
      Out to Old Aunt Mary's!

And then in the dust of the road again;
And the teams we met, and the countrymen;
And the long highway, with sunshine spread
As thick as butter on country bread,
Our cares behind, our hearts ahead,
      Out to Old Aunt Mary's.

For only, now, at the road's next bend
To the right we could make out the gable-end
Of the fine old Huston homestead—not
Half a mile from the sacred spot
Where dwelt our Saint in her simple cot—
      Out to Old Aunt Mary's.

Why, I see her now in the open door
Where the little gourds grew up the sides and o'er
The clapboard roof!—And her face—ah, me!
Wasn't it good for a boy to see—
And wasn't it good for a boy to be

---

[4] crookedly
[5] delayed
[6] pretend
[7] laughter, joy

Out to Old Aunt Mary's?—

The jelly, the jam, and the marmalade,
And the cherry and quince "preserves" she made!
And the sweet-sour pickles of peach and pear,
With cinnamon in 'em and all things rare!—
And the more we ate was the more to spare
      Out to Old Aunt Mary's!

Ah, was there, ever, so kind a face
And gentle as hers, and such a grace
Of welcoming, as she cut the cake
Or the juicy pies she joyed to make
Just for the visiting children's sake—
      Out to Old Aunt Mary's!

The honey, too, in its amber[8] comb
One only finds in an old farm-home;
And the coffee, fragrant and sweet, and ho!
So hot that we gloried to drink it so,
With spangles of tears in our eyes, you know—
      Out to Old Aunt Mary's.

And the romps we took, in our glad unrest!—
Was it the lawn that we loved the best,
With its swooping swing in the locust trees,
Or was it the grove, with its leafy breeze,
Or the dim haymow, with its fragrancies—
      Out to Old Aunt Mary's.

Far fields, bottom-lands, creek-banks— all
We ranged at will.— Where the waterfall
Laughed all day as it slowly poured
Over the dam by the old mill-ford,
While the tail-race writhed, and the mill-wheel roared—
      Out to Old Aunt Mary's.

But home, with Aunty in nearer call,
That was the best place, after all!—
The talks on the back porch, in the low
Slanting sun and the evening glow,
With the voice of counsel that touched us so,
      Out to Old Aunt Mary's.

---

[8] brownish-yellow

And then, in the garden—near the side
Where the beehives were and the path was wide—
The apple-house—like a fairy cell—
With the little square door we knew so well,
And the wealth inside but our tongues could tell—
      Out to Old Aunt Mary's.

And the old spring-house, the cool green gloom
Of the willow trees—and the cooler room
Where the swinging shelves and the crocks were kept,
Where the cream in a golden languor[9] slept,
While the waters gurgled and laughed and wept—
      Out to Old Aunt Mary's.

And as many a time as you and I—
Barefoot boys in the days gone by—
Knelt in the tremulous ecstasies

---

[9] stillness

Dipped our lips into sweets like these—
Memory now is on her knees
        Out to Old Aunt Mary's.

For O my brother so far away,
This is to tell you—she waits today
To welcome us:—Aunt Mary fell
Asleep this morning, whispering, "Tell
The boys to come."...And all is well,
        Out to Old Aunt Mary's.

Questions for Review

1. List several things that stuck in your mind that the poet loved about going to Old Aunt Mary's house.

2. Do you have a relative like Old Aunt Mary, whose home you love to visit? What about that relative's home do you enjoy?

3. Write a five-line poem like one of the stanzas of this poem about a relative you like to visit, or a place you love to go. Try to follow the same rhyme scheme as "Old Aunt Mary's."

4. Listen to a recording of James Whitcomb Riley himself reading "Old Aunt Mary's" online. (You can find a 1911 recording by searching the web site **www.archive.org**.) Here's the link if you can't find it:

https://archive.org/details/James_Whitcomb_Riley-Out_To_Old_Aunt_Marys

Do Insects Think?

By Robert Benchley

One of America's funniest writers, the great Robert Benchley (1889-1945) observed people, culture, and the world, and then wrote his often-hilarious thoughts on what he saw. One of the things he observed was the tendency of scientists to be a little pompous and sure of themselves. The below essay, which Benchley wrote in 1922, was in response to The Psychic Life of Insects, *a book written four years earlier by French scientist Eugene Louis Bouvier.*[1]

· · · · ·

In a recent book entitled *The Psychic Life of Insects*, Professor Bouvier says that we must be careful not to credit the little winged fellows with intelligence when they behave in what seems like an intelligent manner. They may be only reacting. I would like to confront the Professor with an instance of reasoning power on the part of an insect which cannot be explained away in any such manner.

During the summer of 1899, while I was at work on my treatise[2] *Do Larvae Laugh?*, we kept a female wasp at our cottage in the Adirondacks. It really was more like a child of our own than a wasp, except that it *looked* more like a wasp than a child of our own. That was one of the ways we told the difference.

It was still a young wasp when we got it (thirteen or fourteen years old), and for some time we could not get it to eat or drink, it was so shy. Since it was a female, we decided to call it Miriam, but soon the children's nickname for it—"Pudge"—became a fixture, and "Pudge" it was from that time on.

One evening I had been working late in my laboratory, fooling around with some gin and other chemicals, and in leaving the room I tripped over a nine of diamonds which someone had left lying on the floor and knocked over my card catalogue containing the names and addresses of all the larvae worth knowing in North America. The cards went everywhere.

I was too tired to stop to pick them up that night, and went sobbing to bed, just as mad as I could be. As I went, however, I noticed the wasp flying about in circles over the scattered cards. "Maybe Pudge will pick them

---

[1] "Psychic" means having to do with thinking or mental abilities.
[2] article

up," I said half-laughingly to myself, never thinking for one moment that such would be the case.

When I came down the next morning Pudge was still asleep over in her box, evidently tired out. And well she might have been. For there on the floor lay the cards scattered all about just as I had left them the night before. The faithful little insect had buzzed about all night trying to come to some decision about picking them up and arranging them in the catalogue box, and then, figuring out for herself that, as she knew practically nothing about larvae of any sort except wasp larvae, she would probably make more of a mess of rearranging them than as if she left them on the floor for me to

fix. It was just too much for her to tackle, and, discouraged, she went over and lay down in her box, where she cried herself to sleep.

If this is not an answer to Professor Bouvier's statement that insects have no reasoning power, I do not know what is.

Questions for Review

1. Finish this sentence in your own words: "The 'Do Insects Think?' author says (with a sense of humor, of course!) that he knows Pudge is a good thinker, because ___." What is ridiculous about this claim?

2. Write an original paragraph of your own—make it about anything you want—that follows the pattern of the author's absurdly funny claim.

Missionary Travels and Researches (Excerpts)

By David Livingstone

British missionary to Africa David Livingstone (1813-1873) was one of the great men of the nineteenth century. In 1840 he sailed to Africa and journeyed to its interior, going places no non-African had been before. His high character made Africans trust him thoroughly, which allowed him to do greater work for Jesus Christ with the natives. After he lost contact with the outside world for several years, American journalist Henry Stanley found him in 1871.

• • • • •

Chapter I. Early Experiences

My own inclination would lead me to say as little as possible about myself. My great grandfather fell at Culloden,[1] my grandfather used to tell us national stories, and my grandmother sang Gaelic[2] songs. To my father and the other children the dying injunction[3] was, "Now, in my lifetime I have searched most carefully through all the traditions I could find of our family, and I never could discover that there was a dishonest man among our forefathers. If, therefore, any of you or any of your children should take to dishonest ways, it will not be because it runs in your blood; it does not belong to you. I leave this precept with you—be honest."

As a boy I worked at a cotton factory at Blantyre[4] to lessen the family anxieties, and bought my *Rudiments of Latin* out of my first week's wages, pursuing the study of that language at an evening school, followed up till twelve o'clock or later, if my mother did not interfere by jumping up and snatching the books out of my hands. Reading everything I could lay my hands on, except novels, scientific works and books of travel were my especial delight. Great pains had been taken by my parents to instill the doctrines of Christianity into my mind. My early desire was to become a pioneer missionary in China, and eventually I offered my services to the London Missionary Society, having passed my medical examination at Glasgow University.

---

[1] a battle in 1746 in Scotland
[2] an Irish or Scottish language
[3] command
[4] a town in Scotland

I embarked for Africa in 1840, and from Cape Town[5] traveled up country seven hundred miles to Kuruman, where I joined Mr. Moffat[6] in his work, and after four years as a bachelor, I married his daughter Mary.

Settling among the Mabotsa tribe, I found that they were troubled with attacks from lions, so one day I went with my gun into the bush and shot one, but the wounded beast sprang upon me, and felled me to the ground. While perfectly conscious, I lost all sense of fear or feeling, and narrowly escaped with my life. Besides crunching the bone into splinters, he left eleven teeth wounds on the upper part of my arm.

I attached myself to the tribe called Bakwains, whose chief, Sechele, a most intelligent man, became my fast friend, and a convert to Christianity. The Bakwains had many excellent qualities, which might have been developed by association with European nations. An adverse[7] influence, however, is exercised by the Boers,[8] for, while claiming for themselves the title of Christians, they treat these natives as black property, and their system of domestic slavery and robbery is a disgrace to the white man. For my defense of the rights of Sechele and the Bakwains, I was treated as conniving[9] at their resistance, and my house was destroyed, my library, the solace[10] of our solitude, torn to pieces, my stock of medicines smashed, and our furniture and clothing sold at public auction to pay the expenses of the foray.[11]

---

[5] in South Africa
[6] Robert Moffat, a Scottish missionary
[7] harmful
[8] British farmers who came to live in Africa ("Boer" means "farmer")
[9] dishonest
[10] comfort
[11] raid

In traveling we sometimes suffered from a scarcity of meat, and the natives, to show their sympathy for the children, often gave them caterpillars to eat; but one of the dishes they most enjoyed was cooked "mathametlo," a large frog, which, during a period of drought, takes refuge in a hole in the root of certain bushes, and over the orifice[12] a large variety of spider weaves its web. The scavenger beetle, which keeps the Kuruman villages sweet and clean, rolls the dirt into a ball, and carries it, like Atlas,[13] on its back.

In passing across the great Kalahari desert we met with the Bushmen, or Bakalahari, who, from dread of visits from strange tribes, choose their residences far away from water, hiding their supplies of this necessity for life in pits filled up by women, who pass every drop through their mouths as a pump, using a straw to guide the stream into the vessel. They will never disclose this supply to strangers, but by sitting down and waiting with patience until the villagers were led to form a favorable opinion of us, a woman would bring out a shell full of the precious fluid from I knew not where.

At Nchokotsa we came upon a number of salt pans, which, in the setting sun, produced a most beautiful mirage[14] as of distant water, foliage,[15] and animals. We discovered the river Zouga, and eventually, on August 1, 1849, we were the first Europeans to gaze upon the broad waters of Lake Ngami. My chief object in coming to this lake was to visit Sebituane, the great chief of the Makololo, a man of immense influence, who had conquered the black tribes of the country and made himself dreaded even by the terrible Mosilikatse.

During our stay with him he treated us with great respect, and was pleased with the confidence we had shown in bringing our children to him. He was stricken with inflammation of the lungs, and knew it meant death, though his native doctors said, "Sebituane can never die." I visited him with my little boy Robert. "Come near," said he, "and see if I am any longer a man. I am done." After sitting with him some time and commending him to the mercy of God, I rose to depart, when the dying chieftain, raising himself up a little from his prone[16] position, called a servant, and said, "Take Robert to Maunku (one of his wives), and tell her to give him some milk." These were the last words of Sebituane.

---

[12] opening

[13] Atlas is a figure in Greek mythology who carries the earth on his back.

[14] illusion

[15] plants, vegetation

[16] lying down

Chapter II. Among the Makololo

On questioning intelligent men amongst these natives as to a knowledge of good and evil, of God and the future state, they possessed a tolerably clear perception on these subjects. Their want, however, of any form of public worship, or of idols, or of formal prayers and sacrifices, make both the Caffres and Bechuanas appear as amongst the most godless races of mortals known anywhere. When an old Bushman on one occasion was sitting by the fire relating his adventures, including his murder of five other natives, he was remonstrated[17] with. "What will God say when you appear before Him?" "He will say," replied he, "that I was a very clever fellow." But I found afterwards in speaking of the Deity they had only the idea of a chief, and when I knew this, I did not make any mistake afterwards.

The country round Unku was covered with grass, and the flowers were in full bloom. The thermometer in the shade generally stood at 98 degrees from 1 to 3 p.m., but it sank as low as 65 degrees by night, so that the heat was by no means exhausting. At the surface of the ground in the sun it marked 125 degrees, and three inches below 138 degrees. The hand cannot be held on the ground, and even the horny soles of the natives are protected by hide sandals, yet the ants were busy working in it. The water in the floods was as high as 100 degrees, but as water does not conduct heat readily

---

[17] protested

downwards, deliriously cool water may be obtained by anyone walking into the middle and lifting up the water from the bottom to the surface by the hands.

We at last reached a spot where, by climbing the highest tree, we could see a fine large sheet of water, surrounded on all sides by an impenetrable belt of reeds. This was the river Chobe, and is called Zambesi. We struggled through the high, serrated[18] grass, the heat stifling for want of air, and when we reached one of the islands, my strong moleskins were worn through at the knees, and the leather trousers of my companion were torn, and his legs bleeding. The Makololo said in their figurative language: "He has dropped among us from the clouds, yet came riding on the back of a hippopotamus. We Makololo thought no one could cross the Chobe without our knowledge, but here he drops among us like a bird."

On our arrival at Linyanti, the capital, the chief, Sekelutu, took me aside and pressed me to mention those things I liked best and hoped to get from him. Anything either in or out of the town should be freely given if I would only mention it. I explained to him that my object was to elevate him and his people to be Christians; but he replied that he did not wish to learn to read the Book, for he was afraid "it might change his heart and make him content with one wife like Sechele." I liked the frankness of Sekelutu, for nothing is so wearying to the spirit as talking to those who agree with everything advanced.

While at Linyanti I was taken with fever, from chills caught by leaving my warm wagon in the evening to conduct family worship at my people's fires. Anxious to ascertain[19] whether the natives possessed the knowledge of any remedy, I sent for one of their doctors. He put some roots into a pot with water, and when it was boiling, placed it beneath a blanket thrown around both me and it. This produced no effect, and after being stewed in their vapor baths, smoked like a red herring over green twigs, and charmed *secundem artem*,[20] I concluded I could cure my fever more quickly than they could.

Leaving Linyanti, we passed up the Lecambye River into the Barotse country, and on making inquiries whether Santuru, the Moloiana, had ever been visited by white men, I could find no vestige[21] of any such visit before my arrival in 1851.

In our ascent up the River Leeba, we reached the village of Manenko, a female chief, of whose power of tongue we soon had ample proof. She was a woman of fine physique, and insisted on accompanying us some distance

---

[18] jagged, saw-like
[19] determine
[20] according to common practice
[21] trace

with her husband and drummer, the latter thumping most vigorously, until a heavy, drizzling mist set in and compelled him to desist. Her husband used various incantations and vociferations[22] to drive away the rain, but down it poured incessantly, and on our Amazon went, in the very lightest marching order, and at a pace that few men could keep up with....My men, in admiration of her pedestrian[23] powers, every now and then remarked, "Manenko is a soldier!" Thoroughly wet and cold, we were all glad when she proposed a halt to prepare for our night's lodging on the banks of a stream.

Questions for Review

1. Describe how Livingstone is attacked by a lion and by British farmers.

2. What does Livingstone find about many natives' ideas of God and the afterlife? What does Sekelutu say to Livingstone about Christianity?

3. Name several memorable events that Livingstone writes about in these two chapters.

Missionary Travels and Researches

By David Livingstone

• • • • •

Chapter III. Peril and Patience

When we arrived at the foot of the Kasai[24] we were badly in want of food, and there seemed little hope of getting any; one of our guides, however, caught a light-blue mole and two mice for his supper. Katende, the chief, sent for me the following morning, and on my walking into his hut I was told that he wanted a man, a tusk, beads, copper rings, and a shell as payment for leave to pass through his country. Having humbly explained our circumstances and that he could not expect to "catch a humble cow by the horns"—a proverb similar to ours that "You cannot draw milk out of a stone"—we were told to go home, and he would speak to us next day. I could not avoid a hearty laugh at the cool impudence[25] of the savage. Eventually I sent him one of my worst shirts, but added that when I should reach my own chief naked, and was asked what I had done

---

[22] "incantations and vociferations": chants and cries
[23] hiking
[24] a river in central Africa
[25] boldness, nerve

with my clothes, I should be obliged to confess I had left them with Katende.

Passing onwards, we crossed a small rivulet, the Sengko, and another and larger one with a bridge over it. At the farther end of this structure stood a negro who demanded fees. He said the bridge was his, the guides were his children, and if we did not pay him, he would prevent further progress. This piece of civilization I was not prepared to meet, and stood a few seconds looking at our bold tollkeeper, when one of our men took off three copper bracelets, which paid for the whole party. The negro was a better man than he at first seemed, for he immediately went into his garden and brought us some leaves of tobacco as a present.

We were brought to a stand on the banks of the Loajima, a tributary of the Kasai, by the severity of my fever, being in a state of partial coma, until late at night, I found we were in the midst of enemies; and the Chiboque natives insisting upon a present, I had to give them a tired-out ox. Later on we marched through the gloomy forest in gloomier silence; the thick atmosphere prevented my seeing the creeping plants in time to avoid them; I was often caught, and as there is no stopping the oxen when they have the prospect of giving the rider a tumble, came frequently to the ground. In addition to these mishaps, my ox Sinbad went off at a plunging gallop, the bridle broke, and I came down behind on the crown of my head. He gave me a kick in the thigh at the same time. I felt none the worse for this rough treatment, but would not recommend it to others as a palliative[26] in cases of fever.

We shortly afterwards met a hostile party of natives, who refused us further passage. Seeing that these people had plenty of iron-headed arrows and some guns, I called a halt, and ordered my men to put the luggage in the center in case of actual attack. I then dismounted, and advancing a little towards our principal opponent, showed him how easily I could kill him, but pointed upwards, saying, "I fear God." He did the same, placing his hand on his heart, pointing upwards, and saying, "I fear to kill, but come to our village; come, do come."

During these exciting scenes I always forgot my fever, but a terrible sense of sinking came back with the feeling of safety. These people stole our beads, and though we offered all our ornaments and my shirts, they refused us passage. My men were so disheartened that they proposed a return home, which distressed me exceedingly. After using all my powers of persuasion, I declared to them that if they returned, I would go on alone, and went into my little tent with the mind directed to Him Who hears the sighing of the soul, and was soon followed by the head of Mohorisi, saying, "We will never leave you. Do not be disheartened. Wherever you lead, we will

---

[26] painkiller

follow. Our remarks were made only on account of the injustice of these people."

We were soon on the banks of the Quango, and after some difficulties reached the opposite bank.

The village of Cassenge is composed of thirty or forty traders' houses on an elevated flat spot in the great Quango, or Cassenge, valley. As I always preferred to appear in my own proper character, I was an object of curiosity to the hospitable Portuguese. They evidently looked upon me as an agent of the English government, engaged in some new movement for the suppression of slavery. They could not divine what a "missionario" had to do with the latitudes and longitudes which I was intent on observing.

On coming across the plains to Loanda we first beheld the sea; my companions looked upon the boundless ocean with awe. In describing their feelings afterwards, they remarked, "We marched along with our father thinking that what the ancients had always told us was true, that the world has no end, but all at once the world said to us, 'I am finished, there is no more of me.'"

Here in this city, among its population of 12,000 souls there was but one genuine English gentleman, who bade me welcome, and seeing me ill,

benevolently[27] offered me his bed. Never shall I forget the luxuriant pleasure I enjoyed feeling myself again on a good English couch, after six
months sleeping on the ground.

Chapter IV. Into the Wilderness Again

For the sake of my Makololo companions I refused the tempting offer of a
passage home in one of her majesty's cruisers.[28]

During my journey through Angola I received at Cassenge a packet of
the *Times* from home with news of the Russian war up to the terrible charge
of the light cavalry. The intense anxiety I felt to hear more may be imagined
by every true patriot.

After leaving the Kasai country, we entered upon a great level plain,
which we had formerly found in a flooded condition. We forded the Lo-
tembwa on June 8, and found that the little Lake Dilolo, by giving a portion to our Kasai and another to the Zambesi, distributes its waters to the
Atlantic and Indian oceans. From information derived from Arabs at Zan-
zibar, whom I met at Naliele in the middle of the country, a large shallow
lake is pointed out in the region east of Loanda, named Tanganyenka, which
requires three days in crossing in canoes. It is connected with another
named Kalagwe (Garague?), farther north, and may be the Nyanja of the
Maravim.

Although I was warned that the Batoka tribe would be hostile, I decided
on going down the Zambesi, and on my way I visited the falls of Victoria,
called by the natives Mosioatunya, or more anciently, Shongwe. No one can
imagine the beauty of the view from anything witnessed in England. It has
never been seen before by European eyes, but scenes so lovely must have
been gazed upon by angels in their flight. Five columns of "smoke" arose,
bending in the direction of the wind. The entire falls is simply a crack made
in a hard basaltic rock from the right to the left bank of the Zambesi, and
then prolonged from the left bank away through thirty or forty miles of hills.
The whole scene was extremely beautiful; the banks and islands dotted over
the river are adorned with sylvan[29] vegetation of great variety of color and
form. At the period of our visit several of the trees were spangled over with
blossoms.

In due time we reached the confluence of the Loangwa and the Zambesi,
most thankful to God for His great mercies in helping us thus far. I felt some
turmoil of spirit in the evening at the prospect of having all my efforts for
the welfare of this great region and its teeming[30] population knocked on the

---

[27] kindly
[28] Her Majesty at this time was Queen Victoria.
[29] forest
[30] crowded, full

head by savages tomorrow, who might be said to "know not what they do."[31]

When at last we reached within eight miles of Tete I was too fatigued to go on, but sent the commandant the letters of recommendation of the bishop and lay down to rest. Next morning two officers and some soldiers came to fetch us, and when I had partaken of a good breakfast, though I had just before been too tired to sleep, all my fatigue vanished.

Questions for Review

1. What difficulties does Livingstone face while traveling to the center of Africa? Why does he have to submit to some tribes and persons, even though he could easily overwhelm them with his weapons?

2. Look up some information about and film footage of Victoria Falls.

3. Research the meeting between David Livingstone and American reporter Henry Stanley, and the end of David Livingstone's life.

---

[31] When Jesus was killed on the cross, of those who did it to Him, He said, "Father, forgive them, for they know not what they do" (Luke 23:34).

Songs for My Mother

By Anna Hempstead Branch

Mary Bolles Branch, the mother of Connecticut-born Anna Hempstead Branch (1875-1937), was also a poet, so no doubt she taught Anna a great deal. Branch began to write poems in college and enjoyed success as a poet throughout her life. "Songs for My Mother" is a lovely tribute to two of her mother's beautiful features.

• • • • •

I
HER HANDS

My mother's hands are cool and fair;
   They can do anything.
Delicate mercies hide them there
   Like flowers in the spring.

When I was small and could not sleep,
   She used to come to me,
And with my cheek upon her hand
   How sure my rest would be.

For everything she ever touched
   Of beautiful or fine,
Their memories living in her hands
   Would warm that sleep of mine.

Her hands remember how they played
   One time in meadow streams—
And all the flickering song and shade
   Of water took my dreams.

Swift through her haunted fingers pass
   Memories of garden things—
I dipped my face in flowers and grass
   And sounds of hidden wings.

One time she touched the cloud that kissed
   Brown pastures bleak and far—
I leaned my cheek into a mist
   And thought I was a star.

All this was very long ago
    And I am grown; but yet
The hand that lured my slumber so
    I never can forget.

For still when drowsiness comes on
    It seems so soft and cool,
Shaped happily beneath my cheek,
    Hollow and beautiful.

II
HER WORDS

My mother has the prettiest tricks
    Of words and words and words.
Her talk comes out as smooth and sleek
    As breasts of singing birds.

She shapes her speech all silver fine
    Because she loves it so.
And her own eyes begin to shine
    To hear her stories grow.

And if she goes to make a call
    Or out to take a walk
We leave our work when she returns
    And run to hear her talk.

We had not dreamed these things were so
    Of sorrow and of mirth.[1]
Her speech is as a thousand eyes
    Through which we see the earth.

God wove a web of loveliness,
    Of clouds and stars and birds,
But made not any thing at all
    So beautiful as words.

They shine around our simple earth
    With golden shadowings,
And every common thing they touch
    Is exquisite[2] with wings.

---

[1] joy
[2] beautiful, delightful

There's nothing poor and nothing small
    But is made fair with them.
They are the hands of living faith
    That touch the garment's hem.[3]

They are as fair as bloom or air,
    They shine like any star,
And I am rich who learned from her
    How beautiful they are.

Questions for Review

1. What beautiful, loving things does the author remember about her mother's hands?

2. Explain what the phrase "She shapes her speech all silver fine" means.

3. What does the author say about the power of words?

---

[3] See Matthew 9:19-22.

My Mother's Bible

By George P. Morris

George Pope Morris (1802-1864) was a songwriter and a poet. He also helped start and write for several newspapers. Morris was popular with both the public and other writers, including famous American writer Edgar Allan Poe, who highly praised his work. The following poem, with its moving subject, was written and sung as a hymn.

• • • • •

This book is all that's left me now,
    Tears will unbidden[1] start,
With faltering lip and throbbing brow
    I press it to my heart.
For many generations past
    Here is our family tree;[2]
My mother's hands this Bible clasped;
    She, dying, gave it me.

Ah! well do I remember those
    Whose names these records bear;
Who round the hearthstone used to close,
    After the evening prayer,
And speak of what these pages said
    In tones my heart would thrill!
Though they are with the silent dead,
    Here are they living still!

My father read this holy hook
    To brothers, sisters, dear;
How calm was my poor mother's look,
    Who loved God's word to hear!
Her angel face—I see it yet!
    What thronging[3] memories come!
Again that little group is met
    Within the walls of home!

---

[1] not asked for
[2] Many family Bibles at the time contained "family trees" written down in the front.
[3] flooding

Thou truest friend man ever knew,
    Thy constancy I've tried;[4]
When all were false, I found thee true,[5]
    My counselor and guide.
The mines of earth no treasures give
    That could this volume buy;
In teaching me the way to live,
    It taught me how to die.

Questions for Review

1. List several images that this poem made you "see" in your mind.

2. What does the poet mean by the lines in the second stanza, "Though they are with the silent dead, here are they living still!"?

3. How can the Bible teach someone "how to die," as the poet says?

4. Name one way that God's Word has been a comfort to you.

---

[4] "constancy I've tried": faithfulness I've tested
[5] "...[L]et God be true, but every man a liar" (Romans 3:4).

Zero Hour

By Ray Bradbury

*Ray Bradbury (1920-2012) was one of the most fa-
mous American science fiction writers of all time. Science fiction (or "sci-fi") is a **genre**, or type of writing.
It focuses on creative stories often set in the future,
with imagined scientific technologies and inventions
that have changed life drastically. Other common sci-
fi topics include space travel and creatures from other
planets. "Zero Hour" was first published in a magazine called* Planet Stories *in 1947.*

· · · · ·

Oh, it was to be so jolly! What a game! Such excitement they hadn't
known in years. The children catapulted[1] this way and that across
the green lawns, shouting at each other, holding hands, flying in
circles, climbing trees, laughing....Overhead, the rockets flew and beetle-
cars whispered by on the streets, but the children played on. Such fun, such
tremulous[2] joy, such tumbling and hearty screaming.

Mink ran into the house, all dirt and sweat. For her seven years she was
loud and strong and definite. Her mother, Mrs. Morris, hardly saw her as
she yanked out drawers and rattled pans and tools into a large sack.

"Heavens, Mink, what's going on?"

"The most exciting game ever!" gasped Mink, pink-faced.

"Stop and get your breath," said the mother.

"No, I'm all right," gasped Mink. "Okay I take these things, Mom?"

"But don't dent them," said Mrs. Morris.

"Thank you, thank you!" cried Mink and—boom! she was gone, like a
rocket.

Mrs. Morris surveyed the fleeing tot. "What's the name of the game?"

"Invasion!" said Mink. The door slammed.

In every yard on the street children brought out knives and forks and
pokers and old stove pipes and can openers.

It was an interesting fact that this fury and bustle occurred only among
the younger children. The older ones, those ten years and more, disdained[3]
the affair and marched scornfully off on hikes or played a more dignified
version of hide-and-seek on their own.

---

[1] ran, jumped
[2] trembling
[3] looked down on

Meanwhile, parents came and went in chromium beetles. Repair men came to repair the vacuum elevators in houses, to fix fluttering television sets, or to hammer upon stubborn food-delivery tubes. The adult civilization passed and repassed the busy youngsters, jealous of the fierce energy of the wild tots, tolerantly amused at their flourishings, longing to join in themselves.

"This and this and *this*," said Mink, instructing the others with their assorted spoons and wrenches. "Do that, and bring *that* over here. No! *Here*, ninnie! Right. Now, get back while I fix this—" Tongue in teeth, face wrinkled in thought. "Like that. See?"

"Yayyyy!" shouted the kids.

Twelve-year-old Joseph Connors ran up.

"Go away," said Mink straight at him.

"I wanna play," said Joseph.

"Can't!" said Mink.

"Why not?"

"You'd just make fun of us."

"Honest, I wouldn't."

"No. We know *you*. Go away or we'll kick you."

Another twelve-year-old boy whirred by on little motor-skates. "Aye, Joe! Come on! Let them sissies play!"

Joseph showed reluctance and a certain wistfulness.[4] "I *want* to play," he said.

"You're old," said Mink, firmly.

"Not *that* old," said Joe sensibly.

"You'd only laugh and spoil the Invasion."

The boy on the motor-skates made a rude lip noise. "Come on, Joe! Them and their fairies! Nuts!"

Joseph walked off slowly. He kept looking back, all down the block.

Mink was already busy again. She made a kind of apparatus[5] with her gathered equipment. She had appointed another little girl with a pad and pencil to take down notes in painful slow scribbles. Their voices rose and fell in the warm sunlight.

All around them the city hummed. The streets were lined with good green and peaceful trees. Only the wind made a conflict across the city, across the country, across the continent. In a thousand other cities there were trees and children and avenues, businessmen in their quiet offices taping their voices, or watching televisors. Rockets hovered like darning needles in the blue sky. There was the universal, quiet conceit[6] and easiness of men accus-

---

[4] dreaminess
[5] gadget, machine
[6] pride

tomed to peace, quite certain there would never be trouble again. Arm in arm, men all over earth were a united front. The perfect weapons were held in equal trust by all nations. A situation of incredibly beautiful balance had been brought about. There were no traitors among men, no unhappy ones, no disgruntled ones; therefore, the world was based upon a stable ground. Sunlight illumined half the world, and the trees drowsed in a tide of warm air.

Mink's mother, from her upstairs window, gazed down.

The children.

She looked upon them and shook her head. Well, they'd eat well, sleep well, and be in school on Monday. Bless their vigorous little bodies. She listened.

Mink talked earnestly to someone near the rosebush—though there was no one there.

These odd children. And the little girl, what was her name? Anna? Anna took notes on a pad. First, Mink asked the rosebush a question, then called the answer to Anna.

"Triangle," said Mink.

"What's a tri," said Anna with difficulty, "angle?"

"Never mind," said Mink.

"How you spell it?" asked Anna.

"T-R-I-" spelled Mink, slowly, then snapped, "Oh, spell it yourself!" She went on to other words. "Beam," she said.

"I haven't got tri," said Anna, "angle down yet!"

"Well, hurry, hurry!" cried Mink.

Mink's mother leaned out the upstairs window. "A-N-G-L-E," she spelled down at Anna.

"Oh, thanks, Mrs. Morris," said Anna.

"Certainly," said Mink's mother and withdrew, laughing, to dust the hall with an electro-duster-magnet.

The voices wavered on the shimmery air. "Beam," said Anna. Fading.

"Four-nine-seven-A-and-B-and-X," said Mink, far away, seriously. "And a fork and a string and a—hex-hex-agony...hexagon*al*!"

• • • • •

At lunch, Mink gulped milk at one toss and was at the door. Her mother slapped the table.

"You sit right back down," commanded Mrs. Morris. "Hot soup in a minute." She poked a red button on the kitchen butler, and ten seconds later something landed with a bump in the rubber receiver. Mrs. Morris opened it, took out a can with a pair of aluminum holders, unsealed it with a flick, and poured hot soup into a bowl.

During all this, Mink fidgeted. "Hurry, Mom! This is a matter of life and death! Aw—!"

"I was the same way at your age. Always life and death. I know."

Mink banged away at the soup.

"Slow down," said Mom.

"Can't," said Mink. "Drill's waiting for me."

"Who's Drill? What a peculiar name," said Mom.

"You don't know him," said Mink.

"A new boy in the neighborhood?" asked Mom.

"He's new all right," said Mink. She started on her second bowl.

"Which one is Drill?" asked Mom.

"He's around," said Mink, evasively.[7] "You'll make fun. Everybody pokes fun. Gee."

"Is Drill shy?"

"Yes. No. In a way. Mom, I got to run if we want to have the Invasion!"

"Who's invading what?"

"Martians invading Earth—well, not exactly Martians. They're—I don't know. From up." She pointed with her spoon.

"And *inside*," said Mom, touching Mink's feverish brow.

Mink rebelled. "You're laughing! You'll kill Drill and *every*body."

"I didn't mean to," said Mom. "Drill's a Martian?"

"No. He's—well—maybe from Jupiter or Saturn or Venus. Anyway, he's had a hard time."

"I imagine." Mrs. Morris hid her mouth behind her hand.

"They couldn't figure a way to attack earth."

"We're impregnable,[8]" said Mom, in mock-seriousness.

"That's the word Drill used! Impreg—that was the word, Mom."

"My, my. Drill's a brilliant little boy. Two-bit words."

"They couldn't figure a way to attack, Mom. Drill says—he says in order to make a good fight you got to have a new way of surprising people. That way you win. And he says also you got to have help from your enemy."

"A fifth column,"[9] said Mom.

"Yeah. That's what Drill said. And they couldn't figure a way to surprise Earth or get help."

"No wonder. We're pretty strong," laughed Mom, cleaning up. Mink sat there, staring at the table, seeing what she was talking about.

---

[7] carefully, deceptively

[8] unconquerable

[9] A "fifth column" is a group of traitors within a nation that helps an outside enemy defeat the nation it's part of.

"Until, one day," whispered Mink, melodramatically, "they thought of children!"

"*Well!*" said Mrs. Morris brightly.

"And they thought of how grownups are so busy they never look under rosebushes or on lawns!"

"Only for snails and fungus."

"And then there's something about dim-dims."

"Dim-dims?"

"Dimens-shuns."

"Dimensions?"

"Four of 'em! And there's something about kids under nine and imagination. It's real funny to hear Drill talk."

Mrs. Morris was tired. "Well, it must be funny. You're keeping Drill waiting now. It's getting late in the day and, if you want to have your Invasion before your supper bath, you'd better jump."

"Do I have to take a bath?" growled Mink.

"You do. Why is it children hate water? No matter what age you live in, children hate water behind the ears!"

"Drill says I won't have to take baths," said Mink.

"Oh, he does, does he?"

"He told all the kids that. No more baths. And we can stay up till ten o'clock and go to two televisor shows on Saturday 'stead of one!"

"Well, Mr. Drill better mind his p's and q's.[10] I'll call up his mother and—"

Mink went to the door. "We're having trouble with guys like Pete Britz and Dale Jerrick. They're growing up. They make fun. They're worse than parents. They just won't believe in Drill. They're so snooty, cause they're growing up. You'd think they'd know better. They were little only a coupla years ago. I hate them worst. We'll kill them *first.*"

"Your father and I, last?"

"Drill says you're dangerous. Know why? Cause you don't believe in Martians! They're going to let *us* run the world. Well, not just us, but the kids over in the next block, too. I might be queen." She opened the door. "Mom?"

"Yes?"

"What's—lodge...ick?"

"Logic? Why, dear, logic is knowing what things are true and not true."

"He *mentioned* that," said Mink. "And what's im—pres—sion—able?" It took her a minute to say it.

"Why, it means—" Her mother looked at the floor, laughing gently. "It means—to be a child, dear."

---

[10] To "mind your p's and q's" means to watch out and behave yourself.

"Thanks for lunch!" Mink ran out, then stuck her head back in. "Mom, I'll be sure you won't be hurt, much, really!"

"Well, thanks," said Mom.

Slam went the door.

$$\bullet\ \bullet\ \bullet\ \bullet\ \bullet$$

At four o'clock the audio-visor buzzed. Mrs. Morris flipped the tab. "Hello, Helen!" she said, in welcome.

"Hello, Mary. How are things in New York?"

"Fine, how are things in Scranton? You look tired."

"So do you. The children. Underfoot," said Helen.

Mrs. Morris sighed, "My Mink, too. The super Invasion."

Helen laughed. "Are your kids playing that game, too?"

"Heavens, yes. Tomorrow it'll be geometrical jacks and motorized hop-scotch. Were we this bad when we were kids in '48?"

"Worse. Don't know how my parents put up with me. Tomboy."

"Parents learn to shut their ears."

A silence.

"What's wrong, Mary?" asked Helen.

Mrs. Morris's eyes were half-closed; her tongue slid slowly, thoughtfully over her lower lip. "Eh," She jerked. "Oh, nothing. Just thought about *that*. Shutting ears and such. Never mind. Where were we?"

"My boy Tim's got a crush on some guy named—*Drill*, I think it was."

"Must be a new password. Mink likes him, too."

"Didn't know it got as far as New York. Word of mouth, I imagine. Looks like a scrap drive. I talked to Josephine, and she said her kids—that's in Boston—are wild on this new game. It's sweeping the country."

At this moment, Mink trotted into the kitchen to gulp a glass of water. Mrs. Morris turned. "How're things going?"

"Almost finished," said Mink.

"Swell," said Mrs. Morris. "What's *that*?"

"A yo-yo," said Mink. "Watch."

She flung the yo-yo down its string. Reaching the end it—

It vanished.

"See?" said Mink. "Ope!" Dibbling her finger she made the yo-yo reappear and zip up the string.

"Do that again," said her mother.

"Can't. Zero hour's five o'clock! 'Bye."

Mink exited, zipping her yo-yo.

On the audio-visor, Helen laughed. "Tim brought one of those yo-yo's in this morning, but when I got curious he said he wouldn't show it to me, and when I tried to work it, finally, it wouldn't work."

"You're not *impressionable*," said Mrs. Morris.

"What?"

"Never mind. Something I thought of. Can I help you, Helen?"

"I wanted to get that black-and-white cake recipe—"

• • • • •

The hour drowsed by. The day waned.[11] The sun lowered in the peaceful blue sky. Shadows lengthened on the green lawns. The laughter and excitement continued. One little girl ran away, crying.

Mrs. Morris came out the front door.

"Mink, was that Peggy Ann crying?"

Mink was bent over in the yard, near the rosebush. "Yeah. She's a scarebaby. We won't let her play, now. She's getting too old to play. I guess she grew up all of a sudden."

"Is that why she cried? Nonsense. Give me a civil answer, young lady, or inside you come!"

Mink whirled in consternation,[12] mixed with irritation. "I can't quit now. It's almost time. I'll be good. I'm sorry."

"Did you hit Peggy Ann?"

"No, honest. You ask her. It was something—well, she's just a scaredy-pants."

The ring of children drew in around Mink where she scowled at her work with spoons and a kind of square shaped arrangement of hammers and pipes. "There and there," murmured Mink.

"What's wrong?" said Mrs. Morris.

"Drill's stuck. Halfway. If we could only get him all the way through, it'll be easier. Then all the others could come through after him."

"Can I help?"

"No'm, thanks. I'll fix it."

"All right. I'll call you for your bath in half an hour. I'm tired of watching you."

She went in and sat in the electric-relaxing chair. The chair massaged her back. Children, children. Children and love and hate, side by side. Sometimes children loved you, hated you, all in half a second. Strange children; did they ever forget or forgive the whippings and the harsh, strict words of command? She wondered. How can you ever forget or forgive those over and above you, those tall and silly dictators?

Time passed. A curious, waiting silence came upon the street, deepening.

---

[11] faded into night

[12] alarm

Five o'clock. A clock sang softly somewhere in the house, in a quiet, musical voice, "Five o'clock...five o'clock. Time's a-wasting. Five o'clock," and purred away into silence.

Zero hour.

Mrs. Morris chuckled in her throat. Zero hour.

A beetle-car hummed into the driveway. Mr. Morris. Mrs. Morris smiled. Mr. Morris got out of the beetle, locked it, and called hello to Mink at her work. Mink ignored him. He laughed and stood for a moment watching the children in their business. Then he walked up the front steps.

"Hello, darling."

"Hello, Henry."

She strained forward on the edge of the chair, listening. The children were silent. Too silent.

He emptied his pipe, refilled it. "Swell day. Makes you glad to be alive."

Buzz.

"What's that?" asked Henry.

"I don't know." She got up, suddenly, her eyes widening. She was going to say something. She stopped it. Ridiculous. Her nerves jumped. "Those children haven't anything dangerous out there, have they?" she said.

"Nothing but pipes and hammers. Why?"

"Nothing electrical?"

"Heck, no," said Henry. "I looked."

She walked to the kitchen. The buzzing continued. "Just the same you'd better go tell them to quit. It's after five. Tell them—" Her eyes widened and narrowed. "Tell them to put off their Invasion until tomorrow." She laughed, nervously.

The buzzing grew louder.

"What are they up to? I'd better go look, all right."

The explosion!

• • • • •

The house shook with dull sound. There were other explosions in other yards on other streets.

Involuntarily, Mrs. Morris screamed. "Up this way!" she cried, senselessly, knowing no sense, no reason. Perhaps she saw something from the corners of her eyes, perhaps she smelled a new odor or heard a new noise. There was no time to argue with Henry to convince him. Let him think her insane. Yes, insane! Shrieking, she ran upstairs. He ran after her to see what she was up to. "In the attic!" she screamed. "That's where it is!" It was only a poor excuse to get him in the attic in time—in time!

Another explosion outside. The children screamed with delight, as if at a great fireworks display.

"It's not in the attic!" cried Henry. "It's outside!"

"No, no!" Wheezing, gasping, she fumbled at the attic door. "I'll show you. Hurry! I'll show you!"

They tumbled into the attic. She slammed the door, locked it, took the key, threw it into a far, cluttered corner.

She was babbling wild stuff now. It came out of her. All the subconscious suspicion and fear that had gathered secretly all afternoon and fermented like a wine in her. All the little revelations and knowledges and sense that had bothered her all day and which she had logically and carefully and sensibly rejected and censored. Now it exploded in her and shook her to bits.

"There, there," she said, sobbing against the door. "We're safe until tonight. Maybe we can sneak out, maybe we can escape!"

Henry blew up, too, but for another reason. "Are you crazy? Why'd you throw that key away?"

"Yes, yes, I'm crazy, if it helps, but stay here with me!"

"I don't know how I *can* get out!"

"Quiet. They'll hear us. Oh, they'll find us soon enough—"

Below them, Mink's voice. The husband stopped. There was a great universal humming and sizzling, a screaming and giggling. Downstairs, the audio-televisor buzzed and buzzed insistently, alarmingly, violently. *Is that Helen calling?* thought Mrs. Morris. *And is she calling about what I* think *she's calling about?*

Footsteps came into the house. Heavy footsteps.

"Who's coming in my house?" demanded Henry, angrily. "Who's tramping around down there?"

Heavy feet. Twenty, thirty, forty, fifty of them. Fifty persons crowding into the house. The humming. The giggling of the children. "This way!" cried Mink, below.

"Who's downstairs?" roared Henry. "Who's there!"

"Hush, oh, nonononono!" said his wife, weakly, holding him. "Please, be quiet. They might go away."

"Mom?" called Mink, "Dad?" A pause. "Where are you?"

Heavy footsteps, heavy, heavy, *very* HEAVY footsteps came up the stairs. Mink leading them.

"Mom?" A hesitation. "Dad?" A waiting, a silence.

Humming. Footsteps toward the attic. Mink's first.

They trembled together in silence in the attic, Mr. and Mrs. Morris. For some reason the electric humming, the queer cold light suddenly visible under the door crack, the strange odor, and the alien sound of eagerness in Mink's voice, finally got through to Henry Morris, too. He stood, shivering, in the dark silence, his wife beside him.

"Mom! Dad!"

Footsteps. A little humming sound. The attic lock melted. The door opened. Mink peered inside, tall blue shadows behind her.

"Peek-a-boo," said Mink.

Questions for Review

1. Look up the term *zero hour*. Why do you think the author used that term for the story's title?

2. Why are children only under nine allowed to play "invasion"? How does the author describe the world's situation at the story's opening?

3. When does the story start to get a little creepy for you, or make you concerned for Earth and/or the parents?

4. What do you think a "televisor" is? What modern device is it quite similar to?

5. What message do you think the author is sending to parents in this story? And besides the aliens in "Zero Hour," can you think of another organization that often turns children against their parents? (Hint: It's one of the reasons your parents homeschool you!)

A Manual on Education

By Stephen Leacock

*Last time we checked in on Stephen Leacock, he was slinking out of a bank after trying to open an account, with the whole building laughing at him. (The **people** in the building were laughing at him, too.) Today, Leacock shares with you, the young reader—don't you feel lucky?—many golden nuggets of rich wisdom he remembers from going to school all those years. This piece is taken from his 1910 book* Literary Lapses.

• • • • •

The few selections below are offered as a specimen[1] page of a little book which I have in course of preparation.

Every man has somewhere in the back of his head the wreck of a thing which he calls his education. My book is intended to embody[2] in concise[3] form these remnants[4] of early instruction.

Educations are divided into splendid educations, thorough classical educations, and average educations. All very old men have splendid educations; all men who apparently know nothing else have thorough classical educations; nobody has an average education.

An education, when it is all written out on foolscap,[5] covers nearly ten sheets. It takes about six years of severe college training to acquire it. Even then a man often finds that he somehow hasn't got his education just where he can put his thumb on it. When my little book of eight or ten pages has appeared, everybody may carry his education in his hip pocket.

Those who have not had the advantage of an early training will be enabled, by a few hours of conscientious application,[6] to put themselves on an equal footing with the most scholarly.

The selections are chosen entirely at random.

I. Remains of Astronomy

Astronomy teaches the correct use of the sun and the planets. These may be put on a frame of little sticks and turned round. This causes the tides. Those at the ends of the sticks are enormously far away. From time to time a diligent searching of the sticks reveals new planets. The orbit of a planet is the

---

[1] sample
[2] express
[3] short, to the point
[4] remains
[5] writing paper
[6] "conscientious application": careful, hard work

distance the stick goes round in going round. Astronomy is intensely interesting; it should be done at night, in a high tower in Spitzbergen.[7] This is to avoid the astronomy being interrupted. A really good astronomer can tell when a comet is coming too near him by the warning buzz of the revolving sticks.

II. Remains of History

Aztecs: A fabulous race—half man, half horse, half mound-builder. They flourished at about the same time as the early Calithumpians. They have left some awfully stupendous monuments of themselves somewhere.

Life of Caesar: A famous Roman general, the last who ever landed in Britain without being stopped at the custom house.[8] On returning to his Sabine farm (to fetch something), he was stabbed by Brutus, and died with the words "Veni, vidi, tekel, upharsim"[9] in his throat. The jury returned a verdict of strangulation.

Life of Voltaire:[10] A Frenchman; very bitter.

Life of Schopenhauer:[11] A German; very deep; but it was not really noticeable when he sat down.

Life of Dante:[12] An Italian; the first to introduce the banana and the class of street organ known as "Dante's Inferno."

Peter the Great,
Alfred the Great,
Frederick the Great,
John the Great,
Tom the Great,
Jim the Great,
Jo the Great, etc., etc.

It is impossible for a busy man to keep these apart. They sought a living as kings and apostles and pugilists[13] and so on.

III. Remains of Botany

Botany is the art of plants. Plants are divided into trees, flowers, and vegetables. The true botanist knows a tree as soon as he sees it. He learns to distinguish it from a vegetable by merely putting his ear to it.

---

[7] a group of islands (part of Norway) just about at the "top" of the world
[8] where import taxes are collected by government agents
[9] See Daniel 5:1-25.
[10] French philosopher François-Marie Arouet (1694-1788)
[11] pessimistic philosopher Arthur Schopenhauer (1788-1860)
[12] Italian writer Dante Alighieri (1265-1321)
[13] boxers, fighters

IV. Remains of Natural Science

Natural Science treats of motion and force. Many of its teachings remain as part of an educated man's permanent equipment in life. Such are:

(a)   The harder you shove a bicycle the faster it will go. This is because of natural science.

(b)   If you fall from a high tower, you fall quicker and quicker and quicker; a judicious[14] selection of a tower will ensure any rate of speed.

(c)   If you put your thumb in between two cogs[15] it will go on and on, until the wheels are arrested,[16] by your suspenders. This is machinery.

(d)   Electricity is of two kinds, positive and negative. The difference is, I presume, that one kind comes a little more expensive, but is more durable; the other is a cheaper thing, but the moths get into it.

Questions for Review

1.   Read out loud to Mom or Dad this line from the second paragraph: *"Every man has somewhere in the back of his head the wreck of a thing which he calls his education."* Then ask your parent(s) if they can identify with Leacock's statement.

2.   Name some of the funny remarks that the author makes about various "school topics."

3.   What do you think "Calithumpians" are? (You can look up the word if you'd like—it's a real word!)

4.   What point do you think the author is making by writing this humorous take on his education?

---

[14] wise
[15] mechanical gears
[16] stopped, blocked

The Night Express

By Fred M. White

English writer Fred Merrick White (1859-1935) was a specialist in science fiction and spy/detective stories. His output was incredible—he wrote hundreds of both novels and short stories, many of which were quite popular. "The Night Express," written in 1905, tells the tale of a crime that seems impossible to have taken place. See if you can piece together the clues revealed in the story to come up with a reasonable way to explain how it happened!

•••••

A pelting rain volleyed against the great glass dome of the terminus,[1] a roaring wind boomed in the roof. Passengers, hurrying along the platform, glistened in big coats and tweed caps pulled close over their ears. By the platform the night express was drawn up—a glittering mass of green and gold, shimmering with electric lights, warm, inviting, and cozy.

---

[1] train station

Most of the corridor carriages and sleeping berths were full. A few late-comers were looking anxiously out for the guard. He came presently, an alert figure in blue and silver. Really, he was very sorry. But the train was unusually crowded, and he was doing the best he could. He was perfectly aware of the fact that his questioners represented a Cabinet Minister on his way to Balmoral[2] and a prominent Lothian[3] baronet, but there are limits even to the power of an express guard, on the Grand Coast Railway.

"Well, what's the matter with this?" the Minister demanded. "Here is an ordinary first-class coach[4] that will do very well for us. Now, Catesby, un-lock one of these doors and turn the lights on."

"Very sorry, my lord," the guard explained, "but it can't be done. Two of the carriages in the coach are quite full, as you see, and the other two are reserved. As a matter of fact, my lord, we are taking a body down to Lyd-mouth. Gentleman who is going to be buried there. And the other carriage is for the Imperial Bank of Scotland. Cashier going up north with specie,[5] you understand."

It was all plain enough, and disgustingly logical. To intrude upon the presence of a body was perfectly impossible; to try and force the hand of the bank cashier equally out of the question. As head of a great financial house, the Minister knew that. A platform inspector bustled along present-ly, with his hand to his gold-laced cap.

"Saloon carriage being coupled up behind, my lord," he said.

The problem was solved. The guard glanced at his watch. It seemed to him that both the bank messenger and the undertaker[6] were cutting it fine. The coffin came presently on a hand-truck—a black velvet pall lay over it, and on the somber cloth a wreath or two of white lilies. The door of the car-riage was closed presently, and the blinds drawn discreetly close. Following behind this came a barrow in charge of a couple of platform police. On the barrow were two square deal boxes, heavy out of all proportion to their size. These were deposited presently to the satisfaction of a little nervous-looking man in gold-rimmed glasses. Mr. George Skidmore, of the Imperial Bank, had his share of ordinary courage, but he had an imagination, too, and he particularly disliked these periodical trips to branch banks, in convoy, so to speak. He took no risks.

"Awful night, sir," the guard observed. "Rather lucky to get a carriage to yourself, sir. Don't suppose you would have done so, only we're taking a corpse as far as Lydmouth, which is our first stop."

---

[2] a region in southeastern Australia
[3] from southeastern Scotland
[4] a cheaper seat
[5] gold or silver
[6] funeral director

"Really?" Skidmore said carelessly. "Ill wind that blows nobody good, Catesby. I may be overcautious, but I much prefer a carriage to myself. And my people prefer it, too. That's why we always give the railway authorities a few days' notice. One can't be too careful, Catesby."

The guard supposed not. He was slightly, yet discreetly, amused to see Mr. Skidmore glance under the seats of the first-class carriage. Certainly there was nobody either there or on the racks. The carriage at the far side was locked, and so, now, was the door next the platform. The great glass dome was brilliantly lighted so that anything suspicious would have been detected instantly. The guard's whistle rang out shrill and clear, and Catesby had a glimpse of Mr. Skidmore making himself comfortable as he swung himself into his van. The great green and gold serpent with the brilliant electric eyes fought its way sinuously[7] into the throat of the wet and riotous night on its first stage of over two hundred miles. Lydmouth would be the first stop.

So far Mr. Skidmore had nothing to worry him—nothing, that is, except the outside chance of a bad accident. He did not anticipate, however, that some miscreant[8] might deliberately wreck the train on the off chance of looting those plain deal boxes. The class of thief that banks have to fear is not guilty of such clumsiness. Unquestionably nothing could happen on this side of Lydmouth. The train was roaring along now through the fierce gale at sixty odd miles an hour, Skidmore had the carriage to himself, and was not the snug, brilliantly lighted compartment made of steel? On one side was the carriage with the coffin; on the other side another compartment filled with a party of sportsmen going North. Skidmore had noticed the four of them playing bridge just before he slipped into his own carriage. Really, he had nothing to fear. He lay back comfortably wondering how Poe or Gaboriau[9] would have handled such a situation with a successful robbery behind it. There are limits, of course, both to a novelist's imagination and a clever thief's process of invention. So, therefore....

Three hours and twenty minutes later the express pulled up at Lydmouth. The station clock indicated the hour to be 11:23. Catesby swung himself out of his van on to the shining wet platform. Only one passenger was waiting there, but nobody alighted.[10] Catesby was sure of this, because he was on the flags before a door could be opened. He came forward to give a hand with the coffin in the compartment next to Skidmore's. Then he noticed, to his surprise, that the glass in the carriage window was smashed; he could

---

[7] gracefully
[8] villain
[9] Edgar Allan Poe and Emile Gaboriau, detective story writers
[10] got off

see that the little cashier was huddled up strangely in one corner. And Catesby could see also that the two boxes of bullion[11] were gone!

Catesby's heart was thumping against his ribs as he fumbled with his key. He laid his hand upon Skidmore's shoulder, but the latter did not move. The fair hair hung in a mass on the side of his forehead, and here it was fair no longer. The carpet on the floor was piled up in a heap; there was red on the cushions. It was quite evident that a struggle had taken place here. The shattered glass in the window testified to that. And the boxes were gone, and Skidmore had been murdered by some assailant who had shot him. And this mysterious antagonist had got off with the bullion, too.

A thing incredible, amazing, impossible; but there it was. By some extraordinary method or another the audacious[12] criminal had boarded an express train traveling at sixty miles an hour in the teeth of a gale.[13] He had contrived to enter the cashier's carriage and remove specie to the amount of eight thousand pounds![14] It was impossible that only one man could have carried it. But all the same it was gone.

Catesby pulled himself together. He was perfectly certain that nobody at present on the train had been guilty of this thing. He was perfectly certain that nobody had left the train. Nobody could have done so after entering the station without the guard's knowledge, and to have attempted such a thing on the far side of the river bridge would have been certain death to anybody. There was a long viaduct[15] here—posts and pillars and chains, with tragedy lurking anywhere for the madman who attempted such a thing. And until the viaduct was reached the express had not slackened speed. Besides, the thief who had the courage and intelligence and daring to carry out a robbery like this was not the man to leave an express train traveling at a speed of upwards of sixty miles an hour.

The train had to proceed; there was no help for it. There was a hurried conference between Catesby and the stationmaster; after that the electric lamps in the dead man's carriage were unshipped,[16] and the blinds pulled down. The matter would be fully investigated when Edinburgh was reached; meanwhile the stationmaster at Lydmouth would telephone the Scotch capital and let them know there what they had to expect. Catesby crept into his van again, very queer and dizzy, and with a sensation in his legs suggestive of creeping paralysis.

---

[11] gold and silver
[12] gutsy
[13] strong wind
[14] This is at least $1 million today.
[15] railway bridge
[16] removed

• • • • •

Naturally, the mystery of the night express caused a great sensation. Nothing like it had been known since the great crime on the South Coast. But that was not so much a mystery as a man hunt. There the criminal had been identified. But here there was no trace and no clue whatever. It was in vain that the Scotland Yard authorities tried to shake the evidence of the guard, Catesby. He refused to make any admissions that would permit the police even to build up a theory. He was absolutely certain that Mr. Skidmore had been alone in the carriage at the moment that the express left London; he was absolutely certain that he had locked the door of the compartment, and the engine driver could testify that the train had never traveled at a less speed than sixty miles an hour until the bridge over the river leading into Lydmouth station was reached; even then nobody could have dropped off the train without the risk of certain death. Inspector Merrick was bound to admit this himself when he went over the spot. And the problem of the missing bullion boxes was quite as puzzling in its way as the mysterious way in which Mr. Skidmore had met his death.

There was no clue to this either. Certainly there had been a struggle, or there would not have been blood, and the window would have remained intact. Skidmore had probably been forced back into his seat, or he had collapsed there after the fatal shot was fired. The unfortunate man had been shot with an ordinary revolver of common pattern, so that for the purpose of proof the bullet was useless. There were no finger marks on the carriage door, a proof that the murderer had either worn gloves or that he had carefully removed all traces with a cloth of some kind. It was obvious, too, that a criminal of this class would take no risks, especially as there was no chance of his being hurried, seeing that he had had three clear hours for his work. The more the police went into the matter, the more puzzled they were. It was not a difficult matter to establish the bona fides[17] of the passengers who traveled in the next coach with Skidmore, and as to the rest it did not matter. Nobody could possibly have left any of the corridor coaches without attracting notice; indeed, the very suggestion was absurd. And there the matter rested for three days.

It must not be supposed that the authorities had been altogether idle. Inspector Merrick spent most of his time traveling up and down the line by slow local trains on the off-chance of hearing some significant incident that might lead to a clue. There was one thing obvious—the bullion boxes must have been thrown off the train at some spot arranged between the active thief and his confederates. For this was too big a thing to be entirely the work of one man. Some of the gang must have been waiting along the line

---

[17] identifications

in readiness to receive the boxes and carry them to a place of safety. By this time, no doubt, the boxes themselves had been destroyed; but eight thousand pounds in gold takes some moving, and probably a conveyance, a motor for choice, had been employed for this purpose. But nobody appeared to have seen or heard anything suspicious on the night of the murder; no prowling gamekeeper or watcher had noticed anything out of the common. Along the Essex and Norfolk marshes, where the Grand Coast Railway wound along like a steel snake, they had taken their desolate and dreary way. True, the dead body of a man had been found in the fowling nets up in the mouth of the Little Ouse, and nobody seemed to know who he was; but there could be no connection between this unhappy individual and the express criminal. Merrick shook his head as he listened to this from a laborer in a roadside public house where he was making a frugal[18] lunch on bread and cheese.

"What do you call fowling nets?" Merrick asked.

"Why, what they catches the birds in," the rustic explained. "Thousands and thousands of duck and teel and widgeon they catches at this time of year. There's miles of nets along the road—great big nets like fowl runs. Ye didn't happen to see any on 'em as ye came along in the train?"

"Now I come to think of it, yes," Merrick said thoughtfully. "I was rather struck by all that netting. So they catch sea birds that way?"

"Catches 'em by the thousand, they does. Birds fly against the netting in the dark and get entangled. Ducks they get by 'ticing 'em into a sort of cage with decoys. There's some of 'em stan's the best part of half a mile long. Covered in over the top like great cages. Ain't bad sport, either."

Merrick nodded. He recollected it all clearly now. He recalled the wide, desolate mud flats running right up to the railway embankment for some miles. At high tide the mud flats were under water, and out of these the great mass of network rose both horizontally and perpendicular. And in this tangle the dead body of a man had been found after the storm.

There was nothing really significant in the fact that the body had been discovered soon after the murder of Mr. George Skidmore. Still, there might be a connection between the two incidents. Merrick was going to make inquiries; he was after what looked like a million to one chance. But then Merrick was a detective with an imagination, which was one of the reasons why he had been appointed to the job. It was essentially a case for the theoretical[19] man. It baffled all the established rules of the game.

Late the same afternoon Merrick arrived at Little Warlingham by means of a baker's cart. It was here that the body of the drowned man lay awaiting the slim chances of identity. If nothing transpired during the next eight and

---

[18] simple, cheap
[19] imaginative

forty hours, the corpse would be buried by the parish authorities. The village policeman acted as Merrick's guide. It was an event in his life that he was not likely to forget.

"A stranger to these parts, I should say, sir," the local officer said. "He's in a shed at the back of the 'Blue Anchor,' where the inquest was held. If you come this way, I'll show him to you."

"Anything found on the body?"

"Absolutely nothing, sir. No mark on the clothing or linen, either. Probably washed off some ship in the storm. Pockets were quite empty, too. And no signs of foul play. *There* you are, sir!"

Casually enough Merrick bent over the still, white form lying there. The dead face was turned up to the light, coming through the door. The detective straightened himself suddenly, and wiped his forehead.

"Stranger to you, sir, of course?" the local man said grimly.

"Well, no," Merrick retorted. "I happen to know the fellow quite well. I'm glad I came here."

• • • • •

Until it was quite too dark to see any longer Merrick was out on the mud flats asking questions. He appeared to be greatly interested in the wild-fowlers and the many methods of catching their prey. He learned, incidentally, that on the night of the express murder most of the nets and lures had been washed away. He took minute[20] particulars as to the state of the tide on the night in question; he wanted to know if the nets were capable of holding up against any great force. For instance, if a school of porpoises came along? Or if a fish eagle or an osprey found itself entangled in the meshes?

The fowlers smiled. They invited Merrick to try it for himself. On that stormy east coast it was foolish to take any risks. And Merrick was satisfied. As a matter of fact, he was more than satisfied.

He was really beginning to see his way at last. By the time he got back to his headquarters again he had practically reconstructed the crime. As he stood on the railway permanent way, gazing down into the network of the fowlers below, he smiled to himself. He could have tossed a biscuit on to the top of the long lengths of tarred and knotted rigging. Later on he telephoned to the London terminus of the Grand Coast Railway for the people there to place the services of Catesby at his disposal for a day or two. Could Catesby meet him at Lydmouth tomorrow?

The guard could and did. He frankly admitted that he was grateful for the little holiday. He looked as if he wanted it. The corners of his mouth twitched, his hands were shaky.

---

[20] detailed

"It's nerves, Mr. Merrick," he explained. "We all suffer from them at times. Only we don't like the company to know it, ye understand? To tell the truth, I've never got over that affair at the Junction here eight years ago. I expect you remember that."

Merrick nodded. Catesby was alluding[21] to a great railway tragedy which had taken place outside Lydmouth station some few years back. It had been a most disastrous affair for a local express, and Catesby had been acting as guard to the train. He spoke of it under his breath.

"I dream of it occasionally even now," he said. "The engine left the line and dragged the train over the embankment into the river. If you ask me how I managed to escape, I can't tell you. I never come into Lydmouth with the night express now without my head out of the window of the van right away from the viaduct till she pulls up at the station. And what's more, I never shall. It isn't fear, mind you, because I've as much pluck as any man. It's just nerves."

"We get 'em in our profession, too," Merrick smiled. "Did you happen to be looking out of the window on the night of the murder?"

"Yes, and every other night, too. Haven't I just told you so? Directly we strike the viaduct I come to my feet by instinct."

"Always look out the same side, I suppose?"

"Yes, on the left. That's the platform side, you understand."

"Then if anybody had left the train there—"

"Anybody left the train! Why we were traveling at fifty miles an hour when we reached the viaduct. Oh, yes, if anybody *had* left the train I should have been bound to see them, of course."

"But you can't see out of both windows at once."

"Nobody could leave the train by the other side. The stone parapet[22] of the viaduct almost touches the footboard, and there's a drop of ninety feet below that. Of course I see what you are driving at, Mr. Merrick. Now look here. I locked Mr. Skidmore in the carriage myself, and I can *prove* that nobody got in before we left London. That would have been too dangerous a game so long as the train was passing any number of brilliantly lighted stations, and by the time we got into the open we were going at sixty miles an hour. That speed never slackened till we were just outside Lydmouth, and I was watching at the moment that our pace dropped. I had my head out of the window of my van till we pulled up by the platform. I am prepared to swear to all this if you like. Lord knows how the thing was done, and I don't suppose anybody else ever will."

"You are mistaken there," said Merrick drily. "Now, what puzzles you, of course, is the manner in which the murderer left the train."

---

[21] referring
[22] low wall

"Well, isn't that the whole mystery?"

"Not to me. That's the part I really do know. Not that I can take any great credit to myself, because luck helped me. It was, perhaps, the most amazing piece of luck I have ever had. It was my duty, of course, to take no chances, and I didn't. But we'll come to that presently. Let it suffice for the moment that I know how the murderer left the train. What puzzles me is to know how he got on it. We can dismiss every other passenger in the train, and we need not look for an accomplice. There *were* accomplices, of course, but they were not on the express. Why didn't Mr. Skidmore travel in one of the corridor coaches?"

"He was too nervous. He always had a first-class carriage to himself. We knew he was coming, and that was why we attached an ordinary first-class coach to the train. We shouldn't do it for anybody, but Lord Rendelmore, the chairman of Mr. Skidmore's bank, is also one of our directors. The coach came in handy the other night because we had an order from a London undertaker to bring a corpse as far as here—to Lydmouth."

"Really! You would have to have a separate carriage for that."

"Naturally, Mr. Merrick. It was sort of killing two birds with one stone."

"I see. When did you hear about the undertaking job?"

"The same morning we heard from the bank that Mr. Skidmore was going to Lydmouth. We reserved a coach at once, and had it attached to the Express. The other carriages were filled with ordinary passengers."

"Why didn't I hear of this before?" Merrick asked.

"*I* don't know. It doesn't seem to me to be of much importance. You might just as well ask me questions as to the passengers' baggage."

"Everything is of importance," Merrick said sententiously.[23] "In our profession, there are no such things as trifles.[24] I suppose there will be no difficulty in getting at the facts of this corpse business. I'll make inquiries here presently."

So far Merrick professed himself to be satisfied. But there were still difficulties in the way. The station people had a clear recollection of the receipt of a coffin on the night of the tragedy, and, late as it was, the gruesome thing had been fetched away by the people whom it was consigned to. A plain hearse, drawn by one horse, had been driven into the station yard, the consignment note had been receipted in the usual way, and there was an end of the matter. Lydmouth was a big place, with nearly a quarter of a million of inhabitants, and would necessarily contain a good many people in the undertaking line. Clearly it was no business of the railway company to take this thing any further.

---

[23] sharply
[24] unimportant details

Merrick admitted that freely enough. It was nearly dark when he came back to the station, profoundly dissatisfied with a wasted afternoon.

"No good," he told Catesby. "At the same time there are consolations.[25] And, after all, I am merely confirming my suspicions. I suppose your people here are on the telephone. If so, I should like to send a message to your head office. I want the name of the firm in London who consigned the coffin here. I suppose the stationmaster could manage this for me."

An hour or so later the information came. Merrick, at the telephone, wanted a little further assistance. Would the Grand Coast Railway call up the undertaker's firm whilst he held the line and ask the full particulars as to the body sent from London to Lydmouth. For half an hour Merrick stood patiently there till the reply came.

"Are you there? Is that Inspector Merrick? Oh, yes. Well, we have called up Lincoln & Co., the undertakers. We got on to the manager himself. He declares that the whole thing is a mistake. They have not sent a corpse over our trunk system for two months. I read the manager the letter asking for special facilities, a letter on the firm's own paper. The manager does not hesitate to say the whole thing is a forgery. I think he is right, Inspector. If we can do anything else for you—"

Merrick hung up the receiver and smiled as if pleased with himself. He turned to his companion, Catesby.

"It's all right," he said. "Is there any way we can get back to London tonight? The whole thing is perfectly plain, now."

· · · · ·

Though Merrick returned to London thoroughly satisfied, he knew that the sequel was not just yet. There was much work to be done before it would be possible to place all the cards on the table. The Christmas holidays had arrived before Merrick obtained a couple of warrants, and, armed with these, he went down to Brighton on Boxing Day,[26] and put up at the Hotel Regina, registering himself as Colonel Beaumont, sometime of the United States Field Forces. Merrick could pose as an authority on Cuba, for on one occasion he had been there for six months on the lookout for a defaulting bank manager. He had made certain changes in his appearance, and just now he bore little resemblance to Inspector Merrick of New Scotland Yard.

The big hotel on the front was full. There was a smart dance that same night, preceded by a children's party and Christmas tree. The house swarmed with young folks, and a good many nationalities were represented. On occasions like these somebody generally takes the lead, and by com-

---

[25] comforts
[26] the day after Christmas

mon consent the part of the chief of the events had been allotted to the Marquis de Branza.

To begin with, he was immensely rich. He had vast estates in Italy. He had been staying at the Regina for the past month, and it was whispered that his bill had reached three figures.[27] He entertained lavishly; he was the soul of hospitality; he was going to buy a palace in Kings' Gardens, and more or less settle down in Brighton.

In addition to all this the Marquis was a handsome man, very fascinating, and a prime favorite with all the boys and girls at the Regina. He had his little peculiarities, of course—for instance, he paid for everything in gold. All his hotel bills were met with current coin.

Merrick had gleaned all this before he had been a day at the Regina. They were quite a happy family, and the Colonel speedily found himself at home. The Marquis welcomed him as if he owned the hotel, and as if everybody was his guest. The dance was a great success, as also were the presents in connection with the cotillon[28] promoted by the Marquis.

At two o'clock the following morning the Marquis was entertaining a select party in the smoking room. The ladies had all vanished by this time. The Marquis was speaking of his adventures. He really had quite a talent in that direction. Naturally, a man of his wealth was certain to be the mark for swindlers. Merrick listened with an approving smile. He knew that most of these stories were true, for they had all been recorded from time to time at Scotland Yard.

"You would have made an excellent detective, Marquis," he said. "You have made it quite clear where the police blundered over that Glasgow tragedy. I suppose you read all about the Grand Coast Railway murder."

The Marquis started[29] ever so slightly. There was a questioning look in his eyes.

"Did you?" he said. "Naturally one would, Colonel. But a matter the most inexplicable. I gave him up. From the very first I gave him up. If the guard Catesby was not the guilty person, then I admit I have no theory."

One by one, the smoking-room company faded away. Presently only Merrick and the Marquis remained, save one guest who had fallen asleep in his chair. A sleepy waiter looked in and vanished again. The hotel was absolutely quiet now. Merrick, however, was wide awake enough; so, apparently, was the Marquis. All the same, he yawned.

"Let us to bed," he said. "Tomorrow, perhaps—"

"No," Merrick said somewhat curtly. "I prefer tonight. Sit down."

---

[27] That is, at least £100 (100 "pounds"), around $15,000 today.
[28] dance
[29] flinched

The last two words came crisply and with a ring of command in them. The Marquis bowed as he dropped into a chair and lighted a fresh cigarette. A little red spot glowed on either of his brown cheeks; his eyes glittered.

"You want to speak to me, Colonel?" he said.

"Very much indeed. Now, you are an exceedingly clever man, Marquis, and you may be able to help me. It happens that I am deeply interested in the Grand Coast Express murder; in fact, I have devoted the last two months to its solution."

"With no success whatever, my dear Colonel?" the Marquis murmured.

"On the contrary, my dear Marquis, with absolute satisfaction. I am quite sure that you will be interested in my story."

The Marquis raised his cigarette graciously.

"You are very good to give me your confidence," he said. "Pray proceed."

"Thank you. I will not bore you with any preliminary[30] details, for they are too recent to have faded from your memory. Sufficient that we have a murder committed in an express train; we have the disappearance of eight thousand pounds in gold, without any trace of the criminal. That he was on the train at the start is obvious. That he was not in any of the carriages conveying ordinary passengers is equally obvious. It is also certain that he left the train after the commission of the crime. Doubtless you read the evidence of the guard to prove that nobody left the train after the viaduct leading to Lydmouth station was reached. Therefore, the murderer contrived to make his escape when the express was traveling at sixty miles per hour."

"Is not all this superfluous?"[31] the Marquis asked.

"Well, not quite. I am going to tell you how the murderer joined the train and how he left it after the murder and the robbery."

"You are going to tell me that! Is it possible?"

"I think so," Merrick said modestly. "Now, Mr. Skidmore had a compartment to himself. He was locked in the very last thing, and nobody joined the train afterward. Naturally a—well—an amateur detective like myself wanted to know who was in the adjoining compartments. Three of these could be dismissed at once. But in the fourth there was a corpse—"

"A corpse! But there was no mention of that at the inquest."

"No, but the fact remains. A corpse in a coffin. In a dark compartment with the blinds down. And, strangely enough, the firm of undertakers who consigned, or were supposed to consign, the body to Lydmouth denied the whole business. Therefore, it is only fair to suppose that the whole thing was a put-up job to get a compartment in the coach that Mr. Skidmore trav-

---

[30] introductory
[31] unnecessary

eled by. I am going to assume that in that coffin the murderer lay concealed. But let me give you a light—your cigarette is out."

"I smoke no more," the Marquis said. "My throat is dry. And then—"

"Well, then, the first part is easy. The man gets out of the coffin and proceeds to fill it with some heavy substance which has been smuggled into the carriage under the pall. He screws the lid down and presently makes his way along the footboard to the next compartment. An athlete in good condition could do that; in fact, a sailor has done it in a drunken freak more than once. Mind you, I don't say that murder was intended in the first instance; but will presume that there was a struggle. The thief probably lost his temper, and perhaps Mr. Skidmore irritated him. Now, the rest was easy. It was easy to pack up the gold in leather bags, each containing a thousand sovereigns, and to drop them along the line at some spot previously agreed upon. I have no doubt that the murderer and his accomplices traveled many times up and down the line before the details were finally settled. Anyway, there was no risk here. The broken packing cases were pitched out also, probably in some thick wood. Or they might have been weighted and cast into a stream. Are you interested?"

The Marquis gurgled. He had some difficulty in speaking.

"A little dangerous," he said. "Our ingenious friend could not possibly screw himself down in the coffin after returning to his compartment. And have you perceived the danger of discovery at Lydmouth?"

"Precisely," Merrick said drily. "It is refreshing to meet with so luminous[32] a mind as yours. There were many dangers, many risks to take. The train might have been stopped, lots of things might have happened. It would be far better for the man to leave the express. And he did so!"

"The express at top speed! Impossible!"

"To the ordinary individual, yes. But then, you see, this was not an ordinary individual. He was—let us suppose—an acrobat, a man of great nerve and courage, accustomed to trapeze work and the use of the diving net."

"But Colonel, pardon me, where does the net come in?"

"The net came in at a place near Little Warlingham, on the Norfolk coast. There are miles of net up there, trap and flight nets close by the side of the line. These nets are wide and strong; they run many furlongs[33] without supports, so that an acrobat could easily turn a somersault on to one of these at a given spot without the slightest risk. He could study out the precise spot carefully beforehand—there are lightships on the sands to act as guides. I have been down to the spot and studied it all out for myself. The thing is quite easy for the class of man I mean. I am not taking any great credit to

---

[32] bright
[33] A furlong is an eighth of a mile (220 yards).

myself, because I happened to see the body of the man who essayed that experiment. I recognized him for—"

"You recognized him! You knew who he was?"

"Certainly. He was Luigi Bianca, who used to perform in London years ago, with his brother Joseph, on the high trapeze. Then one of them got into trouble and subsequently embarked...on a career of crime. And when I saw the body of Luigi I knew at once that he had had a hand in the murder of Mr. Skidmore. When the right spot was reached the fellow took a header in the dark boldly enough, but he did not know that the storm had come with a very high October tide, and washed the nets away. He fell on the sands and dislocated his neck. But I had something to go on with. When I found out about the bogus corpse I began to see my way. I have been making careful inquiries ever since for the other criminal—"

"The other criminal! You mean to insinuate—"[34]

"I insinuate nothing," Merrick said coldly; "naturally enough I wanted to find Joseph Bianca. He was the man who picked up the gold; he was the man who hired a car in London from Moss & Co., in Regent Street, for a week. This was to recover the gold and incidentally also to take up the thief who stole it. I wanted to find Joseph Bianca, and *I've done it!*"

The Marquis leaped to his feet. As he did so the man in the distant chair woke up and moved across the room.

"Don't make a fuss!" Merrick said quietly. "You will be able to explain presently—perhaps what you are doing here posing as a Marquis, and where you got all that ready money from. Meanwhile, let me inform you that I am Inspector Merrick, of Scotland Yard, and that this is Sergeant Matthews. Joseph Bianca, you are my prisoner, and I have a warrant for your arrest as an accessory before and after the fact for the murder of Mr. George Skidmore. Ask them to call us a cab, Matthews!"

Questions for Review

1. What facts make it incredible to Catesby that the crime occurred?

2. What is the importance of the man's body found in the birding nets? Why does Merrick ask the locals if the nets could hold up against a large animal?

3. How does Catesby's testimony about looking out the window help with the case?

4. How was the crime committed?

---

[34] suggest

I Know Whom I Have Believed

By Daniel Webster Whittle

Massachusetts-born Daniel Webster Whittle (1840-1901) was an evangelist and a prolific hymnwriter; he wrote more than 200 hymns, including "There Shall Be Showers of Blessing." Before you read the beautiful below hymn, read 2 Timothy 1:1-12, Matthew 24:29-36, and 1 Thessalonians 4:13-18 in a King James Bible.

• • • • •

I know not why God's wondrous grace
   To me He hath made known,
Nor why—unworthy—Christ in love
   Redeemed me for His own.

But "I know whom I have believèd,
   And am persuaded that He is able
To keep that which I've committed
   Unto Him against that day."

I know not how this saving faith
   To me He did impart,
Nor how believing in His word
   Wrought peace within my heart.

But "I know whom I have believèd,
   And am persuaded that He is able
To keep that which I've committed
   Unto Him against that day."

I know not how the Spirit moves,
   Convincing men of sin,
Revealing Jesus through the word,
   Creating faith in Him.

But "I know whom I have believèd,
   And am persuaded that He is able
To keep that which I've committed
   Unto Him against that day."

I know not what of good or ill
   May be reserved for me,

Of weary ways or golden days,
    Before His face I see.

But "I know whom I have believèd,
    And am persuaded that He is able
To keep that which I've committed
    Unto Him against that day."

I know not when my Lord may come,
    At night or noonday fair,
Nor if I'll walk the vale with Him,
    Or "meet Him in the air."

But "I know whom I have believèd,
    And am persuaded that He is able
To keep that which I've committed
    Unto Him against that day."

Questions for Review

1. How does the first line of each of the five stanzas contrast with the first line of the chorus (which starts, "But 'I know whom I have believed")?

2. Find and listen to this song sung by a choir.

3. If you're feeling creative and poetic, write your own sixth stanza, in the same style as the first five (four lines, with the second and fourth lines rhyming).

Mabel Ashton's Dream

By Courtenay H. Fenn

A fascinating story by the American missionary to China Courtenay Hughes Fenn (1866-1953), "Mabel Ashton's Dream" was written in 1913. What would you *do if you found yourself in Mabel's shoes?*

• • • • •

As the guests came together in the brilliantly lighted parlors at the home of Mabel Ashton that crisp winter evening, there was nothing unusual in the appearance of the rooms to indicate that the party to which they had been invited was to be in any respect different from the round of gaiety[1] to which they had been devoting themselves for the greater part of the winter. Some of the guests, as they greeted their young hostess, noticed an unusual degree of nervousness in her manner, but, attributing it to the excitement of preparation and anticipation, thought no more of it, and all were soon engaged in conversation.

The musicians were in their places, and the young people were beginning to wonder why the signal was not given for the orchestra to strike up, when Mabel Ashton, her sweet face flushed and pale by turns, took her stand near the musicians. After closing her eyes for a moment, during which the room became perfectly still, in a voice at first trembling, but clear and steady, she said:

"Friends, I know you will think me very queer; but before we do anything else, I must tell you a little story.

"I had a dream last night, which has made such an impression on my mind and heart that I must tell it to you. I dreamed that tonight had arrived, and you had all assembled in these rooms, when there came to the door, and was ushered in, a guest who seemed strangely familiar, and yet whom I could not recognize. He had a rare face, peaceful, yet a little sad in its expression, and his eyes were more penetrating than any that I had ever before seen. He was dressed in neat yet very plain clothing, but there was something in his appearance which marked him as no ordinary man.

"While I was trying to think where I had seen him, he advanced to me, took my hand, and said, gently, 'You do not recognize me, Mabel?' Surprised at such a form of salutation[2] from a stranger, I could only say, 'Your face, sir, seems familiar, yet I cannot recall your name.'

---

[1] fun
[2] greeting

"'Yet I am one whom you have invited here this evening, or, I should rather say, one to whom both you and your parents have extended many invitations to be present here whenever I am able to come. You have even invited me to make my home here; and I have come tonight to join your little company.'

"'I beg a thousand pardons,' I replied, 'but you mystify me all the more, and I beg you will relieve me by telling me whom I have the pleasure of greeting.'

"Then he offered to my view the palms of his hands, in which were scars as of nail wounds, and looked me through and through with those piercing yet tender eyes; and I did not need that he should say to me, 'I am Jesus Christ, your Lord.'

"To say that I was startled would be to express only a very small part of my feelings. For a moment I stood still, not knowing what to do or say. Why could I not fall at his feet and say with all my heart, 'I am filled with joy at seeing you here, Lord Jesus'?

"With those eyes looking into mine, I could not say it; for it was not true. For some reason, on the instant only half comprehended by myself, I was sorry he had come. It was an awful thought, to be glad to have all the rest of you here, yet sorry to see my Savior! Could it be that I was ashamed of Him, or was I ashamed of something in myself?

"At length I recovered myself in a degree, and said, 'You wish to speak to my parents, I am sure.'

"'Yes, Mabel,' as he accompanied me to where my mother and father sat gazing in surprise at my evident confusion in greeting an unexpected guest; 'but I came this evening chiefly to be with you and your young friends; for I have often heard you speak enthusiastically in your young people's meetings about how delightful it would be if you could have me visibly present with you.'

"Again the blush came to my cheeks as the thought flashed through my mind, Tomorrow night is prayer-meeting night; I should have been delighted to see Him then. But why not tonight, on this pleasant occasion? I led him to my parents, and, in a somewhat shamefaced fashion, introduced him.

"They both gave a start[3] of amazed surprise, but, convinced by his appearance that there was no mistake, my father recovered a degree of self-possession, and bade him welcome, as he offered him a seat, remarking that this was an unexpected pleasure. After a somewhat lengthy pause, he explained to Jesus that his daughter Mabel, being very closely occupied with her studies, and having little variety in life, had been allowed to invite a few friends in for a social evening, with a little quiet dancing by way of healthful exercise. Her friends were all of the very choicest, and he felt that this was

---

[3] little jump

a harmless amusement, which the church had come to look upon in a somewhat different light from that in which it was viewed forty years ago. Removing the objectionable feature of bad company, had made this pleasant pastime a safe indulgence.[4]

"As my father stammered out, in the presence of Jesus, these words of apology, which had fallen from my own lips, I felt myself flush crimson with shame both for my dear father and for myself. Why should he apologize at all for what he considered unquestionably right? How hollow it all sounded there in the presence of the Lord! Did not Jesus know that my studies were not so pressing but that I could keep late hours, sometimes several nights in the week, at parties?

"Then father, anxious to relieve my evident embarrassment, said, 'I am sure we can leave these young people safely to themselves, and nothing would please me so well as to take you, my Lord Jesus, off into my study for a talk.'

"'No,' said Jesus, 'Mabel has often invited me, and I came tonight especially to be with her. Will you introduce me to your friends, Mabel? Some of them I know, but some I do not know.'

"Of course, all this time you, friends, were looking much in our direction, wondering at our embarrassment, and perhaps guessing that we had been made uncomfortable by the arrival of a not altogether welcome guest. I led him first to some of the church-members among you, and there was not one of you who looked so comfortable after the introduction as before.

"As it became known who the guest was, faces changed color, and some of you looked very much as if you would like to leave the room. It really seemed as if the church members were quite as unwilling to meet Jesus as those who were not Christians.

"One of you came up quietly and whispered to me, 'Shall I tell the musicians not to play the dance music, but to look up some sacred pieces?' Jesus caught the question, and, looking us both squarely in the face, he simply asked, 'Why should you?' and we could not answer. Some one else suggested that we could have a very pleasant and profitable evening if we should change our original plans, and invite Jesus to talk to us. And he also was met with that searching question, 'Why should my presence change your plans?'

"After I had introduced the Lord Jesus to you all, and no one knew what to do next, Jesus turned to me and said: 'You were planning for dancing, were you not? It is high time you began, or you cannot complete your program before daylight. Will you not give the word to the musicians, Mabel?'

"I was much embarrassed. If my original plan was all right, his presence ought only to add joy to the occasion; yet here were all my guests, as well

---

[4] treat, pleasure

as myself, made wretchedly uncomfortable by the presence of him whom most of us called our best Friend. Determined to throw off this feeling and be myself, at his word I ordered the musicians to play for the first dance.

"The young man with whom I was engaged for that dance did not come to claim me, and no one went upon the floor. This was still worse embarrassment. The orchestra played once more, and two or three couples, more to relieve me than for any other reason, began to dance in a rather formal fashion. I was almost beside myself with shame and confusion, when the Lord Jesus turned to me and said: 'Mabel, your guests do not seem at ease. Why do you not, as their hostess, relieve their embarrassment by dancing, yourself? Would it help you any if I should offer to dance with you?'

"My confusion gave way to an expression almost of horror, as I looked into those tenderly sad eyes and cried, 'You dance! You cannot mean it!'

"'Why not, Mabel? If my disciples may dance, may not I? Did you think all this winter, when you and others of my disciples have gathered for the dance, or the card party, or at the theater, that you left me at home or in the church? You prayed for my presence in the prayer meeting; you did not quite want it here; but why not, my dear child? Why have you not welcomed me tonight, Mabel? Why has my presence spoiled your pleasure? Though I am "a Man of sorrows, and acquainted with grief,"[5] yet I delight to share and increase all the pure joys of my disciples. Is it possible that you leave me out of any of your pleasures, Mabel? If so, is it not because you feel that they do not help you to become like me and to glorify me; that they take your time and strength and thought to such an extent that you have less delight in my Word and in communion with me? You have been asking, "What's the harm?" Have you asked, "What is the gain?" Have you done these things for the glory of God?'

"It was plain to me now. Overcome with self-reproach and profound sorrow, I threw myself on the floor at his feet, and sobbed out my repentance.

"With a 'Daughter, go in peace; thy sins be forgiven thee,'[6] he was gone. I awoke and found that it was all a dream. And now I want to ask you, my friends, shall we go on with the program tonight, or shall we take these lists which we have prepared, and discuss for a time with our partners the question, 'What can young people do to make the world better for their having lived in it'?"

As the vote was unanimous in favor of the latter plan, which was followed by other wholesome recreations, and as the social evening was declared the most delightful of the winter, it is safe to say that the Lord Jesus had sent that dream for others besides Mabel Ashton.

---

[5] See Isaiah 53:3.
[6] See Luke 7:36-50.

An <u>Incredibly</u> Important Question for Review

"Mabel Ashton's Dream" is a fictional story about what Jesus might say to some-one in a more modern situation. But in the beginning of this book, we read John, Chapter 1. Here's what verses 9-13 say about Jesus Christ:

That was the true Light, which lighteth every man that cometh into the world. He was in the world, and the world was made by him, and the world knew him not. He came unto his own, and his own received him not. But as many as received him, to them gave he power to become the sons of God, even to them that believe on his name: Which were born, not of blood, nor of the will of the flesh, nor of the will of man, but of God.

And here's the most important question of the year:

Have <u>you</u> "received" Jesus Christ, as verse 12 says, and become one of the "sons [or daughters] of God"—one of those God gives this power to because they "believe on his name"?

If you haven't, I urge you to put your faith in Jesus Christ, who will save you from your sins and give you eternal life with Him. We all know that we've sinned against God; in fact, the Bible says that *"all have sinned, and come short of the glory of God"* (Romans 3:23). But the Bible also says God *"hath made him [Jesus] to be sin for us, who knew no sin; that we might be made the righteousness of God in Him"* (2 Corinthians 5:21).

And the Bible says this about Jesus: that He *"was made a little lower than the angels for the suffering of death, crowned with glory and honour; that he by the grace of God should taste death for every man"* (Hebrews 2:9). Jesus "taste[d] death for every man"; *that means you.*

So how do you have your sins forgiven and make peace with God—and have a life with Him after you die? The Bible says that *"if thou shalt confess with thy mouth the Lord Jesus, and shalt believe in thine heart that God hath raised him from the dead, thou shalt be saved"* (Romans 10:9). When a Roman jailer asked the apostle Paul and his assistant Silas what he had to do to be saved, they told him this: *"Believe on the Lord Jesus Christ, and thou shalt be saved"* (Acts 16:31).

If you've never put your faith in Jesus, do so right away! You don't have to say exactly the right words or change your ways first. Call out to God and ask Him to forgive your sins and save you through Jesus Christ. Find a Bible-believing church and get an old Authorized Version ("King James") Bible and start reading the rest of the book of John.

And if you have any questions or need prayer about anything, feel free to email me any time: **scott@homeschoolpartners.net.**

Many blessings,
Scott Clifton

Answer Key to Questions for Review

Week 1, Day 1: "John 1:1-14"

1. *The holiness of Jesus shined like a light in the darkness of sin, and those who love sin and "darkness" do not understand Jesus and His works.*
2. *To bear witness of Jesus, so all people on earth might believe in Him.*
3. *Just as John the Baptist was sent to bear witness of Jesus so "all men" might believe, Jesus is the Light that lights "every man that cometh into the world."*
4. *By receiving Jesus and believing on His name (verse 13). God gets the credit, since He gives a new birth to those who believe in Jesus Christ.*

Week 1, Day 2: "The Highest Education"

1. *It is to teach someone how to learn what he wants and how to achieve it, and finds truth, most importantly. To get an orderly mind that knows **how** to learn, not just a mind that memorizes dates and places on a map and grammar rules.*
2. *Proverbs 23:23 says, "Buy the truth, and sell it not," and in John 14:6 Jesus says, "I am the way, the truth, and the life: no man cometh unto the Father, but by me." A young Christian can see that the whole reason we exist is to serve the Truth: Jesus Christ.*
3. *That person treats everyone, regardless of "race" or condition, with love and respect. He also looks for beauty in God's creation, gives generously to others, and lives in a clean and decorated home.*
4. *Answers will vary (AWV).*

Week 1, Day 3: "Casey at the Bat"

1. *AWV, but maybe cheering crowds who scream at the umpire or referee.*
2. *He's showing off for the crowd, because he's so sure he can clobber any pitch he wants to and doesn't think there's any chance he'll strike out.*
3. *AWV.*

Week 1, Day 4: "Rikki-Tikki-Tavi"

1. *AWV, but his friendliness, loyalty to the English family, courage, willingness to help Darzee's family, and so on. Practically all the animals acted in some ways as humans; Kipling even says that "Darzee was very like a man in some ways."*
2. *They plan to kill the English family, so Rikki-tikki has no family to live with, and he will leave the area so he's no danger to them anymore. Rikki-tikki asks Darzee to pretend to be hurt to draw away Nagaina, so he can grab her eggs and goad her into a fight.*
3. *Snakes have long been a symbol of evil, beginning with the serpent—the devil who tempted Eve—in the Garden of Eden.*

Week 2, Day 1: "The First Telegraph Instrument"

1. *AWV, but his persistence and his knowledge of so many types of machinery is impressive, especially the ways they can work together, and the endless possibilities of failure.*
2. *He almost went broke, and he lived meagerly, with barely enough to eat, in a little room; he also faced the possibility of ridicule if his invention failed.*
3. *No doubt he was grieved at not finding out soon enough to attend her funeral, and he might have wanted to spare anyone else that grief, which happened only because communication was so slow. Telegraphy changed the world by its immediate communication.*

Week 2, Day 2: "The Leak"

1. *Because they're never caught, so nobody knows they've committed crimes!*
2. *Others are finding out his plans within minutes of his dictating them to Miss Winthrop. TTM says either the leak is via Grayson or Miss Winthrop.*
3. *Miss Winthrop types her notes in Morse Code, which is wired to send the information to someone else in another room.*

Week 2, Day 3: "The Boat"

1. *It's called "ABAB" on the odd stanzas; even lines rhyme on the even stanzas.*
2. *He does things his own way, owns the boat, follows his own will; but slowly as he encounters Jesus, he changes his ways to conform to and obey the will of Jesus.*

Week 2, Day 4: "My Financial Career"

AWV.

Week 4, Day 1: "An Address to Young Converts"

1. *He says it's critical to young believers to read it prayerfully, thoughtfully, and with prayer that the Holy Spirit would open up the meaning of it to us.*
2. *Not just reading the Bible like a storybook, but by taking its words as God's own words. Müller says to be happy, we must be doers of God's word.*
3. *That we should pray all the time—not just about problems that come up, but about "little things," too. He says that even if a parcel came in the mail and we couldn't open it, to pray about it too.*
4. *AWV.*

Week 4, Day 2: "John G."

1. *Twenty-two years old, alert, strong, clean-limbed, and brave, even though he's not as strong as he was!*

2. *A potential violent riot that they must reach and prevent, or at least stop. It turns out to be a false alarm, but John G. travels many miles in a terrible storm, calmly and carefully leading all the other horses there and back.*
3. *They are appreciative of him and love the horse. They take three hours to dry and brush him off!*
4. *Proverbs 12:10 says, "A righteous man regardeth the life of his beast: but the tender mercies of the wicked are cruel." The men in this story treat their horses well! Often how a man treats the animals he owns is a good indicator of his character.*

Week 4, Day 3: "He Leadeth Me"

1. *Philippians 2:14-16 tells Christians to "Do all things without murmurings and disputings," so we will be blameless and shine as lights in a crooked and perverse world.*
2. *AWV.*

Week 4, Day 3: "Temptation Resisted"

1. *As "the intent to deceive."*
2. *It takes away half of it, wondering if he'll be found out, and knowing he disobeyed to be able to do it.*
3. *AWV.*

Week 4, Day 4: "In the Country of the Sioux"

AWV.

Week 5, Day 1: "Psalm 1, Psalm 97"

1. *To listen and follow the advice of those who don't love God, to join sinners in their evil, and to join those arrogant persons who mock God and others.*
2. *No, because so many Christians who delight in God's word are not rich financially; it means that God will direct their efforts to be successful in a way that pleases Him.*
3. *Anyone who sees the creation of the skies can see that God created it*
4. *Hate evil, rejoice in the Lord, give thanks when we remember God's holiness.*

Week 5, Day 2: "The Largest Statues in the World"

1. *They both are huge, to honor someone/something, took many man-hours and technology to build. They're different in that the Rameses II statue was to honor a king, and the Statue of Liberty was to honor liberty.*
2. *AWV.*

Week 5, Day 2: "The Story of Alaska"

1. *AWV.*
2. *It increased settlement greatly, with everyone trying to strike it rich.*
3. *AWV.*

Week 5, Day 3: "A Poison Tree"

1. *He tells his friend, and they resolve their argument; he keeps it from his foe, and his anger towards him grows worse and worse.*
2. *It gets worse and worse, because he doesn't resolve it.*
3. *The apple likely represents sin and then death, which is what Adam and Eve were threatened with by God if they ate the forbidden fruit in Genesis 3. Similarly, the poet's foe dies after eating the poisoned apple in the poet's garden.*
4. *He dies, killed by the poet. The Bible passages command us not to e angry with someone without a cause, to love our enemies and do good to them, and to "be angry and sin not" and not to "let the sun go down upon your wrath."*

Week 5, Day 3: "A Ballad of Trees and the Master"

1. *They both have similar first lines, their second lines rhyme, they both have a line with "came" and one with "shame," they end with a similar line.*
2. *The poem is about the willingness of Jesus to suffer and die for the world's sins, and the verses tell us that Jesus humbled himself and was willing to die on the cross, and He was made a curse for us, fulfilling the passage in Deuteronomy 21:23.*

Week 5, Day 4: "Benjamin Franklin"

1. *It's stealing! One of government's proper duties, according to Jeremiah 22:3, is to deliver the spoiled out of the hand of the oppressor." The government, therefore, is there to stop or punish stealing.*
2. *Any government that does something supposedly to benefit everybody, while at the same time violating an individual's rights, puts EVERYBODY'S rights in jeopardy, because if the government can violate one person's rights to "benefit all," it can violate ANYBODY'S rights and claim to do the same thing.*
3. *AWV.*

Week 6, Day 1: *The Merry Adventures of Robin Hood*

1. *AWV.*
2. *Robin Hood, in Pyle's version (and others), actually protected the poor from the government's stealing their money—stealing it back!*

Week 6, Day 2: *The Merry Adventures of Robin Hood*

1. *He's really angry about being shown up by Robin Hood and his men, and being made to look foolish.*
2. *AWV.*
3. *AWV, but the sheriff didn't know the identity of the prize-winning archer, and when he gets the message that it was Robin Hood, he blows up in anger, and the reader feels that justice has been served!*

Week 6, Day 3: "My Kate"

1. *Nearly every line has 11 syllables; the accented syllables there are syllables 2, 5, 8, and 11. For the few lines that are 12 syllables, the accented syllables are 3, 6, 9, and 12.*
2. *Her gracefulness, soft-spoken manner, her ability to make others nobler and purer, and so on.*
3. *She ennobles them, makes them want to please God and act more purely. In the last stanza, the author vows to Kate, who has died, that she will carry on Kate's work*
4. *Proverbs 31:30 says "Favour [charm, grace] is deceitful, and beauty is vain: but a woman that feareth the LORD, she shall be praised." 1 Peter 3:1-5 commands Christian wives to be pure in their conversation, to "adorn" themselves with a "meek and quiet spirit" instead of jewels and hairdos, and to honor their husbands.*

Week 6, Day 4: "Cicely"

1. *Her cold, selfish attitude toward the hard-working girls in the dressmaking shop, demanding that some of them be made to stay to get her the dress she wants for her cousin. Rhoda gives Cicely a smile!*
2. *She and her sister Marcelle have to pay their father's debts; Cicely is hanging on for a year of working in the dressmaking store until the debt is paid, and she can return home.*
3. *Rhoda realizes that Cicely has literally spilled her blood to make her (Rhoda) happy, and that she feels ashamed of making Cicely go through so much just to make her happy.*
4. *She shares them with Miss Waite during the day, and Miss Waite returns her favor by inviting her to a delicious supper and helping her save the petals. Cicely appreciates the note from Rhoda that says, "Sincerely, your friend" just as much as the roses, because it lightened her heart knowing that someone in the big city cared about her.*

Week 9, Day 1: "Puc-Puggy and His Notes on the Rattlesnake"

1. *It means "Flower Hunter," since Bartram was a botanist. He seems to have a pretty good relationship with the Indians he encounters.*

2. *They say he's too "heroic and violent," so they say they need to take out some of his blood! Bartram's writings don't make himself out to be any kind of hero—just a scientist and explorer who's trying to learn about the area's nature.*
3. *AWV.*
4. *Talented writing! He remarks on how they aren't aggressive, they don't slither even as fast as a child could run, they could have attacked him several times when he was within inches of them but didn't, and they're easily killed with just a blow to the head with a stick. He also feels bad about killing the rattler at the end of the selection, and can't even eat it because he feels so bad about its death.*

Week 9, Day 2: "From Morning Till Night on a Florida River"

1. *AWV, but might include how Lanier starts off with an interesting opening sentence, includes lively details, uses strong nouns and verbs to paint pictures in the reader's mind, and closes with an effective paragraph that wraps up the day.*
2. *AWV.*

Week 9, Day 3: "On the Grasshopper and the Cricket"

1. *It has 10 syllables per line, five "beats," and an accent on the even-numbered beats. The poem's rhyme scheme is ABBA, ABBA, CDECDE.*
2. *"The poetry of earth is never dead" and "The poetry of earth is ceasing never." The two parts are similar in that they express how nature is like poetry; they're different in that the first describes summer (and is linked to the grasshopper), while the second describes winter (and its linked to the cricket).*
3. *AWV, but possibly that the parts of nature like grasshoppers and crickets and birds "speak" almost like lines of poetry from the earth.*

Week 9, Day 4: "The 'Gator'"

1. *"Cannibalistic" fathers, who eat their young.*
2. *They can be killed by bullets, they will eat almost anything, they travel great distances on land, they can grow to great lengths, they rarely attack unless it's a female defending her young.*
3. *U. S. alligators fear man more than Amazon ones, so Amazon ones are more aggressive and dangerous to humans. Amazon alligators are less hunted than U. S. alligators, so they can grow to spectacular lengths.*

Week 10, Day 1: "Matthew, Chapter 5"

1. *AWV, but someone who helps stop arguments and creates peace among those who disagree, or between themselves and their enemies.*
2. *It says they should rejoice and be very glad, for it proves they're righteous with God.*
3. *AWV.*

Week 10, Day 2: "Uncle Remus Stories"

1. *The first reminds readers: mind your own business! And keep your noses out of trouble when possible; the second shows how we often fail to act bravely, but make excuses so others won't know we have faults.*
2. *Reverse psychology is trying to make someone do the opposite of what you say, counting on the hope that the person will want to defy your wish. That's what Brer Rabbit does to Brer Fox in the story, since he really wants to be thrown into the briar patch!*

Week 10, Day 3: "What a Friend We Have in Jesus"

They tell Jesus followers to pray to God for help, because he's much more righteous than our friends we ask help of and trust they'll help us, or the wicked judge the widow got to help her; they also tell us to pray without ceasing.

Week 10, Day 4: "The Lumber Room"

1. *He's a little troublemaker, but still somewhat likable, because he's not vicious, and the aunts who try to punish him are even more unlikable!*
2. *He uses a forbidden key, and he finds all kinds of things that are treasures to a young boy.*
3. *He pretends to believe his "aunt" is the devil, so as she calls out to him to help her (she's fallen into the rainwater tank), he won't, to get even about being punished. Nicholas probably focuses on the huntsman's potential escape, because he's wondering if HE will escape without more punishment as well!*

Week 15, Day 1: "Safety Match"

1. *He claims his daughter is lonely and would be glad to marry any man who showed interest in her. Dick's attempt to speak to her along bombs; she barely even looks at him, preferring to read instead.*
2. *He thinks Kate just wants to win an argument with her father, so he sets up Raggett to try to woo Kate, so he can say he doesn't approve of Dick, so Kate will try to resist her father and be attracted to Dick. Kate has already called Raggett an "old chap with one foot in the grave and a face like a dried herring." Raggett understandably balks!*
3. *She agrees to marry him! He gurgles and chokes when she talks about a three-week honeymoon in London, then when she goes to bed, he blames her father for getting him into this mess.*
4. *He tells her she's getting a good man in Raggett, and she tells him she knew all the time it was a setup, since she heard Raggett and her father discussing the idea. Then she says she'd like to marry Dick, and he is glad to hear it!*
5. *A safety match is a newer type of match that didn't use white phosphorus, which was dangerous to people. The term "safety match" in the story's case refers to the "match" between Kate and Dick.*

Week 15, Day 2: "On Raising Questions"

1. *It's okay to work through doubts in your Christian faith, but to actively try to find problems with Christianity and the Bible is weird and unproductive—why would you try to undercut your only hope for salvation?*
2. *The two philosophers waste time debating this and that about food, while the countryman just believes and eats and is full. This is like someone who simply believes God's word and is spiritually "full," as opposed to someone who thinks up endless questions against God that don't help him at all.*
3. *Because that undercuts the whole Bible; if parts are incorrect, why isn't ALL of it wrong or untrustworthy? What are we going to put our faith in, if some parts—who knows which is true and which isn't—are wrong?*

Week 15, Day 3: "Thankfulness"

1. *It keeps our lives from being "too perfect," so we appreciate the idea of heaven more, and we lean on God to take us through these times.*
2. *Like the first question, it keeps us focused more on the life to come than this temporary earthly life.*

Week 15, Day 4: "The Pimentia Pancakes"

1. *He uses fancy vocabulary a great deal, but he (a) acts like an uncultured, gun-toting, violent cowboy who settles things with his gun instead of his brains, when he's first with Jackson Bird; and (b) acts awkwardly around Willella when he's courting her, talking of weird things like skinning cows and doing rattlesnake imitations when she's wanting to sing opera songs.*
2. *Jackson tells Willella and Uncle Emsley that Jud got hit on the head with a frying pan while somebody was cooking pancakes, and that he now acts crazy and starts talking about pancakes. Willella and Uncle Emsley think Jud is going nuts, asking about a pancake recipe...but, of course, Jackson has put Jud up to it, so Willella will think Jud's crazy and be sure to marry Jackson!*
3. *Cowboy riding and talk of cattle herding, saloons, a lot of western lingo, and the threat of guns (although the only gunplay is Jud's shooting a few animals to intimidate Jackson, and it's a battle of wits to win the hand of Willella, instead of some typical gunfight at high noon).*

Week 19, Day 1: "Have You Done Your Best?"

1. *AWV.*
2. *Christian slaves are told to obey their masters, working "heartily, as to the Lord." If SLAVES are commanded that, surely we who aren't slaves can work hard at our not-as-hard jobs and responsibilities.*
3. *AWV.*

Week 19, Day 2: *"Billy" Sunday: The Man and His Message*

1. *It is plain and down to earth, a speaking style much like the way people normally talk, instead of a highly formal style many preachers use today.*
2. *AWV.*
3. *He tells non-Christians they need to stop messing around and believe on Jesus Christ, and he tells those who identify as Christians to start acting like it!*

Week 19, Day 3: "Jim, Who Ran Away from His Nurse, and Was Eaten by a Lion"

1. *The poem qualifies as a parody because it exaggerates and pokes fun at stories like "Temptation Resisted," which are trying to teach an actual moral; Belloc's poem is mocking this type of story, in a lighthearted way.*
2. *AWV.*

Week 19, Day 4: "The Adventure of the Norwood Builder"

1. *His walking stick with blood on it, Oldacre's disappearance, papers scattered around, and the charred remains of someone in the fire set by Oldacre's home.*
2. *Oldacre wants to make it look as if McFarlane killed him for the money.*
3. *He doesn't think he would kill Oldacre the same day he was made his heir, do it right after a housekeeper who can identify him let him in, or conceal the body while leaving his stick.*
4. *To the police, it "proves" that McFarlane committed the crime, but to Holmes, who already examined the exact place and found nothing, it means that somebody put that thumbprint there recently.*
5. *Hatred of McFarlane's mother for rejecting his marriage proposal many years ago; Oldacre planned to disappear and take his money under another identity, and at the same time, get even with her.*

Week 20, Day 1: "The Eagle"

1. *The alliteration is the line "clasps the crag with crooked hands"; the simile is "like a thunderbolt he falls."*
2. *AAA, BBB. Each line has nine syllables.*
3. *It is surrounded by blue things: the sky and the ocean.*

Week 20, Day 1: "Ingratitude"

1. *Not being thankful.*
2. *The winter wind and the frozen sky. This is called an "apostrophe."*
3. *Man's ingratitude, and a friend who fails to remember your faithfulness as a friend.*
4. *It says that God loves and blesses all people, even the unthankful, and that in the last days, men will be lovers of their own selves, and overcome by sins, including being unthankful.*

Week 20, Day 2: "The Golden Windows"

1. *It is short, the characters are never named, and the writing style resembles a fable or fairy tale.*
2. *That his house has windows of gold and diamond. He really means that it looks beautiful to others who see it from the other side of the valley—that is, he has something to be thankful for that he didn't "see."*
3. *AWV.*

Week 20, Day 2: "A Dilemma"

1. *He remembers his uncle, all right; all he can do is think about how cruel of a trick he's played on him for the rest of his life!*
2. *Would a man who read his Bible a lot pull such a cruel trick on someone, and talk about how he hates the poor, and how much he hates his sister-in-law?*
3. *AWV.*

Week 20, Day 3: "Inscriptions on a Sun-Dial"

1. *The sun-dial itself!*
2. *It's another way of saying that just because a "shadow" (misfortune or sadness) has fallen over your life is no reason to despair: The presence of a shadow means there must be a light, too!*

Week 20, Day 3: "Four Things"

AWV.

Week 20, Day 4: "The Revolt of Mother"

1. *She's a hard worker, loyal and thankful to her husband, resourceful, and strong-minded. He's cheap, and grunts instead of talking; he also seems to be more concerned about making money than taking care of Sarah's needs.*
2. *Adoniram had promised her before to build a house, not another barn; they need a new house built before they build a new barn to put four cows in, since their present house is so old and in bad shape.*
3. *She says she's too embarrassed to have her wedding in the house, but would be willing to have it in the new barn, because it will be nicer!*
4. *They talk endlessly about it; some think she's insane, and some say she's rebellious. They hang around the Penn farm when Adoniram is due back to see the possible fireworks!*
5. *AWV, but maybe he feels bad for neglecting the needs of his wife for so long.*

Week 22, Day 1: "What Can I Do?"

1. *Ephesians 2:8-9 says, "For by grace are ye saved through faith; and that not of yourselves: it is the gift of God: not of works, lest any man should boast."*
2. *Tom becomes a blessing to Croft by reading to him, and he blesses the boys by instructing them and talking about noble and holy things. Croft is rewarded by the townspeople for doing this for Tom, and Tom is rewarded for helping the boys by eventually becoming a schoolmaster.*
3. *AWV.*

Week 22, Day 2: "A Pioneer Mother"

1. *She longed for her husband to return from war, endured hardship, cracked jokes, taught the author to read, forgave, was beloved by all, she patiently endured diseases like smallpox with no complaint, she moved respectfully when her husband wanted to, and so on. AWV on the second question.*
2. *She becomes "middle aged" to her sons, because her grief "ages" her, but keeps her cheerfulness.*
3. *They buy her rich gifts—silverware and glassware; Mrs. Garland cannot even speak her thanks. Their neighbors weep when they say goodbye, knowing that they will almost surely never see each other again.*
4. *To make other weary older mothers happy, and to encourage children to visit their elderly parents—to pay them back for the hard work that the parents went through to provide for them.*
5. *AWV.*
6. *AWV.*

Week 22, Day 3: "Up Hill"

1. *It shows that the poem is a conversation between two persons.*
2. *It likely stands for life itself—how it is like a journey that's sometimes difficult, but with "rest" at the end of the journey.*
3. *Those lines say that there is rest at the end of the journey; in Matthew 11:28-30, Jesus tells His followers to come to Him, and He will give them rest.*

Week 22, Day 4: "Quality"

1. *They're German shoemakers, hardworking and pleasant, and their shoes are works of art, lasting a long time.*
2. *First, they're not the Gesslers' boots; second, the larger firms are taking away much of the Gesslers' business; third, they're not as good as the Gesslers' boots; fourth, the Gesslers are struggling to survive, and Mr. Gessler looks much older suddenly. To sooth his guilt, he buys several pairs of boots, and they are so well made that he doesn't have to go back for two years.*
3. *He enters and learns that the elder Gessler has died, then comes in some time later and learns that the younger Gessler has also died. The Gesslers were expert shoemakers, but they couldn't compete with other shoe stores and their*

advertising. They didn't keep up with the times, so nobody knew about their high-quality boots.
4. *Because of the quality of work the Gesslers did.*

Week 23, Day 1: "Proverbs 13"

1. *AWV, but something like (in order): "A person can stay out of trouble by keeping his mouth shut and not talking too much (or foolishly), but can get into trouble by talking too much"; "Many rich persons have lots of money, but nothing really valuable, and many poor persons have little money, but great riches that aren't money"; "Obeying God's Word keeps a person out of trouble"; and "A parent that doesn't spank his child really hates his child, but a parent who loves his child trains him up starting when he's young."*
2. *AWV.*

Week 23, Day 2: "Bears of High and Low Degree"

1. *They have many of the same faults and strengths of humans: protectiveness about their children, grouchiness, the desire for food, and so on.*
2. *AWV.*
3. *AWV.*

Week 23, Day 3: "The Children's Hour"

1. *AWV.*
2. *AWV.*
3. *The legend of Bishop Hatto has him in a castle with a tower across the river in Bingen, Germany. Hatto supposedly kept food from the townspeople, and even tricked them into going into a barn to wait for food, then locking them in and killing them, saying, "Listen to the mice squeak!" Hatto then was attacked by mice, which ate him alive. The poem compares the author's daughters climbing up and surrounding him like the mice attacking Hatto.*

Week 23, Day 3: "I Like to See It Lap the Miles"

1. *It's a train!*
2. *In the first stanza, the train travels fast around the country; in the second, it goes around mountains and rock beds; in the third, it goes into tunnels loudly; in the fourth, it roars loudly again and comes to the station and stops.*

Week 23, Day 4: "A Doctor's Cow"

1. *It was just a mistake by a careless boy, not a malicious act; Harry has improved since coming to the farm; it won't bring back the cow if they do get rid of him; Harry is heartbroken over his mistake; it will hurt Harry's ability to find another place if they let him go; and Harry's future is more important than a cow!*

2. *Besides the natural and most important one of saving Harry's future and giving him a chance at a new life, Harry does well, marries well, becomes a father, and rises as an honest senator. And he repays the doctor with a monetary gift as well.*

3. *2 Peter 3:9 says, "The Lord is not slack concerning his promise, as some men count slackness; but is longsuffering to us-ward, not willing that any should perish, but that all should come to repentance." God is patient with His creation, and wants everyone to repent and be saved, much like the doctor showed great patience with Harry.*

Week 24, Day 1: "Giving Up the Right to Our Standard of Living"

1. *She'd never have anything in her house that would prevent ordinary poor people from coming in it. It's to keep from creating a stumbling block for others who might believe, but see the missionaries as rich people.*

2. *The principle is that they should try to blend in with the natives to win them over and win their confidence, and so they'll know that the missionaries aren't snooty or looking down on them. But if a practice violates their Christian faith, those missionaries shouldn't conform to it.*

3. *AWV.*

Week 24, Day 2: "Shandon Waters"

1. *She was orphaned at six, grew up a rough and untamed girl, and didn't know social customs very well. The people are stunned to see her, because since becoming a widow six months ago she hasn't left her home.*

2. *She becomes even more withdrawn and anti-social, and never visits anybody.*

3. *She's upset because Mary seems to have everything, and she's more upset because she's marrying the doctor who operated on Dan, who didn't survive. Shandon is furious at the doctor, and she lashes him in the face with her whip.*

4. *Mary and the doctor gladly postpone a huge wedding to help Danny when he's poisoned, even when the doctor still has a scar on his face from Shandon's whip. AWV on the second question, but surely Shandon will try to interact more with the Deaneville residents after this!*

Week 24, Day 3: "Old Aunt Mary's"

AWV.

Week 24, Day 4: "Do Insects Think?"

1. *AWV, but could include something like, "when he got up in the morning, Pudge had not touched the pile of scattered cards on the floor, which showed that Pudge knew she would make more of a mess trying to refile them—proving that Pudge was thinking carefully!" The claim is ridiculous, of course, because there's no evidence at all that Pudge, a wasp, did this at all!*

2. *AWV.*

Week 29, Day 1: *Missionary Travels and Researches*, Chapters I-II

1. *The lion nearly kills him, breaking his arm after being wounded with a shotgun. The Boers, because he speaks out against their shameful treatment of African natives, destroy his home, library, and medicine, and steal and sell his furniture and clothing.*
2. *He says they have a general understanding of good and evil, and God, but sometimes think of him as just a chief, like the old bushman who brags about murdering five persons. Sekelutu doesn't want to read the Bible, because he says it might make him want just one wife, like Sechele, a native chief who converted to Christianity.*
3. *AWV.*

Week 29, Day 2: *Missionary Travels and Researches*, Chapters III-IV

1. *Tribes and individuals demand payment to travel through, and steal his and his group's property. He could have just used his guns to overwhelm these, but fears God and refuses to murder others. It would hurt his Christian testimony to do something like that.*
2. *AWV.*
3. *AWV.*

Week 29, Day 3: "Songs for My Mother"

1. *How they touched her cheek, lulled her to sleep, and told of memories when she was a little girl.*
2. *Her mother chose her words carefully to make them lovely and descriptive and beautiful. Proverbs 25:11 says, "A word fitly spoken is like apples of gold in pictures of silver," which is close to saying the same thing.*
3. *She says they're the most beautiful thing on earth, they can enrich and enlarge even the poorest and most common, simple things, and they can make others feel better. Colossians 4:6 says, "Let your speech be alway with grace, seasoned with salt, that ye may know how ye ought to answer every man." Our speech is to be graceful and kind, well-spoken to others.*

Week 29, Day 3: "My Mother's Bible"

1. *AWV.*
2. *The names of the dead written in his mother's Bible are "alive" in the Bible, reminding him of their lives.*
3. *It puts confidence and peace in the hearts of those who trust God with their lives and deaths, knowing that they'll be in heaven with Jesus when they die.*
4. *AWV.*

Week 29, Day 4: "Zero Hour"

1. *"Zero hour" is the time that an operation—often a military operation—is scheduled to begin. It's the story's title because the climax is the invasion of Earth, scheduled for 5 PM.*
2. *The invaders believe they have imagination and pay attention better than older children and adults. The world's situation is described as perfectly in balance and peaceful—even smug about it.*
3. *AWV.*
4. *It seems to look and operate like a smart phone!*
5. *AWV, but something like, "Stop staring at your televisor all day and pay attention to your children!" The organization: the government school system.*

Week 30, Day 1: "A Manual on Education"

1. *AWV.*
2. *AWV.*
3. *It's just a nonsense group that Leacock sticks in the list of various peoples kids are taught about in history. The name actually refers to a group of loud partiers or noisy rioters.*
4. *AWV, but something like, "Much of the information I learned in school was useless, or just focused on memorizing names and dates and so on."*

Week 30, Day 2: "The Night Express"

1. *He's sure Skidmore was alone in his compartment, he's sure he locked his door, he's sure the train ever stopped going under 60 miles per hour, and he's sure no one could have left the train without attracting attention.*
2. *Inspector Merrick recognizes him; he asks because he suspects a man jumped out of the window of the train into one.*
3. *He's positive he was looking out the one side, because he always does since he was involved in a train accident years ago, because of his nerves. Anyone leaving the train could only have jumped out the other side of the train into the fowling nets.*
4. *The Bianca brothers, who are trapeze artists, did it. Luigi hid in the coffin, crawled out, went on the side of the train to Skidmore's cabin, killed him, and took the gold and threw it out the window. He then waited for the fowling nets to jump into, having experience in landing on nets as a trapeze artist. But the nets had been torn down by the water, and he was killed. His brother, Joseph, was posing as a Marquis and was involved in the crime.*

Week 30, Day 3: "I Know Whom I Have Believed"

The stanzas start "I know NOT" something, which contrasts with the chorus, which says, "I KNOW."

Did you enjoy this book?

If so, I would be extremely grateful if you'd leave a brief review on Amazon.com!

It's fast and easy to leave a review; here's how:

- Search for "Middle School Literature for Christian Homeschoolers" at Amazon.com, and
- Hit "Ctrl+F" (for "Find") and type "Write a customer review."

Thank you so much!
Scott Clifton

Homeschool Humor

Do you like to laugh? (For example, "Ha, ha!")

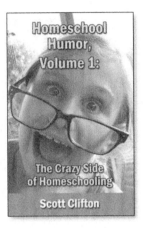

Would you like to feel much better about your family's weird homeschooling experiences, since the ones in these books are even loonier?

Are you interested in soft, luxurious, and more man-ageable hair?

If you happened to answer "Yes" to any of those ques-tions, *Homeschool Humor* books can help! (Except for the one about the soft, luxurious hair; maybe you should try egg whites or something.)

The two volumes of *Homeschool Humor* are packed with hilarious stories of the pitfalls and wackiness occurring in a somewhat-normal homeschool family, including chapters like...

- Let's Go Camping! Some Other Time!

- Naming Your Homeschooled Child

- Helping Your Children Build Strong Character by Smashing People Right in the Face

- Science and Other Mythical Creatures

- A Brief History of Homeschooling That Briefly Shows Homeschooling Throughout History, in a Brief Way That Is Also Historical

Also included: juicy lists of how to answer those complete strangers who ask, "Are those all your children?" or "What are those kids doing out of school?"

Homeschool Humor books are available here:

homeschoolpartners.net/books

7th–12th Grade Literature for Christian Homeschoolers:

Here's what you get with the above sets of literature books for Christian middle school and high school homeschoolers:

- **Great Reads!** Many wonderful essays, short stories, speeches, poems, letters, and novels—in conveniently arranged sets for seventh grade, eighth grade, and four years of high school.

- **A 30-Week, Four-Days-Per-Week Reading Schedule.** No more asking, "What should we read this week?"

- **Introductions, Footnotes, Questions for Review.** These place writings into his-torical context, help students understand archaic terms, clear up potentially hazy passages, and help the student think about important ideas.

- **A Christian Worldview.** This worldview is reflected in the introductions, foot-notes, and review questions.

- **Free Answer Keys to Review Questions.** Parents, you can discuss the review questions—fully armed with answer keys!

homeschoolpartners.net/books

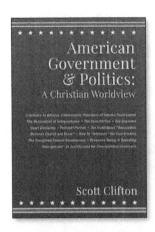

American Government & Politics: A Christian Worldview

• A helpful, 30-week, two-to-four-day-per-week reading schedule

• A good overview of American Government, in clear, short sections

• A Christian view of government and government types, the Constitution and how to interpret it, political parties, taxes, and more

• Review questions for each day's reading

• Free review question answer key

Civics for Christian Homeschoolers

• A helpful, 15-week, four-day-per-week schedule

• A good overview of Civics, in clear, short sections

• A Christian view of citizenship, types of law, types of government, the Declaration of Independence, a Christian's rights and responsibilities, juries, voting, and more

• Review questions for each day's reading

• Free review question answer key

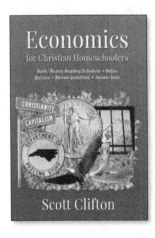

Economics for Christian Homeschoolers

• A helpful, 15-week, four-day-per-week schedule

• Clear, short sections

• A Christian view of economics, with a pro-free market viewpoint

• Explanations of the dangers of socialism, inflation, bureaucracies, taxes and business regulations, and other government meddling

• Review questions for each day's reading

• Free review question answer key

homeschoolpartners.net/books

About Scott Clifton

North Carolina is where Scott Clifton makes his home, with his wife Julie and their children. Scott is a fervent homeschooling advocate, and just *seconds* after his first child was born, as he took his little baby boy and held him close to his chest, he looked down and immediately knew—right then in his heart—that he would never be able to wear that particular shirt again. (Also, that he and Julie would homeschool their children, which they have done since 1994.)

Scott earned his B.A. in Journalism from the University of Central Florida and his M.Ed. from York University. He began his career writing and editing for a family newspaper and a state banking association. In 2002, the Lord led Scott into the field of home school education, and that year he began teaching classes full time as the owner and operator of Home School Partners (**homeschoolpartners.net**).